ZERO 22

Also by Chris Ryan

CHRIS RYAN

ZERO 22

CORONET

First published in Great Britain in 2020 by Coronet
An Imprint of Hodder & Stoughton
An Hachette UK company

This paperback edition published in 2021

1

A CIP catalogue record for this title is available from the British Library

Paperback ISBN 9781473667976
eBook ISBN 9781473667945

Typeset in Bembo by Hewer Text UK Ltd, Edinburgh
Printed and bound in Great Britain by Clays Ltd, Elcograf S.p.A.

Hodder & Stoughton policy is to use papers that are natural, renewable
and recyclable products and made from wood grown in sustainable
forests. The logging and manufacturing processes are expected to
conform to the environmental regulations of the country of origin.

Hodder & Stoughton Ltd
Carmelite House
50 Victoria Embankment
London EC4Y 0DZ

www.hodder.co.uk

ONE

23.45 hrs, Eastern European Time

The convoy headed west.

It comprised four vehicles. Three sand-coloured Jackals, each containing three guys and mounted with two general-purpose machine guns. The Gimpys had an effective range of two thousand metres in sustained-fire mode. Regular infantry would need two men to operate each weapon. Not the SAS. Each gun was constantly manned by a single Regiment guy wearing night-vision goggles, surveying the desert terrain and ready for whatever threats they might encounter. The fourth vehicle was a Bushmaster. Camouflage paint. Sturdy, rear-mounted spare tyres. A safe, sealed, air-conditioned unit. Five guys. Remote weapon station with a manned 40mm grenade launcher. Heavily armoured. It led the convoy as it trundled through the night along a rough, unmade road.

The Iraqi border was seventy-five klicks to the east. Thirty klicks north: Turkey. This bleak, blasted patch of desert was officially Syrian territory, and there was always the risk that the convoy would encounter Syrian government forces. Unofficially? Emboldened by the American withdrawal and the backing of the Russians, the Turks were making frequent sorties across the border. The militants of Islamic State still infested the region. The Kurds, fierce fighters with good reason to fight, viewed this land as part of their tribal territory of Kurdistan and were still in situ, despite their supposed friends the Yanks fucking off and leaving them to the non-existent mercy of the Turks. The Russians had Spetsnaz special forces on the ground and some remaining Delta Force were here.

1

Try to untangle that little web of enmity and alliances. Try to distinguish your friends from your enemies in this messed-up part of north-eastern Syria.

Danny Black didn't care to. He was happy to follow orders and so were the rest of his troop. They were heavily armed and confident in their ability and firepower. They knew they could handle anything they came across.

B Squadron SAS had been in-country for a month now. At first, Danny had been glad of the distraction after the rigours of his previous op: a mission to hunt down a lone-wolf killer called Ibrahim Khan that had not gone at all the way anyone had expected. Now Danny was throwing himself into B Squadron's current objective: regular sorties mounted from a base in Iraq, over the border into Syria to take out known IS targets. It had been a blood-soaked month. A month of night raids on isolated villages. Of 9mm rounds discharged ruthlessly into the skulls of IS scumbags. Danny had no problem with that. None of the guys did. Each IS militant they put in the ground made the world a better place. But it had also been a month of screaming wives and suddenly orphaned children. It would get to even the most cold-hearted Regiment death squad eventually.

Their latest orders, delivered to Danny that morning over the encrypted radio, felt like a momentary relief. Even Bullethead had said so. Implacable, relentless Bullethead, who had more kills to his name than anybody Danny knew. He was so called because of the pointed shape and shine of his bald head, which beaded with sweat in the heat whenever he wasn't wearing a helmet. He had the lowest voice Danny had ever heard. When he spoke, it was like the engine of a motorbike turning over. 'Change is as good as a rest,' he had growled, as Danny told them they had new instructions.

'There's a secure prison facility three hundred klicks south-west,' Danny said. 'Up until a couple of months ago it housed IS prisoners and was guarded by Kurds.'

'So, when we say prison facility, we mean torture facility, right?' Bullethead said. 'Otherwise the Kurds would have just killed the fuckers.'

'I guess,' said Danny. 'Anyway, the Kurds came under attack and had to abandon the site. The IS prisoners escaped. Chances are we've shot a few of them in the last few weeks. The facility's been deserted since the breakout, but a Kurdish unit have just returned. They've got some documentation that might help identify further targets. And reading between the lines, they're shitting themselves. They want an escort out of Syria in return for the intel. That's us. Operation call sign, Zero 22.'

Which was why, as the rest of B Squadron continued their dark work across the area, Danny now found himself sitting in the Bushmaster, the constant groan of the engine grinding in his ears. The vehicle had two places up front and two vertical rows of four seats in the back, facing each other. It was cramped and hardly luxurious, but it was a hell of a sight better than the tin ovens that were the Jackals. As the senior guy, Danny reckoned he'd earned his place here. When they grew closer to the target, however, he'd transfer to one of the Jackals. If anything went wrong, he wanted to be in the best position to call the shots, not stuck inside this armoured beast.

Bullethead sat opposite him, staring into the middle distance, his body moving with the vehicle. Next to him was Dougie, an acerbic Glaswegian which a shock of ginger hair. They were all in their early thirties. Tough men in the prime of life and peak of fitness. They were dressed similarly. Crye Precision camouflage gear with knee pads sewn into the trousers. Armoured flaps to cover their groin area, currently clipped up. Plate hangars with magazines for their personal weapons stashed round the front and side. Personal radios at shoulder height with a stubby antenna pointing upwards and coax cables coiling round their bodies. Boom mikes and earpieces. Helmets, cut away around the ears, with night-vision goggles fitted to the top, ready to pull down when necessary. GPS units on their wrists. Their personal weapons – suppressed C8 rifles and Glock 17s – were sprayed in olive camouflage colours. Dougie had a black bandana over his mouth and nose. In other circumstances, it would be there to conceal his identity. Out here, it was a filter from the dust that stuck to everything. Lots of the guys wore them. Danny didn't bother. He'd operated in this part of the world so often that clean air was now a novelty to him.

Dougie's head was resting against the wall of the Bushmaster and his eyes were closed. Other members of the troop were driving and manning the weapons stations. It was probably a good shout to get some shut-eye while you could.

Danny couldn't. He wasn't wired like that. On the face of it, this was a straightforward op. It would be a stupid move for anybody to take on this heavily armed convoy. But it was in Danny's nature to repeat the operational details in his head, over and over. The prison facility was a three-pronged building with a high perimeter fence. The vehicular entrance to the fence would be open, but the convoy would not cross the perimeter until the Kurds on site had given a pre-arranged sign that it was safe to approach: three flashes from a torch, repeated at one-minute intervals. Once the troop had the all clear, one of the Jackals would enter the facility grounds and pick up the Kurds. They were expecting three men. The Jackal would take them back to the convoy. Then the troop would escort them through the night, back across the Iraqi border to the safety of the British military base. It was up to the head shed what happened to them after that.

Danny's earpiece burst into life. It was Ollie Macalister, who was driving the Bushmaster. Danny could see the back of his head, and that of Chinese Mike, who had that name because he preferred Asian women. He was sitting up front in the passenger seat. Beyond them, through the toughened windscreen of the armoured vehicle, a milky half-moon hung in the sky. From time to time, Danny could see the silhouetted outline of a distant mountain range. Other than that, nothing. They were driving without headlamps so they couldn't be seen from a distance. Ollie had his night vision engaged.

'*Okay, lads,*' said Ollie over the radio, '*we're on the edge of govern-ment-held territory. We're going to head off road now. Follow my lead. ETA to target, ninety minutes.*'

Danny felt the Bushmaster swerve off road. The terrain instantly became bumpier and Dougie, who had appeared to doze through Ollie's radio transmission, opened his eyes. There was no sign of sleepiness. Instant alertness. The guys in the back all began to raise their hands to their helmets to engage their NV. Immediately the interior of the Bushmaster turned a hazy green colour and small details appeared that had been invisible before. A first-aid kit strapped to one of the doors. A holster on Dougie's lower leg containing a tiny snubnose pistol. Extra-curricular, but that was okay. In the badlands of Syria, each man took whatever he felt he needed.

'It's ma kid's birthday today,' Dougie said in his deep Glaswegian accent. It was a surprising admission. Normally, on ops, the guys kept personal stuff like that to themselves. Neither Danny nor Bullethead said anything. If Dougie wanted to open up, he'd do it of his own accord. 'The missus wants tae give her a fuckin' iPhone. Eleven years of age, man, and we give her a fuckin' Batphone to every paedo on the net.' Dougie had a particular obsession with paedophiles. If he ever found himself behind bars – and that wasn't unlikely for a guy of Dougie's temperament – the sex-case criminals would be in for a rough time.

'She'll be fine, buddy,' Danny said. 'It'll be Candy Crush and Ariana Grande all the way.'

Dougie made a non-committal grunt and Danny found himself thinking about his own daughter, Rose, who he hardly ever saw. He'd met her mother Clara in Syria all those years ago, but Clara didn't like Rose having a killer for a father. Danny preferred not to dwell on it, so he was pleased when Ollie brought the Bushmaster to a halt, announced that they were thirty klicks from target and called for a changeover. Bullethead took the wheel while Danny climbed on top and manned the grenade launcher. It was good to be out of the vehicle and in the open, even though it was much hotter and his eyes immediately started to sting from the dust kicked up by the convoy. They were back on a road now. The desert glowed green around him. Rough scrub here and there. Boulders dotted around. The occasional distant glint of an animal's eyes.

But no people. No threats. The surrounding terrain was quiet and effectively empty. It somehow made Danny twice as alert. He scanned the area carefully up ahead, left and right. When he turned a full 360 he saw the three Jackals following, and his troop mates manning the double-mounted Gimpys, also searching for threats.

Nothing.

After forty-five minutes, something appeared up ahead. A low building, probably three klicks distant, but visible because of the largely flat terrain. Danny was about to alert the others when Bullethead's voice came over the comms. '*Eyes on the target. Repeat, eyes on the target. Go static.*'

The convoy came to a halt. Danny continued to scan the surrounding area. There appeared to be no infrastructure in the vicinity of the prison. This road in, and the occasional drainage ditch on either side. Otherwise, this was a solitary facility. And abandoned, as he expected. There were no vehicles nearby, or any sign of life. He flicked a switch on his radio pack, changing to the satellite channel that would put him in touch with the ops base back in Iraq. 'Alpha, this is Zero 22. Over.'

A brief pause. Then: '*Zero 22, this is Alpha. Go ahead. Over.*'

'We're three klicks east of the target and we have eyes on. Have you heard from the Kurds? Over.'

'*Roger that. They made contact at 22.00 hours and confirmed the approach procedures. You're clear to advance on target at will. Over.*'

'Understood. Out.'

Danny switched the radio back to the troop's personal comms frequency. 'We have the all-clear from base. We'll advance to a klick from target then recce on foot.'

The convoy moved off, trundling slowly over the hard-baked desert earth.

Ten minutes later they came to a halt again. Danny and Dougie dismounted from the Bushmaster and silently jogged towards the target. They stopped five hundred metres out. Danny noticed a deep drainage ditch heading off at right angles to the road. He wondered if this area was prone to flooding in the winter months. The prison complex was clearer now. It was a surprisingly modern building, low and sleek. The guys back at base had described it to Danny as a symmetrical three-pronged construction, each prong leading from a circular central space. They were approaching from the east, heading to the area between two of the prongs. Danny retrieved a telescopic night sight from his ops waistcoat as he and Dougie hit the ground to put in surveillance. He identified the perimeter fence, topped with rolls of razor wire, and three security towers evenly spaced about it. There was a gap in the fence where a gate had been opened, and a small guard house next to it. The perimeter didn't look massively secure to Danny, but one glance at the surrounding terrain explained why that would be the case: escape from here on foot and in this unforgiving landscape, you'd likely be dead in a couple of days anyway.

'*Any sign of the safe-approach signal?*' Bullethead asked over comms.

'Not yet,' Danny said. 'Hold your positions.' He raised his night sight again and scanned the prison buildings. Still nothing. No vehicles. No personnel. No movement.

'Where the fuck are they?' Dougie said.

Danny continued to watch. He was looking out for three flashes from a torch in quick succession. None came.

A minute passed.

Two.

Nothing.

Danny switched his radio frequency. 'Alpha, this is Zero 22. Over.'

'*Go ahead, Zero 22. Over.*'

'We're on target. There's no sign of the Kurds. No safe-approach signal. Can you make contact with them? Over.'

'*Roger that. Wait out. Over.*'

Two minutes passed. Then: '*Zero 22, this is Alpha. We've lost contact with the Kurds. Looks like a comms outage. Over.*'

Danny swore. Losing radio contact was an occupational hazard. But why was there no safe-approach signal?

'*Zero 22, are you in a position to make an approach and recce the target?*'

Danny narrowed his eyes. He didn't like it. But the only option was a full retreat, and he didn't like that either. 'Roger that,' he said. 'Wait out.'

He switched frequency to speak to the rest of the troop. 'The Kurds have lost contact with base. They want us to make a recce. Advance with care.'

Danny and Dougie stayed on the ground, keeping eyes on the target while the convoy approached. Once the three Jackals and the Bushmaster had caught them up, Danny and Dougie rejoined them. 'Place looks deserted,' Dougie said. 'Maybe the Kurds got cold feet and fucked off.'

Yeah, Danny thought. *Maybe.*

'This is the plan,' he said. 'Jackal One, make an approach. Jackals Two and Three remain static to provide covering fire. The Bushmaster will hold back in a protective position. I'll take the top gun in Jackal Two.

Danny took his position at one of the Gimpys on Jackal Two. As Jackal One advanced towards the target, Jackals Two and Three positioned themselves on either side of the road that led towards the prison, which was four hundred metres distant. The Bushmaster was thirty metres behind them. To Danny's right was another drainage ditch leading at right angles from the road. Danny and the other three Gimpy operators rotated their weapons towards the prison compound, ready to give covering fire if necessary. Jackal One trundled towards the prison at a slow, steady rate. In his peripheral vision, Danny was aware of Chinese Mike aiming the Bushmaster's grenade launcher towards one of the security towers. Danny raised his night sight again, looking for the three regular flashes of the torch. They didn't come.

He switched his radio frequency to speak to the ops base. 'Alpha, this is Zero 22. We have one vehicle approaching the target now. Over.'

A pause and a hiss. '*Roger that. Over.*'

Jackal One was ten metres from the entrance. It stopped. Through his sight, Danny saw the top-gunners making a precautionary sweep of the compound. A voice in his earpiece said, '*Clear.*' Jackal One sustained its slow advance towards the guard house. Danny continued to watch through his sight.

It happened suddenly. One moment the Jackal was advancing. The next, there was an explosion so fierce that, even from a distance, it sent a shock wave through Danny's body. There was a brief flash, bright enough to dazzle him. When his sight returned, he saw smoke belching from the position the Jackal had held, it was so thick that it completely obscured the vehicle.

Danny screamed into his radio. 'Land mine! Contact! Contact! One vehicle down! Three guys!'

But it was already going noisy. Tracer fire shot through the air from positions inside the prison. It lit up the night, burning through and over the perimeter fence, at first landing only in the vicinity of the convoy vehicles and spitting up vicious explosions of desert dust. It took only seconds for the shooters to fine-tune their aim. Before any of the team could return fire, the tracer rounds – .40 and .50 cal, Danny estimated – slammed into the two remaining Jackals and the Bushmaster. Each time a tracer round hit, there was a sickening metallic crunch and a multicoloured burst of ricochet, like fireworks.

After a few seconds' delay, the air exploded with the thunder of the SAS team returning fire. The night split with the cacophony of the four Gimpys on Jackals Two and Three pumping ordnance back towards the prison. Danny fired bursts of three to five rounds – the most effective and accurate way to operate a Gimpy. The empty rounds spat out of the weapon and the 7.62s flew through the thick plume of smoke billowing from the wrecked Jackal One. Grenades smashed through the perimeter fence and exploded in the vicinity of the prison. But sustained and relentless and brutal though the SAS's counterattack was, it seemed to have no effect. If anything, the incoming fire increased in intensity. More lines of tracer fire sliced towards them, slamming into the Jackals and the Bushmaster, which were rocking and smouldering with the impact. Two RPGs starburst in the air, showering the area with shrapnel. Two more exploded on the ground fifteen metres behind the Bushmaster. The incoming grew heavier and heavier, high-calibre rounds drilling into the armoured panels of the vehicles.

'Bullethead!' Danny screamed through comms at the driver of the Bushmaster. 'Advance, *advance!* We need more covering fire!' He could feel the heat coming off the barrel of his Gimpy.

As the Bushmaster moved forwards, Danny switched frequency. Immediately he heard a stressed voice at the other end of the radio. '*Zero 22, what is your sitrep?*'

'We're under heavy fire! We need air support! Now!'

Even as he spoke, things got worse.

Through his night vision he saw a flare from inside the prison. In the two seconds that followed, he became aware of an anti-tank missile hurtling through the air directly at Jackal Three. The vehicle was to his three o'clock, no more than twenty metres away. Against a weapon like that, it didn't stand a chance. The missile slammed hard into the Jackal. The extremity of the explosion punched all the air from Danny's lungs. Jackal Three was thrown on to its side like a toy. Flames engulfed it. Within the space of ninety seconds, whoever was lying in wait at the prison had demolished two Jackals and six men, and things were only going to get worse. Danny fired more bursts from the Gimpy. The barrel was glowing faintly, and smoking. He was going to burn it out if he kept this rate of fire, but there was no chance of changing out the barrel. 'Fast air!' Danny shouted into comms. 'FAST AIR!'

He didn't hear the response, because right then the Bushmaster hit an IED in the road that the rest of the convoy had miraculously missed. The gutting crack of the explosion cut through the noise of tracer rounds and Gimpy fire. The front end of the Bushmaster crumpled horrifically and the whole vehicle tipped over on to its side with an ominous creak.

And then its problems really started.

Three anti-tank missiles slammed into the Bushmaster's undercarriage. The noise and devastation were immense. Metal ripped. Smoke belched. Fuel ignited. It was obvious at a glance that everyone inside the vehicle was fucked. Danny quickly switched his radio to personal comms. He wished he hadn't. All he could hear was inhuman screams from inside the Bushmaster. Macalister? Bullethead? He couldn't tell. Danny tried to concentrate on keeping the rounds from his Gimpy raining down on the prison, but now he was aware of someone moving away from the Bushmaster. It had to be Chinese Mike, thrown from the remote weapon station. He was staggering towards Jackal Two, then he stumbled and fell perhaps fifteen metres away, Danny could hear him screaming.

Danny's reaction was instinctive. He threw himself from the Jackal, hitting the ground with a heavy, deadened thump. Chinese Mike was in trouble. He needed help. Danny struggled to his feet, the air around him a riot of tracer fire and shrapnel. He sprinted towards Chinese Mike, who had managed to get to his knees.

He was only five metres away when the rounds hit. If the effect of the tracer rounds on the armoured shells of the convoy vehicles was brutal, their effect on a human body was obscene. They cut through Chinese Mike's neck, abdomen and groin like he was made of warm butter. Blood and the hot mush of decimated internal organs and fragments of bone showered everywhere. Danny hit the ground, pressing himself hard on to the desert floor to avoid meeting the same grisly fate as his mate. He looked back towards Jackal Two. It was ten metres from where he was lying and only had one Gimpy operational since Danny had gone to Mike's rescue.

He evaluated his options. Jackal Two was the only remaining vehicle. He had to get back to it.

No chance.

Less than a second later, a missile hit the Jackal. The shock wave physically threw him several metres away from the vehicle and on to Chinese Mike's gruesome remains. There was a sudden wave of intense heat as the thermobaric warhead did its work. Danny thought he was on fire. He roared with pain, but somehow had the presence of mind to push himself back to his feet and sprint away from the conflagration. A secondary explosion from the Bushmaster threw him to the ground again. Danny was horribly aware of the stench of his scorched clothes and the constant barrage of tracer fire devouring the remains of the convoy. He was gasping, gulping for air. Still pressed into the ground, he fumbled for his radio and switched frequencies again. 'Thirteen men down!' he shouted. 'Where's that fucking fast air?'

'*Incoming from Northern Iraq. ETA five minutes.*'

Danny swore and looked around. He saw four individual fires: the four vehicles, still burning, spewing black smoke. Jackal Two had fallen into the drainage ditch that led from the road. The air wavered with the heat haze and the prison was barely visible beyond the glare, although he could make out gobbets of fire rising from the perimeter fence. The incoming had subsided. There was an ominous silence. It was only when he raised his night sight, which was still hanging by a lanyard round his neck, that he could discern the movement of personnel near the prison. Enemy advancing. Was it the Kurds? Had this been a catastrophic blue on blue? Or an elaborate trick? He didn't think so. Why would they have ditched the safe-approach signal if they wanted to ambush the troop? Would they have access to that kind of fire-power? No. This was someone else. Islamic State? Perhaps. They'd have gladly butchered the Kurds that had once guarded this facility, and might have forced the intel of the SAS's imminent arrival out of them. But even that didn't quite ring true. Those anti-tank missiles were serious bits of kit, and the shock and awe tactics they'd used to get the better of an SAS troop smacked to Danny of special forces operators.

SF operators who had, without question, been expecting them.

He had no rifle. He'd left it in the Jackal. His Glock 17 was holstered, but it was a poor replacement, useless for long-range firing. The terrain was flat and featureless. If he ran, the enemy would see him, no question. His only hope of finding cover, he realised, was in the drainage ditch where Jackal Two had ended up. He crawled towards it, grimacing against the heat radiating from the burning Jackal. His body hurt and he moved slowly. It took twenty seconds to cover the ten metres to the ditch. He rolled down into it. It was a little cooler here, below the level of the burning Jackal. He saw the circular opening of a culvert, an underground drainage pipe perhaps a metre in diameter. It would do as a hiding place, but as he prepared to climb in, a voice came over his earpiece. '*Zero 22, this is Alpha, patching you through to fast air.*'

'Go ahead,' Danny said. His own voice surprised him: raw, dry and hoarse.

A new voice. '*We're one minute from target. Repeat, one minute from target. What is your location?*'

'Forget my location,' Danny barked. 'Drop everything you've got on the prison!'

'*Blast area's going to be big. Are you in a position of safety?*'

'Thirteen men down and I'm next. Drop the fucking payload!'

'*Roger that. Out.*'

He could hear the fast air approaching, very quiet at first, very distant, but the noise of its engines increasing by the second. He scrambled a few feet into the culvert and screwed his body up into a ball, his arms protecting his face and covering the hard kevlar of his helmet. His only hope was that the culvert, the kevlar and the burning bulk of the Jackal would protect him from the payload. It wasn't much of a hope, but it was something.

The crescendo of the fast air became more intense. Danny screwed up his eyes as the deafening roar of the aircraft passed overhead and the vibration thrummed even here under the ground.

And then the bombs hit.

The noise was unreal. Five explosions so loud that they caused stabbing pains in Danny's ears. But the noise was not the worst thing. The overpressures, so close to the blast site, were like nothing he had ever experienced. His mouth, his head, his lungs all felt as though they'd had the air sucked out of them. The ground shook and his body shook with it. There was a cracking sound and he knew that the concrete culvert was collapsing around him. He felt dust in his mouth and could hear, outside his hiding place, the brutal, relentless rain of shrapnel pelting the ground. There was another enormous, metallic crash and crunch nearby and several afterblasts, each of them sending a vibrating shock through Danny's body.

And then, suddenly, silence.

Danny gasped noisily, his lungs suddenly working again. His mouth filled with grit and dust. He opened his eyes. Everything was spinning. It was dark, and he realised that the air was still so full of dust it was completely obscuring his vision. He crawled out of the culvert. As he moved, he heard the concrete collapse behind him. Out in the ditch, he coughed and retched as the thick, polluted air seemed to suck its way into his nose, mouth and ears. His right ear, where his earpiece was fitted, felt clogged. There was moistness on his left earlobe. He realised that his eardrums were bleeding.

It took a minute for the dust to settle sufficiently that it was worth Danny re-engaging his NV goggles. Astonishingly they were still working. He recced the surrounding area and immediately saw the source of the nearby metallic crash. The force of the blast had thrown the nearby Jackal into the air and out of the ditch. It lay on its back, crunched and smouldering, ten metres away. Danny raised his goggles, fumbled with trembling fingers for his night sight, and looked back towards the prison.

It barely existed. Two minutes ago there had been a strong, secure edifice. Now it was rubble. Several individual fires glowed where the prison had once been and the perimeter fence, still standing in places, was aflame. Danny knew how lucky he was to be alive. It was obvious to him that the air strike must have taken out any other person in the immediate vicinity.

'*Zero 22, this is Alpha. Do you copy? Over.*' The voice in Danny's ear was muffled because of the blood. He removed the earpiece and tried to clear out the earhole with a thick, dirty forefinger. When he replaced the earpiece, the guy back at base was repeating his communication. '*Zero 22, this is Alpha. Do you copy? Over.*'

'They're gone . . .' Danny muttered. His voice was slurred. Slow. He could barely understand himself.

'*What is your status? Over?*'

'Everyone's gone . . .'

Danny surveyed the bleak scene again. The guys were dead. All of them. Ambushed by a force with superior fire power who had known — Danny was certain of this — that they were coming. Thirteen good guys. Thirteen friends. He felt a surge of anger boil through him. '*Zero 22. Danny? Activate your personal tracking device. Over.*'

He stared into the distance for a full ten seconds before the instruction registered. His tracking device resembled a smart-phone in a tough, rugged case. He fumbled for it, his attention still on the blazing bomb site. He swiped and tapped the screen to transmit his distress beacon back to base.

'*Listen up, Danny. We need to get you out of there. Your nearest patrol is a day's drive away, so we're going to despatch a chopper. That blast site's going to attract attention, so you need to get the hell away from it. Keep walking east. Don't stop walking. Get away from that place as quickly as possible. Do you copy?*'

Danny didn't reply. He realised he was stumbling around aimlessly.

'*Danny! Do you copy?*'

'They were waiting for us,' Danny muttered.

'*You need to calm down, Danny. You need to listen carefully. Get away from the blast site. There could be . . .*'

Danny switched of his radio and the voice died.

The Bushmaster and the two remaining Jackals were mere shells. He went through the motions of checking for survivors, but he knew it was useless. He couldn't even recognise the remains of his unit mates. Their skin was scorched away, their features

14

melted. They stank of burned flesh and hair. Beyond the vehicles, closer to the remains of the prison, he encountered dismembered body parts among the chunks of rubble and pockmarked craters in the earth. He picked some of them up. A forearm. A lower leg. He felt he should do something with them, but he didn't know what, so he dropped them on the ground again. None of them helped him with his objective: to identify the fighters who had been lying in wait for them, and who had killed Danny's team. And so he started stumbling groggily in the direction of the bomb site.

He was 200 metres from ground zero when he found his first piece of evidence. To the untrained eye, it would look like nothing more than a hunk of twisted, mangled metal. But when Danny pulled out his torch and examined it more closely, he knew immediately what it was, or at least what it had once been: a metal tripod with a thick cylindrical tube atop, still warm to the touch. This was one of the anti-tank missile launchers that had made such short work of the convoy. It was a Kornet-EM. Laser-beam guidance system. Range of eight to ten kilometres.

And Russian.

Danny spat the dust from his mouth. His mind was clearing. He pulled out his camera and photographed the Kornet. He staggered on. A minute later, he came across a body. It was almost as mangled as the missile launcher, its limbs pointing at strange angles from broken bones, patches of clothing burned away and whatever skin remained on the face covered with a thick, sooty layer. Danny knelt down beside it. He took his water canteen from his ops vest and poured a little water on the dead man's face, before scrubbing away the dirt and rinsing it again. There was no doubt about it: this was not the body of Kurd or an IS fighter. This was white skin.

He photographed the dead body then got back to his feet and stared down at the corpse. A wave of overwhelming anger rose in his gut. He drew his pistol and aimed it at the body. Discharged a full magazine into its torso and then, when it was empty, threw the weapon at its face. And then he felt stupid, he'd lost control and he had no spare magazines. Now he was without a useable weapon.

15

He muttered to himself. The Kornet. The white skin. They both pointed to a single fact: they'd been ambushed by Russians. How or why, he didn't know. He bitterly turned his back on the burning bomb site and retraced his steps away from the prison. He switched his radio back on. Almost immediately, the voice was barking down the line. *'Zero 22. Do you copy? Repeat, do you copy? Over.'*

'Yeah, I copy,' Danny said, as he staggered towards the smouldering vehicles that contained the remnants of his mates, finally heading east like he'd been told. 'Send that chopper in.'

'Roger that,' the voice said. Danny barely heard it. He had just seen something. A single light. A vehicle was approaching from a distance. A motorbike? Perhaps. The headlamp bumped over the rough terrain. It was coming from the north and advancing quickly. Danny tried to judge the distance. It was tough to do at night and with his head dazed. A mile? Maybe a little more? Who the hell was it? One of the Kurds, late to the party? No. The Kurds were dead. He'd put money on it. More likely, this was part of the hostile force. One of the guys, or maybe two, who had been coordinating the ambush from a distance and were now approaching to see what the hell had happened and if any of their men were still alive.

'Fuck,' Danny muttered to himself. He faced east and started to run. He didn't get far. His ears were still bleeding, and his balance was all over the place. He tripped and fell, and the world started to spin. He was half aware of the bumping headlamp. It etched neon lines across his vision as he tried to stand up. He only managed to get as far as a kneeling position when he had to bend over to vomit. He felt an urgency to get away from there, but his body wouldn't do what his mind demanded. He stayed there, hunched in a ball next to his own puke, resisting nausea and mustering strength. Then he managed to straighten up again. The bumping headlamp wasn't bumping any more. It had stopped. It was twenty metres away and it dazzled him as he squinted at it.

A distended silhouette appeared in front of the headlamp. It approached slowly, preceded by its long shadow. Danny staggered to his feet, cursing himself for wasting his ammunition. The incoming danger forced his mind to achieve more clarity. Whoever this was, he wasn't shooting. Did that mean he was friendly? No. It meant he'd calculated that Danny was unarmed, since Danny hadn't drawn a weapon either.

He was ten metres away when Danny was able to get a proper look at him. He was huge. Danny was a big man. This guy was bigger. A head height taller and another foot around the shoulders. He wore standard military camo gear, but the sleeves of his jacket had been torn off to reveal thick, muscular arms, grimy with sweat. They were the arms of a bodybuilder, with perhaps a few steroids thrown in for good measure. His head was shaved, with the exception of a thick, black mohawk down the centre of his scalp, buzz cut to a height of a centimetre. The skin on one side of his head was horrifically marked with an embossed network of red scars. He had a weapon in his belt but he didn't draw it. Obviously his hands were weapons enough. He was clenching and releasing them, like he was loosening them up, ready for action.

He stopped five metres from Danny, who staggered to his feet. The man looked him up and down, then he grinned. It was the kind of grin that had a very particular meaning: *I'm going to rip you apart with my bare hands, motherfucker.*

'Fuck,' Danny repeated under his breath.

The guy took a step forwards. Danny took a step back. He noticed something else. The guy had two patches sewn on to the chest of his jacket. They were SAS squadron patches. The A Squadron patch portrayed an animal that looked like a cross between a tick and a scorpion. The D Squadron patch was an Indonesian Kris sword. They looked like trophies.

Danny evaluated his options. He couldn't run. The guy had a handgun and a vehicle. He couldn't shoot. He had only one path open to him. This guy looked like he was spoiling for a fight. Danny had no choice but to give him one, when it was all he could do to stay upright.

'*Fuck!*' he said for a third time. If this guy hit him, Danny would be on the floor in an instant. No question. And there was a good chance he'd never get back up.

The guy stepped forwards again. His fists were permanently clenched now and the grin had morphed into a strained scowl.

The guy lunged towards him, raising one fist to deliver a hammer blow to Danny's head. Danny sidestepped. The guy overshot and Danny managed to raise his right heel and kick him hard in the kidney.

If he'd done that to anyone else, they'd have been floored, groaning in pain and possibly unconscious. This guy barely seemed to notice it. Danny felt like a wasp stinging an elephant – a minor inconvenience at worst. He glanced over at the motorbike. He could hear the engine turning over. Perhaps he could get to it. Not at the moment. The mohawk guy would just pull his weapon and shoot Danny in the back. Danny would have to play this out a little longer.

The guy turned and bore down on him again. This time he was ready for Danny's sidestep. His fist clipped Danny's right shoulder. It was enough to send him staggering back. His arm went numb. The mohawk guy pressed his advantage. When he charged again, Danny was too dizzy from the last hit to get out of his way, and he landed his first proper hit. It was a solid punch to the solar plexus, and it delivered all the raw power that the guy's physique promised. Danny's legs collapsed beneath him and the air shot from his lungs. The pain was excruciating – he wondered if he'd cracked a rib or even his sternum. His respiratory system didn't seem to work, and he felt a moment of panic as he tried to inhale but couldn't.

The next blow came to the side of Danny's face. It came from the thick sole of the mohawk guy's boot, and it nearly took Danny's head off. He felt blood spurt from his nose as he hit the dirt, and it was flowing more freely from his left ear again. He choked and coughed and tried to grab some loose earth in the hope that he could throw it at his assailant to blind him. But the ground was baked; his fingernails only scraped the hard earth and one of them tore.

Then the mohawk guy was standing above him, huge and threatening. Danny looked up at him through a film of sweat. He noted that the guy hadn't yet pulled his weapon. He obviously wanted to finish Danny off manually. But he wanted to gloat first.

'SAS scum,' he said. He spoke English, but his accent was definitely Russian. He tapped the two patches on his jacket. 'I killed two of your comrades with my hands. You will be an easy third.' He laughed, as if he'd just told a great joke. Then he took a couple of steps back, like a rugby player preparing to take a kick. And Danny's head was the ball.

His mistake was not finishing Danny off the moment he was on the ground. In a weird way, Danny was disappointed in him. This guy and his men had just ambushed and massacred an SAS team. They were pros. They knew what they were about. And the first rule of hand-to-hand combat? Fight to win. Finish your opponent quickly and by whatever means possible. No second chances.

Danny had a second chance.

The Russian took his run up. Before he could take his kick, Danny rolled fast towards him and into the foot that remained on the ground. The guy tripped and fell, and now he was on the ground, face up, and Danny was on his feet. Danny stamped his heel into the Russian's face and he roared in pain as his nose broke and blood spread and spattered over the scarring on the side of his scalp. He was fumbling for his weapon now and Danny had a split-second call to make. Observe the first rule? Grab his gun and finish him? He couldn't. His arm was still numb. He wasn't sure he could operate the handgun effectively and in any case the Russian had gripped it now.

So he ran like hell towards the motorbike. It was twenty metres away. He moved in a zig zag, out of the beam of the headlamp, so he was hard to see and harder to hit. He figured that, big as his opponent was, a boot in the face and a broken nose will at least have stunned the Russian and give Danny time to reach the vehicle.

He figured right. Danny threw himself on to the bike – just as he heard the retort of a handgun behind him. There was no sound of the bullet impacting. Danny forced the bike into a tight turning circle. The tyres protested against the desert floor as he moved the vehicle and accelerated hard. The gap between him and the mohawk guy began to widen: thirty metres, then forty.

Danny braked and skidded. The headlamp lit up the terrain in front of him. He could taste the fight in his mouth; a taste of blood and dust and pain. Around him, he was aware of the burning fires of the Jackals and the Bushmaster and the bomb site, and he felt again the bitterness of losing his unit mates. He turned the bike to face his enemy and revved the engine, fully intent on accelerating towards his assailant and hitting him with the full momentum of a heavy vehicle at speed.

The Russian was now on his feet again. He had his weapon raised and pointing at Danny. There was no chance of him landing a shot on target at that range. Their eyes locked. The guy had blood streaming down his face. Danny knew he himself probably looked twice as bad. He let the guy's features imprint themselves on his mind. The buzz-cut mohawk. The horrific scarring on the scalp. The SAS flashes on his jacket. 'One day,' he muttered to himself. 'One fucking day.'

It was almost as if the Russian could hear him. He grinned, inclined his head and then he spat on the ground. But he didn't lower his weapon.

Danny turned the bike and accelerated again, heading east. He only glanced in the side mirror once to see the burning remnants of the Zero 22 op and the fading silhouette of the man who had just tried to kill him, and failed.

TWO

Devon. One week later.

Half past three. Going-home time.

The rain was incessant. The kids were spilling out of the play-ground, anonymous in their raincoats with the hoods crimped tight around their faces. They shook their teacher's hand before being allowed off the premises to meet their parents. The mums and one or two dads congregated around the gates, a phalanx of umbrellas protecting them from the unusually heavy rain. When they each saw their child, they bustled them under their umbrella and hurried them to the car.

One of the kids was called Danny White. He didn't have many friends. In fact, he didn't have *any* friends. He'd arrived halfway through the school year. Friendship groups were established and, try though he might, he hadn't been able to break into any of them. So he was alone as he shook soggy hands with the teacher. 'Where's your mum, Danny?' she asked. He pointed to the yellow umbrella that he recognised, set slightly apart from the crowd. 'Alright then. Good afternoon. Have a nice weekend.'

Danny didn't think he would have a nice weekend. His week-end would be like all the others. Solitary. Since moving down here with his mum, she had been different. She was kind enough, alright, and she looked after him, made sure he had enough to eat and his clothes were clean and he got to school on time every morning. But she was distracted. She kept the curtains closed during the day but often slightly parted them to look outside, as if checking for something or someone. When Danny asked if they could go to the park, she always found a reason to say, 'Another time, sweetie.' She only went out to do the school run and make the occasional trip to the supermarket, and even then, she always wanted to get back as quickly as possible.

His mum was standing next to the lamp post as usual. Danny's shoes were wet through as he approached her. He was looking down at them, thinking about how much darker they looked when they were wet, so it wasn't until he was under the umbrella that he realised that the person holding it wasn't his mum. It was a man. Danny was embarrassed and was about to turn away when the man took his shoulder. He had a cheery, friendly face.

'Danny?' he asked.

Danny nodded. The man wore brown leather shoes, smart new jeans that were wet from the knee down and a black leather jacket. He offered him a Maoam chew. 'Your mum said these were your favourite,' he said.

They *were* Danny's favourite. He took the Maoam and started to peel the wrapper, but then decided he might keep it for later and put it in his pocket. 'Where's my mummy?' he said.

'Her car broke down,' said the man. 'She asked me to come and get you. Shall we go?'

Danny frowned. He knew about stranger danger. 'What's your name?' he said.

'Sorry. I'm Andy. You've probably seen me around?' Danny shook his head. 'Well, I live next door. Come on, let's get you home.'

Danny hesitated. The man had very broad shoulders and he'd just noticed a scar on the right-hand side of his nose.

'Why didn't my mummy come with you?' he said.

'Her car broke down on the way.'

'I have to tell my teacher.'

'Don't worry about that,' said the man. 'We'll get soaked if we don't get back to my car.' He pulled a mobile phone from his pocket. 'We'll call your mum, shall we?'

'Okay,' said Danny.

'I'm parked just down here. Want to hold the umbrella?' He handed it to Danny, who had to walk on tiptoes and hold it aloft in order to cover them both. The man offered Danny his free hand.

'I thought you were going to call my mummy.'

'I've got her number in here somewhere,' the man said, swiping the screen. He took Danny's hand in his and started to walk away from the school. There was a firmness to his grip and Danny found he had to walk quickly to keep up. The man showed him the phone as if to indicate that he'd located his mum's number then put it to his ear. They turned a corner at the end of the street, into a tree-lined avenue with cars parked on both sides. 'She's not answering,' said the man. 'We'll try her again in a minute.'

Danny stopped. 'Where did you get her umbrella from?' he said.

'She lent it to me. Didn't want you getting wet. You know what mums are like, hey?'

'She keeps it in the car,' Danny said.

He might only be six, but he wasn't stupid. He could tell the man was lying. He tried to release himself from his grip, but he couldn't. The big hand enveloped his and the man was too strong. Danny wriggled. 'Let go of me!' he said. And then he shouted it: '*Let go of me!*' The noise of the rain against the umbrella was loud and the nearest person was on the other side of the street. He knew nobody had heard him.

The man didn't reply. He put his phone back in his pocket and gripped Danny's hand a little harder. Danny tried to stop walking, to drag his heels. It made no difference to the man, who walked faster, pulling Danny along the pavement. Danny tried to hit him with the umbrella, but the man simply grabbed the umbrella back.

Danny started to cry. He wanted to scream, but suddenly found he was too scared to do it. It was like someone had punched him in the stomach. He could barely catch his breath through the sobs. He looked back over his shoulder, hoping somebody might see them. But nobody did. There were very few people in the street. Those that were had their heads down and their umbrellas up. Danny was invisible to them.

Up ahead, there was a white van. The rear windows were blacked out. As they approached it, in the side mirror Danny saw the reflection of somebody watching in the passenger seat. The door opened and the person stepped out. He looked similar to

Andy. The same broad shoulders. The same thick neck. But he wasn't smiling. He closed the passenger door and banged against the side of the white van with a clenched fist. The rear doors opened, by which time the new guy had grabbed Danny's other arm. Danny wriggled and writhed even more strenuously. He even managed to shout out despite his breathlessness. But he was completely overpowered by the two men. They lifted him from the pavement while Danny's kicks simply bounced off their shins. They manoeuvred him over a puddle of water that had collected by the kerb and towards the back of the van. Through his tears, Danny saw two more men in the vehicle, but it was gloomy in there so he couldn't fully make out their features. All he heard was a gruff voice saying: 'Get him in!'

Danny knew he only had one last chance. He screamed as loudly as he could, then raised his legs and struck Andy with all the force he could muster. He obviously hurt him, because Andy said, 'Little shit!'

One of the guys in the van said, 'Just throw him in!'

The two men hurled him into the van. Roughly. He caught his foot on a lip in the doorway. It caused his body to twist and he hit his head hard, once on the side of the van and a second time on the floor.

And that was the last Danny knew of his abduction.

'Fuck's sake,' said KitKat.

They called him that because he only has four fingers on his right hand, like the chocolate bar. His thumb was missing in action, last seen spinning through the air when his SBS team were providing a training package to a group of rebels in the DRC. He'd been demonstrating how to use a Russian landmine as a booby trap when it went off prematurely, earning him not only a nickname, but also the loss of sight in one eye and a career henceforth limited to carrying out the SBS's donkey work. Work like this, abducting a six-year-old kid.

Nobody joined the SBS to abduct six-year-old kids.

'Fuck's *sake*!' KitKat repeated. What were they playing at? There was nothing to the boy. Why did they have to throw him in so hard? KitKat winced when he saw the kid's head hit the side of the van. His neck had jarred to the right and there might even have been a crack, he wasn't sure. He lurched forward to catch him, but too late. The boy had gone limp and his head slammed hard against the floor.

The kid lay there, still as a corpse. One of his feet was still poking through the door opening. 'Get him in!' said the guy outside. KitKat grabbed the kid's shoulders and pulled him further into the van as the doors slammed shut and they were plunged into darkness. Rain hammered on the roof and the engine turned over. By the time KitKat had pulled his Maglite torch from his pocket, the van had pulled away. He shone the torch at the kid and rolled him over on to his back.

Every special forces operator is well trained in field medicine. The training kicks in when it's needed. Automatic. Instinctive. KitKat reached out with his good hand and placed his index and middle fingers against the kid's neck. He knew he wouldn't find a pulse. When you'd seen as many corpses as he had, you learned to recognise the signs. The rictus of the mouth. The heavy stillness of the body. KitKat went through the motions, blowing rescue breaths into the kid's mouth, performing chest compressions. But he knew it was hopeless. The kid was dead. Roughed up by a four-man SBS unit whose instructions had been to abduct him and keep him safe.

'*Fuck's sake!*' he said for a third time as he gave up on the CPR. He turned to his mate who was watching from the corner of the van. 'He's a fucking goner,' he spat. 'And we're toast.'

He slammed a fist against the inside of the van in frustration. The van accelerated. KitKat switched off the torch. He didn't want to look at the boy's pale face any more than was necessary.

THREE

Back in the day, when Danny Black had first joined the Regiment, an old-timer told him that there were two kinds of SAS men. The ones whose minds gave up before their bodies and the ones whose bodies gave up before their minds. Danny was beginning to think that he was the latter.

That wasn't to say he slept easy. How could anyone do that, when they'd seen the things he had? The Zero 22 debacle was a week old and it stuck with him. The image of Bullethead's burned face kept returning. He'd visited Dougie's missus. He'd put on a clean shirt and even shaved. His face had felt naked after months of wearing a beard on ops. There'd been no sign of Dougie's daughter, but Danny couldn't help noticing the precious new iPhone that had so worried her dad. It was sitting on the kitchen table in a Hello Kitty case.

But there was no doubting that his body was sore and tired, much more so than it would have been during his early days in the Regiment. His shoulder still ached where the Russian had hit him. The bruising on his face had only just started to fade and his ears were still clogged. Back at base, they'd offered him a little R and R, but he'd turned it down. He preferred to keep his fitness sharp, his strength and endurance at their peak. It wasn't his style to put his feet up.

Even so, he was surprised to get the call.

He'd clocked in to base early, ready for a morning on the range. One of the clerks who manned the Kremlin – the inner sanctum of RAF Credenhill, where the CO and all the other Ruperts had their offices – approached him outside the B Squadron hangar and told him his presence was required in briefing room C at 09.30 hrs. He made his way there alone, ignoring the looks from the administrative staff that followed him as he went. Word of the Zero 22 op had spread. Of course it had. The loss of thirteen men on a single mission was a wound the Regiment would carry for a long time. Danny knew that those inquisitive glances masked many different questions. Was Danny Black the hero of the hour for making it out alive, or was he in some way responsible for the death of the guys in his troop? Could he have done more to save them? Had he just saved his own skin?

Danny ignored those glances. They weren't posing any questions he hadn't asked himself. He was comfortable that he'd done all he could. Like he'd said in his debrief, they'd been ambushed by a heavily armed force that hit them hard and fast. He'd reported his suspicion that the enemy had been Russian. Maybe the Kurds had set them up. Who knows what impenetrable alliances existed in that part of the world. Bottom line: Zero 22 had been played by someone.

He knocked on the door of briefing room C. A suit with a funereal expression opened it, looked Danny up and down, then opened the door wider and indicated that he should enter. Danny stepped in. Aside from the suit who had opened the door, there were three other men in there. His CO, Mike Williamson, sat at a round table dressed in military camo. He had a handsome, leathery face and a pale scar on his chin. Danny liked him. To his left was George Attwood, Director Special Forces. Grey bushy hair, sparkling blue eyes. He had his hand over his mouth and Danny saw the old bullet wound that had scarred the space between his thumb and forefinger. Danny liked him too. To the CO's right was a gaunt, skinny man with yellowing eyes and thinning black hair. An immaculate suit and a neat tie in an Oxford knot. His fingertips were pressed together and he watched Danny from over them. This was Alan Sturrock, Chief of MI6. When a patronising politician had suggested that the victims of Grenfell Tower had lacked common sense, Danny had shared the public's distaste. At the same time, he had thought of Sturrock. That was the sort of thing *he* would say. Danny loathed him.

Danny felt a sense of déjà vu. Barely six months earlier, these three men had briefed Danny in the matter of Ibrahim Khan. It had led to an op with an MI6 agent called Bethany White, who had turned out not to be quite who she seemed. On the outside, an MI6 agent and single mother. On the inside, a killer of SAS men. Had Bethany White not been in possession of intelligence that could have deeply harmed MI6, and Alan Sturrock in particular, Danny would no doubt have received the order to kill her. But she had, and he hadn't.

Danny would have preferred never to lay eyes on Sturrock again. Now here he was, giving him a smarmy smile as he opened a small bottle of lotion and started to moisturise his hands. 'My dear chap,' said Sturrock. 'You're looking very well, all things considered.'

Danny ignored him and addressed the CO. 'You wanted to see me, boss?'

'Sit down, Danny.'

'I prefer to stand.'

'Sit the fuck down, will you?'

Danny inclined his head and took a seat opposite the three men. Sturrock nodded to the suit at the door. He left the room. There was a moment of silence. Then George Attwood spoke. 'I'm not going to sugar-coat it, Black. Questions are being asked about the Zero 22 clusterfuck. Plenty of bleeding-heart liberals in Whitehall think Hereford is a drain on the public purse. They'd love to use this as a reason to shut us down.'

'Tell them I'm sorry my unit mates chose to die for their country before they'd earned out,' Danny said.

'I'd love to, Black. Believe you me, I'd love to.' He glanced at the CO and Sturrock before continuing. 'Zero 22 was compromised. Somebody knew you were coming. They were expecting you.'

'Tell me something I don't know,' Danny replied.

'I'm about to. That photograph of the enemy combatant that you took. We've had some people look at it. We think we have a positive ID.'

'Russian?' Danny said.

Attwood nodded. 'Leonid Bogatov. Former *Spetznaz*. Retired in 2013 to join the Wagner Group.'

'You're aware of the Wagner Group?' Sturrock asked.

Yeah, Danny was aware of the Wagner Group. It was a private military company, several thousand men strong, run and in part manned by former special forces agents. Except of course, like most PMCs, it wasn't really private. The Wagner Group was in practice an extension of the Russian administration, called in to bolster their armed forces and to perform deniable operations. It existed to carry out the whims of the Russian president, and to cover the trail leading back to him.

Danny nodded.

'We have a high degree of certainty that it was the Wagner Group who hit you,' Attwood said.

'Why?'

'Two reasons.'

'I'd have thought the first was obvious,' Sturrock cut in. 'You were extracting high-level Kurdish personnel. The Syrian regime wanted them dead and for us to lose our taste for defending them. The Russians are Syria's de facto protectors.' He gave Danny a thin smile. 'Are you keeping up?'

Danny was more than keeping up. His mind was racing ahead. How could the Wagner Group possibly have known the details of Zero 22's arrival? It was a secret SAS operation.

Attwood and the CO were watching him carefully. It was almost as if they could see his line of reasoning as it unfolded.

'What's the second reason?' Danny said.

Sturrock held up a photograph. Danny caught his breath. The photograph showed a huge man standing in front of a sand-coloured Jeep with a desert background. He wore a camouflage jacket with the sleeves cut off. He had a black mohawk and prominent, grotesque scarring on one side of his shaved head, almost as if his veins and capillaries were on the outside of his skin. He was holding up the heads of two men by their hair. Their necks were cleanly severed, and the skin was not yet waxy, which told Danny that they were freshly executed. He recognised the man, of course. It was the guy he had fought in Syria. He recognised the victims too. They were young SAS men – Hal Robbins and Tommy Evans – who had been reported KIA some months ago.

'Friend of yours?' Sturrock asked.

'That's him,' Danny said. He had described the man in his debrief.

'His name is Alexander Turgenev. He's a self-appointed colonel in the Wagner Group. He has quite a CV. Putting to one side the fact that he was responsible for the deaths of two SAS men—'

'Fifteen SAS men,' Danny interrupted him, 'if you add the Zero 22 guys. And if it's all the same to you, I don't think I will put that to one side.'

Sturrock continued as if Danny hadn't spoken. 'He was a Spetsnaz operator for seven years, very highly prized despite having a criminal record as long as your arm. The unofficial record suggests he has a history of the extrajudicial killing of gay men in Chechnya. He was discharged from Spetsnaz for gun running – they didn't have a choice about that – but the Wagner Group welcomed him with open arms. Our working theory is that he was coordinating the Zero 22 ambush.'

'If he's the guy you saw,' Attwood said, 'it's the smoking gun that puts the Wagner Group in the right place at the right time.'

'He's the guy,' Danny said. 'No question.' He stared at the picture and remembered the devastation of the op, and the fight that followed, and the two SAS patches on Turgenev's jacket, and his taunt. *SAS scum. I killed two of your comrades with my hands. You will be an easy third.* 'When do I get to waste him?' Danny said. He was trying hard to keep his voice level.

'You don't,' Sturrock said. 'Turgenev is very far from being our principal target.'

Danny remained stony faced. 'Speak for yourself,' he said. 'How did the Wagner Group know we were coming?'

'Does the name General Frank O'Brien mean anything to you?' Attwood said.

'Rings a bell,' Danny said.

'He's American. Five-star general. Popular with the men, thorn in the side of the guy in the Oval Office.' Attwood glanced at the other two men in the room. Danny could tell he was about to deliver some sensitive information. 'It's obvious that the Russians received information about your movements from someone with inside knowledge. The CIA believe that person is O'Brien.'

Danny did not think he could dislike Sturrock any more, but at that moment the spook proved him wrong. A self-satisfied smirk crossed Sturrock's face. Danny wanted to grab him by the throat, pin him to the wall and ask him exactly why he found the death of thirteen Regiment men so amusing.

He restrained himself. He just said: 'Something funny?'

'You wouldn't understand,' said Sturrock. The three men stared at him. 'Very well,' he said. 'For the Americans to have a Russian mole at that level is a matter of extreme embarrassment to them. You wouldn't understand if you didn't work in the service. Back in the fifties, Kim Philby was our principal liaison with the Americans. He was exposed as a Russian spy. I'm not exaggerating when I say that the CIA have been holding that episode over our heads for the past seventy years.'

'They should get a life.'

'Administrations have long memories, Black. MI6 has an ill-deserved reputation for being leaky. But a five-star general passing operational information to the Russians? That's bigger than Philby. For all we know, O'Brien's been sharing classified information for the past two decades. Our transatlantic cousins are eating some humble pie just at the moment.'

'How do you know it's him?' Danny said.

'It's him,' Sturrock replied, as if that ended the matter.

'The Yanks have shared their intel with us,' Attwood said. 'Look, if they hadn't withdrawn from Syria, it would have been them picking those Kurds up from the prison. Truth is, we were extracting those guys at the Americans' request, so there were elements in the American military who knew what you were doing that night. O'Brien was one of them.' Attwood picked up a tablet from the table in front of him. 'Three nights before the Zero 22 operation, O'Brien was in Crete on holiday. He was staying in a hotel outside Chania. Turns out there was another guest there by the name of Dmitri Poliakov. Poliakov is a known FSB agent.' Attwood held up the tablet and showed Danny a picture. It looked like a still from a CCTV camera and showed two men sitting at a bar. One of them was well built, with a straw Trilby hat and a tropical shirt. He had a flamboyant cocktail in front him. The other was much skinnier, with short dark hair and a sober sleeveless shirt. He wore dark sunglasses and his lips were pursed. In front of him was a small coffee cup. 'O'Brien and Poliakov having a cosy little chinwag.'

'And let's be clear,' said Sturrock. 'They weren't discussing the temperature of the pool.'

'We know what they were discussing?' said Danny in a tone of disbelief.

Attwood looked at him. 'It's a fairly busy bar. Lots of smart-phones around. You don't need me to tell you that the CIA have ways of remotely accessing data on these devices. Video snippets intended for social media. Voice assistant recordings. They've managed to piece together bits of their conversation. It's not the whole thing, not by any means. Just a patchwork really. But it's enough. They supplied us with the recording. This is the transcript.'

He handed Danny a piece of paper, stamped TOP SECRET.

O'BRIEN: . . . we shouldn't be seen together . . . blow everything apart . . .
POLIAKOV: . . . I need to know that you mean what you say . . .
O'BRIEN: You don't need to worry about that . . .
. . .
O'BRIEN: . . . fourteen men . . . night-time raid . . . Zero 22 . . .
. . .
POLIAKOV: This is the biggest operation we've worked on. We need to be careful we don't make a mistake.
O'BRIEN: I need to be careful nobody points the finger at me . . .

Danny let the paper drop to the table. He felt sick. 'You have this on tape?' he said.

They nodded.

'Where's the General now?' Danny asked quietly.

The three men shared another glance. 'We'll come to that, Danny,' said the CO. 'You want some water or something?'

Danny shook his head. Water was the last thing he wanted. Sturrock cleared his throat. 'Clearly,' he announced, 'something needs to be done about O'Brien.'

'Something involving a nine-millimetre round and his skull,' Danny said. 'Delta will deal with it like that.' He clicked his fingers.

Sturrock gave another bland smile. 'There are good reasons for keeping Delta Force well clear of this,' he said. 'Like I said, General

O'Brien is popular with the men. Particularly with the special forces. Fights their corner when the liberals start making noises about war crimes. Sending in an American SF force to deal with him would be high risk.'

'They'd do what they have to do,' Danny said.

'Forgive me, Black, but you yourself are walking proof that special forces operators are not entirely averse to going off-piste.' He raised a sarcastic eyebrow.

'The Yanks have passed it over to us,' Atwood said. 'They're dressing it up as a favour, giving us the chance to hit back at the guy responsible for our boys' deaths. It's bullshit, of course. O'Brien's a big problem for them, but they want to keep the solution at arm's length. Ordinarily, we'd leave them to clean up their own mess. But the PM's been informed of the situation and he doesn't see it that way. Politically, it suits him to do the Yanks a favour. Brexit and all that. When a big US–UK trade deal's on offer, it helps grease the wheels if we can remind them how we helped out with their little problem.'

'We don't need to worry about the politics,' said the CO. 'Frank O'Brien as good as killed thirteen of our guys, Danny. Nobody gets away with doing that.'

'You want me to nail him?' Danny asked.

There was a moment of silence.

'We want you to help someone do it,' the CO said.

'I think I've got the skillset.'

Attwood gave a bleak smile. 'No doubt,' he said.

'So why don't I just do it.' The thought of avenging his mates was a comforting one.

'That's one possible plan,' said Attwood. 'But there are several reasons why it might need a little . . . tweaking.'

'Like what?'

'O'Brien's not easy to get to.'

Danny pointed at the transcript on the table. 'Poliakov managed it.'

'Of course. But that meeting would have been set up by the General himself. In the normal course of events, he has a ring of steel around him. Bodyguards wherever he goes. Special forces, mostly. And especially in the next few days. He's attending a summit in Jordan, laying down the basis for a peace deal between the Turks and the Kurds. O'Brien's the main event. Like we told you, he's a popular fellow, very charming, very diplomatic. He's well liked by certain elements high up in the Turkish administration, and the Kurds trust him. If he's there, the warring parties will at least come to the table.'

'You want to take him out in the middle of a peace conference?'

'Of course not. We want to take him out before the conference even starts. We know he'll be staying in the Hotel Grand in Amman for two days before the conference begins, prepping for the talks.'

'What about the peace deal?' Danny said. 'You take him out before it happens, the Turks are going to carry on butchering the Kurds.'

'It's a good job,' said Sturrock, 'that men like you are set to fighting rather than thinking. The man's a Russian agent, for heaven's sake. Isn't it obvious that he'll simply do what he can to destabilise the peace talks? The Russians are quite happy for the Kurds to be wiped out. There'll be no peace agreement while O'Brien's involved.'

'He's right,' said Attwood. 'We can kill two birds with one stone here.' He narrowed his eyes. 'Actually, perhaps we can kill three.'

'What are you talking about?' said Danny.

'O'Brien will be well guarded in the hotel, but he has a weak spot. It's about six inches long and hangs between his legs. It's a common enough flaw in these people.'

'We all remember Petraeus,' Sturrock muttered.

'O'Brien's cut from the same cloth. Can't keep his dick in his pants. He's got a reputation for picking up girls in hotel bars when he's abroad, even on work tours. Everyone hushes it up because he's so respected. Of course, it's going to be hard for you to get close to him because you don't have blonde hair and big tits. But if you hook up with somebody who does, all of a sudden we have a strategy.'

'Except you need a blonde with big tits who you can trust to kill him.'

Another silence. Another long glance between the three men.

'We believe we have someone who fits the bill,' said Sturrock. Danny had never heard him sound more weaselly. Sturrock moisturised his hands again. There was an unpleasant slippery sound as he did it. 'Show him,' he said.

The CO handed a sheaf of photographs over the table. They were scene-of-crime pictures and they were grotesque. One showed a corpse bound to a pole with a cable tie round his neck, his ears missing, blood streaking down the sides of his face. Another showed a dead man on a bed in the position of a crucifix, fingers removed and lying on his chest, blood blooming into the bedclothes from his butchered hands. A third picture – the worst – showed a male body with a cut throat and the genitals removed.

Danny had seen these pictures before. He put them down on the table. 'You've got to be fucking kidding me,' he said.

He knew that these killings were the handiwork of the former MI6 agent Bethany White. The victims were ex-SAS, and Bethany had taken them out in a bloody spree of anger and revenge. She would have killed Danny if she'd had the chance. It was only because her kid had begged her not to that Danny was still alive. 'You're insane. She'll never do it. She's got you over a fucking barrel.'

This was true. Bethany White had hard documentary evidence of British war crimes. Copies were secretly stashed with various lawyers around the world. She'd made it very clear that if anything ever happened to her or her son, the lawyers would release the evidence to the world.

'It may be true,' Sturrock said, a hint of self-satisfaction in his voice, 'that at one time Bethany White had some leverage. That time has passed. She made it particularly hard to track down the lawyers she'd engaged, but we managed it. The guardians of her precious so-called evidence have been dealt with.'

The phrase 'dealt with' had a note of finality about it. Danny didn't probe any further. 'There's still no reason why she should do what you ask her,' he said. 'She fucking hates you. She hates all of us. Plus, she's a psycho.'

'I can't disagree with you there,' Sturrock said. 'But you're quite wrong in other respects. Bethany White *will* do as she's told. We've arranged some leverage of our own.'

'Yesterday afternoon,' Attwood said, 'an SBS team abducted her son. I believe he's also called Danny?'

'Yeah,' Danny said. 'He is.' And though he would never have admitted, nor even let it show in his face, he felt a moment of queasiness. No matter what Bethany White's faults – and they were many – her boy was a good kid. Dragging *him* into the mess? Danny didn't like it.

'The boy's being held in a secure location,' Sturrock continued. 'He's safe, he's well looked after. Rather better looked after than he was with his mother, I should think.'

'Does Bethany know?'

He nodded grimly. 'Her reaction was extreme.'

'I bet it was,' Danny muttered. There was an awkward silence, then Danny shook his head. 'This doesn't add up,' he said. 'There are other ways to deal with O'Brien. Why does it have to be Bethany White?'

Sturrock looked at the two military men. It looked like he didn't want to articulate whatever was coming next. It was Attwood who took over. 'Let's be plain,' he said. 'We're green-lighting a British op to take out an American five-star general. The fallout is potentially catastrophic. It's all very well doing the Yanks a favour, but who's to say they won't use our complicity against us at some time in the future? If that happens, it either compromises the assassin, or it gives them a great deal of leverage over us. It's much better if, once the job is complete, the assassin is taken out of the picture.'

And suddenly, it all became clear to Danny. 'You want me to kill Bethany White when she's done it. You want to use her because she's ruthless and expendable.'

'More than expendable,' Sturrock said. 'She's a rogue MI6 agent and she has intel that cannot enter the public domain.' He pressed his fingers together once more. 'Like I said, three birds with one stone.'

Again, silence. It was Danny who broke it. 'What about the kid?' he said.

'He will be well looked after,' Sturrock said. 'We have the budget for it. He'll be re-homed in a more stable environment. To be perfectly honest with you, the outcome will be much better for him. Once he's got over the initial distress of losing his mother, of course.'

'You reckon?' He couldn't help thinking of his own daughter Rose. The daughter he seldom saw. Was his absence the best outcome for her too?

The three men were staring at him. There was no sense that they were waiting for his agreement. Danny had been a soldier for long enough to understand that was not how it worked. They were waiting for an acknowledgement that he understood his orders. 'Just to be clear: you want me to babysit Bethany White on a mission to assassinate General O'Brien. When it's done, you want me to kill her.'

'It's more than babysitting,' Attwood said. 'Of course you need to make sure that she does what she's told. But getting her into Jordan isn't straightforward.'

'For obvious reasons,' Sturrock said, 'we've wanted to keep tabs on her movements. She'll be pinged at any border with facial recognition technology. It means we don't want her making a standard border entry into Jordan. You'll have to get her in covertly.'

'We're proposing a tandem HALO,' said the CO. 'We'll get you into the Jordanian desert and you can make your way cross country into Amman. Once you're there, we'll have counterfeit IDs and press passes waiting. We'll arrange for you to be on the press list for access to the hotel where O'Brien is staying. Our intelligence suggests that his routine is to go to the hotel bar every evening at 18.00 hours sharp for a cocktail. That's where you'll need to make contact. Get the job done and get her out of there and out of Amman.'

'We don't need to worry about getting her out of the country, of course,' Sturrock said. His self-satisfied smile had returned.

'What's the timescale?' Danny said.

'O'Brien is already in Amman,' said the CO. 'The drop happens tonight.'

'Where's Bethany now?'

'On her way to Brize Norton,' said Sturrock. 'By all accounts, she's making rather a nuisance of herself.'

'No shit,' Danny muttered.

'A van's waiting for you,' the CO said. 'Check out anything you need from the armoury.' He pushed a folder of documents across the table. 'That's your target pack. It has your movement orders, details of the location of the hotel in Amman where the General's staying, everything you need to know. The rest is up to you.'

Danny nodded, stood and left the room.

The door clicked shut. Sturrock, Attwood and Williamson remained silent for a full minute.

'Can he be trusted?' Sturrock said finally.

'You asked us that once before,' Attwood said. 'I think it's safe to say that Danny Black has proved himself.'

'Frankly, Sturrock, I'm surprised he sat in the same room as you for so long,' said the CO. Another long pause. 'We should have told him that Bethany White's little boy is dead.'

Both Attwood and Sturrock shook their heads. A rare moment of solidarity between them. 'The boy's the only leverage we have over White,' said Sturrock. 'If she finds out he's dead, we have nothing over her.' He coughed. 'It's all very tragic, of course,' he added.

'He's right, Mike,' said Attwood. 'We can't risk Black letting it slip.'

'Danny Black's a professional,' said the CO.

'Agreed,' said Attwood. 'But he's also a decent guy beneath it all. Not always an advantage, in situations like this.'

Nobody had anything to say to that. The three men collected their papers and left the room.

FOUR

Alice Goodenough was married to her job. All her friends said so. But they didn't know what her job was.

They *thought* they did. Something boring and desk-bound in the civil service that kept her in the office way past six o'clock. It was a big joke that she was always too late to get a round in. As long as she smiled and joined in on the joke, nobody asked what had kept her.

Alice was twenty-nine. They'd recruited her at a university careers fair. She thought her degree in Russian Language and Literature might lead her into the Foreign Office, so had chatted with a bookish civil servant. No, he had assured her. Being a woman of colour would not impede her application in any way. He encouraged her to put her name and email address down on a clipboard list. She received an invitation to come in for an 'informal chat' the next day. It took place in a bland office near Victoria Station. One chat led to another, and another. Gradually it became clear to Alice that she was being recruited into something more interesting than the civil service.

Alice accepted the need for secrecy. In the seven years she had worked at the MI6 building in Vauxhall, she never told her friends or even her widowed mother, who lived in a council flat in Peckham, what she really did for a living. She sometimes wondered what would happen if she found herself in a serious relationship. Would she be able to keep the secret then? That was academic anyway. Yes, Alice Goodenough was truly married to her job.

And she was good at it. Very good. She had an enquiring mind and an eye for detail. It could make her unpopular. Hers was not a workplace where young black women from poor backgrounds were expected, or even intended, to thrive. She endured all the usual slurs, racist and sexist. The pale, male and stale contingent – the PMS, as she liked to think of them – routinely raised their eyebrows at her south London accent. As for the coloured strands in her braided hair, her elaborately painted nails and the tiny stud in her nose: Alice stood out in the offices of MI6. People stared and talked behind her back. She ignored all this as best she could, and concentrated on her work.

Right now, her work involved research into an FSB agent called Dmitri Poliakov.

The assignment came from the top. Alice could practically hear the muttering from the PMS contingent when she was summoned to the fifth floor to see the head of the Russian desk, Maxwell Stark. Stark was a powerful guy, second only to the Chief, the odious Sturrock. You wouldn't have thought it to look at him. He was a tubby old-timer in his late sixties with eyebrows so bushy Alice wanted to reach for the tweezers every time she saw him. He wore thick-rimmed spectacles that often looked as though they needed a good clean. And he had a helpless addiction to extra strong mints. The tang of peppermint accompanied him at all times, and his teeth were shocking. Stark was a mild-mannered old boy, though. He wielded his authority lightly and treated Alice with respect. He clearly saw something in her. He asked her opinion on important matters when he didn't need to and listened carefully to her replies. If he was male and pale, perhaps he wasn't quite so stale as some of the others.

The brief was concise. 'We'll be needing every last bit of intel you can find on an FSB agent called Dmitri Poliakov, especially in respect to any contact he may have had with the American General Frank O'Brien. We think O'Brien's dirty. Would you be okay with that, Alice? That's very good of you. Needless to say, we can't allow this to go any further.'

Alice fully understood. A five-star general on the Russian books? In her world, that was as big as it could be. The need for secrecy was obvious. Equally obvious was that putting Alice on the job was a vote of confidence in her abilities. If she worked this case well, there might be a promotion. That, she thought, would silence the PMS contingent for good.

Stark briefed her more fully about the reasons for this research. She learned about a disastrous SAS mission in north-eastern Syria. Thirteen men dead at the hands of a Russian paramilitary force. He showed her the transcript of a recording made by the CIA in Crete between O'Brien and Poliakov that incriminated the American general. And she knew not to ask too many questions when Stark said, 'The O'Brien situation is being dealt with.' His statement had an air of impropriety about it, and Alice was smart enough not to probe further. Her job was to do some digging on Poliakov. Nothing more.

Alice had a small office – more of a cupboard, really – on the fourth floor overlooking the train line into Waterloo. River views were not for people like her. It was neat and adequate for her needs. She sat at her desk. To one side was a laptop displaying a screensaver image of a Caribbean beach. She had a file open in front of her, fresh from the records office in the basement. Her index finger guided her eyes down the page as she read. She felt she had a good idea of who Poliakov was already.

Born 3 September 1970. Father: an intelligence analyst for the KGB. Mother: no job listed. Married to Alexa, a florist in Moscow, with two children, one boy, one girl, Ivan and Sophia. Poliakov had been a known field operative for at least fifteen years and likely been working for Russian Intelligence for much longer than that. He'd been active, so far as MI6 knew, in Georgia, Ukraine and South America. Alice studied a picture of him meeting with a contact in a Bogota cafe in 1998. He was a handsome man, or at least he had been then. Short black hair, an aquiline nose, a mole on his left cheek, heavy stubble and – according to this photo at least – a charming smile. Charm was the most important attribute in an intelligence officer working in the field. You couldn't learn it. Charm was either there or it wasn't. Alice continued to look through the file. Here was Poliakov in Rio de Janeiro. Here he was in Tbilisi. Here he was with his wife and kids waving at the camera under the Eiffel Tower.

Nothing in the file suggested that Poliakov was an especially important or successful FSB agent. He had recruited a minor Dutch member of the European Parliament and had been responsible for spreading some low-level misinformation about elements in the

Gilets Jaunes in Paris. Alice wasn't fooled. She had learned, back in her days on the council estate, that the criminals to fear were not the famous, showy ones who had spent more time inside than out, but the quiet, clever ones. The ones the police could never pin anything on. So it was with spies. A thin file didn't necessarily suggest a lack of activity. Sometimes it just meant they were good.

Was Poliakov good? It was impossible to say from the information available. But if he'd been assigned contact with General O'Brien, the smart money was surely on him being higher up the tree than his file suggested. She kept this in mind as she continued to work her way through it. She found copies of his children's school reports, and the transcript of a Skype conversation between his wife and her mother in Kiev. There was an unconfirmed report from an agent in Moscow that he had a penchant for cocaine. Someone had written, in red pen, the word 'Blackmail?', and circled it twice.

Then, at the back of the file, she found something interesting.

It was a one-page report from a British agent she knew well. His name was Mark Cawley and he worked under diplomatic cover at the British Embassy in Moscow. He was a sleazy old dinosaur, but his information was usually reliable. She read his memo greedily. It was dated just two days ago and reported a rumour that Dmitri Poliakov had been missing for one week. Ordinarily, this would not merit any kind of comment. Poliakov could be anywhere, for any reason. He was a spy, after all. However, his wife and two children were also missing. And for anybody who knew anything about Russia, that was alarming. The families of FSB agents were protected citizens, but only for so long as the agent was in favour. If the agent messed up in any way, the family could expect to pay a price.

Alice put the file down and stared out of the window over the train tracks. A South Western service trundled by, glinting in the bright sunshine. She thought it through. Poliakov was General O'Brien's point man. But he'd messed up. He'd been spotted with the General in Crete, their conversation overheard. Did the Russians know this? If so, they would most certainly want to eliminate Poliakov. So, was he still alive? Was his family still alive?

So many questions, impossible to answer from a broom cupboard in Vauxhall. She picked up her work phone.

It was a regular smartphone, but with a dedicated app for making encrypted calls. She used it to dial Mark Cawley in Moscow. He answered quickly.

'Cawley,' he said. He had the affable, patrician voice of British diplomats all over the world.

'Mark, it's Alice. From the Office.'

'What can I do you for, Alice?'

'You can speak openly?'

'As openly as anyone can speak in Moscow, my dear.'

Alice let the 'my dear' pass. 'I'm looking at your communication regarding Dmitri Poliakov.'

'Yes,' said Cawley. He elongated the word. *Yeeeessss.* 'I have an intelligence source who is a friend of his. He's rather unreliable, to be honest. Bit too fond of the old Stolichnaya. Told me about Poliakov and his family after a sherbert too many. Didn't think it would be of much interest, if I'm honest.'

'Can you find out more?' Alice said. 'Is he still missing? Do we have any idea of his whereabouts?'

'Of course, my dear. Might it be important?'

'Just putting my ducks in a row, Mark.' She made a face. It was the sort of thing the PMS contingent said, but she used it now because this was Cawley's language. 'Could you make it a priority? I've got the fifth floor breathing down my neck.'

'Say no more,' Cawley said. 'And maybe we could have a spot of lunch next time I'm over?'

Alice made a sour face. 'That would be super, Mark,' she said. 'You'll call me as soon as you know anything?'

'The very moment, my dear.'

The line went dead.

FIVE

Hamoud Al Asmar's sheets were soaked in sweat every morning when he woke. Today his thin, boney, naked body was clammy, the mattress uncomfortably damp.

At least he hadn't woken to the sound of his own screams. That happened two or three times a week, and it made him feel bad all day. Not bad for himself, but for his wife, Rabia, and his children, Malick and Melissa. It distressed them terribly to hear their father in such anguish. No matter how often he tried to persuade them that it was just a silly bad dream, that it was really nothing to worry about, that he was absolutely fine, they never believed him. Why would they? They weren't stupid.

Hamoud's night terrors had haunted him ever since the blessed day he had left Guantanamo Bay. During his two years as an inmate, he'd never dreamed at all. The horrors had happened when he was awake. When he was asleep, his mind blocked them out.

Now a free man, he relived them every night. This time it had been the salt water. In his dream, as in real life, rough men had woken him in his cell. That cell! Empty but for Hamoud, the flies and the two bowls in the corner. One bowl was his toilet. The other contained dirty water to wipe himself clean. They changed the bowls only every three or four days. He slept on the hard floor and the flies would crawl over his waste and drink at the foul water and then settle on his face. In the early days he would flick those germ-ridden insects away. As time passed and his spirit broke, he lacked the motivation and the energy even to do that.

The men had arrived in his cell without warning. Perhaps it was midnight, perhaps midday, Hamoud had no way of knowing. There

44

were four of them. Two carried five-gallon containers full of water. Two carried a piece of apparatus that resembled a child's see-saw. He knew what it was for and he panicked. He tried to fight the men, but he was thin and malnourished, and they were burly and strong. One of them hit him. He fell and hit his face against the raised end of the see-saw. It collapsed under his weight, but the corner was sharp and it cut him badly. He could still remember the agony of the skin tearing in a line up his right cheek, over his eyelid and up over his right eyebrow. He could feel the hot blood stinging his eye, and the panic that he might be blinded.

They strapped him to the see-saw. They pivoted the see-saw so Hamoud's feet were higher than his head. They placed a bucket under his head and a thick, wet cloth over his face. Hamoud's eye was agony and he found it difficult to breathe. He strained against the strapping and emitted a muffled cry. He knew what was coming.

They had waterboarded him before. They had poured fresh water over his covered face. That was bad enough. Within seconds he had been screaming at them to stop. When they repeated the process, he had shouted at them whatever he thought they wanted to hear. Yes! He was a jihadist! Yes! He had come to America from his native Mauritania with the express intention of murdering American citizens! Yes! He could name others! Mohammad! Ahmed! Kalil! Never mind that these so-called accomplices were entirely made up. Never mind that Hamoud would never hurt another living creature, let alone murder an American. If they needed to hear these confessions to make it stop, he would say them.

This time was worse. The five-gallon containers contained not fresh water but salt water, which burned his throat as well as the wound on his eye. It made him want to retch, which only made him ingest more and increased the terrifying, paralysing suffocation. And when the sluicing stopped, although he tried to gasp for breath, his burning throat was so full of salt water that he could do nothing but splutter and choke. And then, after only a few seconds, they started again.

Hamoud would never be able to say how long the torture lasted. He only knew that, when it was over, his throat and lungs throbbed with pain, that he was dizzy and nauseous and disoriented, that the wound on his eye had been numbed into insensitivity. In the brief intervals when they had removed the cloth, he had rasped information at his torturers. *Any* information. Names, made up. Places, invented. Plots, fabricated. All now forgotten, by him at least.

He had shivered in the corner of the room as they silently removed their equipment. When they'd left, he had noticed through his good eye that the bowl of dirty water had been upturned and was spreading across the floor of his cell, and a fly was circling the rim of the toilet bowl . . .

Hamoud had dreamed vividly about that torture last night. For a moment, in the twilight between sleeping and waking, he thought his salty sweat was the salt water from the five-gallon containers, and that it was all happening again. Even as he woke more fully, clutching his right eye, he thought he was lying in his cell. It was only the calming voice of Rabia, and the touch of her cool hand on his brow, that told him he was safely at home. The memory of Guantanamo Bay was just that: a memory.

It was dark in their tiny bedroom. They couldn't afford curtains, let alone blackout curtains, so he knew it was before dawn. He crept out of bed and pulled on his plain white robe. He had to wear loose clothing because anything too tight hurt the scars on his abdomen. But even the robe clung to his sweaty skin and he winced with discomfort. He tiptoed sideways round the bed because there was so little space, and walked lightly so he didn't disturb the two children who shared a thin mattress on the floor in the next room. Rabia kept the bathroom scrupulously clean even though the constant condensation made the walls sweat even more than Hamoud. Here, he splashed water on his face and looked in the mirror. There was enough moonlight for him to see his reflection. Hamoud was only thirty-two but he looked at least ten years older. His skin was dark but the rings around his eyes were darker. His beard was flecked with grey. It was long and soft. The children liked to put their hands through it. Hamoud would have preferred to shave it off because he knew that it made him look more Muslim, and that could be difficult. But Rabia persuaded him to keep it. She liked it, she said, and he should not be ashamed of who he was, any more than he should be ashamed by the scar on his eye. He looked at it now. It was white and embossed. It stretched in a straight vertical line from his right eyebrow, over his eyelids and down his cheek. It made him look like a criminal. People stared at it, at him, and he knew what they were thinking: that his appearance indicated a hatred of America.

The dream had stayed with him as he sat at the table in their living space. He could almost taste the brine in the back of his throat. He scratched his palms. It was a habit of his from his time in Guantanamo. They were red and inflamed. The more he scratched them, the sorer they became, but he couldn't stop doing it. He poured himself a glass of water and drank deeply. To Hamoud, who had spent so many days in prison starved of water, this was a real luxury. He felt much better when he'd finished it. Calmer.

Hamoud owned a box. It wasn't a special or expensive box. Just a plywood thing that he'd bought in a thrift store. He kept it on the top shelf of the bookcase, out of the children's reach. Rabia had wanted Hamoud to dispose of the contents, but they were important to him. He fetched the box now, placed it on the table and opened it up. It was brimful of newspaper clippings, neatly trimmed and folded. He removed the top clipping. A face stared out at him. A man with brown skin, like Hamoud. He looked sinister. Scary, almost. The caption under the photograph read: 'Former Guantanamo Bay inmate Ahmed Kenan'. Hamoud had never met Ahmed Kenan. They had segregated him from all other prisoners during his time in the camp. He had never met any of them. He didn't know whether Ahmed Kenan was falsely accused, like him, or a violent terrorist. He would never know. They would never meet. But he felt a connection with the man who stared out of the newspaper clipping. He felt a connection with all the former inmates whose details he had meticulously collected and stored in this cheap box. He selected another picture, a more friendly looking fellow with an unnaturally long face and a beard that seemed to elongate it even further. Hamoud liked looking at this man. There was something appealing about him. He thought in a different life they could have been friends.

It grew light outside. He could hear Rabia moving around. He folded up the clippings and returned the box to its place on the bookcase. He knew she would tell him off for looking through it. *Why are you looking at those pictures?* she would say. *How many of those men are criminals? It's almost like you want to be back in that cursed place!* There was nothing Hamoud wanted less and he couldn't explain why he found the pictures such a comfort. Perhaps it was just the thought that there were other people who knew – who *truly* knew – what he had been through. He worried that she would one day throw them out, but for now she at least seemed to accept that they were important to him, even if she didn't like it.

He heard her enter the bathroom. Soon she would leave for work, cleaning houses, and she would not be back until it was dark. Hamoud would take the children to school and return to the apartment, where he would remain until it was time to pick them up. There was no question of him getting a job. His nerves were not up to it and his wife would never allow it. Not until he was 'better', whatever that meant. And anyway, at some point he would have to let an employer know where he had spent two years of his life, and who in their right minds would give a job to a former Guantanamo inmate? It would make no difference to them that he had been released without charge. It would make no difference that he was a US citizen. Nobody wanted Hamoud to help make America great again.

So, he would spend today, as every day, alone in this tiny apartment with its musty carpets and patches of damp, provided by the American government as a meagre acknowledgement that they had inflicted two years of horror on an innocent man. And when his family returned from their full days, he would be diminished. Less of a man than he had been when he'd said goodbye to them. Each day chipped away at him. Soon, he thought to himself, there would be nothing left.

As these thoughts raced through his mind, he heard something. Footsteps in the corridor outside. The walls of this apartment block were thin. Sound travelled. No doubt his neighbours heard his regular night-time screams. It was unusual, however, to hear footsteps at this time in the morning. He checked his watch. Two minutes to six. Normally he didn't hear anybody until six thirty. The footsteps stopped outside the door to the apartment. An envelope appeared under the door. Hamoud, sitting cross-legged on the threadbare sofa they had salvaged from a street corner, watched it with quiet astonishment.

He stood up, hurried to the door and opened it, peering outside to see who the delivery person was. The corridor was empty. The door at the end which led to the stairwell slammed shut.

Silence.

Hamoud picked up the envelope. It was addressed to him, and there was a stamp and postmark. It felt heavy. Distracted, he closed the apartment door with his foot and walked back to the sofa where he opened the envelope and emptied out its contents.

There was a letter inside, and a brochure for Walt Disney World in Florida. His eyes lingered on the brochure first. There was a boy and a girl on the front cover. Each had pale skin, blue eyes and blonde, tousled hair. They were hugging Mickey Mouse and they looked so happy that Hamoud smiled. Then he felt sad. He wished *his* children might one day look as happy as that. It seemed unlikely. They were only eight and ten, and already they had the tired expressions of the world-weary.

He turned his attention to the letter. At the top, beneath a letterhead that depicted the Cinderella Castle showered in fire-works, was the word 'Congratulations!' in a big, cheery typeface.

It was just a piece of junk mail. On another day, Hamoud might have chucked it in the bin. But this morning he felt like reading. He'd loved to read as a child, but since Guantanamo he couldn't hope to focus on something as long as a book. So he read on.

Congratulations!
You and your family have been chosen, in our special
summertime bonanza, for an ALL EXPENSES
PAID trip to Walt Disney World Florida!

He blinked, then glanced back at the brochure. A tiny flame of excitement ignited inside him. He snuffed it out quickly. There was obviously a catch. He read on.

As part of our special promotion, you will receive complimentary
flights and $2000 spending money, to ensure your family has
the trip of a lifetime! Just call this number to claim your prize!

There was a 1-800 number at the bottom of the page, and a pre-printed signature. Hamoud read the letter again and then, when he heard Rabia coming, stuffed the envelope and its contents under the cushions of the sofa. He didn't quite know why he wanted to hide them. Perhaps it was because he didn't want his family to get their hopes up. Perhaps it was because he felt embarrassed at the idea that his wife might think he believed this was anything but a scam.

'Was there someone at the door?' Rabia said as she entered. Her hair was tied back and she looked very beautiful. Hamoud shook his head. 'I thought I heard it,' she said.

The family always spoke English together, rather than their native Arabic. It helped Malick and Melissa to integrate and was a symbol of their intention to forgive the Americans for what they had done to Hamoud. Rabia walked over to him and put a hand on his cheek. 'Are you okay?' she asked.

He knew she was talking about the dream and nodded. 'We should wake them,' he said. 'They'll be late for school.'

Their morning routine was the same as ever. Sleepy children, reluctantly dressed. Bowls of Cheerios, slowly eaten. Hamoud made little jokes with the kids and gradually their sleepiness was replaced by smiles. They were so different from each other: Melissa boisterous and loud, Malick quiet and reserved like Hamoud. But both kind and sensitive. Occasionally Hamoud caught them glancing at him with concern, because they knew that sometimes their dad was sad even when he pretended to be happy. But they didn't say anything and soon they were kissing their mum good-bye as she left for work. Hamoud urged them to pack their schoolbags and hurried them out of the apartment.

They lived in a poor area, here on the outskirts of Cincinnati. They weren't the only brown-skinned people, but they still drew stares from some of the passers-by, many of them unfriendly. Hamoud and his family were used to it, or so they liked to pretend. The children were clingy at the school gates, holding on to their dad for a few seconds longer than most other kids, unwilling to say goodbye. Hamoud stayed at the gates, one hand raised in fare-well, until they were out of sight. Then he returned home.

The apartment was so quiet without them. Ordinarily he hated this moment, facing a day enclosed by the walls and his thoughts.

As usual, he locked himself inside. When you'd been a prisoner, some habits were hard to shake. Normally he would now sit in front of the TV and watch the shopping channel all day in an attempt to distract himself from his worries. But not today. Today he felt a tinge of anticipation.

He removed the letter from under the cushion and read it again. Then he pulled his cheap, scuffed, second-hand cell phone from his pocket. He keyed in the 1-800 number, but his finger hovered over the dial button for several minutes. Anxiety burned in his chest. He wasn't good at making phone calls at the best of times. He put the phone to one side and scratched at his palms so hard he thought they might bleed. He breathed deeply. His gaze fell on the Walt Disney World brochure, and the smiling children on the front, and that gave him the courage to pick up the phone again and press call.

It rang four times.

Five.

Nobody was going to answer. He should just hang up . . .

'*Hello, Walt Disney World, where all your dreams come true!*'

A cheerful female voice.

'Uh . . . Hello?' said Hamoud.

'*How may I help you sir?*'

'Well, you see . . . it's probably nothing . . . I mean, it's probably a hoax. But I received the letter about a special summertime offer . . . an all-expenses paid trip . . .' It sounded ridiculous even as he said it.

'*Of course, sir. May I take your name please?*'

'Hamoud . . . Hamoud Al Asmar.' He said it apologetically.

'*And your address please, sir?*'

He gave his address.

'*One moment please, sir.*'

There was a click. A swooning orchestra played 'When You Wish Upon A Star'. It continued for perhaps a minute, then there was another click and the voice returned. '*Mr Al Asmar?*'

'Uh . . . yes?'

'*Congratulations! You and your family are going to Walt Disney World for five magical days and nights, starting Wednesday! . . . Mr Al Asmar? Mr Al Asmar, are you there?*'

'I'm here, yes. I'm here. It's just . . . I don't understand. Why are you giving us this? Why . . . why us?'

Your names have been chosen at random, sir. All we ask in return is the opportunity to take a few pictures of you and your beautiful family while you're enjoying the magic of Walt Disney World. We'll be FedExing your plane tickets today!

'But, can't we choose when to go? My wife has to work and the children are at school.'

I'm afraid the dates are fixed, Mr Al Asmar. Your flights are booked for Wednesday and we have rooms booked for you until Sunday night.

'Wednesday? But that's tomorrow.'

The dates are fixed Mr Al Asmar. But if you're unable to take advantage of the offer, we do understand and will find another family who have more flexibility.

'No,' said Hamoud quickly. 'No, we'll go. Uh . . . my wife can ask for some time off.'

That's great to hear, sir. Everything you need will be with you first thing in the morning. You'll be flying from Cincinatti to Orlando. Is there anything else I can help you with?

Hamoud shook his head even though there was nobody to see it. 'No,' he said. 'No, thank you.'

Then you have a great day, sir. Thank you for choosing Walt Disney World for your vacation.

The line went dead. Hamoud stared at the phone for a little while. I didn't choose Walt Disney World, he wanted to say. Walt Disney World chose me. His hand was trembling. That was nothing new. But this time it was out of excitement rather than stress. He flicked through the Walt Disney World brochure and, instead of the happy American children screaming with joy on Space Mountain, he saw Malick and Melissa. It brought a smile to his face.

He dialled Rabia's number to tell her the good news but hung up before the call could connect. Better to tell her tonight, when she was not distracted by her cleaning job.

The days passed slowly for Hamoud. He prepared himself for today to pass more slowly than most.

SIX

Danny Black was always ready to deploy. He kept a grab-bag in the squadron hangar and his personal weapons were waiting for him in the armoury. It took an hour to prepare himself, by which time the gear needed for his HALO drop into the Jordanian desert had been stowed in the back of the unmarked transit van waiting for him. He didn't recognise the driver, nor did he want to speak to him. He took his seat in the back and sat silently.

His mind churned. Events were happening quickly. An operation like this, to take out such a sensitive target, would usually be weeks in the planning. It would require a substantial team of guys. This wasn't the first time that Danny had felt he was taking on the work of more than one man, but he understood why it was necessary. It wasn't just the covert nature of the op. It was the difficulty of dealing with the other person involved.

Bethany White.

She was the most complicated person Danny had ever met. A mother and a killer. A grieving widow and a psychopath. A high-level MI6 operator and MI6's worst nightmare. She was poison and honey. Light and dark. In his experience, the security services attracted many psychotic types, highly manipulative and able to kill without a flicker of fellow feeling. But Bethany White was an extreme case. She had manipulated Danny with skill and apparent ease. Danny would be lying if he said he wasn't attracted to her, but she repelled him too. He'd never hoped or expected to see her again and the thought that they were to come face to face in a couple of hours made him apprehensive. Funny, he thought to himself, how calmly he could deal with whatever threats the life of an SAS soldier threw at him, but the thought of meeting a beautiful, blonde thirty-year-old woman again dumped acid in his gut.

The journey to Brize Norton took two hours. It gave him time to examine the target pack they'd given him back in Hereford. He committed to memory details of the forthcoming HALO drop, maps of the area and plans Hereford had put in place to get them out of the desert into Amman and close to the General. Hereford's strategy was good, but it relied on a single, scarcely knowable factor: Bethany White's compliance. Danny suspected it would be unwillingly delivered.

A Globemaster was taking off as they arrived at their destination. The deafening roar of its engines made the unmarked van shake as the driver flashed some ID at a security point that led straight on to the airfield. They slalomed around fuel lorries and military trucks as they crossed to the far side of the airfield, where a long solitary Portakabin was manned by a couple of armed guys in camouflage gear. It was a hot day, unusually hot for the UK, and the airfield shimmered in the heat haze. A couple of hundred metres away, a Hercules was taxiing across the tarmac. Once Danny had alighted, carrying a grey sports bag stuffed with clothes, the van headed up in the direction of the Herc. Danny approached the Portakabin. Blackout linings covered the inside of the windows. The two armed guards were young and pimply. Danny could tell they were nervous. He smiled to put them at ease, but then realised he wasn't the reason they were on edge.

'Is it locked?' he asked them, dumping the sports bag on the ground.

They nodded.

'Give me the key.'

One of the guys handed it over.

'Has she been searched?' Danny asked.

'Yeah,' said the guy. 'Three times. But keep your distance, if I was you. When we was bringing her in, she had a blade in the lining of her top that we missed. Cut my mate's face something nasty. Took three of us to get it off her.'

Danny nodded. That sounded like her. He felt for his Glock and made sure it was secure in its holster. He walked up the steps to the Portakabin door, unlocked it, then kicked it. The door clattered as it swung open. Danny entered.

There were a couple of tables. Chairs scattered around, some on their sides as if there had been a fight in here. White boards on the wall. The blackout linings on the windows were fixed with layers of brown tape.

And there was Bethany White.

She was huddled in a corner, clutching her knees. There was a table between them, but it didn't block his view. Her blonde hair was matted and dirty. There were mascara streaks on her cheeks that partially covered the golden freckles underneath. Her eyes were red. She was breathing heavily. And she was staring at him.

The Bethany that Danny knew had always shown the world a smart, confident face. This pale creature, her face bleached both by the overhead light and her own distress, was wretched. Her shoulders shook. Her left eye twitched. There was an unpleasant smell in the Portakabin. Danny was pretty sure it came from her. There was a smear of blood on her cheek and Danny remembered what the guy outside had said about the blade. He looked around the room, searching for anything that might present itself as an incidental weapon. There was nothing, but that didn't mean she hadn't located any dangerous items before his arrival.

'Stand up,' he said.

She stared at him without moving.

'You heard me, I said—'

'Yeah, I heard you,' she rasped. Her voice was hoarse, but that didn't hide her faint West Country burr.

They locked gazes. Bethany pushed herself to her feet, her back sliding up against the wall. She was wearing what Danny supposed were the clothes she had on when she was brought in. Tatty jeans and an oversized sweatshirt. The sweatshirt was streaked with blood. So were her hands. They were clawed, as though she was ready to scratch someone's eyes out. 'I didn't think I'd be seeing you again,' she said.

'Makes two of us. I hear you've been getting handy with a razor blade.'

She managed to make an insouciant shrug. 'He got too close.' A smile crossed her lips and, despite her feral appearance, Danny saw a hint of her dazzling good looks. 'I seem to remember you

55

trying to get quite close too, Danny. What is it? Have you gone off me?' He saw her clawed fingers relax.

'I don't want to be here any more than you want me here,' Danny replied.

'Did I say that?' said Bethany. She moved a strand of matted hair from her face. 'They took my son,' she said.

'I know. He's safe.'

'You want to know what I'm going to do when I find the people who took him?'

'You'll never find them,' he said.

'You want to bet?'

'You're too smart, Bethany. You know what they'll do to you if you start going after people again. You won't give them any option, and Danny won't have his mother.'

'He doesn't have his mother now.'

'But he will do. If you do what you're told, he will do. You have my word on that.'

She laughed scornfully. 'Your word? What's that worth?'

Danny stared her down. 'Something,' he said. 'Your boy stopped you from killing me, remember? Maybe I owe him one.'

Bethany watched him uncertainly. She clearly didn't know if she believed him. But Danny was telling the truth. No matter what he thought of Bethany, he liked her kid. He tried not to think too hard about his instruction to make him an orphan. 'Listen,' he said, 'I don't have any great love for the spooks. They've lied to me more times than I can count, and I don't like the way they've played this. I've got a kid too. I get it. I want yours to go back home. No matter what I think of you.'

'What a pretty speech.' She slow-clapped sarcastically and gazed around. 'So do we get to leave this room? Those two boys outside looked like they might soil themselves.'

'This room is secure,' said Danny. 'I can brief you here. We're heading to Jordan. Tonight.'

She was obviously trying to hide it, but a flicker of interest crossed Bethany's face. *You can take the girl out of MI6*, Danny thought to himself. 'I haven't agreed to anything yet,' she said. And then, unable to withhold her curiosity. 'Why would we go to Jordan?'

'We have a target. An American five-star general. His name's Frank O'Brien. He's been a bad boy.'

'Show me a soldier who hasn't been,' Bethany said.

'No one else has been bad like this.' An image of the smoke-filled wasteland outside the Syrian prison flashed in his mind. 'He's passing sensitive military information to the Russians. Including information about British troop movements. Thanks to him, my team was massacred. Now he gets paid back.'

'So the Yanks have got a mole.' Her dismissive tone of voice angered Danny, but he did his best not to show it. 'It was only a matter of time. What's it got to do with me?'

'The General's in Jordan for a peace conference. He has a CP team wherever he goes. It's hard for me to get close. But he also has an eye for the ladies.'

Danny didn't have to say any more. Bethany gave a cynical smile. 'Are you suggesting that you and your friends at MI6 suddenly feel a little less queasy about my methods?'

'We do what we have to do,' Danny said.

'Obviously. Which is why you don't mind stealing a six-year-old boy from his mother.' She took a step towards him. There was something in her gait. The Bethany Danny had seen when he walked in here had looked broken. Somehow, in the course of their conversation, she had started to put herself back together again. 'The trouble is, you seem to have forgotten something. I've lodged details of MI6's illegal actions with solicitors all over the world. One word from me and they'll release that information. So I don't think I need to do a single thing you say. And if my former employees don't get my son back to me, they'll only have themselves to blame.'

Danny put one hand in his pocket and removed his mobile phone. He offered it to Bethany. 'Go ahead,' he said. 'Call your lawyers. Any of them. I think you might find that each of them has met with a nasty accident.'

'What do you mean?'

'Come on,' Danny said. 'You're not stupid. You really think you could give GCHQ six months and they wouldn't trace your precious solicitors?'

Bethany didn't seem to have a response to that. Her shoulders slumped again. But then, in an instant, she regained her poise. 'It doesn't matter,' she said. 'So let's say I agree. How do we go about this?'

'We can't make a regular border entry,' Danny said. 'Your face will ping every facial recognition system in the world – MI6 have seen to it. So we need to make a covert entry. There's a Hercules waiting for us. Tonight, we fly along the Israel–Jordan border and we do a tandem HALO jump into the Jordanian side. They'll drop a quad bike in alongside us and we'll make our way across the desert into Jordan. We'll have passes waiting for us that will get us in to the General's hotel, then you flutter your eyelashes at him.'

Bethany took a moment to absorb that. 'A HALO jump?' she said.

Danny nodded. 'I'll talk you through it.'

'I'm not one for heights,' she said. 'You'll have to hold me tight.'

Danny gave her a level look. He was only human. He couldn't help being physically attracted to Bethany White, but he knew how dangerous that was and how ruthlessly she would use it against him. 'You weren't thrilled to see me walk into this room,' he said. 'I'm not thrilled to be here. I've got a job to do and so do you. Any of that other shit, forget it. If you want your kid back, let's get this done and we never have to see each other again.'

Silence.

'I need to shower,' said Bethany. 'Do you think the boys at the door will let me leave without peeing their pants?'

Danny held up his Glock. 'Don't make a mistake,' he said. 'I *will* do it.'

'And then who's going to nail your precious general for you?' Bethany said. 'Put the gun down, Danny. You're not going to shoot me and I'm not going to give you any trouble. At least, not until I have my boy back.' She turned her back on him. 'Tell the kids I'm coming out,' she said. 'I wouldn't want to scare them.'

Danny left the Portakabin. The two guys outside were gripping the weapons slung across their fronts. 'I'm taking her out,' Danny said. 'She needs to get cleaned up.'

'We have orders,' said one of them. He held up a pair of hand-cuffs. 'As long as she's on site, she wears these.'

Danny took the cuffs. 'You got the key?' he said. The soldier handed it over. Danny clunked the cuffs shut, dropped them on the ground and pocketed the key. 'She's with me,' he said. 'She doesn't need those.'

The two soldiers eyed each other uncomfortably. Danny re-entered the Portakabin. 'No cuffs?' Bethany said.

'They wanted to. I said no.'

Bethany shrugged, as if to suggest that she wasn't fussed. Danny wasn't fooled. He could sense that she was suddenly more at her ease. Ditching the handcuffs had been the right call.

He knew Brize Norton well, having deployed from here more times than he could count. There was a functional shower and toilet block to the back of the main terminal. Danny led Bethany out of the Portakabin, picked up the sports bag full of clothes and handed it to her. She smiled at the two soldiers keeping guard, but looked gruesome with her dirty, bloodied face framed by her wild, matted hair. They crossed the tarmac in silence. When they reached the shower block, Danny stood outside. He wasn't really guarding the entrance. He knew that if Bethany wanted to escape the block, she'd find some way to do it. But he was certain that she wouldn't. Bethany White was many things. A killer. A traitor, even. But everything she'd done had been for family. She wasn't about to throw all that away. 'No peeking!' she shouted over her shoulder as she entered the block.

Danny was sweating heavily. The afternoon sun beat hard on the airfield and he had to shield his eyes to look across at the Hercules. The tailgate was down and gear was being loaded up, though from this distance he couldn't quite make it out in detail. Otherwise, all he saw were troops moving around in open-top trucks and fuel vehicles circling the perimeter: the regular sights and sounds of a working military airfield.

Ten minutes later, Bethany re-emerged. She looked amazing. Her clean skin glowed, her long blonde hair was damp and shiny. There was no vestige of the crazy-looking woman Danny had found in the Portakabin. She was wearing the camouflage gear Danny had supplied her with. It too was damp where her hair touched it. 'A perfect fit,' she said, indicating the clothes. 'It's almost as if you knew my size.'

Danny ignored her flirtatious comment. He pointed towards the Hercules. 'That's our ride,' he said. 'You ever done a HALO drop before?'

'What do you think?'

'I'll explain everything once we're in the air.'

'This is all pretty fast, Danny. It's not like the Hereford I know. Don't they want a week of briefings and a full squadron in case somebody stubs their toe?'

'No time for that,' Danny said. 'And sometimes you need a scalpel, not a hammer.'

'Very poetic. Shall we go?'

Bethany strode forwards. If she was feeling any anxiety, she didn't show it. He reminded himself that she had fooled him once before. Nothing, with Bethany, was quite what it seemed, and Danny didn't intend to make the same mistake twice.

He caught up with her and they walked side by side back to the Portakabin. The two soldiers were still there, sweating in the heat. Danny pulled out his phone and made a call. Seconds later, the white van pulled away from the Hercules and headed across the tarmac towards them.

SEVEN

Danny knew from past experience that Bethany White was as skilled an actress as she was an assassin. She was apparently a completely different person now she'd emerged from the shower. There was no sign of the broken, distressed mother crouching in the corner of a locked Portakabin. She walked with confidence, shoulders pinned back, head held high. Nobody would even begin to guess what she had learned in the last hour, nor what she had agreed to do. It made Danny even more wary. He knew plenty of killers. He knew female soldiers more ruthless than even the most ferocious Regiment guys. But he'd never met a person who could slip into a role quite so easily. It was impossible to tell what such a person was thinking, or what they intended to do. Bethany White was probably more dangerous than anyone he'd ever met.

The unmarked white van deposited them at the bottom of the Hercules's tailgate. Five loadmasters stood together, drinking coffee from plastic cups. Two older men stood slightly apart. Each had aviator shades hanging from the top pocket of their fatigues. They were clearly the pilot and co-pilot. Danny walked up to them and shook their hands. Formalities over. 'What's our flight path?' he asked.

'We're heading across the Med and over Cyprus. The Israelis have given us permission to enter their airspace, but my instructions are to keep the Jordanians in the dark. So we're going to head south along the Israel–Jordan border and make the drop when we're directly west of Amman. That'll put you down somewhere between the West Bank and the Jordanian village of As-Salt.'

'What's the status in the West Bank? Any fighting?'

'None reported, but it's volatile, as I'm sure you know. If we can nudge over to the Jordanian side of the border, we will.' He looked at his watch. 'It's 19.00,' he said. 'Wheels up in thirty minutes. We'll look to make the drop some time after 01.30 local, if that suits you?'

Danny nodded his agreement, shook the pilot's hand again and walked over to the loadmasters. One of them, a bald guy with a crusty cold sore on his lower lip, stepped forward. He was clearly the main loadie.

'Is the quad bike strapped up?' Danny said.

'Trussed up like a Christmas turkey,' the loadie replied. 'Ready to go.'

'The rest of my gear?'

The loadie nodded in the direction of the tailgate. Danny thanked him and gave the remaining loadies a thumbs-up. In advance of a HALO jump, these were the guys you needed on your side. He was under no illusion, though, that they were more interested in Bethany, with her damp blonde hair and the pout that Danny knew was entirely affected, than him. He ushered her up the tailgate into the belly of the Hercules.

Danny remembered how, as a kid, the smell of his dog's damp fur had a calming effect on him. Nowadays, the smell of a military aircraft fulfilled the same role. It wasn't a pleasant smell. It was greasy and thick. The stench of aviation fuel caught at the back of your throat. But it was a smell that told Danny he was in an environment where he knew what he was doing. He'd thrown himself out of these aircraft more times than he could count. This was his turf.

The same couldn't be said of Bethany. As they entered the Hercules, her show of cool confidence faltered momentarily. He'd seen it before: the tightening of the eyes and the slump in the shoulders of arrogant young rookies, all piss and vinegar, as they entered an aircraft for their first freefall and were hit with the realisation of what they were about to do. When Bethany caught Danny looking at her, she quickly straightened herself up and made a show of looking around the inside of the aircraft.

It was functional. There were benches along either side of the plane, with webbing straps and medical boxes fixed to the interior fuselage. The space was dominated by a pallet with a quad bike strapped to it. The bike itself was a couple of metres long with large, solid tyres that still held remnants of dust and mud from its last use. It was heavily strapped to the pallet, almost as if somebody had attempted to bandage it, and its bodywork was sprayed in desert khaki colours. A robust, dependable piece of kit which, in a few hours, would be dropped into the desert from 30,000 feet. An enormous parachute pack was strapped to the top of the quad bike and the pallet itself was resting on a set of rails that ran along the centre of the Hercules, all the way to the tailgate.

Danny's gear was stashed by one of the benches. He walked over to it, crouched down and double-checked the kit. First off, the tandem chute. He examined the release rings and cables, the routing of the strapping and the cutaway handles. Bethany watched him intently as he performed these standard checks.

'So, you never jumped before?' Danny said.

'Never.' She sounded a bit reluctant to admit her lack of experience.

'You'll be strapped to me.'

'What are they for?' Bethany pointed at a couple of canisters.

'Oxygen. It'll be thin where we're jumping from. We'll need it for the first few thousand feet. Otherwise hypoxia – oxygen starvation. We don't want to pass out before we deploy the chute.'

Bethany looked a bit queasy. 'What if it goes wrong?' she said.

'It's only the last inch that kills you.'

'Is that supposed to be funny?'

Danny stood up and walked over to her. 'Which wrist do you wear your watch on?'

'My left,' she said. She held up her left wrist to show him.

'If anything happens,' Danny said, 'that's the arm you want to hold in the air.'

She looked confused. 'Why?'

'You want to break your watch?'

'Fuck off.'

'Nothing's going to go wrong,' Danny said. He went back to the gear and held up the tandem rig. 'You're going to wear this,' he said. 'I'll be securely clipped in behind you and I'll operate the chute. As soon as the quad goes out, we'll follow. Put your arms across your chest and keep your head up. Don't worry if we go upside down, it happens sometimes and we'll soon right ourselves. Do what I tell you and you'll be fine. I've done this thousands of times before.' He managed a smile. 'It's going to be the best ride of your life.'

Bethany looked deeply uncertain. She pointed at the quad bike. 'I'm guessing we don't intend to drive that thing up to the front entrance of a swanky hotel in Amman.'

'Right,' Danny said. He had instant recall of the instructions in his target pack. 'There are some old Roman ruins in the desert on the outskirts of the city. We'll head for that location where we'll RV with a local fixer at dawn. He'll have a more suitable vehicle for us and will show us a place to hide the quad bike.'

'Can we trust him?'

'Course not. But he won't get paid until we're out of country and he's not doing it for the shits and giggles. Once we have the new vehicle, we'll head to a safe house in Amman where there'll be civvies and press passes waiting for us, so we can get into the General's hotel.' He could see her assimilating this information. 'Just do as I tell you,' he said.

She gave him a contemptuous look. He went back to checking over the kit: wrist-mounted altimeter, twice the size of a normal watch, and a smaller wrist-mounted Garmin GPS unit; personal weapons and ammunition; oxygen masks; two sets of night-vision goggles for when they were on the ground; NV scopes; day packs; an entrenching tool. When he was happy that everything was in order, he turned his attention to the quad bike. He tugged at the strapping to ensure everything was secure. He checked the fuel tank was closed. The keys to the quad were hanging in the ignition. He removed them and placed them in a secure pouch in his camo gear.

By now the loadies were all aboard, performing their own final checks and readying the Herc for flight. The engines started up. The aircraft thrummed and the tailgate closed, blocking out the daylight. Lights along the fuselage illuminated the interior, but only dimly. Danny and Bethany strapped themselves into the benches, sitting opposite each other, as the Herc began to move.

It taxied for ten minutes, stopped for a few seconds and then accelerated. Moments later they were airborne.

Danny watched Bethany carefully as the Herc gained altitude. Her eyes were closed and she was resting her head against the fuselage. She had looked almost inhuman a couple of hours ago. Now, despite her anxiety about the drop and her anger about being manoeuvred into this situation, she looked entirely calm. Danny wished he knew what was going on in her head. Which version of Bethany existed behind that impenetrable exterior?He thought about what he had been tasked to do to her once she had served her purpose, as the Hercules banked steeply, straightened up and set its course for the Jordanian border.

Alice had worked late, as usual. She had left the MI6 building just after ten and taken a train from Vauxhall to Mitcham where she lived alone in a tiny one-bedroom maisonette. She'd called her mum who told her, as she did every single day, that Alice was working too hard. Then she'd eaten some cold pasta bake from the fridge, drank a cup of herbal tea, removed her make-up and fallen into bed.

Alice's phone was on silent, but it still vibrated noisily on her bedside table as a call came through. She groped for it in the darkness, almost dropped it, then answered it sleepily. 'Hello?'

'Alice, my dear!'

'Who is this?' Her bedside clock read 11.55.

'It's me, my dear. Mark. Mark Cawley.'

His voice was slightly slurred. He'd been drinking.Alice quickly calculated that it must be just after 2 a.m. in Moscow. 'It's late, Mark,' she said.

'Never too late to hear your delightful voice. When are you going to visit me in Moscow? I know a cracking—'

'Why are you calling, Mark?' She was fully awake now and keeping her voice level and patient.This was by no means the first time an officer in the field had contacted her in a state of inebriation. Drunkenness, for many of them, seemed almost unavoidable. The best way to persuade a target or informant to release information was to ply them with alcohol. It worked both ways, of course.You could hardly pour your guest vodka all night, while drinking nothing but sparkling water yourself. A spy needed many attributes: bravery, inquisitiveness, tradecraft. But as much as anything else, they needed a sturdy liver and the ability to hold their drink. 'It's not really to hear my delightful voice, is it? Do you have information for me? Mark? Mark, are you there?'

There was no reply, but she could just make out the sound of splashing water. She realised he was urinating and screwed up her nose in distaste. Holding the phone between her ear and shoulder, she took the notepad and pencil that she always kept by her bed and waited for him to finish. 'Where was I?' he said finally.

'In the bathroom?'

'Ah, yes, excuse me, my dear. Nature calls!'

'Do you have information for me, Mark?'

'I certainly do.'

'Is it safe for you to talk?'

'I checked into a hotel room for that precise purpose. I've been with my informant, Roman.'

A pause.

'And?' Alice said, trying to keep her voice calm.

'Dreadful place he lives in. One of those Soviet monstrosities on the edge of Moscow. Concrete as far as the eye can see. No wonder the poor fellow wanted to get blasted. He's been out of work for a year. Wife and three kids to support. Hardly room to swing the proverbial cat. Walls like cardboard.'

'Did he know anything about Poliakov?'

'They're old mates, my dear. Went to school together. Of course, that was back in the eighties, before *glasnost* and *peri . . . peri . . .*' He tried a few times to say the word *perestroika*, then gave up. 'He became a teacher while Poliakov went into government work. But they stayed in touch and their children are friends.' Cawley belched fruitily. 'S'cuse me,' he said.

'So has he heard anything?'

'Eh?'

'Your informant. Has he heard anything about Poliakov?'

'Bloody clever kids,' said Cawley. 'We should tap them up for GCHQ. Course, the Russkies will get there first.'

'*Mark!*'

'Computer mad. Boffins, really. They're young. They drive my informant to distraction, you know. Always playing computer games on these damned Xbox contraptions. Did you know that they play with their friends online wherever they are in the world, and even *record* their gaming sessions?'

Alice smiled to herself. Cawley was a decent agent, but he was one of the old school and he was showing his age with his astonishment at the simplest piece of technology. She refrained from telling him that she herself had done the same thing with her friends ten years ago, hoping instead to keep him on track.

'Poliakov, Mark?' she said.

'Sorry, my dear, sorry. So, it turns out that one of my informant's children, Sergei, has been playing online computer console games with one of Poliakov's children.'

Alice fell silent, and now it was Cawley's turn to nudge her. 'My dear?'

'How recently?'

'Yesterday.'

Relief flowed through her. Alice knew Poliakov was a typical FSB hood. A bad guy who had done bad things. She wasn't fooled by the slimness of his MI6 file, and his disappearance was hardly regrettable. But she didn't feel the same about his family. Chances were, they didn't know a thing about his secret activities. They certainly didn't deserve to be killed just because Poliakov had been exposed, which Alice had presumed had happened. But it sounded as if the family might – might *just* – still be alive.

'How certain was your informant?'

'He was drunk, my dear. Very drunk. Poor fellow could barely string a sentence together. Feel rather sorry for him, for the way he'll feel in the morning.' He chuckled. 'Feel rather sorry for myself, too.'

'How certain was he, Mark?'

'Neither certain nor uncertain,' said Cawley. For the first time during their conversation, Alice had the sensation that although he *sounded* drunk, his mental faculties were all in order. 'He rather mentioned it in passing. Mumbled it, really. I didn't have the impression that he was trying to feed me false information. I didn't have the impression he was trying to feed me *any* information. It was just a drunken comment and then we moved on.'

Alice's mind was moving rapidly. Mark Cawley might be an un-PC old dinosaur, but this was good work. 'Listen to me carefully, Mark. I need you to go back to your informant's apartment. Do it first thing in the morning if you can. The kid's Xbox will be connected to an external hard drive. I need you to get that drive for me. If the kid's been recording gaming sessions with Poliakov's son, we need to hear that conversation.'

'My dear thing,' said Cawley. 'I'm a step ahead of you.'

'What?'

'I have the drive in front of me as we speak. Roman doesn't quite have my iron bladder. I popped into the other room and took it while he was splashing his boots.'

Alice smiled again. She was more certain than ever now that Cawley's drunkenness was in part an act. He'd been having her on. 'You need to upload the contents of that drive for me,' she said.

'As it happens,' said Cawley, 'I have my laptop open in front of me. Not for the usual reason single men in hotel rooms have their laptops open, you understand.'

Alice was out of bed now, pulling on her jeans. 'Upload it to the secure server,' she said. 'I'll be at the office in an hour. And Mark —'

'Yes, my dear?'

'Good work. *Great* work.'

'Thank you, my dear. I haven't forgotten about that lunch you promised me, next time I'm in London.'

'I'm looking forward to it,' Alice said as she squeezed her feet into her Fila trainers. And she even half meant it.

She hung up, finished getting dressed and ordered an Uber.

EIGHT

The Hercules was heading south. They were somewhere over Lebanon, heading down to the Israel–Jordan border. It was time to get ready.

Danny gave the quad bike a final once-over – two loadies were doing the same – then headed over to Bethany. They had to communicate with gestures due to the noise. Danny fitted her tandem harness, helmet and visor. He showed her how to clip her oxygen canister to the side of her body and fit her mask with its elephant-trunk oxygen tube to her face. He also showed her how to strap both their packs to her legs, then encouraged her to sit down while he prepared himself. The tandem chute was bigger than a regular one, and slightly heavier. Its strapping was as thick as seatbelts. He put on the pack, then clipped his suppressed C8 assault rifle to his side, his pistol already securely holstered across his chest. He put his boxy altimeter on to his wrist – it told him they were at 27,000 feet and climbing – then strapped his GPS device next to it. He fitted and checked his own helmet, oxygen canister and mask, then looked over at the main loadie. He was holding up ten fingers, which told Danny they were ten minutes out. At the back of the aircraft, a red light appeared. Two of the other loadies were cracking lumisticks and tying the glowing plastic tubes to the top of the quad bike. Danny moved over to Bethany and got her to stand up. He checked that the day sacks were firmly strapped to her legs, then stood behind her and clipped the tandem harness together. He noticed the familiar smell of her sweat. It smelled good.

One of the loadies joined them. He pointed at the quad bike on its pallet and shouted above the noise of the engines, 'Automatic deployment at three thousand five hundred feet!'

Danny gave a thumbs up to indicate he understood. With the help of another loadie, they waddled awkwardly but carefully to the back of the plane. They stood to one side of the rails that carried the quad bike. Danny grabbed a piece of strapping on the side of the fuselage and gripped it tightly as the tailgate started to open.

There was a distinct change in the atmosphere. Cold air hit the exposed parts of Danny's face. Although he knew that the next few hours were dangerous, that he was freefalling into hostile territory with a woman he couldn't trust, to carry out an operation that everyone involved with would deny should it go wrong, he couldn't help but feel a thrill. If you didn't get a buzz from a HALO jump, the SAS wasn't for you.

The tailgate was fully open. There was no sign of the moon, but Danny could see the stars and, far away and far below, arteries of light on the ground. The head loadie held up three fingers to indicate three minutes out. Danny waited for the red light to turn green while the other guys prepped the quad bike's pallet. He could sense that Bethany's nervousness was increasing. Her limbs were rigid and she was breathing fast. The oxygen mask amplified the sound of Danny's own breathing, which was slow and composed. It was impossible to ask Bethany if she was okay, so he squeezed her arm reassuringly. She flinched and withdrew it.

Two minutes out. They edged a little closer to the tailgate, Danny still gripping the strapping.

One minute out.

Green light.

Everything happened in a moment. The quad bike on its pallet shot along the rails and out into the sky, a tiny stabilising drogue chute stretching out behind it, flapping wildly. Danny threw himself and Bethany after it, arching his outstretched arms and legs back to ensure that they fell stably. They slid over the familiar curve of the Herc's slipstream. The deafening roar of the aircraft's engines instantly disappeared, replaced with the fierce, icy rush of wind in their ears as they accelerated towards the earth, their clothes and gear flapping madly. He needn't have worried Bethany about the risk of turning over. His body was arched rigidly and they were falling face down to the earth, her legs tucked inside his. He quickly felt for his own drogue chute, which was folded into a side pouch of his rig. He grabbed it, threw it out and immediately felt its steadying influence as they continued their acceleration towards terminal velocity.

There was light everywhere. Danny could see the moon now, crescent and hanging low. Infinite stars clouded the sky. From this great height he could see villages and towns on the ground, glowing yellow masses with arterial routes spreading in all directions. The curvature of the earth glowed faintly even in the darkness. He concentrated on the glowing lumisticks tied to the quad bike. There they were, red and blue, below them. It was not easy to judge distances in the air, but he estimated that they were separated by a constant fifty feet of altitude. He altered his body position so that they were falling a little closer to the vertical, but not so close that they would get tangled in the quad bike's parachute when the automatic deployment device activated.

He checked the glowing altimeter on his wrist. The number on the display was decreasing rapidly.

25,000.

20,000.

They had certainly reached their maximum rate of descent, well in excess of 120 miles per hour. The rush of air was louder, the lift of air resistance at its peak. Here, closer to the earth, Danny's field of view was smaller and diminishing. Fewer settlements. Fewer towns. He had a much greater sense now that they were freefalling into a large, uninhabited expanse. The thick darkness of the desert at night. He saw spots of light here and there. Bedouin encampments, maybe, or vehicles traversing the bare terrain. Civilian or military? Impossible to know. Either way, they were to be avoided. Directly below them, however, he saw nothing. The drop zone had been well chosen.

15,000.

10,000.

5,000.

Any moment now, the quad bike's automatic deployment device would kick in.

4,000.

3,500.

Suddenly he saw the quad bike's enormous chute deploy and billow, blocking his view of the lumisticks. He immediately deployed his own rig and sensed the rigging lines shoot up above him. He felt the instant pull of deceleration. The wind noise diminished. Almost complete silence. Just the gentle flapping of the spreader bar, a rectangular piece of material above him that held the rigging lines in place and stopped the chute from inflating too quickly and messily.

They didn't need oxygen at this altitude. Danny reached for Bethany's mask, pulled it away and removed his own. 'You okay?' he said. There was no need to raise his voice.

'What if I said I wasn't?' Her voice had a slightly wired timbre, half thrill, half fear.

'You're doing great,' Danny said, and instantly regretted it.

'I'm not a child.'

Danny reached for the toggle lines of their parachute, which he could use to follow the quad bike to the ground and guide them on to target. They drifted quietly. The air, so cold when they'd left the Herc, grew warmer. Danny scanned the earth below, checking for threats or obstacles on the landing zone. It was a clear night, well lit by the moon, and he had a good view of the ground. He saw nothing to worry him.

The quad bike made contact with the earth and its chute started to deflate. Danny guided himself and Bethany to one side of it. When they were almost on the ground, he pulled both the toggle lines to flare the tandem chute and put them safely down. Their feet touched the ground and he could sense Bethany's tension releasing. He immediately unclipped her from the tandem rig. She disentangled herself from the day packs round her legs and staggered forwards, plainly relieved to be on solid ground again. Danny gathered the chute. Once he had an armful of crumpled canvas, he took off his freefall rig. He opened his day pack and retrieved his collapsible entrenching tool. He unfolded it while scanning the area all around. The moon lit the terrain up well, but there was little to see. It was barren and almost featureless. Hard earth, with the occasional sturdy desert weed. The ground was level, giving Danny a 360 view of a couple of hundred metres into the distance. There was a shallow wadi, only a couple of metres wide and less than a metre deep, a little beyond the quad bike. He saw no vehicle marks on the ground, but that didn't mean people never came here, and Danny couldn't risk just leaving the parachutes. He would have to dig them in.

'Gather that chute,' he told Bethany, pointing at the quad bike's rig. 'Then keep watch. Let me know if you see anything.' Bethany nodded. Danny took his entrenching tool over to the wadi. The ground would be softer in the ditch, easier to excavate. He jumped inside and started to dig.

It was hot, hard work. The entrenching tool could only cut into the earth inch by inch, with the metronomic scraping of a gravedigger's shovel. It took a full twenty minutes for Danny to make a hole big enough to conceal both chutes, while Bethany kept watch. By the time he'd stuffed them inside, he was drenched with sweat. Before filling the hole in, he jumped up out of the wadi and turned his attention to the quad bike. It was still fastened to its wooden pallet with a tangled mess of strapping. He loosened, undid and removed the straps, then carried them over to the hole and buried them. He shovelled the dislodged earth back over the stash, flattened it down with his boots and redistributed the surplus. He rejoined Bethany, took the quad bike's keys from the secure pouch, climbed on board and drove it off the pallet.

'What do we do with that?' Bethany said, pointing at the pallet.

'We take it with us,' Danny said. 'Dump it somewhere else. If anybody comes across it in this location, chances are they'll start nosing around and find where I've buried the chutes.'

'How are we going to carry it?'

'*We're* not going to carry it,' Danny said. '*You're* going to carry it.' He climbed off the quad bike and took the night-vision gear from one of the day packs. 'We'll be driving blind,' he told her as he fitted one set of goggles to her helmet. 'No headlamps. The moon's pretty bright, but we might need these.'

Bethany pulled the goggles over her eyes, looked around for a few seconds, then raised them and stared at Danny. 'They suit you,' she said.

Danny ignored her. He loaded the day packs on to the bike. 'Get on,' he said.

Bethany mounted the bike. Danny lifted the pallet, upended it and handed it to her so it was positioned vertically with one edge resting on her lap. He took the driving seat again. 'This isn't easy to hold,' Bethany complained.

'I guess not,' Danny said. He checked the quad bike's GPS unit. It was set to night mode, so it gave off very little light. The coordinates of their destination were pre-set, and it gave them an estimated journey time of three hours. That meant they would hit the Roman ruins just before dawn, assuming they didn't encounter any problems on the way.

They moved off, slowly at first but with increasing speed as Danny got a feel for the terrain and the level of light. The moon was sufficiently bright to cast a faint shadow from the quad bike, which trundled quietly over the rough ground. Only after they'd been going for five minutes did Danny stop and allow Bethany to discard the pallet. It broke up a little as she threw it to the ground. Danny drove off again immediately.

His senses were keen. He scanned the horizon as he drove, aware of Bethany watching to the side and behind them now that she no longer had to handle the pallet. There was something strangely reassuring about her manner. Bethany was a difficult, dangerous woman, but Danny had almost forgotten what a capable operator she was. At least as capable as many of the guys back at Hereford. He respected her, in a peculiar way.

He drove without the aid of his NV goggles for twenty minutes. But then a bank of cloud drifted across the moon, severely limiting his vision. He lowered the goggles and viewed the world through a green haze. The NV gave him a good sense of the detail of his surroundings. Small undulations in the terrain became more distinct and he could make out straggly patches of low brush. The use of goggles for extended periods could be tiring on the eyes, but right now it was necessary.

Half an hour passed. In the distance, maybe three hundred metres away, there was a road heading east-west. Danny's preprogrammed GPS route took them that way, but they had to stay clear of the road itself, dressed and tooled up like this. Danny turned right a hundred metres before they met it, then followed the road's direction without getting any closer to it.

The road was deserted, which made sense. It was a minor road leading straight to the Israeli border and into the West Bank. Any normal person wanting to travel in that direction would be safer taking a properly policed main supply route. A journey into that territory could go either way. It just depended if it was one of those days when the Arabs and the Israelis were taking chunks out of each other. But deserted or not, Danny kept to the unmade desert. There might be Jordanian police vehicles in the area. There might be Hezbollah militants. There might be ordinary citizens. None of them would react well to the presence of two British operatives. Much better to remain unseen.

Danny raised his NV goggles to relieve the strain on his eyes and allow some of his natural night vision to return. The moon was hazy but not completely obscured. There was just enough light to see by. He focused on the ground ahead. It had become slightly bumpier and required more of his attention.

Which was why he didn't see the threat until Bethany alerted him. 'Over there!' she hissed.

Danny brought the quad bike to a sudden halt and killed the engine. Bethany was pointing up towards the road. They had been travelling parallel to it, but now it was curving round to the south. If they continued on the same trajectory, they would hit it in about 200 metres. Danny cursed himself for his momentary lack of awareness. Parked up by the road were several vehicles: at least three, perhaps more hidden behind those he could see. A saloon car. Two heavy trucks. There was movement of personnel around the trucks. Danny raised his night sight and surveyed the scene.

Something was going down. The men moving around the vehicles – Danny counted four of them – were armed. Two had rifles. Two had something heavier – RPG launchers, Danny guessed, though it was hard to be certain. Shamags covered their heads and they were facing away from the vehicles, out into the desert, in Danny and Bethany's direction. They were obviously guarding whatever was in the trucks.

And they had just as obviously clocked the quad bike and its two passengers.

They started shouting at each other. Hoarse, curt instructions in Arabic that travelled clearly across the still desert air. Danny recognised the tone of these shouts, even if he couldn't discern the words. He knew that he and Bethany were about to come under fire. He swore under his breath, twisted round and, with all the force he could muster, pushed her from the bike. Danny grabbed his C8 as she fell to the ground, leapt off the other side of the bike and crawled quickly away from it. 'Keep down!' he shouted, pressing himself as closely as possible to the ground. 'Get away from the bike! Contact!'

The distant fizz of an RPG launch was a sound Danny knew well. Every time he'd heard it in the past it had given him the same sensation: the bite of anticipation and fear, not knowing how or where the grenade would land, or what damage its shrapnel would inflict. Tonight, the fizz triggered a specific memory. He was back in north-eastern Syria, with eyes on an abandoned prison, and his team were unexpectedly under fire from a Russian ambush. For the briefest moment, he saw not the enemy before him, but a flashback of his burned and mangled unit mates, encased in coffins of twisted metal. He saw missiles hurtling through the air. He saw himself crouched in a cramped culvert as an earth-shaking fast air strike detonated above him.

He was there, and not here.

An explosion returned him to the present as the RPG hit the quad bike. The impact shook Danny from his moment of inattention. He felt a sour wave of self-loathing at his lack of focus as shrapnel showered around him and a second RPG flew towards the quad bike.

His training kicked in. Instinct. Situational awareness. He didn't know who these people were or why they had engaged him and Bethany. He didn't know if they had been expecting them, or if they were simply in the wrong place or the wrong time. But none of that mattered. All that mattered was the fight, and right now Danny was at the wrong end of it. That had to change. The second RPG hit the quad bike, knocking it back. As another shower of shrapnel fell, he heard the unmistakeable bang of an exploding tyre. The quad bike was fucked. But it told him one thing: the enemy targets were focusing on the bike. It suggested that they couldn't see Danny and

Bethany. Here, exposed and in open ground, that was their only strategic advantage. He had to make use of it, and quickly.

'Stay down!' he told Bethany. 'Don't move! If you move, they'll see you!'

There was no response from Bethany. He couldn't see her and had no idea if she was hit. He suspected not. He knew how a person screamed when they'd been injured by hot shrapnel. Not even Bethany, cold-hearted and self-controlled as she was, would be able to suppress that kind of pain. And if she had been hit? There was nothing he could do. Priorities. He had to deal with the threat first.

His C8, with its full thirty-round magazine, was by his side. He placed it in front of him in the firing position. Through the sight he could see the enemy targets: four guys, artlessly standing in a line with no apparent thought for taking defensive positions. He would have to pick them off, one by one, and quickly before they were able to work out his position.

The bad news for the four targets was that Danny Black had clocked up more hours on the range in Hereford than almost any other soldier, in this precise position, preparing for this precise moment. His weapon was also suppressed, which meant that although it was not silent, it would be difficult for the targets to identify the source of the dull knock of its retort.

He rested his finger on the trigger, breathed in and held his breath to keep his body as still as possible. Then he squeezed.

He knew the shot was good the moment the empty casing ejected itself from the rifle and his shoulder absorbed the weapon's recoil. He half saw the first target crumple suddenly and heavily to the ground as he re-aimed and positioned the second target in his sight, the crosshair directly over his chest. It was one of the RPG guys. He had the launcher by his side and was scanning the desert, plainly not yet aware that his mate had been shot. Danny didn't give him time to twig what was happening. His second shot was as swift and accurate as the first. The target hit the ground.

There was immediate panic now. The two remaining targets realised that events were not unfolding as they intended. They were shouting. Danny could hear their stressed voices. If they had any sense, they would run, but they were too busy yelling instructions at each other. Danny's third target was standing side on, waving his arms and rifle at his companion. His movement and position made this a more challenging shot. Danny raised the rifle just a little, so the crosshairs were aligned with the target's body. He fired and made no mistake.

The fourth man ran. Danny tried to follow him with his sights, but he sprinted behind the nearest truck before Danny could release a fourth round.

There was a deep silence. No movement.

Danny glanced to the left. The quad bike was smouldering. There was still no sign of Bethany on the other side, nor any indication that she was alright. He didn't budge. He could feel his heart beating strong, but his pulse was slow, controlled by his regular breathing as he turned his attention back to the vehicles. He appraised the situation. There was at least one enemy target left, but there could well be more, and he might be calling for help. The four guys had looked like they'd been guarding something or someone. Danny's money was on more personnel waiting. What would their next move be? Either they'd make a run for it, or they'd continue their attack. Stalemate wasn't an option. So Danny needed to be ready to suppress any contact from the targets. He continued to look through his rifle sight, panning the area from left to right. Truck. Open ground. Truck. Open ground. Saloon car. And then back again. Saloon car. Open ground. Truck. Open ground. Truck.

A minute passed. No movement.

Another minute. Danny's mouth felt dry. He knew something was coming. Any moment now . . .

He nearly wasn't fast enough. The target appeared from behind the middle truck just as Danny's sights had panned past him. He only saw a clip of movement on the edge of the sight. By the time he had panned back, the militant was in plain view, an RPG launcher on his shoulder, ready to fire. From the angle at which he was standing, Danny knew the target was not now aiming at the quad bike, but at him.

He released three rounds in quick succession. The first missed, striking the side of the truck. The second hit its mark. As the target crumpled uselessly to the ground, the third round flew over his head and into the desert beyond.

Silence again. Stillness. And then, seemingly from nowhere, more movement and noise. Two of the vehicles pulled away: the saloon car and the truck that had remained untouched by Danny's ammo. Danny followed the vehicles with his weapon but let them go. Shooting out their tyres meant prolonging the contact. He'd kept the upper hand so far, but firefights when you were as heavily outnumbered as this were unpredictable. Much better for him if the remaining targets got the hell out of here.

The distant sound of the vehicles' screaming engines faded. The vehicles themselves disappeared along the road.

Danny lay still for a further two minutes. He could see one truck and four corpses, but it would be a mistake to assume the threat had disappeared. There could still be targets behind or inside the truck.

'You okay?' he called to Bethany.

'Just lying here enjoying the show.'

'No injuries?'

'I'm okay, alright? Who they hell were those people?'

'Your guess is as good as mine. They weren't pros. My guess is we stumbled over some sort of deal. Drugs, maybe.' He glanced at the quad bike again. One tyre was smoking, but that wasn't the full extent of the damage. The bodywork at the front was gnarled and twisted, and the whole thing was leaning to one side in a way that suggested a broken axle. 'The bike's fucked,' he said. 'We're going to need another vehicle.'

'Only one vehicle that I can see,' Bethany said.

Danny examined the distant truck. There was no option: if their journey was to progress, he would have to approach it at some point. 'Stay where you are,' he said. 'I'm going to recce the truck.'

A pause.

'Be careful, Danny,' Bethany said. She had momentarily lost the edge in her voice.

'Stay where you are until I give you a signal.'

He got up in two movements; firstly on to one knee, weapon still engaged and pointing at the truck. He flicked his weapon to the automatic setting. Then, a minute later, when there was still no sign of enemy personnel, he got to his feet. The truck was 200 metres away. He advanced, the butt of his weapon pressed hard into his shoulder, his finger resting lightly on the trigger. His boots crunched on the hard earth as he advanced, ready to fire at the slightest hint of a threat.

Distance to target: 150 metres. No sign of enemy personnel.

100 metres.

75.

The attack, when it came, was sudden. A figure appeared at the front of the truck, head wrapped in a shamag, an ostentatious bandolier of ammo slung round his chest. He appeared crazed, screaming some kind of war cry, which served no other purpose than to alert Danny to his position. It only took a short burst of three rounds to silence him. His body was thrown back against the truck, then it slid to the ground. Even from this distance, Danny could see the dark swab of blood he left on the bodywork.

He knelt down again in the firing position, waited a minute, then continued his advance.

There was no further contact. As Danny reached the truck, he circled it, searching for enemy personnel. Nobody was left alive. He checked in the cab, under the body and finally placed himself in front of the back doors. He lowered his rifle, pulled his hand-gun and, with his free hand, opened the back of the truck.

It was stuffed full of weapons. Serious weapons. Assault rifles with underslung grenade launchers, sniper rifles, RPG launchers and wooden crates full of warheads, Claymore mines, plastic explosives, detonators, coils of wire, boxes of ammunition. They hadn't stumbled on a drugs deal. They'd stumbled on a weapons deal. If the guys involved had had more tactical nous, they might have realised that they had enough gear here to take out an entire squadron, let alone a solitary SAS man and an unarmed former spook. He closed the truck up and checked the ignition. No keys. They had to be here somewhere. He approached the body of his final target. The man was lying at a gruesome angle by the front wheel and the three rounds from Danny's burst had made a real mess of him. They had torn open his thoracic cavity. His chest still oozed blood and fragments of rib and lung poked through the tears in his clothes. Danny's hands became bloodied and sticky as he patted his victim down, searching for the keys that he finally found in a back trouser pocket. He took them, then jogged back to Bethany and the wrecked quad bike.

She stood up as he approached. Danny raised his NV goggles so he could see her properly.

'All clear?' she asked, with the strained inflexion of a stressed person trying to sound calm.

Danny nodded. 'Enough weapons in that truck to sink a battleship.'

'Smugglers?' she said.

'Probably.'

Bethany looked over at the vehicle. 'Probably Jordanian criminals selling weapons to West Bank Palestinians,' she said. 'We know it goes on.' She frowned, clearly aware that she'd just inadvertently put herself back in the role of an active MI6 officer. 'I mean—'

'I know what you mean.' He nodded at the quad bike. 'We have to deal with this.'

'What do you mean, deal with it?'

'It's a British quad bike, covered with our DNA, nowhere to hide it. If the Jordanian authorities come across it, they'll start asking questions.'

'So what do we do?'

'Burn it. Stand back.'

Danny unloaded all their gear from the quad bike, removed the GPS unit and set it all in a pile fifteen metres from the bike itself. Then he located the quad bike's fuel line, detached it and allowed fuel to spill over the chassis and on to the ground. He located a stash of waterproof matches in his day pack, lit one and threw it on to the fuel. It ignited immediately. He hurried back to where Bethany was standing and waited for the explosion of the fuel tank. It happened within seconds and, before a minute was out, the entire bike was alight, flames licking high and a plume of black greasy smoke pumping into the desert night.

'Fetch your gear,' Danny said. 'That fire's going to be visible from a distance. We need to get out of here.'

They grabbed their stuff, slung their day packs over their shoulders and ran back up to the truck. Bethany stared at the corpses as they passed. There was a blankness to her expression that chilled Danny. She showed no sign of being disturbed by the sight. She'd seen worse. She'd *done* worse. That was why she was here in the first place.

'Israeli plates,' Bethany said, pointing at the truck.

They climbed up into the truck. It was old and dirty and stank of fuel. Danny placed the GPS unit on the dashboard and familiarised himself with the vehicle. The gear stick was stiff, hard to manoeuvre, but when Danny put the keys in the ignition the engine turned over easily. Bethany looked out of the window, staring at the bodies again. 'You've killed a lot of men, Danny,' she said.

'That makes two of us.'

'When do you stop counting?' she asked.

'The trick is not to start in the first place.'

She turned to face him. 'I was going to stop,' she said. 'For my son's sake. I promised myself. No more. But here I am.'

Danny shrugged. He didn't want her to see that the catch in her voice had triggered something like sympathy in him. 'Turns out it becomes a habit,' he said. 'As long as you limit it to the bad guys, you can rest easy at night.'

'And this general you all want me to deal with. He's one of the bad guys?'

'One of the worst.' For the second time in half an hour, he remembered the ambush in Syria and his dead mates.

'Will they look after him?'

'What do you mean?' Danny was confused.

'My boy. He's the only reason I'm giving you the time of day, you know. Will they look after him? Is he okay?'

Danny couldn't bring himself to look her in the eye. He knocked the vehicle into first gear. 'He'll be fine. You'll see him again in a couple of days. He'll have forgotten about all this before you know it. Kids are like that.' It wasn't true, of course. In a couple of days, Bethany would be dead. She was one of the bad guys. And her son? Danny told himself that wasn't his problem. 'We need to stay off the road. The smugglers will want their gear and if anybody stops us with half a ton of heavy weaponry, it's going to take some explaining.' He released the clutch and the vehicle rolled off the road and back on to the desert terrain. The quad bike was still burning and smouldering. He turned away from it, following the directions given him by the GPS.

'He talks about you, you know?'

'Who?' Danny said, even though he knew exactly what she meant.

'Danny. My son. You made an impression.' They drove in silence for a few seconds. 'Don't worry,' she said. 'I'm not about to suggest a cosy reunion.'

'Good.' He checked the GPS again. 'We should be at the RV point in about an hour.'

'The Roman ruins?'

'Right. Dawn is at ten minutes past five, but I want to make sure we're early. I'd prefer to see our contact arrive than the other way round. So I need to concentrate.'

'Concentrate away.' Bethany looked out of her window and fell silent.

Danny killed the vehicle's lights, flicked down his NV goggles, and drove.

NINE

The MI6 building was different at night. Alternative faces and a quieter atmosphere. Alice attracted some curious glances at security, dressed in casual clothes and shiny white Filas. She looked even less like the typical MI6 employee than usual. She made her impatient way through security and hurried not to the fourth floor, but to the basement.

Alice did not often venture to the sunless depths of the building. There were areas here for which she didn't have clearance. But this was also where the techies lived. Where the huge cluster of comms satellites atop the building sent their incoming messages from around the world. Where the secure servers were located. It was to this part of the basement that she headed. There were further security checks before she could gain access. A biometric iris scanner, a fingerprint check. All was good, and she entered the techies' lair.

It was gloomy in here. The only light came from laptops and a few large screens on the far wall. There were perhaps fifteen people working down here, all men, all under twenty-five. They wore single-ear headsets and there was a constant clickety-clack of fingers on keyboards. Alice strode up to the nearest techie. He had a hipster beard and a black polo neck, and he pretended not to notice Alice approaching. Alice had no time for such games. She didn't humour him with a polite clearing of the throat or a diffident 'excuse me'. 'I need access to files that have been uploaded from an agent in Moscow,' she said.

The techie held up one finger and continued to type for twenty seconds before turning on his swivel seat and finally acknowledging her. Alice was used to the barely perceptible look of surprise when people saw her for the first time, and she recognised it now. The techie's demeanour visibly softened. He gently stroked his beard. Alice recognised that gesture too. If they were in a bar, the techie would start hitting on her about now. Here at work, he wouldn't dare. He wasn't of the old school like Mark Cawley. 'Say again?' he said.

Alice repeated her request, even though she knew he'd heard every word of it.

'What's your asset's identification code?' the techie asked.

Alice recited it. The techie did his thing at the keyboard. 'Here it is,' he said. He frowned. 'Are these from a games console?'

'Xbox,' Alice said. 'I need to know if there's any audio files we can extract.'

It was always the same with the techies. They pretended to be so laid back, but as soon as you gave them a problem to solve, their inner geek presented itself. Alice watched his expression change from the self-confidence of a man who knew this wouldn't be a problem, to the anxiety of man who had encountered an unexpected difficulty, to the satisfaction of a man who'd cracked it. 'Just the audio files?' he asked after a couple of minutes' work.

'For now.'

The techie took a new memory stick from his desk drawer, inserted it into his computer and transferred the file. Then he handed the memory stick to Alice and stroked his beard again. 'Anything else?' he asked.

Alice shook her head, rewarded him with a smile for his usefulness, then left the basement and headed back up to her tiny office.

There were no trains passing outside her window at this hour, but there were several workmen on the tracks with hi-vis jackets and head torches. Alice paid them little attention as she inserted the memory card into her computer and opened up the audio files. There were about thirty, but the metadata told her that only five had been recorded since Poliakov's disappearance, so she decided to focus on those. She moved the file icons to a separate part of her desktop, plugged in some headphones, took out a pencil and notepad and clicked on the first of the five.

The recording was obviously of a Call of Duty-type game and the first sound she heard was the loud drilling of a computer-generated automatic weapon, and the over-the-top screams of computer-generated death. She reduced the volume and listened to a good two minutes of gameplay before she heard any human dialogue. There were two boys, their unbroken voices teetering on the edge of adolescence. Their conversation was in Russian, of course, but that was no problem for Alice. At first, she heard little more than monosyllabic grunts or the occasional whoop of delight when an on-screen enemy was killed. But gradually the conversation became more varied, if no more interesting: comments about homework left undone, or female classmates unkissed. There was one dominant voice on the first recording, and that was clearly the informant's son, the owner of the Xbox. She knew this, because the second voice constantly referred to him as Sergei. After seven or eight minutes, Sergei referred to his friend as Alexander. This was not Poliakov's son, whose name was Ivan.

Alice killed the recording and opened the next file. To her surprise, Sergei was talking to a girl called Masha.

Recording three was more interesting.

The metadata on the file told Alice that it had been recorded three days ago, and she knew within seconds that Sergei's gaming partner was named Ivan, because he shouted his name as a massive explosion from the game resonated in her ears.

— *Ivan, you bastard!*

Alice scribbled her translation of the Russian on her notepad. Her brow was furrowed with concentration, and she squinted slightly as she listened hard.

For several minutes there was nothing but gameplay. Then both boys shouted as there was another explosion. The gameplay fell silent.

— *When are you coming back to school?*
— *I don't know.*
— *Are you on holiday?*
— *Not exactly. Do you want another game?*
— *OK.*

The violent noise of the gameplay started up again. The kids' conversation reverted to grunts and the occasional expletive. When it was over, they said a curt goodbye. End of recording.

None of the remaining recordings featured the voice of Ivan Poliakov. Alice was disappointed. It was gone three in the morning now, and what she had thought would be a very substantial lead had turned out to be less fruitful than she'd hoped. She removed her headphones, rubbed her tired eyes and looked back at the notepad. The fragment of conversation between the two boys yielded nothing, other than proof that Ivan had been alive three days ago and was staying somewhere with an internet connection and an Xbox. She considered her next move. Maybe they could access the Microsoft servers, find out the IP address of Ivan's console. Worth a try, but her gut told her it wouldn't lead anywhere. These kids, especially the Russian ones, were smart enough to keep their devices behind a VPN. Maybe GCHQ could do something with the hard drive, but she wasn't hopeful.

She put the headphones back on and started up the recording of the two boys again, scrubbing forwards to the fragment of conversation. She replayed it several times, not quite certain what she was listening out for. Whatever it was, she didn't hear it. After listening to the fragment for the fourth time, she let the recording continue playing as she stared at the workmen on the railway track below. The Call of Duty explosions continued. In the distance, very faint yet just discernible despite the headphones, she heard the distinctive sound of Big Ben striking the hour.

She blinked and looked at her watch. It was 03.27. And she had never – *never* – heard Big Ben from her office.

She hadn't heard it in real time. She'd heard it on the recording.

She scrubbed back. The chimes had happened just after a particularly long burst of computer-generated fire, and a howl of frustration from one of the boys. It was faint and distant, and the second half of the peals was drowned out by more game noise. But it was unmistakeable, and it meant Alice had a lead: three days ago, Ivan Poliakov had been in London. Had his father Dimitri been with him? Alice didn't know, but she was determined to find out.

And to do that, she needed some more help from the techies.

★   ★   ★

Hamoud's wife Rabia routinely returned home at 8 p.m. The final two hours of waiting for her were always the slowest. The kids were watching Nickelodeon. Hamoud would ordinarily pretend – to himself and to the children – that he was busy. Folding and refolding clothes left on the floor. Preparing food for a frugal meal that he knew Rabia would finish cooking when she got back, shooing him from the kitchen. Sometimes he would panic that she wasn't coming back. That she had met someone else. That she had grown tired of his constant anxiety. He knew it was paranoia. And he knew paranoia was a symptom of everything he had experienced at Guantanamo. But sometimes those paranoid thoughts multiplied in his mind and he wasn't able to control them. It was a disease.

Tonight, however, he sat at the table while *Spongebob Squarepants* played in the background. He constantly swiped his phone to refresh the page that indicated Rabia's location with a little blue dot. She had left her final cleaning job three blocks away and was making her way home. Hamoud was impatient for her to walk through the door.

Impatient and nervous. He hadn't told the kids about Walt Disney World. He hadn't the heart to raise their hopes when he wasn't certain that Rabia would agree to the trip. There were, now he thought about it, many reasons not to. They would lose several days' income, for a start. There was no sick pay for domestic cleaners. His wife never missed a day's work, no matter how unwell she was. And it would mean removing the children from school. She was very strict about that. She wanted her children to have the benefit of a proper education, and not end up like their parents. And perhaps the biggest obstacle was her pride. She didn't want to rely on anybody's charity. They were not victims. She often used those precise words, glossing over the inescapable truth that Hamoud was – or, at least once, had been – exactly that.

He put his phone down when he knew she was close and busied himself in the kitchen. A couple of minutes later, the door clicked open and Melissa ran to meet her mother. It was as if a champagne cork had been pulled from a bottle. She started babbling about her lessons, her friends and what had happened in the school yard. Malick quietly joined her and even offered a few quiet observations about his day. Rabia enveloped them in her arms, laughing at their jokes and commiserating with their tiny problems at just the right moments. Only when they had finished talking to her and drifted back to the TV did she approach Hamoud, smile warmly, place one hand on his cheek and say: 'And how are you, my love?'

Ordinarily, it was the most difficult question of the day. Because how could he tell her the truth? How could he tell her that all day he had been counting the seconds of his solitude, wrestling with the memories and dark thoughts that swirled in his mind? How could he tell her that today had been worse than yesterday, which had been worse than the day before? He had heard it said that a problem shared was a problem halved. But not for him. To share his problems would be to infect others with his negative thoughts. He could not do that to Rabia when she was so kind and worked so hard. So he would always reply with the same words. 'Today was better.' And she would smile, and nod, and go to the kitchen.

This evening, however, he said: 'Today was *interesting*.'

Rabia raised an eyebrow. 'How so?' she asked.

He tried to scratch his palms, but she gently stopped him. 'How so?' she repeated.

He told her about the letter. About the call. How they'd won a prize and, if they wanted to, they could take the children to Walt Disney World. He didn't tell her about the peculiar way the letter had been delivered. He knew she would find that suspicious. When he had finished explaining it all, he took Rabia's hand. 'I know it means taking some time away from your work,' he said, 'and removing the children from school for a few days. But we could hold back some of the spending money to cover what you don't earn. And when will we ever have this chance again?'

'Are you sure it's genuine?' she said.

'I spoke to the lady. She was very kind. The tickets will arrive in the morning.'

She nodded her head slowly. For a moment, Hamoud thought the crease on her forehead meant she was going to say no. But then she smiled. 'We deserve some good luck,' she said. 'Heaven knows we haven't had much of it.' Her eyes shone. 'We'll go! I'll call my clients, and I'm sure the school will understand.'

For the first time in years, Hamoud felt light. He had something to look forward to, not just the relentless march of the days. 'You tell them,' Rabia said, nodding towards the children who were still transfixed by Spongebob.

Hamoud nodded gratefully. He released his hands from hers and went over to the kids. 'Children,' he said. 'Turn off the TV. I have something to tell you.'

And once he'd told them, he was certain that he would never, until the day he died, forget the look on their faces.

There were more CCTV cameras in London than anywhere else in Europe. Or so they said. Alice didn't know if it was true, but she knew this: if the security services had a picture of your face, and they wanted to track your movements in London, they had a good chance of finding you quickly. It was becoming a common strategy. The lawyers were increasingly queasy about phone taps, and the resources to track targets in person were desperately limited. But there was a vast network of surveillance cameras, and the advances in facial recognition technology meant the computers could do most of the heavy lifting.

Of course, it also meant that the techies in the facial recognition department were permanently overworked. And they liked you to know it. Alice prepared herself to break through a brick wall as she returned to the basement with a photograph of Dimitri Poliakov. She swiped herself through to the correct department and found herself in another room dominated by computer screens, laptops and the low hum of fans and electronics.

A woman approached. She was about Alice's age with pale, freckly skin, red hair and black-rimmed glasses. 'You need something?' she asked.

Alice nodded and handed over the photograph. 'I think this guy is in London. I've no other leads. Can you help me out?'

The woman glanced at the photo. 'We're running quite a few checks at the moment,' she started to say. 'I'm not sure how quickly we can get to it.'

Alice had a choice. She could invoke her superiors, explain that her instructions came from the top and hint that if she didn't get what she wanted, it might be all the worse for this woman and her department. Or she could take the more effective path. In situations like this she had learned a little girl power went a long way. She glanced over her shoulder, as though worried someone might be listening or approaching. 'Do me a favour,' she said, as appealingly as she could. 'I've got this bloody man in the department, always putting me down. If I could ID this suspect before he hauls his arse out of bed in the morning, it would just put me a step ahead of him.' She flashed her a smile.

The woman's demeanour softened. She gave the photograph a more detailed look. 'Come on,' she said. 'Let's see what we can do.'

TEN

Hereford's target pack had included satellite imagery of the old Roman ruins. There was enough weaponry in the back of this smuggler's truck to mount a small siege. Hooking up with a local fixer ought to be routine. But he was on edge.

The flashbacks he'd experienced earlier in the night had stayed with him. As he drove the truck towards the RV with the benefit of his night-vision goggles, he couldn't help noticing the similarities with the Zero 22 op. This, too, was a covert night-time approach on a supposedly friendly target. As a Regiment man, Danny had learned to treat all operational situations with a degree of uncertainty. He had reason to be more uncertain than usual, with an unpredictable Bethany White sitting next to him, driving a vehicle that the fixer wasn't expecting.

An hour had passed since the contact with the smugglers. They had driven in silence. This truck was less suited to the terrain they were crossing than the quad bike; Danny drove slowly and with extra care. He winced each time a wheel hit an unexpected dip and the weaponry in the back of the truck shook noisily. But they crossed twenty-five miles of desert with no further incident and now were close to their destination. Danny stopped the truck, took his rifle and night sight and stepped outside to scan the area.

The word 'ruins' was definitely apt. There was barely anything to see here. Through his sight, he picked out some stones protruding from the ground in regular patterns about 300 metres away, and an old stone wall. This was no tourist site. There was a narrow road, little more than a track, leading from the far side. To Danny's two o'clock there was a copse of cypress trees, atypical for the terrain. Danny figured there must be some kind of underground water source. If they poked around the ruins, they'd probably find an old well somewhere. He guessed that the copse was where the fixer planned to hide their quad bike. It was just about the only place Danny had seen for the last hour that offered enough cover to hide a vehicle. Hopefully they'd be able to hide the truck there.

Time check: 04.20 hrs. Dawn, the time of the RV, was at 05.10. This was open ground; there was very little cover. Danny drove the truck round the ruins and parked on the far side of the copse from the road, hidden from anybody approaching. He removed and stowed the GPS unit. Took the keys and buried them at the foot of a tree with a distinctive knot on the trunk. 'Come with me,' he told Bethany.

They entered the copse together and headed through the trees to the other side. They could see the road from here. Danny knelt behind the tree line. Bethany took her position next to him. They waited.

The desert was silent. Just the whisper of leaves in a faint, cold wind. Danny kept his eyes on the road. He could feel Bethany looking at him and sensed that she wanted to say something. Danny didn't yield. His instruction to deal with her when the op was over was weighing heavily. He would do it, but he was only human: the more time he spent with someone, the greater the connection he felt.

Headlamps appeared at 05.00 exactly. Two sets. The temperature had suddenly dropped and the sky had started to lighten, though there was no sign of the sun yet. Danny was breathing clouds of condensation. He raised his weapon and followed the lead vehicle with the barrel as the two cars drew closer and stopped. Distance: fifty metres. Both drivers' doors opened. Two figures appeared, silhouetted by the headlamps. One of them stood in front of the car, blocking the left light. The other stepped towards the copse. 'Hello?' he called. '*Salam?*'

Danny and Bethany stood. Danny flicked a switch and the red dot of a laser sight appeared on the man's chest. The man noticed immediately and quickly put his hands in the air.

'Keep them there!' Danny called. 'And your friend, too.'

The man shouted something in Arabic. The guy by the car quickly raised his hands. The two men stood statue-still. Danny kept the laser sight on his guy's chest.

He let thirty seconds pass. He could see that they were dressed in regular Arabic garb: plain white *dishdasha* and sandals. They had full beards but looked young, maybe early twenties.

'Follow me,' Danny told Bethany. 'And do exactly as I say. If they sense any tension between us, it gives them the upper hand.'

'So you really don't trust them?'

'I was only expecting one guy. And anyway, they're fixers. They work for whoever pays them. If someone's paying them more than us, guess where their loyalties lie.'

They emerged from the treeline, Danny with his weapon still raised, Bethany walking to one side and a little behind. As they approached the two men, Danny saw that they were younger than he'd first imagined, barely into their twenties. One of them had a chunky gold bracelet, the other an expensive watch. There was something about their wary yet arrogant demeanour that he didn't like. He and Bethany stopped five metres from where they stood. Without lowering his weapon or looking away from his guy, Danny spoke. 'Search them,' he said.

Bethany stepped forwards and started to pat down the first guy. His outrage was clear on his face even before he complained. 'What is this? Why is a woman touching me like this?'

'Trust me,' said Danny, 'she doesn't like you in that way.'

Bethany turned, holding up a pistol she had found on his person.

'Anything else?' Danny said.

'Nothing.'

'You sure?'

Bethany gave him a 'do you want to do this?' look, but kept quiet. 'Do his friend,' Danny said.

The second guy had no weapon. Danny lowered his. 'Okay,' he said. 'Which is ours?'

The fixer pointed to the lead vehicle. 'The keys are in the car, sir,' he said. He licked his lips and looked around. 'We were told there would be a quad bike?'

'Change of plan,' Danny said. He stepped up to the fixer. 'There's a truck behind those trees. When we leave here, you're going to be tempted to open it up and see what's inside. It's booby trapped. You know what that means?' The fixer nodded. 'Good.

Don't touch that truck. If you do—' He made an explosion gesture with two hands. 'And if it's not here when we come back in a day or two, you don't get your money. Is there anything about that that you don't understand?'

The fixer shook his head. 'May I please have my gun back, sir?' he said.

Danny gave him a withering look. He turned to Bethany. 'Get in the car,' he said. They jogged over to the vehicle together. It was a beaten-up Passat, covered in red dust and with several dents in the panel work. That suited Danny just fine – it was the kind of car nobody would look at twice. He stowed his rifle in the boot and took the wheel. With Bethany beside him in the passenger seat, he turned a full 180 and drove round the other vehicle away from the ruins. When he'd gone twenty metres, he held the fixer's pistol out of the window, brandished it for a moment to be sure it could be seen, then dropped it in the sand.

'You think they're going to stay away from the truck?' Bethany said.

'Probably,' Danny said. 'But other people might come nosing around. We need to be sure we have another way of getting back to the pick-up point, if we need it.' He kept his eyes on the road as he spoke, carefully avoiding Bethany's gaze. An image flashed in his mind: he was standing over Bethany somewhere in the Jordanian desert. Bethany was on her knees, a gun to her head. He wondered if she suspected what was waiting for her.

Danny had no need for the GPS unit for this part of the journey. The road headed east, towards the rising sun. He knew that Amman lay in this direction and within fifteen minutes they found themselves on a well-maintained main supply route, busy with early morning traffic. Large road signs in Arabic hung overhead and the desert surroundings gradually became more urban. Warehouses on the outskirts of town. Mosques and grim-looking tenement blocks. In many ways, it could have been any city in the world. He switched back on the GPS unit and set it to direct them to the pre-loaded destination. A couple of klicks further down the road, the GPS directed them off to the left. They followed a winding, maze-like route through a busy, run-down suburb. It was only just gone 06.00 hrs and already the temperature was rising uncomfortably. The vehicle's paltry air-con did not so much keep them cool as recirculate the choking traffic fumes from outside. The roads were filled with the beeping of car horns. Danny, already sweating, drove soberly. He ignored the occasional raised fist from impatient Jordanians. His objective was to get to their safe house without incident, not to demonstrate to the drivers of Amman what a big guy he was.

The GPS led them to a squat four-storey concrete block that wouldn't have been out of place in the scummiest parts of Croydon. Its exterior walls were festooned with old air-conditioning units and lines of washing. There was an open basement car park. Danny reversed the vehicle into a space directly opposite the exit, ready to get out of there quickly if necessary. A few guys in traditional Arabic clothes were getting into their own cars, presumably on the way to work. Danny let them leave before he and Bethany exited the vehicle. The fewer people that saw them, the better.

Danny knew from his target pack that the safe house was apartment number 312 on the third floor. There was a lift from the basement, but he had no desire to put himself in an enclosed space with no exit. They took the stairs. A couple of curious kids playing cards on the ground watched them walk from the stairwell along the third-floor corridor, but by the time Danny and Bethany were outside their apartment, the kids had gone. Danny tried the door. It was unlocked. They stepped inside.

Danny was not expecting luxury. They didn't get it. The four rooms of the apartment were equally grim. The bare concrete floors were peppered with rodent droppings. The kitchen and bathroom had different but similarly foul stenches. The bedroom contained a double bed with a stained old mattress and no bedclothes. There was no furniture in the main room where a dirty window looked out from the tower block towards the hilly urban sprawl of Amman, undulating under the blue morning sky. The city was a ramshackle, chaotic place. The sort of place you could easily lose yourself. Danny's sort of place.

There was a key in the front door. Danny locked it from the inside and put the key in his pocket. 'You want me all to yourself, is that it?' Bethany said. Danny ignored the comment and pushed past her into the bedroom. There were two suitcases in here. He hauled them on to the bed and opened them up. Inside were sets of smart clothes for each of them: a navy suit, white shirt and shiny brown shoes for Danny, a black knee-length skirt, jacket and cream blouse for Bethany, and a bag of make-up. There was a brown envelope containing British passports with Danny and Bethany's photographs but the names of Andy Waldren and Sophia Milton. Two press passes held the same photos and names, Danny's accredited to the *Sunday Times*, Bethany's to the *Telegraph*. A second brown envelope contained a sheaf of Jordanian dinars. There were two shoulder bags: a small leather handbag with detailing on the clasp, and a larger black man-bag. Each contained a blank A5 journalist's notepad and a few rollerball pens, along with a local mobile phone, the number stuck on the back. Danny had his own encrypted mobile, so he'd have no use for it, but he memorised the number on the back of Bethany's and took a moment to write his number on a piece of paper and hand it to her. She read it once, committed it to memory and screwed up the paper.

He wondered who had delivered all this to the safe house. An MI6 agent attached to the British Embassy, he presumed. He didn't much like the idea of the locals spotting an obviously Western person carrying these suitcases up to the flat. He hoped they'd been discreet, and he double-checked that the door was locked before returning to the bedroom where Bethany was waiting for him. 'Not going to lie,' she said. 'I'm quite looking forward to seeing you in a suit.'

Yet again, Danny found himself resisting her flirtation. A tendril of hair had fallen over her face in an appealing way. He wanted to brush it back over her ear. He forced himself to think about something else. 'We need to talk,' he said.

'Oh yeah?'

'We're going to the General's hotel this evening. I need to know how you're going to do it.' She cocked her head. 'How are you going to do it?' he repeated. 'We won't be able to take weapons into the hotel. It's not as simple as a bullet in the head. You need a plan.'

Bethany didn't reply immediately. She walked over to the window, where she looked out over Amman while tracing a shape on the glass with her forefinger. 'I'll improvise,' she said.

'Not good enough,' Danny told her. And when she didn't reply again, he strode over to where she was standing, grabbed her by the shoulder and roughly turned her round to face him. He was surprised to see that tears were welling in her eyes.

'You think I'm a monster,' she said. 'You think I spend my time working out inventive ways to kill people.'

'You've got form.'

'And so do you. But there's more to you than that. And there's more to me, too. The men I killed, I killed for a reason.'

'We're killing this man for a reason too. So how are you going to do it? He's highly trained.'

Bethany gave him a rueful smile and shook her head. She dabbed at her eyes with the same forefinger she'd been tracing on the window and walked over to the bed. 'Once a man has his clothes off,' she said, 'you can do anything. You think you're so damn powerful in the bedroom. You're not. You're putty in the hands of a woman who knows what she's doing.'

'We're talking about a five-star American general here. Don't underestimate him.'

'I'm not underestimating anybody. But trust me, once a guy thinks it's on, he's a child again, I don't care who he is. If I can get him to take me to his room, it's a done deal. I don't need much. A pen. A razor blade. Whatever comes to hand.'

'His room might be guarded. You'll need to keep him quiet while you do it.'

'Trust me. He won't make a peep.' She pointed at the bed. 'I'm going to get some sleep. If I'm going to be all the General's dreams come true, I don't want bags under my eyes. You can stay or go. It's up to you.'

Danny left her in the bedroom, taking his press accreditation and passport. He returned to the front door. Sat opposite it with his back against the wall and his handgun on the floor beside him. He opened up the passport and committed the counterfeit Andy Waldren's place and date of birth to memory. He calculated that Waldren would be thirty-four. He put the documentation to one side. He barely wanted to admit it to himself, but Bethany's tears had affected him. He found himself wanting to comfort her. Maybe more. He did his best to put that thought from his mind as he closed his eyes and prepared to wait out the day.

Alice's lack of sleep was catching up on her. The basement was warm from all the computer equipment, which gave off a hypnotic whirr. Her eyelids were heavy, and she had to keep shaking herself awake.

The young woman who had agreed to help had introduced herself as Karen. She sat by Alice's side at a workstation. Three curved monitors, a keyboard, a trackpad and a fingerprint scanner. The screens displayed a flickering succession of images. They changed so quickly that Alice couldn't identify any of them individually. Rather, she had a sense of a jumble of generic types of pictures: individuals standing at a zebra crossing, or queueing in a coffee shop, or stepping out of a bus. A bewildering blur of young and old, male and female, black and white. After scanning in Alice's picture of Poliakov, Karen had sat and stared at these screens for at least two hours, as if her brain was processing the tens of thousands of CCTV images that the systems were checking. Alice could see the flickering pictures reflecting in her glasses, which somehow made the whole experience more disorientating. Every twenty minutes or so, the pictures would stop, and Karen's fingers would fly over the keyboard. The first time this happened, she'd explained that she was changing to a new CCTV zone, but now they sat in silence as she went about her work and Alice grew sleepier and sleepier.

Her chin was on her chest when Karen's voice jolted her awake. 'I'm sorry. It doesn't look like we have any matches. We can set an alert, if you like? If your guy turns up, we'll let you know.'

Alice found it hard to conceal her disappointment. 'Are you sure you've tried everything?' she said. 'It's really important I find this guy soon.' She knew instantly that Karen was holding something back. It was the tightness around the eyes. The hesitation. 'Please, Karen,' she said. 'I *know* he's been in London. If there's *anything* you can do?'

'There are some other CCTV databases,' Karen said. 'We're not really supposed to access them without prior authorisation. The lawyers get antsy.'

Alice was wide awake now. 'Please,' she repeated. 'I *promise* I'll get you any authorisation you need. But the sooner I get a lead . . .'

Karen bit her lower lip, then nodded. She turned back to her screen and started typing again. The blur of images reappeared. The two women stared expectantly at the screen. Five minutes passed. Ten minutes.

And then the blur stopped. A single image filled the screen. Alice felt her stomach lurch.

It was him. Poliakov. Even though the CCTV image was monochrome and blurred, there was no doubt. It looked like he had just entered a building through a revolving door. He wore a black beanie hat and a heavy coat, and there was something decidedly shifty in the way he was half looking over his shoulder, half looking up, as if searching for the camera that was filming him, but failing to see it. He had several days' stubble and dark rings under his eyes. It was, in Alice's experience, the image of an anxious man in hiding.

'Where was this taken?' Alice said.

Karen brought up a table of metadata. It meant nothing to Alice, but her colleague seemed to decipher it with ease. She launched some mapping software on one of her screens and keyed in some coordinates. The map zoomed into a location in central London. 'Battersea,' Karen said. And then, after a few more taps of the keyboard: 'One of the new residential blocks at the old power station.'

'Which one?'

'The Pump House. The footage was taken by a camera in the reception area.'

'When?'

'Yesterday. 22.13 hours.'

Alice felt a surge of heat through her veins. Even as she'd been researching him last night, Poliakov had been been active in London. Doing what? Was he planning something? Every instinct she had told her that if so, it needed to be stopped. Quickly.

'The Mansion House,' she repeated, her voice much calmer than her insides. 'Do me a favour, Karen. Keep the search running.

If he crops up anywhere else, let me know?' There must have been something about the way she looked or spoke, because Karen's demeanour changed. She seemed more alert as Alice stood up before hurrying out of the basement and up to her office on the fourth floor.

Back at her computer, it was a moment's work to access all the information on the MI6 servers pertaining to the Battersea Mansion House. There was a full set of architect's plans, a record of police callouts to the building and, of course, a complete list of apartment owners and residents pulled from the Land Registry and council tax records. It was a big tower and a long list, but Alice didn't have to scan very far down it until a particular name jumped out at her. The penthouse apartment had been bought only six months previously for a sum of £17 million by a certain Boris Rostropovic. Alice recognised the name but couldn't quite place it. She keyed his name into the database. A photograph of an elderly Russian man appeared. His face was deeply lined, his hawkish eyes hooded. His security services biography, printed below the photograph, was a melting pot of Soviet KGB collusion, post-Soviet asset stripping and personal acquaintance with high-ranking members of Russian administrations past and present. He was your classic oligarch, the type that was buying up high-end property in London by the sackful. And according to the immigration authority records, he had entered the UK on a private Learjet into London City Airport the previous week. So far as Alice could tell, he was still in the country.

Alice sat back for a moment on her office chair, staring at the screen, re-reading the biog and nodding thoughtfully. She wondered what kind of influence he had, that would require the need to put his building on a special CCTV database. More importantly, was it chance that an FSB agent high on MI6's wanted list had, less than twelve hours previously, been visiting with an individual whose past and present was as murky as Boris Rostropovic's? Hardly likely. She picked up Poliakov's file, flicked through it one more time and gazed at the image of Rostropovic that stared out from her computer. Then she picked up her office phone and dialled a number.

Her boss, Maxwell Stark, head of the Russian desk, was clearly still in bed. He was a mild, polite man who nevertheless couldn't quite hide his annoyance at being woken. It fell from his voice as soon as Alice said Poliakov's name. She gave him a précis of her investigations and he listened attentively. When she'd finished there was a moment of silence. 'Good work, Alice,' Stark said. '*Excellent* work.' The sound of his voice almost made her smell peppermint.

'What's our next move, sir?'

Another silence.

'There's a high probability that we'll find either Poliakov or Rostropovic or both in the penthouse apartment of the Mansion House,' said Stark.

'I agree, sir.'

'Then we need to make a hard arrest. It's politically sensitive and Poliakov is a trained FSB agent, so we can't hand this over to the Met.'

'No sir.'

'I'm going to mobilise Hereford. We need an SAS team. Would you be so good as to stay where you are? We're going to force entry into the penthouse today. I'm on my way in.'

The line went dead.

ELEVEN

Four members of the SAS anti-terrorist team were already on the ground in London. Their base: a run-down flat in Victoria, the look and smell of which hadn't been improved by the presence of four military guys over the period of the last month. Their names were Bobby Hunter, Mike Cracknell, Dan Finch and Craig Knowles. Hunter was the smallest guy in the Regiment, but what he lacked in height he more than made up for in toughness. He was a broad-shouldered, stocky guy with a square chin and a taste for a fight. When the call came in from Hereford at 08.30 hrs, of the four men in the flat, he was the only one awake. That was the standard operating procedure: one guy on stag at any given time, ready to take instructions and mobilise the unit if necessary.

Hunter was making his fourth coffee of the morning when his phone rang and the terse voice of Ray Hammond, the ops officer back at Hereford, delivered their instructions. 'The Mansion House, Battersea Power Station. A hard arrest of two Russian suspects.'

'We could do with more guys, boss,' Hunter said.

'There's another team mobilising from Hereford right now. They're flying in and they'll put down in the gardens of the Honourable Artillery Company at approximately 10.00 hours.'

'Who's on the team?'

'Cunningham, Moore, Parsons, Hobbs. While they're inbound, get your arses down to Battersea and put in surveillance on the apartment block. I've uploaded pictures of the two Russkies to the secure server. If you see either of them leaving the Mansion House, follow and apprehend. If not, you'll force entry into the penthouse at 17.00 hours. Assuming we get the go-ahead from Whitehall.'

Hunter gulped down the rest of his coffee and unceremoniously woke the others. They were sleeping on mattresses in the living room, holsters and personal weapons on the carpet next to them. There was a ripe, male smell in the air. They grumbled at Hunter's booming voice for only a fraction of second before they realised that he was hauling them out of bed for a good reason. And as soon as he told them the details, they rapidly started to get ready. Each guy put his personal weapon in his waist holster. They fitted their radio packs and concealed earpieces. Hunter sat squat at his laptop and downloaded the images of Boris Rostropovic and Dmitri Poliakov and distributed them to the unit's encrypted mobiles. Within ten minutes of waking, the guys were ready to go.

They had two vehicles: a black Audi and a midnight-blue Kia. Ordinary cars to look at, but souped up and with toughened glass. Hunter and Cracknell took one, Finch and Knowles the other. The London traffic was slow. It took twenty minutes to get to Battersea Bridge and across the river. They parked up in the shadow of the old Battersea Power Station and put their disabled-driver badges on the dashboards of their vehicles. Then they performed a recce of the Mansion House.

It was a shiny new building in an area still largely under construction. Cranes and scaffolding loomed tall against the grey morning sky, but at ground level many things were finished. Fresh paving and newly planted trees surrounded the office workers walking briskly past, phones to their ears or in front of their noses. None of them paid any attention to four burly men circling the apartment block, identifying exits and planning their observation points. Aside from the main entrance at the front of the apartment building, there was a goods entrance round the back and three further side entrances at irregular points around the building. It was possible for one person to keep eyes on the two side entrances of the western edge of the block. Cracknell positioned himself on a bench in the shade of a plane tree. A service road led to the goods entrance at the back, where a bus stop offered an adequate OP, which Knowles occupied. Twenty metres from the entrance on the eastern side was a busy cab rank, where at any one time there were five or ten people milling around. Finch expertly lost himself in that ever-changing crowd, while Hunter took the front of the apartment building. Here, a coffee shop conveniently faced the entrance. Hunter installed himself at an outside table, ordered a large Americano, and watched.

Hunter had set up OPs in some desperate shitholes in his time. His diminutive stature meant he found it easier than most to conceal himself in muddy ditches in Afghanistan fertilised by the locals' raw sewage; in wadis in the desert, covered by hessian sacks, where you sweated faster than you could get water into your system; snow holes in sub-zero temperatures, so cold you couldn't feel your extremities. As surveillance gigs went, this was a peach. A seat. A hot drink. But in a weird way, that made it more difficult. Comfort, he well knew, could make you complacent. An SAS man was trained to thrive in extreme situations. When the elements and your surroundings were against you, it sharpened the mind. Made you more alert. When things were easy, you had to up your concentration. Force yourself to see past the ordinary. Nobody passing the coffee shop would have looked twice at Hunter as he sat facing the Mansion House, sipping his drink. Nobody would have imagined that he was making accurate note of his surroundings with an almost robotic efficiency. He clocked the face of every person exiting the building. The blonde woman in an elegant business suit carrying a burgundy briefcase. The man in his fifties with a deep tan and a v-neck golfing sweater. The teenage girl – an au pair, maybe? – with two kids in tow. The podgy guy in an expensive suit, smaller even than Hunter himself, accompanied by two blondes who almost certainly charged for their services. When his earpiece crackled and Knowles made a lewd comment about a woman he'd seen exiting from the back of the apartment building – 'I wouldn't mind seeing her goods entrance ...' – Hunter smiled inwardly, but showed no sign that he was in contact with anybody else. The first rule of surveillance: expect counter-surveillance. Hunter continued to sip his coffee and watch.

An hour passed and there was no sign of Poliakov or Rostropovic. The SAS men swapped positions, because to stay too long in one location would be a red flag for any counter-surveillance operatives. From his new position on the bench on the western side of the building, he maintained his high level of situational awareness. But something told him that their targets weren't going to appear. He glanced skywards. Up close, perspective made the building dizzyingly tall. He wondered what was going on in the penthouse apartment. Who were these two Russian men Hereford was so interested in?

He snapped his attention back down to the exits. His curiosity would be satisfied soon enough. In the meantime, he needed to keep his focus.

He watched and waited.

As Hunter and his team staked out the ground floor of the Mansion House, a Dauphin 2 helicopter in civilian colours was already airborne from Hereford. Excluding the flight crew, four men were onboard: Dennis Cunningham, Johnny Moore, Rick Parsons, Ken Hobbs. They wore civvies and, as the chopper flew over the outskirts of the capital, were studying architectural plans of the Mansion House, as well as the same images of Dimitri Poliakov and Boris Rostropovic that the ops officer had sent the London team. 'Service lift?' Cunningham shouted at the others over the noise of the chopper, in his broad Scottish accent. His three unit mates nodded their agreement.

The chopper set down in the grounds of the Honourable Artillery Company in East London. A transit van was waiting for them here. It was marked with the Amazon logo, but there were no packages inside. Instead, there were three CO19 armed police officers and enough space for the SAS team and the two flight cases of gear that they carried off the chopper. The police officers – a woman and two men – had an anxious air about them. Cunningham recognised the woman from a previous job, but he couldn't remember her name. She nodded at him in recognition. 'Who's dying tonight?' she asked with a raised eyebrow.

'Depends who's been a wee scunner,' Cunningham said.

'Can't you talk in fucking English?' Parsons said, and Cunningham grinned at him.

'What's the plan?' asked one of the policemen as the doors of the van slammed shut and it started to move.

'We'll go over it once we're on site,' Cunningham told him. They drove on in silence.

Danny woke suddenly. He was still crouched on the ground, opposite the door to the safe house. His neck muscles ached, and he was sweating. The distant sound of a call to prayer had woken him and he spent a moment listening to the weirdly tinny chant. Danny had spent so much time operating in the Middle East that it was a familiar sound. But not comforting. It took him back to Damascus, and Oman, to Afghanistan and to Yemen. It forced him to recall moments of his life he would prefer to keep locked away. Amman was a thriving, modern city. Friendly, welcoming to tourists, relatively safe. He grimaced. Safe? Nowhere in this part of the world was truly safe for a Regiment man. Like Northern Ireland in the eighties, these countries were full of violent men who would give their lives for the opportunity to take out a member of the British SAS. He was certain that here, holed up in this grim safe house, he was a literal stone's throw from an IS or Al-Qaeda sympathiser. He couldn't relax for a minute.

The call to prayer fell silent. Danny was left with only the sound of his own breathing. And a new thought. His enemies were not crazed Jihadists or Middle Eastern terrorist sympathisers. They were Western, and Russian. It would be easy to lose track of that, here in this desert city surrounded by mosques and people whose skin colour soldiers like him had – wrongly – been conditioned to think of as the enemy. An American general was feeding sensitive military information to the Russians. A former MI6 officer and killer of SAS men was currently lying asleep on a stained mattress in the next room. Danny pushed himself up to his feet and quietly opened the door of the bedroom. She was still there. Lying in a fetal position, her blonde hair splayed over the mattress, her breathing slow and steady, her freckles glowing in the light spilling from the window. She didn't look like an assassin. Did anybody? Danny thought about a conversation they had once had. Bethany had told him about her father, himself a former MI6 officer whose slippery moral code had skewed her view of the world. Danny had a moment of self-doubt. Who was he to talk about slippery moral codes when he was about to make an orphan of Bethany's kid? He put that doubt out of his head, where it belonged. *Do your job, Danny. Leave the thinking for those on a higher pay grade.*

Bethany stirred. Her eyes opened and Danny could tell that she didn't know where she was for a second. She smiled drowsily at him. Not a cynical smile, or a flirtatious one. She looked genuinely glad to see him. Danny closed himself off emotionally. He knew he had to keep his distance if he was to complete this op successfully. 'We need to get ready,' he said.

She sat up and ran one hand through her hair. 'I'll need the shower,' she said. And then, looking Danny up and down: 'So will you. Neither of us will get close to the General looking and smelling like this.'

'It's all yours,' Danny said. He stepped back out of the bedroom and returned to his sentry position opposite the front door. He could hear voices in the corridor outside, and the creaking of floorboards somewhere in the building. But they faded soon enough, and now all he could hear was the sound of water against the shower curtain. The stream stopped. Bethany emerged into the hallway, body and hair wrapped in towels. 'All yours,' she said.

In the bathroom, Danny stripped and ran the water as hot as it would go. He stood under the shower and let the stinging hot torrent flood over him. He washed the grime from his scarred body and he let the water wash away his doubts as well. When he stepped out, dripping on to the bathroom floor, his head was back where he needed it to be. On the job.

He wrapped a towel round his waist and walked back into the bedroom. Bethany was dressed and was adding the finishing touches to her make-up. She looked incredible in her snugly fitting skirt and jacket, an inch of heel and her mouth just slightly plump with lipstick. Nobody would ever guess that in the last twenty-four hours she'd been incarcerated in a grim Portakabin, HALOed into the Jordanian desert and been at the sharp end of a firefight with heavily armed Palestinian smugglers.

'You going to stand around half naked,' she said, 'or are you going to get dressed?'

She left the bedroom without waiting for a reply. Danny put on the suit that had been left for him. Normally he was a weddings- and funerals-only suit man. The jacket felt tight across his shoulders and it took him three attempts to get the knot of his tie right. Bethany entered again. She looked him up and down critically. Then she shook her head. 'You're supposed to be a journalist, not James Bond,' she said. 'Loosen your tie, undo that top button.'

Fair enough, Danny thought. Her attention to detail was good and fashion was hardly his strong point. He did as she said. She approached him, took his right hand and undid the button on his cuff. Up close she smelled good. Danny had to make a conscious effort not to allow her scent to put him off the rails.

'You scrub up okay,' she said, as she adjusted his collar.

'I'll take that as a compliment.'

Bethany half smiled and Danny sensed that she was nervous. 'You going to be alright?' he asked.

'Fine,' she said. 'Once we get going.' She went to look out of the window. 'I want to speak to my son,' she said. 'Before we leave. In case anything goes wrong.'

Danny hesitated. It wasn't such a big thing to ask. He had a phone. He could put a call through to Hereford and make it happen. But what would a conversation with the boy do for Bethany's state of mind? Would it focus her or upset her? Right now, she seemed to Danny to be in the zone. He didn't want anything to mess with that. 'They won't do it,' he said. 'You know Sturrock.'

She turned and looked at him. There was a tightness around her eyes and Danny thought: *does she know? Has she worked out that there's no way MI6 would let her live, after what she was about to do for them?*

The tightness eased. Bethany nodded. 'Yeah,' she said. 'I know Sturrock.' Her voice was full of bitterness. 'Alright then. If we're going to do this, let's do it.' She gathered up her dirty clothes and stuffed them into one of the suitcases. Danny did the same.

Hamoud was spared his nightmares because sleep had been impossible. He was too excited, as excited as his children had been the night before, although he would never have admitted it. When they had finally gone to sleep, he and Rabia had fallen into bed. She slept instantly, exhausted from a hard day of cleaning other people's houses. Hamoud lay awake, staring at the ceiling and enjoying the anticipation of their unexpected family holiday.

Now it was 6 a.m. and, as usual, he was up before everybody else. He had made himself a cup of weak tea and was sitting cross legged on the floor, as he had learned to do in his empty cell at Guantanamo. The Walt Disney World brochure was open in front of him. In his mind, he once again mapped the faces of his children onto the faces of the happy kids in the brochure. It warmed him even more than the tea, and for the first time in years, he felt a sense of calmness and optimism.

His tranquillity was broken by footsteps in the corridor outside. A knock on the door. Hamoud scrambled over to it, spilling his tea in the process. He opened the door. There, on the floor, was a FedEx package. He picked it up and looked at both sides. He'd never before received anything by FedEx and was surprised that nobody had asked him to sign for it. Perhaps they'd made a mistake. He wanted to call back the delivery person, but when he looked along the corridor there was nobody there.

Paranoia was a strange, powerful affliction. One moment you could be entirely free of it. The next, it hit you with tidal force, crashing over you, taking your breath away. It was happening now. Hamoud had to grip the door frame to counteract his dizziness. Where *was* the delivery person? *Why* couldn't he see him?

He drew some deep breaths. Calmed himself. Recognise this for what it is, he said. You are paranoid. You are worrying about problems that don't exist. Perhaps the delivery person hadn't waited for a signature because it was so early. He felt a little better, but the paranoia had not completely subsided.

Back inside the apartment, he carefully opened the package. It was all there. Plane reservations for that afternoon, in their names, from Cincinnati to Orlando. Their hotel booking and passes for the parks. Everything in order. So why did he still feel uneasy? He moved over to the window that overlooked the front of their apartment block. With one bony finger, he parted the curtains and peered out on to the road below. He saw his reflection faintly in the window. The grey-flecked beard. The prominent scar on his eye. He looked through it. He was searching for a FedEx van, but there was none. The road wasn't busy this early in the morning, but on the opposite side he saw a black SUV parked up on the kerb. A man was hurrying across the road, away from the apartment block, towards it. When he reached the sidewalk, he stopped for a moment and looked back over his shoulder. He gazed upwards and Hamoud had the uncomfortable sensation that the man was staring directly at him. He guiltily let the curtain fall closed as an electric shock of anxiety buzzed through him. It was the same feeling that he used to get in the prison camp whenever he drew the attention of someone in authority. Hamoud didn't like to be noticed.

He took several deep breaths to calm himself again. Then he returned to the bedroom, the tickets still in his hand. Rabia was half awake. When Hamoud perched on the edge of the bed, shoulders slumped, she sat up and reached out to stroke his back. 'What is it, my love?' she asked.

He almost didn't say. He knew how the conversation was likely to evolve. She would say to him, 'I think you have PTSD. I think you should see a doctor.' But he didn't want to see a doctor. He wanted to get better by himself. But he also wanted to share his concerns with his wife. He frowned at the tickets in his hand. 'Something's not right,' he said. 'Why would anybody send *us* to Walt Disney World? We're not the sort of family this kind of thing happens to. It feels . . . it feels *wrong*.' He didn't mention the lack of a FedEx van or the man by the SUV.

'Hamoud,' said Rabia, her voice gentle and cajoling, 'Hamoud, you need to stop assuming that nothing good will ever happen to you. The things in your past were terrible, but they are over now. God owes us a bit of luck. Perhaps this is the beginning of a change for us. Let's just enjoy it while we can.'

He nodded and smiled at her as reassuringly as he could. But while she was in the shower, he found his phone and he dialled the same number he'd called when the offer had first dropped through his door.

'*Hello, Walt Disney World, where all your dreams come true!*'

It was the same cheerful female voice as before. It struck Hamoud as a bit odd that he should have been put through to the same operator, but he told himself that it was hardly an impossibility. He stuttered his name. 'I just wanted to check . . . to check that our all-expenses-paid trip . . . to check that it's a real offer.'

'*Of course, sir. We're looking forward to welcoming you at Walt Disney World.*'

'Um . . . don't you need to check?'

'*Mr Al Asmar?*'

'That's right.'

'*We're looking forward to welcoming you! May I help you with anything else today?*'

'No,' Hamoud said. 'No. Nothing else.'

'*Then you have a good day,*' said the voice. Music played over the line. The Mickey Mouse song, its catchy refrain spelling out his name, sung by a choir of children, over and over again. A relentlessly cheerful tune, but somehow menacing to Hamoud as he looked from the door to the window, and heard his little ones moving around in their bedroom, the sound of his wife's shower. His palms started itching again and he wanted to scratch them.

He ended the phone call. The song died. His children ran into the room, as excited as they had been before going to bed last night. They flung their arms round his neck, squealing with delight, and Hamoud didn't have the heart not to join in with them. Rabia was right, he told himself. He needed to stop assuming that nothing good would ever happen to him. This was the beginning of a change for them. He would enjoy his good luck for as long as it lasted.

He would not be paranoid.

TWELVE

11.37 hrs. Hunter had rotated to the rear service entrance of the Mansion House. He was perched on the plastic bench of the bus stop that faced the apartment block. Rush hour was over and there were only three other people at the bus stop, all ignoring each other and staring at their phones. Hunter was watching the vehicles entering and leaving the service entrance. In particular, he was watching a Transit van with the Amazon logo on both sides as it drove down into the basement parking lot. He stepped away from the bus stop so he wouldn't be heard by the other pedestrians, put his sleeve to his mouth and spoke over the team's radio. 'Cunningham and the others are here,' he said. 'Keep your positions. I'm moving in.'

Hunter headed across the street. A very narrow pavement followed the road leading into the underground car park. He walked along it, carefully scanning up ahead. When a green Mercedes overtook him on its way in, he instinctively made use of the side mirrors to check nobody was following him. It was clear.

The tyres of the Mercedes squeaked on the smooth floor as it drove to the far side and parked. Hunter loitered in the cover of a white Range Rover while he listened for the slamming of the Mercedes door to echo around the car park, and footsteps to fade. Only then did he approach the Transit van. It had parked next to a fire door with a no-entry sign. The driver – Hunter didn't recognise him – looked straight ahead without even acknowledging Hunter's presence. When Hunter reached the van the door opened, as if automatically. Dennis Cunningham appeared. There was no superfluous greeting. 'Building manager's name is Ravinder Singh,' Cunningham said. 'Indian laddie. Knows we're coming. He should be waiting for us in reception.'

Hunter nodded his acknowledgement and closed the van door. He quickly crossed the car park, past the green Mercedes, towards a lift on the far side. Inside the lift, he hit the ground-floor button. As the lift ascended, he found himself examining the removable panel in the roof. Force of habit. He could just about reach it if he needed to.

The doors pinged open and Hunter stepped into the reception area. A large, airy, open space, with comfortable sofas and enormous indoor plants. Mirrors everywhere. Piped music. On the opposite side, Hunter saw the revolving doors he'd been watching earlier. There were ten or twelve people here – residents, Hunter reckoned, leaving and arriving – and he immediately identified the building manager. Singh wore a black suit and tie and stood by the reception desk, nervously clutching his hands and blinking frequently. He was looking round, as though searching for someone. When his gaze fell on Hunter, Hunter nodded. The manager swallowed hard, looked around again rather conspicuously, then approached. 'Are you the gentleman I'm waiting for?' he said. He was much taller than Hunter and spoke very precise English with an Indian accent.

'We need a private space where we won't be disturbed,' Hunter said.

The manager was still clutching his hands. 'Follow me please,' he said. He called the lift and took them back down to the basement. He was blinking so often that Hunter assumed he must have something in his eye, but then decided it was a nervous tic. At first, he thought the manager was leading him to the Transit van, but it became apparent that he was heading for the no-entry fire door to its side. He lifted the security bar, opened the door and switched on some flickering overhead strip lights in the room beyond. The space was large but with a low ceiling. Concrete floor, breeze block walls and exposed piping in the roof wrapped in silver lagging. It was warm, and against one wall was some kind of boiler or heat-exchange pump, Hunter didn't know which, rattling noisily. Boxes of cleaning products were piled up, along with a stash of orange traffic cones, barrels of water for dispensers and all manner of random stores required for keeping the Mansion

House running. Most importantly, it was empty of personnel and it was private.

'Stay there,' Hunter told the manager. He returned to the Transit van, checked there was nobody in the car park to view them, and knocked on the back door. The door opened and, at a word from Cunningham, the others filed out, the Regiment guys carrying their flight cases. The driver stayed where he was. The Regiment team and the three police officers joined the manager in the boiler room. Hunter closed the door while Cunningham turned to the manager.

'You've been briefed by our people?'

'In a manner of speaking, sir,' the manager said. He blinked several times and didn't appear to know whether to look at Cunningham's face or the hardware in his ops vest. 'I have to say this is most irregular. The comfort and convenience of our tenants is my first—'

'You need to do exactly what we tell you. You got that?'

The manager swallowed hard again and didn't answer. Cunningham stepped up to him and repeated his question at half the volume. 'You got that?'

The manager nodded nervously.

'What's the personnel set-up on the penthouse?'

The manager spoke hesitantly. 'Mr Rostropovic is in town,' he said. 'He is very infrequently here, but when he is, he keeps himself to himself. He hardly leaves the apartment.'

'Who does he have with him?'

'Some guests, I believe. A family. He is of course not obliged to inform anybody whom he invites into his apartment. We are simply here to ensure our tenants—'

'What about security?'

'Mr Rostropovic takes his security arrangements extremely seriously,' said the manager. 'There are always two gentlemen guarding the corridor outside the penthouse apartment at any one time.'

'Armed?'

The manager glanced uncomfortably at the police officers.

Cunningham took a step closer to him. 'Listen here, laddie, the more we know about what's waiting for us up there, the less chance you have of ending up like the inside of a haggis. Are they armed?'

The manager nodded. 'Mr Rostropovic pays a small surcharge . . .' he mumbled.

Cunningham gave him a bleak smile. 'He slips you a back-hander not tae mention the guns to the police?' The manager looked away. 'We've looked at the plans of the building. The pent-house has its own dedicated elevator, correct?'

'Correct, sir.' The manager seemed pleased that the conversation had taken a different turn. 'Only Mr Rostropovic and those with whom he entrusts a key fob may use it.'

'But the service elevator also goes tae the penthouse?'

'Yes, sir. But that is not for public use.'

'We're not the public,' Cunningham said. 'You have a master key to get intae the penthouse itself?'

The manager looked reluctant to reply. 'A key fob,' he said. 'It accesses all the rooms in the building.'

'You have it on you?'

The manager nodded.

'Hand it over.'

The manager looked from Cunningham to the others and back again. Realising he had no option, he took a fob from his top pocket and handed it over. 'Sir,' he said as Cunningham took the card, 'I must inform you that both elevators sound a brief alarm when they reach the penthouse, to alert security that some-body is arriving. You understand?'

'Aye,' said Cunningham. 'I understand.' He turned to Hunter. 'Your guys are still watching the exits?'

'Yep,' Hunter confirmed.

'Keep them there. Our targets could leave at any time.'

'Wish they fucking would,' Hunter said. 'Save us a job.'

'I don't think that's likely.' Cunningham pointed at one of the flight cases. 'Your missus told me you like a bit of role play. There's a couple of BT engineer uniforms in there. Get one of them on.' He looked over at Parsons. 'You too,' he said.

Hunter didn't much like the way Cunningham was curtly taking charge, but he knew better than to make a meal of it right now. He opened the flight case. It didn't only contain BT uniforms.

There was a canvas bag containing engineering equipment, a thick wodge of sturdy cable ties, three assault rifles nestled at the bottom of the case and several cardboard packs of ammo. The manager's eyes widened when he saw the weaponry. Cunningham, Hobbs and Moore each took a weapon. Hunter took out the uniforms and handed the larger of the two to Parsons. Unembarrassed about changing in front of the others, they switched clothes. The uniforms were creased and had a faint hint of body odour. That was by design: fresh, neatly pressed uniforms were more likely to stand out.

'Very fetching,' Cunningham said. 'Okay everyone, listen up. This is what we're going tae do. You three –' he pointed at the police officers – 'stay down here. Once we've secured our targets, we'll call you in tae process any family members. You –' he pointed at the manager – 'escort Hunter and Parsons tae the penthouse in the service lift. When the guards meet you there, tell them the guys are from BT and they need tae investigate a fault on the line in the penthouse.'

'Sir, they will not believe that. They know I would have made such an appointment well in advance.'

'Then you'd better be convincing when you're up there, laddie. In my experience, oligarch bodyguards are a short-tempered bunch. You don't want them using those secret weapons on you.'

'But I would normally ring in advance, at the very least.'

'We can't risk it. They might tell us not to come, then they'll be suspicious when we turn up anyway.'

'Where ... where will you be?'

'Close behind. Everything goes according to plan, you won't notice us until it's too late. As soon as things go noisy, I want you to get face down on the ground and put your hands over your head. You think you can do that?'

'Please, sir, what do you mean by "go noisy"?'

'You'll work it out, laddie,' Cunningham said. He looked over at Hunter. 'You know what tae do?'

Hunter nodded.

'Alright then.' He pulled out his phone. 'I'm going tae call Hereford. As soon as we get the green light, we move in. While we wait, we'll examine the plans of the building so we know what's waiting for us up there.'

He dialled.

It was twelve thirty. Alice was tired and for the first time since working at MI6, she found herself wishing she was more soberly dressed. She was still wearing the casual gear she'd thrown on the night before. But now she was sitting at a boardroom table on the fifth floor not only with her boss, Maxwell Stark, but also with Alan Sturrock, head of the service. Stark was opening a fresh packet of extra strong mints. The boardroom was heavy with the smell of peppermint, but somehow Alice didn't mind that. Sturrock repelled her: the oily hair, the way he regularly rubbed moisturising lotion into his hands with a repulsive, slimy sound. But these were serious men, seriously dressed on serious business. It was a big deal that she had a seat at the table.

There were two tablets in front of them. One had an open line to SAS headquarters in Hereford, the other to Number 10. Alice had been with Stark when he explained to Sturrock her deduction that Poliakov was being sheltered by Rostropovic, and she sincerely thought the chief's eyes might fall out of his head. Apparently Rostropovic was a no-go area, at least without the say-so of the PM. Alice could only imagine what kind of messy political deal she had stumbled across, but she was certain that Sturrock was not the type to take action that might be detrimental to his career.

A voice came over the Hereford line. '*We have confirmation from our team on the ground that they're ready to make the arrest.*'

'Not until I give the instruction,' said Sturrock. He tapped a button on the tablet connected to Number 10. 'We're ready. Do we have approval?'

A pause.

'*Approval withheld. Repeat, approval withheld.*'

Sturrock's lips thinned. He looked at Alice as if the lack of approval was her fault. Then he spoke again. 'Hereford, this is Sturrock. You have no green light. Repeat, you have no green light.' Sturrock turned to Alice. 'Let's hope your intelligence is good, young lady,' he said. 'This could be an embarrassment for us all if you've made a mistake.'

'Does this mean the operation is over?' she asked.

Sturrock didn't answer her directly. Instead, he continued his communication with Hereford. 'Keep your men on the ground, is that understood?'

'*Understood.*'

Alice glanced at Stark. Her boss gave her a reassuring smile, as if to say: 'Wait and see how this plays out.' Then he leaned across the table and offered her a peppermint.

Alice declined.

Five o'clock, Amman. Danny and Bethany's suitcases were in the boot. Their press passes were in their shoulder bags. Danny's handgun was stowed in the glove compartment. He had the wheel and was once again negotiating the city traffic. The GPS unit was set to take them to the Hotel Grand, but the route it chose was not direct. Amman is a city built on hills. Although there were broad, tree-lined thoroughfares heading through central parts of the city, these main arterial routes were clogged with traffic. And so they found themselves winding carefully through narrow side streets and over cobbled, semi-pedestrianised areas bustling with people. Almost all the women they saw wore headscarves. A very few wore a more concealing niqab. The men seemed more westernised in jeans and T-shirts, though some, mainly the older ones, wore traditional dishdash. Danny had his window down to get some airflow going in the intense afternoon heat. It let in the sounds and smells of the city. Exhaust fumes. Street-food stalls deep-frying falafal. Market traders bellowing outside covered bazaars. Loud Arabic pop blaring from cars and first-floor windows. The buildings were a colourful mixture of browns and mustard yellows. Danny had the impression of a busy but friendly place.

'Amman was originally built on seven hills,' Bethany said as the vehicle laboured up a particularly steep incline, reminding Danny that she was a Middle East specialist. 'Nineteen hills now, they say, with the urban sprawl. Lots of refugees. Palestinians originally, after the Arab–Israeli war. More recently, Syrians.'

'I didn't realise I'd booked a tour guide,' Danny said. He was less interested in the geography of the city than in getting to their destination without incident. As they passed some kind of ancient monument – sand-coloured pillars and a tiered, half-circle arena – he paid it barely any attention. They drove on in silence, through various sprawling districts of the city, up and down hills, until finally the GPS unit returned them to one of the main arterial routes where the traffic had eased and Danny was able to up his speed. Five minutes later, the Hotel Grand appeared.

It was a long building, four storeys high with an elegant roof turreted and tiled. It took up the entire side of a pleasant square, in the middle of which was a flower garden. A couple of palm trees grew by the entrance, their leaves motionless in the still air. Between them, three flags drooped pathetically on flagpoles. The road around the square was fairly busy with traffic, but it was the military vehicles parked right in front of the hotel that drew Danny's attention. There were three khaki-coloured, open-topped trucks parked in a row directly in front of the main entrance, noses pointing outwards. There were at least fifteen soldiers surrounding the vehicles, all armed with assault rifles. 'Looks like our general's got a quite a retinue,' he said.

Bethany didn't reply. She was eyeing the soldiers steadily.

Danny allowed himself to drive a single circuit of the square. He knew there was a good chance that someone was observing the traffic to identify suspicious patterns of behaviour. Any more than twice round, they were likely to be observed and possibly trailed. As they drove past the front of the hotel, he noted the two armed guys at the main door checking the ID of three Middle Eastern men entering the hotel. He glanced upwards and saw an open window on the top floor where another armed man was looking down on to the square. There was no getting away from it: the Yanks in this hotel were on high alert.

'You think someone's tipped them off?' Bethany said, her voice edgy, as Danny continued his circuit of the square.

'No,' Danny said. 'The General's meant to be overseeing a peace treaty between the Turks and the Kurds. It's an obvious target for terrorist activity. If I was them, I'd be jumpy too.'

'They're right to be,' Bethany said quietly.

Danny couldn't argue with that.

He drove down one side of the hotel and then round the back. There were more soldiers here, guarding either end of the street. They passed three exits, one with a cluster of large plastic refuse bins outside. Two soldiers guarded each of the three exits. There was no way of getting in or out of this place without your ID being checked.

'I don't like it,' Bethany said.

'What did you expect?' Danny said. 'A walk in the park?'

She didn't answer.

They were able to park the car about 800 metres from the hotel along a narrow road lined with cafes and small shops. The route back to the hotel would take them to a crossroads, where they would turn right on to a main road that led to the hotel. They parked outside a small shop selling fabrics. Danny stowed his handgun under his seat. He felt naked not wearing it, but there was zero chance of getting into the hotel if he was carrying. If he needed a weapon when he was inside – and he hoped he wouldn't – he'd have to improvise. They exited the vehicle. Danny locked it and pocketed the key. He looked up and down the road. There were plenty of pedestrians, but they all seemed to be going about their business. If any of them were paying any special attention to the two smartly dressed westerners who had just stepped out of the dented old Passat, Danny didn't notice them. And he was trained to do just that.

'This is where we split up,' Danny said. They couldn't enter the hotel together. Once they were inside, nobody could know they were associated, if Bethany was to lay her honeytrap successfully. 'You get in first. I'll be watching.'

'It's almost like you don't trust me.'

'When it's done, we meet back here. Any problems, get a taxi back to the safe house.'

'I'm about to walk unarmed into a hotel heavily guarded by American troops and kill their top guy. What makes you think something's going to go wrong?'

'You have your phone. Contact me if there's a problem, but do it discreetly.'

She gave him what was obviously meant to be a 'don't patronise me' look, but she couldn't hide her anxiety as she glanced over

Danny's shoulder in the direction of the hotel. 'How do I look?' she said.

'Right for the job,' Danny told her, and he meant it. Bethany would turn heads. With any luck, she'd turn the General's.

She set off along the pavement. There was no need for her to weave in and out of the other pedestrians. There was something about her seemingly confident stride that made others get out of her way. He waited until they were separated by a distance of fifty metres before following her. His skin was damp with sweat as he walked past the entrance to a souk, fragrant with incense, and ignored the shouts of a street-food vendor offering him something wrapped in flatbread. Bethany didn't look back. At the end of the street was the crossroads where she turned right, and Danny lost sight of her for a few seconds. As he himself turned right, he saw the back of her head as she continued down the road towards the hotel. They passed one of its side entrances on the opposite side of the road. Then they entered the recently recce'd square at the front of the hotel.

Bethany approached the main hotel entrance. Danny stopped outside a cafe with a green awning where young Jordanians sat in the shade drinking tiny cups of coffee. He noticed, with a certain amount of satisfaction, that a few of the American guys on patrol outside the hotel watched her appreciatively as she passed. One guy, stationed between the two palm trees, risked a bollocking by moving from his post and approaching her. He noted the way she flounced her hair as she walked away from him, and how the soldier made a rueful, arms-in-the-air gesture to one of his mates, as if to say: 'Hey, I tried!'

Bethany trotted up the wide steps leading to the main entrance. Danny could see that the guys on guard here were a more serious prospect. There was nothing about their body language that suggested they had any flirtatious intention. They examined Bethany's ID and press pass for a full thirty seconds. For a moment, Danny thought they had a problem, because the soldier passed the documentation to his mate, who studied it just as intently. After another thirty seconds, however, he handed it back to Bethany. The two soldiers stepped aside and she disappeared into the hotel.

Danny took a seat at the cafe and ordered a coffee. He would give it ten minutes. He watched as an official-looking black car pulled up in front of the hotel and three Jordanian men in suits emerged. They received the same treatment from the American soldiers at the door, and appeared impatient with the security arrangements. It didn't do them much good. The soldiers prolonged the ID check before allowing them in.

There was more movement. A group of guys in Arabic dress exited the hotel. A minute later, the soldiers directed a courier to another entrance round the back. Danny checked his watch. 17.45 hrs. He decided it was time to enter. He put some money on the table and left the cafe.

He attracted considerably less attention than Bethany as he approached the hotel. To the soldier standing between the palm trees, he was invisible. Walking up the steps to the entrance, he fixed one of the two guards with an easy smile. 'State your purpose,' the guard said. Close up, Danny could see that he was carrying an MP5 sub-machine gun, and he noticed the handgun holster bulge under his camouflage jacket. He had a shaved head, and the kind of leathery complexion that Danny recognised from men operating in hot countries for extended periods. He decided this guy was probably part of the General's SF retinue.

'Press,' Danny told him.

There was an uncomfortable moment as the guy looked Danny up and down. Danny knew what he was probably thinking: you're the biggest journalist I ever saw. He felt self-conscious of his size, as though he was squeezed into a suit too small for him, and was glad that Bethany had loosened his tie. He held the guy's gaze with the same, easy smile. If he showed any sign of uncertainty, he might be denied entrance.

'You have ID?' the Yank asked. He had a sturdy New York accent.

Danny dug into his shoulder bag and took out his fake passport and *Sunday Times* press pass. The guy handed the press pass to his mate, who started keying his name into a handheld device. He opened up the passport himself. He checked the photo against Danny's face then continued to examine the details. 'How old are you, Mr Waldren?' he asked.

Danny was glad he'd done his homework. 'Thirty-four,' he said.

The soldier nodded and handed back the passport. 'Let me see the bag.'

Danny handed it over. The soldier removed the notebook and flicked through its empty pages. He replaced it and returned the bag to Danny just as his mate handed back the press pass, saying: 'He's on the list.'

'British, huh?' said the first guy. 'One of yours already came in here, a few minutes ago. Good-looking broad. Maybe you'll get lucky.'

'Business, not pleasure, mate. Lot of interest in the peace talks in London,' Danny said. He smiled more broadly. 'Hey, when do you get off duty? Maybe we could do a little interview. It would be an interesting piece, no? A day-in-the-life kind of thing.'

'Nice try,' said the soldier, clearly free of all suspicion now. He jabbed one thumb over his shoulder. 'You're in.'

'Well, if you change your mind,' Danny said. But the soldier's attention was already on one of his colleagues walking up the steps, perhaps to take over guard duty. Danny entered the hotel.

The interior was rich-Arab gaudy. The entrance hall was lined with glass presentation cases filled with chunky gold jewellery and expensive trinkets. There was an enormous chandelier in the reception area, decorative columns at regular intervals, gold paint on the elaborate architraves and an attractive young woman playing cocktail jazz on a white grand piano in the very middle of the room. There was no overt sign of any military presence inside, but Danny wasn't fooled by that. He saw the white man standing by the ornate elevator, casually dressed, watching Danny as he entered. He saw the man and woman sitting wordlessly at a comfortable sofa, tea things in front of them, both of them checking out all the other guests in the reception area, of whom there must have been at least thirty.

There were several exhibition boards with information in English and Arabic regarding the preliminary talks that were ongoing in the hotel in advance of the main peace talks. A plan of the hotel and its various conference rooms was pinned to one. The day's schedule was pinned to another – hourly meetings between nine and five, and lists of attendees. General O'Brien's name appeared several times. He'd had a busy day, and Danny hoped that once his official duties were over, he'd be ready for a spot of R and R in the hotel bar, as was his habit according to Hereford's intel. Danny took in the hotel plan at a glance. He confirmed that there were three floors, one elevator and one staircase. The bar was ahead of him, the staircase beyond that. A couple of smartly dressed blonde women with clipboards were standing by the exhibition boards. It appeared that they were there to help delegates with information, but the business day was over now, and they looked more interested in their watches than anything else.

Danny kept moving before the blondes could ask him if he needed any help. He calculated that the best way to avoid suspicion was to make contact with a member of the hotel staff: an open display that he had nothing to hide. He walked straight up to the reception desk where a friendly looking Jordanian woman greeted him with a lovely smile. 'May I help you sir?'

'I hope so,' Danny said. 'I'm looking for the bar.'

He already knew its location from the plan on the exhibition board, but he nodded politely as she directed him to a corridor to the right of the elevator. As he walked in that direction, he saw that the watchers all had their attention elsewhere.

The bar was even plusher than the reception area. A thick burgundy carpet, with low glass tables surrounded by comfortable armchairs. The bar itself was twenty metres long with an impressive display of alcohol bottles and optics on the wall behind it. A rare sight in the Arab world but not, apparently, in Jordan. The three bartenders were not busy. There were no punters at the bar itself, and only a smattering of people sitting at the tables. One of those people was Bethany. She had installed herself at a table in the far corner, next to a bookcase filled with leather-bound books. She had a full glass and a mixer bottle in front of her and she sat with her legs crossed, nonchalantly swiping her phone. She made no attempt to acknowledge Danny's presence, but her own was having the desired effect. The three bartenders were staring at her quite openly. One of them even seemed to be making an appreciative comment to his colleague. Danny felt a pang of antagonism towards the guy for doing that, then cursed himself for feeling it.

Mind on the job.

He took a seat in a position where he could keep an eye on Bethany as well as all his exit routes. There was the way he'd come in, two doors leading to the male and female lavatories, and a further corridor at the far end of the bar, leading away from it. One of the bartenders approached. Danny ordered a bottle of water. It came accompanied by a plate of nibbles, a small wallet of hotel-branded matches and an eye-watering bill. Danny put some notes down to pay and pocketed the matches. It was ingrained behaviour for him to take possession of any object that might come in useful at some point in the future.

He found it hard to imagine somewhere he would feel more out of place. The same couldn't be said for Bethany. She looked as if she belonged here. And she looked stunning. Danny did what he needed to do to quell his discomfort. Back in Hereford, the CO had told Danny that they had intelligence about the General's routine: that he was in the habit of coming to the bar for a cocktail at 18.00 hrs every evening. But what if he broke his routine? What if he didn't turn up? Plan B would mean that Bethany had to go looking for him. That could get interesting.

For now, all they could do was stand by. He sipped his drink, surveyed the exit routes, kept Bethany in his peripheral vision, and waited.

THIRTEEN

The room was silent. Alice felt uncomfortable, sitting here with these two older men. They'd been in and out for the past four hours, one person always remaining, waiting for the call from Number 10. Now all three of them were back in the room together. She checked the time. Twenty past four. Sturrock was moisturising his hands again. Stark seemed to be making a special effort not to watch the procedure, but the slick, greasy sound was impossible to ignore. Alice's boss removed his spectacles and made an attempt to clean them with his tie. When he put them back on, they were no less dirty, but Sturrock had finished moisturising his hands, so the process had served its purpose.

'Peppermint, Alan?' Stark offered. Sturrock shook his head bad-temperedly. He obviously wasn't handling the pressure well.

The gravity of the situation was obvious. For Sturrock and Stark, the two top guys in the building, to be running this operation themselves: that was unusual. Unprecedented, so far as Alice knew. They were clearly nervous, in their own ways. When the speaker on one of the tablets burst into life again, Sturrock visibly started. Alice recognised from earlier the voice on the line to Number 10. *'You have a green light to proceed. Repeat, you have a green light to proceed.'*

Sturrock stood up immediately. 'Tell Hereford it's a go,' he said to Stark. 'And keep me updated.'

He left the room without another word. Stark gave Alice a thin smile. 'Let's see what Messrs Rostropovic and Poliakov have to say for themselves, shall we?' he said, and he popped another mint into his mouth.

★   ★   ★

Cunningham's phone rang while the SAS men were still poring over the plans of the building. He put it to his ear for only a few seconds before killing the line. 'Hereford,' he told the others. 'It's a go.'

The five SAS men went silently to work. Cunningham, Hobbs and Moore pulled black balaclavas over their heads and performed one last routine check of their personal weapons. Hunter and Parsons approached the manager. He was sweating profusely, clutching his hands and blinking a couple of times every second. Hunter had two options: to scare him into compliance or to try to calm him down. He knew Cunningham would default to the former strategy. Hunter didn't think that would be the right call. The more nervous the manager looked, the more suspicious the oligarch's bodyguards would be. These wouldn't be goons. Rostropovic sounded to Hunter like a guy who could afford the best. And that meant ex-SF, probably. Hunter put one hand on the manager's shoulder and gave him a reassuring smile. 'It's going to be fine, buddy,' he said. 'We do this kind of thing every day of the week. So long as you do what we say, it'll be a walk in the park.'

The manager gave him an 'I hope you're right' kind of smile. Over his shoulder, Hunter saw Cunningham raise an eyebrow. He ignored it. 'Take me to the service lift,' Hunter said. He picked up the canvas bag of engineer's tools.

The manager led him back out into the car park. The tyre screech of a departing vehicle faded away. Their footsteps echoed against the concrete walls as they walked across to a far corner of the space. Here, tucked away next to another fire exit, was the service lift. A sign read 'Staff Only'. There was a single button next to the doors and beneath it was a keyhole. The manager produced a sizeable bunch of keys and selected one. He slotted it into the keyhole and turned it. Then he pressed the button to call the lift. Thirty seconds later, the doors opened and the empty car presented itself.

Hunter looked back across the car park. Parsons was standing outside the fire door, watching for his signal. Hunter double-checked there was nobody else around – it looked clear – then gave Parsons the thumbs up. 'Keep the doors open,' he told the manager, and he stepped inside the lift. There was enough space for twenty people inside. Its metal walls were scuffed where trolleys had bashed into them. Hunter looked up. As expected, there was a detachable panel in the ceiling. No latch. They just needed to push it up and they would be able to gain access to the top of the lift.

The others arrived: Cunningham, Hobbs and Moore in their civvies. Parsons in his BT uniform. They entered the lift. Moore gave Cunningham a leg up so that he could reach the ceiling panel. Cunningham lifted the panel up and moved it to one side. Then he hauled himself up through the hole and on to the top of the lift. Hunter helped Moore and Hobbs follow him up there. Within thirty seconds the three balaclavad men were out of sight, the detachable panel back in place. Hunter and Parsons were inside the lift alone. The manager was still standing nervously outside. 'Okay, buddy,' Hunter said. 'Get inside. We can close the doors. Let's take her up to the penthouse.'

The manager swallowed hard and blinked again. He removed the key, stepped into the lift and looked up. 'Won't they be crushed when we reach the top?'

Hunter shook his head. 'There's always headroom,' he said. 'Let's go.'

The manager inhaled deeply and pressed the button marked 'P'.

Danny checked the time. 18.20 hrs. No sign of the General. He should have been here twenty minutes ago. He slowly sipped his water. The bar was filling up – there were thirty or forty people in here now – and Danny was anxious. Would they have to go looking for the guy? He still had line of sight to Bethany, but occasionally some hotel guests would get in the way and he'd lose visual contact. Each time that happened, he experienced a twinge of apprehension. Did he trust Bethany to go through with this, even if they found the General? He didn't know.

Movement by the entrance at the end of the bar. Four men walked in. Three of them were in camouflage gear. The fourth wore civvies, but it was clear from his demeanour that he had authority over the others, who walked slightly behind him and with the faint stiffness of gait that Danny recognised as soldiers in the presence of their superior. Danny subtly examined the man in civvies. He was well built and had a deep perma-tan. Silver hair, twinkling eyes. A good-looking man, and a face Danny recognised not only from his target pack, but also from the CCTV still Sturrock and the others had shown him back in Hereford. In that still, the man had been wearing a straw trilby and flamboyant shirt. Here, he was more soberly dressed. His shirt was a pale pink which, to Danny, suggested his flamboyant nature hadn't quite deserted him. A sport jacket. Chinos. For some reason, Danny found himself noticing the General's shoes: expensive brown brogues, very shiny. The whole ensemble was a direct contrast to the camo gear of the soldiers surrounding him and elsewhere in and around the hotel. It was unmistakably General O'Brien, and he was unmistakably different to any top brass Danny had met before. At a glance, Danny could see that there was something unusually easy-going about him. He seemed relaxed, like a wealthy man on a golfing holiday. He turned to speak to his three men and clasped one of them on the shoulder – an unheard-of gesture in Danny's world between men of such different ranks. The three men laughed at whatever it was he said, then left the room chatting to each other. The General remained at the bar, alone. He took a stool and sat with his back to Danny, who could see him raise a finger to attract the attention of one of the barmen and instinctively made a mental note that he was right-handed.

Danny glanced over at Bethany. She hadn't moved. She didn't even seem to have noticed the General's arrival. Danny hoped she was just playing it cool.

He pulled out his phone and made a show of playing with it. In reality, he was simply swiping icons while surreptitiously keeping eyes on the room. A corner of his mind was analysing everything he'd seen. Something about the General didn't seem right. The civvies, the easy-going nature. Danny had met top military guys like this before, and they were all the same: army through and through, straight as the barrel of an assault rifle and twice as threatening. But then it occurred to him that perhaps this easy-going nature was precisely the character trait that made him so suited to this job of brokering peace between warring factions.

The world expected him to be the point man at talks that could cause or save any number of lives in the region. Sturrock expected him to be secretly planning to sabotage those talks, but this outward show of relaxation and friendliness was a good way of confirming his quiet self-confidence. Maybe he cultivated it to distract anyone and everyone from the truth.

Or maybe he just didn't care about what he was doing. About the things he had done.

Danny remembered the Zero 22 patrol. His mates, dead within moments of the Russian ambush. The twisted hunks of metal smouldering on the wasteland of the bomb site. A bitter taste rose in the back of his throat. None of that would have happened had it not been for the man at the bar in front of him. His mates would still be alive. It was all Danny could do to stop himself rising from his chair and dealing with the bastard himself.

But he remained seated and sipped his water again. Bethany had stood up. She walked across the room, weaving her way around the tables, avoiding all eye contact with Danny. He was reminded once more what a skilful actress she was. Her body language had changed again. Her hips sashayed appealingly. A tendril of blonde hair tumbled across the side of her face. Her lips seemed somehow fuller than earlier. Hotel guests – male and female – watched her as she passed. Bethany approached the bar, but not the General. He still had his back to her and was being presented with a cocktail. As Danny reflected that this was the first time he'd ever seen a military man order anything other than a beer or a shot, Bethany continued walking along the bar. She sat next to another guy. He had dark skin and wore a business suit. *Probably a local*, Danny thought. There was an orange juice on the bar in front of him.

Bethany didn't strike up a conversation. She gestured at one of the bartenders, but he was already hurrying to serve her. He leaned, in a deliberately nonchalant way, against the bar as he took her order. Bethany was plainly having the desired effect on the men around her. She ordered a drink and looked pointedly away. The bartender flinched at the rejection before pouring her a glass of champagne. By now, the local man in the suit had noticed her. He swivelled on his chair and started making conversation. There was no way Danny could hear what the guy was saying at this distance, but he could see Bethany's reflection in the mirror behind the bar. It was a study in boredom. She was by some distance the most attractive woman of the fifteen or so in the room, but also the least accessible. A challenge to any alpha male in the vicinity.

Right now, there were two. The guy in the suit was leaning towards her. Danny could see him side on. The forced smile, the fast talking. Bethany remained unimpressed. When her champagne arrived, she idly traced her finger round the rim of the glass, apparently impervious to the guy's charms. It didn't seem to deter him. He leaned a little closer – Danny thought he might be at risk of falling from his stool – and stretched out one arm so that he was almost touching her. Bethany recoiled, but in such a way that made her seem superior rather than threatened. The guy took the hint and retracted his arm. But he was still leaning towards her, still chatting. Still clearly of the opinion that his luck might be in.

However, by now the General had noticed her.

Danny had to hand it to Bethany. She was playing this well. The first rule of a honeytrap was to make the target come to you. Make a clumsy approach and you do nothing but cause suspicion. Let the target think this is all their great idea and you're halfway there. Especially if your target is an oversexed Yank with a highly developed sense of his own attractiveness. The General had picked up his cocktail in its delicate martini glass and was sauntering towards Bethany. Bethany was tracing the rim of her champagne glass again, pointedly ignoring the guy in the suit. As the General sat on the stool to her right, she made no attempt even to acknowledge him.

The arrival of the General had a strange effect on the man in the suit. Maybe he thought this broad-shouldered white guy was there to ensure Bethany wasn't being hassled. Maybe one alpha male had seen off another. The man sat up straight again, made a big show of looking at his watch, then downed his orange juice and left the room.

Danny could immediately see that the General was the more skilful player. He didn't rush it. He didn't appear too keen. Both he and Bethany had their backs to Danny, but so far as he could tell the General hadn't yet initiated a conversation. Danny felt like he was in the presence of two predators slowly circling each other, waiting to go in for the kill. He stood up and headed to the gents. Bethany was handling this well and he didn't want to draw attention to himself by sitting there staring at them for too long.

It was a long time since he'd taken a piss in a room this posh. An obsequious toilet attendant handed him a fresh towel once he'd washed his hands. Danny dropped a bank note in his dish – a failure to tip would make the attendant more likely to remember him – then returned to his seat in the bar. As he passed Bethany and the General, he could see they were talking. A slightly flirtatious smile played across Bethany's lips, and O'Brien was leaning in towards her and waving one hand.

There had still been no eye contact between Danny and Bethany as he took his seat again. He sipped his drink, swiped his phone and, in the quiet of his mind, said to himself: 'Contact made.'

Cunningham, Hobbs and Moore were crouched low on top of the lift. The shaft extended into the darkness above them. Dim service bulbs glowed every ten metres, but there was insufficient light to see to the top of the building. Three sets of cabling extended from the body of the lift up along the chute: the main cable and two security ones. At the front of the lift roof, housed in a grey panel, were a set of external controls for safety and servicing purposes. Cunningham hunkered down over them. There was an override switch, a red button to move the lift up and a green one to move it down. To the left, clipped to the side of the control panel, was a piece of apparatus: a half-metre long metal lever, somewhere between a key and a jemmy. This was to prise the lift doors open from inside if necessary.

In a moment, it *would* be necessary.

Time check: 16.30 hrs. There was a hiss and the lift started to rise. The movement up here, where there were points of reference along the lift shaft, seemed much faster than it ever did in the enclosed confines of the lift itself. They shot up. Every few seconds they passed the doors of each floor, light seeping in through the cracks. The grinding sound of the pulley system was surprisingly loud and grew in volume as they rose. As the top of the shaft came into view, Cunningham, despite having done this before, felt an irrational moment of fear that the lift wouldn't stop in time and they would be crushed. But it did stop, rather suddenly. Cunningham felt his stomach lurch and he gripped on tightly. Three loud pings announced the lift's arrival at the penthouse level. Cunningham listened for the sound of the doors opening.

Hunter and Parsons stood at the back of the lift, side by side, little and large. The manager stood in front of them, facing the doors, his hands behind his back. Hunter held the canvas bag of tools lightly in his right hand. He acutely felt the absence of a weapon, but that was necessary because he knew there was a good chance he was about to be searched.

Nobody spoke. The manager dug his fingernails into his palms and blinked several times.

'Take it easy, buddy,' Hunter said under his breath. 'Don't freak out.'

The doors slid open.

There were two guys standing in front of the lift. Burly. Flat noses. Thick necks. One, brown-haired with a white blotch on his face that looked like an old burn mark, the other, steely grey hair and several days' stubble. They both wore black suits. Hunter immediately clocked the bulges under their jackets that indicated they were armed. The grey-haired guy started shouting. 'Get out of lift! Get against wall!' A rough, heavy voice, Russian or Eastern European. In a partnership like that, the first person to talk is the dominant one. Hunter made a mental note as he allowed a terrified expression to cross his face. He dropped the canvas bag as the manager emitted a weak moan of fear. He raised his palms in a 'hey guys, take it easy' gesture. Parsons, next to him, did the same.

The brown-haired guy entered the lift, grabbed Hunter, pulled him out and threw him hard against the opposite wall. Hunter winced in mock pain as he took in his surroundings. The service lift was at the end of a corridor. Turn left, you hit a wall. Turn right, the corridor extended for fifteen metres before opening out into a larger room. Here, Hunter could see the doors of the main lift, the edge of a painting on the wall next to it and a bright orange designer sofa. There was thick carpet on the floor, good for cushioning the sound of footsteps. 'Mate,' he said, breathless, timid, 'I'm just here to look at your phone lines.'

'What do you mean?' asked the grey-haired gunman. He pulled Parsons out of the lift and threw him against the wall next to Hunter.

The manager stumbled over his words as he crept out of the lift. His blinking was off the scale. It made him look shifty. 'Please, it is nothing serious. These gentlemen are from the telephone company. They would like to check the line coming into Mr Rostropovic's apartment.'

The man sneered. 'Why didn't you fucking call in advance? You know rules.' Each word sounded like he was spitting.

'I . . . I apologise, sir. I'm assured it will only take a few minutes.'

The two guys didn't seem to be listening to the manager. As he jabbered away, they started roughly patting down Hunter and Parsons. Hunter caught a glimpse of a pistol holstered under the brown-haired guy's jacket. The guy clearly saw him noticing. 'Wh-what . . .' Hunter stuttered. 'Is . . . is that a gun?'

The guy didn't answer. He just kept patting him down. When the two guards were satisfied that neither Hunter nor Parsons were armed, the brown-haired guy looked askance at the grey-haired guy. Something passed between them. The grey-haired guy looked at Hunter and pointed at the canvas bag that was still in the lift. 'Get it,' he said.

Hunter entered the lift and retrieved the bag.

'Empty it, short-arse,' said the grey-haired guy. The insult sounded almost comical in his Russian accent. 'All of it.'

Hunter leaned over and emptied the contents of the bag on to the ground. Screwdrivers. Wire cutters and crimpers. An electrician's multimeter. A cable finder. Nothing that a telephone engineer wouldn't be carrying. The brown-haired gunman poked at it with his foot. 'Put them back,' he said.

Hunter crouched down and did as he was told. The brown-haired guy was standing over him, but the atmosphere had changed a little. The guards were less tense. 'Bloody hell, mate,' Hunter said as he crammed the tools back into the canvas bag. 'I nearly peed myself when I saw that –' He made a vague gesture to indicate the pistol. The brown-haired guy with the burn mark sneered at him. Hunter's act had done the job. The guards obviously thought they had a right couple of wimps on their hands. *I'm going to fucking do you later*, Hunter thought to himself as he stood up and maintained his pretence.

'Five minutes,' said the grey-haired gunman. 'You speak to no one in apartment. You ask me before you enter any room. Are you understanding me?'

'Whatever, mate,' said Hunter. 'We'll be in and out. It's no biggie.'

'Yeah,' Parsons said. 'We don't want any trouble.'

'Please,' said the manager. His brow was damp with sweat and he was obsequiously wringing his hands. 'This way. Please, this way.' He started off down the corridor.

The brown-haired guy peered into the lift. Hunter noticed him glance upwards at the ceiling and for a tense moment thought he might investigate further. But then he stepped back into the corridor and pressed the call button. The lift doors slid shut. 'Move,' he said. 'Go on. *Move!*'

Hunter and Parsons followed the manager along the corridor.

Cunningham flicked the override switch on the secondary control panel immediately after hearing the lift doors slide shut. He and the others remained absolutely still and silent. He had his head cocked slightly, listening for the sound of disappearing footsteps, but he could hear none.

A minute passed. There was a noise in the cavity above them. Something flapping around. A bat, maybe. Cunningham ignored it and refocused all his attention on any sound he might be able to discern outside the lift. There was none. He turned to the others, nodded to indicate his intention, then pressed the green button.

The lift descended, but only a couple of metres. Cunningham removed his finger from the button as soon as the top of the lift was in line with the bottom of the penthouse doors. It shuddered to a halt. He unclipped the metal tool from the side of the control panel. He identified a notch halfway up the line where the doors met. The end of the tool fitted into it precisely. All he needed to do was twist the tool and the doors would open silently. He nodded at the others again. Hobbs and Moore raised their hand-guns. Cunningham held up three fingers.

Two.

One.

The doors slid open.

The space in front of the lift was empty. The sound of voices drifted towards them. Cunningham lowered the door opener and jabbed a finger forwards. Hobbs and Moore exited and turned to the right, weapons raised, ready to fire. Cunningham drew his own weapon and stepped outside. The corridor was empty.

They advanced.

The room outside the main lift, with the art on the wall and the orange sofa, was a kind of lobby area. It was gaudy and over the top. There were two marble statues of naked women at either end of the sofa. Against one wall there was a life-sized model of a snarling tiger. There was just one heavy wooden door that led into the penthouse apartment itself – Hunter knew that from his study of the plans. No windows. Subtle lighting, pooling from recessed spotlights. The two guys took up position about five metres from them, facing the door, which meant they couldn't see anyone approaching from the corridor. The manager was standing behind the guards. Good thing too. He looked like he might wet himself. He was blinking so frequently that his eyes looked more shut than open. Hunter took the cable finder from the canvas bag. 'We might be able to do it all out here, avoid disturbing them inside,' he said. He pointed to a section of wall about three metres from the main door and handed Parsons the cable finder. 'You want to see if you can locate it?'

Parsons was making a very good pretence of being scared. *Give that man a fucking Oscar*, Hunter thought. His hand trembled artfully as he took the cable finder, and he glanced with feigned anxiety at the two guards. He put the cable finder to the wall and switched it on. There was a piercing, high-pitched tone. Parsons rotated a dial to get rid of it. Hunter turned to the two guys. They had clearly decided that Hunter and Parsons were no threat because their body language was slack and relaxed. 'It's just noise on the line,' Hunter bluffed. 'If we can trace the cable back . . .'

The guards weren't even listening. Hunter could tell. They were distracted – still facing him, but not looking at him or Parsons, at least not properly. The brown-haired guy had his phone out. He scrolled down and said something to his companion in Russian. They seemed impatient, as though they wanted these two technicians to do their job and then get the hell out of there. That suited Hunter just fine. Because he knew that behind them, advancing round the corner, were the others, their footfall completely silent. They would each have their handgun in their right hand, and their tasers in their left. Each taser had two sharp prongs and the guys would be holding them at shoulder height; a quick, silent way to put the guards down without killing them.

It might have gone smoother if the manager hadn't whimpered. Hunter glanced in his direction. The manager was two metres behind the guards and the other guys were approaching, three abreast, a couple of metres behind him. It was involuntary, no doubt, but when the SAS men were about three metres from their targets, the manager let out a half moan, half sigh, that immediately alerted the two guards to the fact that something wasn't right. It was the grey-haired guy who reacted quickest, spinning round to see what was wrong. He had Cunningham bearing down on him but his reflexes were fast. As Hobbs slammed his handheld taser into the shoulder of the brown-haired guy, his mate reached into his suit jacket and pulled out his pistol.

But if the grey-haired guy was fast, Hunter, crouched by the wall he was pretending to examine, was faster. Having identified him as the dominant shooter, he was ready to attack him from behind. He sprang up and covered the five metres between them in an instant, colliding with the guy a bare fraction of a second before he released a round from his handgun. Cunningham, coming at him from the other direction at great speed, slammed the taser into the grey-haired guy's neck. His body jolted violently and collapsed heavily to the floor. He hit his head badly as he fell and was knocked unconscious. But then there was vicious screaming. The manager was gripping the upper part of his right arm and blood was pissing through his fingers. He must have been clipped by the bullet.

'Shut him up!' Cunningham hissed at Hunter, as he and Hobbs advanced on the door, tasers away, weapons raised. Hunter hurried over to the manager and slammed one hand over his mouth, muffling the screams. Moore removed a bunch of cable ties from his ops vest and threw them to Parsons, who immediately rolled the grey-haired guy's unconscious body on to his front before fastening his wrists behind his back. Blood was pumping from the manager's wound, smearing itself over Hunter's BT uniform. It was flowing fast, bright red, arterial. He was going to bleed out in a couple of minutes without intervention. Hunter didn't need to make the request; Moore chucked a tourniquet his way as he advanced with Cunningham and Hobbs towards the door. Parsons was tying up the brown-haired guy with the burn mark. Hunter had a call to make. Should he remove his hand from the manager's mouth to apply the tourniquet? Tightening it around the wound would be agonising. It would make him scream even more. Would it distract the guys? Alert the targets? They'd have already heard the gunshot. Hardly fucking ideal. The manager's eyes were rolling. Hunter reckoned he had a minute of consciousness left. Cunningham was by the door, tapping the manager's key fob to a pad on the right-hand side, ready to open it. Hobbs and Moore were standing two metres from it. Hobbs had his handgun raised, two-handed, forefinger resting on the trigger. Moore was holding a flashbang grenade. It was about to go very noisy. Hunter elected to hold off for just a few more seconds. He kept his hand clasped over the manager's mouth and tried to ignore the warm blood seeping through the material of his uniform.

Cunningham held up three fingers.

Two fingers.

One.

He yanked the door open. Moore hurled the flashbang inside.

It didn't matter how often you trained with a flashbang. You never totally got used to the shock and awe. Good thing, too. They were designed to disorientate. As the grenade exploded inside the apartment, the shock waves physically jolted Cunningham, rocking him on his feet. His eyesight was protected by the door from the worst of the flash, but there was still a hint of retinal burn. '*Go!*' he said. Weapons raised, Hobbs and Moore rushed into the apartment. Cunningham followed.

A wide, ornate corridor, fifteen metres long. Wood panelling. Small statues of armless figures on plinths. Big oil paintings of boring-looking men in suits. A chandelier. At the end of the corridor was the dining room, doors wide open, apparently empty of people. A large dining table. Silver candlesticks. Three doors on either side, five of them shut, the final one on the left-hand side slightly ajar, light spilling out. Noise from everywhere. Outside the apartment he could hear the manager screaming hoarsely, an absolutely agonising sound, and he knew Hunter must be pulling a tourniquet as tight as possible above his bullet wound. From a room to the right, more screaming. But different screams. Screams of fear. Cunningham could discern three voices: two kids, one adult female. Up ahead, from the dining room but out of sight, male voices. Russian. Shouting at each other. Also scared, but with an edge. Like they were about to take action.

Parsons entered, his handgun raised. Cunningham nodded in the direction of the door behind which the kids and woman were screaming. Ordinarily they would search the apartment room by room, but the direction of the voices gave them an indication of where everybody was. Parsons approached the door to the right as Cunningham, Hobbs and Moore advanced further along the corridor towards the dining room. Moore had taken a second flashbang from his ops vest. He rolled it along the corridor into the dining room. It came to a halt just in front of the dining table, then detonated. Cunningham closed his eyes to protect them from the flash. As the explosion ripped through the apartment, physically jolting him for a second time, the team advanced. The shouting and screaming was louder from all directions now. The manager. The woman and kids. The guys up ahead. Chaos. Cunningham cut through it, focused, mind on what was important. So, when a figure appeared ten metres ahead in the wide-open doors of the dining room, arm extended, holding a gun, eyes half closed because of the flash, Cunningham didn't hesitate. He released a single round, to wound, not kill. It slammed into the figure's shoulder, throwing him backwards so that he hit the table at an awkward angle and went down with a heavy thump. The team continued to advance, Cunningham at the point of their triangular formation, Hobbs and Moore behind him. Cunningham kept half his attention on the man he'd just shot. He was an older guy, maybe sixty. Tufts of hair on either side of his otherwise bald head. A hawkish nose. It was Rostropovic, Cunningham surmised. He'd dropped his weapon and was too busy clutching his wound to be reaching for it. Thank fuck he wasn't screaming. It was like a lunatic asylum in here and there was still no sign of Poliakov. Couldn't Parsons shut those kids up?

They entered the dining room. Broad, floor-to-ceiling windows looked out over the Thames. Expensive furniture. An artificial fireplace. More statues – whoever decked this place out had a liking for naked marble women. There was a big oil-painted portrait of Rostropovic over the fire. A second guy was cringing behind a metre-high plinth moulded like a Greek column. He had his back to them and looked like he was dialling on a mobile phone. Cunningham approached him quickly, leaving Hobbs and Moore to deal with Rostropovic. He freed one hand from his weapon, moved round so he was facing the suspect, then bent down and grabbed him by the scruff of his shirt. He hauled him to his feet, spun him and slammed him against the wall, knocking a painting askew as he did it. The phone went flying. He examined the man's face. Short black hair. A mole on his left cheek that sprouted three tiny hairs. A thin nose. Stubble. It matched the picture of Dmitri Poliakov that the ops officer had provided that morning.

'Positive ID!' he shouted. 'We've got him.'

FOURTEEN

19.00 hrs, Amman.

The General was kind of charming. Bethany had to give him that. He didn't indulge in the usual tired chat-up lines or talk ad nauseum about himself. He seemed – or pretended – to be interested in her. He listened to her responses and laughed at her jokes. That didn't mean Bethany didn't cringe at his outrageous flattery, but she understood how a powerful guy like him would have success with women; his technique made them feel even more important than he was. 'I bet you get all the scoops,' he said, when she told him she was a journalist. 'I bet the guys give you all their secrets.'

'Men have secrets?'

'Not from you, I'm willing to bet.'

'Do *you* have secrets?'

'Why don't I buy you another glass of champagne and you can try to find out.'

Bethany rewarded the General with a smile – the kind of smile that she knew made guys weak – and accepted his offer of a drink.

Fair play to the guy, Danny thought. He was putting the work in. He watched their reflections in the mirror behind the bar, saw the effect of Bethany's smile. The General's eyes gleamed as brightly as his expensive brogues. And well they might. The smile was artful. It filled her expression with promise. She reached out and brushed the General's elbow with her right hand as she said something that made him laugh. A tiny gesture, but Danny knew it would be electrifying for O'Brien. He felt a pang of jealousy.

Under other circumstances, he wouldn't mind being in the General's position right now. A minute later the General returned Bethany's gesture. A little more clumsily, perhaps, but Bethany didn't shrink away when he touched her knee. She smiled at him again.

Something grabbed Danny's attention. He had been aware of the chit-chat around him. It had almost exclusively been in Arabic, although he had tuned in to the occasional sentence in American-accented English. Now he heard a different language. Russian, he was certain, even though he didn't speak it. He glanced over his shoulder. Two men were sitting at a nearby table. One had sandy hair and wore a grey polo neck underneath a tan leather jacket. The other had black hair and a Tom Selleck moustache, and had on an open neck shirt. They had shot glasses of colourless liquid on the table in front of them and were talking quietly. Nothing overtly suspicious, but Danny made a mental note of their presence.

He turned back to the bar. Bethany had one hand on the General's knee. In Danny's eyes, he was as good as dead.

17.03 hrs, GMT.

Rostropovic was being a pain in the arse despite his gun wound. Hobbs was patching him up and he was screaming at him in Russian, with the tone of voice of a man accustomed to being obeyed. Fair play to Hobbs, he was keeping calm, but Cunningham could tell he wanted to shut him up. The rest of the guys had checked there was nobody else in the apartment and now he could hear the police officers, summoned from the basement, talking to the woman and kids in firm, measured voices. Keeping them separate from where the Regiment team was doing its job.

Cunningham turned his attention to Poliakov. On jungle training, he had once caught a fer-de-lance snake. It was nearly two metres long, its body thick and brown. Cunningham had pinned it to the forest floor by the neck with a forked stick, and that snake had hissed and writhed violently in the few seconds it took for him to remove his knife and hack its head off. Poliakov reminded him of that snake. He was face down on the floor, cheek to the carpet, hands behind his back, wrists plasticuffed.

Cunningham had one heavy boot between his shoulder blades to keep him on the floor, but Poliakov still kicked and wriggled and hissed and spat in Russian. He seemed to think Cunningham himself was Russian. Flecks of saliva showered from his lips. Cunningham didn't know what he was saying. Nor did he care. In one hand he had Poliakov's phone and a money clip containing Russian and British currency. His own phone was in his other hand, up to his ear and on the line to Hereford. 'We got him,' he said.

'*Roger that. Patching you through to Vauxhall.*'

A brief pause. Then another male voice, thin and reedy. '*This is Sturrock. What is your status?*'

'I've got a Russky called Poliakov under my boot and another one called Rostropovic who might have tae use his other hand tae tug himself off for a wee bit.'

'*What do you mean, man? Is Rostropovic hurt?*'

'I shot him in the shoulder, so it probably stings a little.' Cunningham didn't know who Sturrock was, but he didn't like the sound of his voice. 'He'll live,' he added. 'But he needs a medic. You want us tae bring Poliakov in?'

'*Immediately. You know where to go?*'

'Aye,' Cunningham said. 'We know where to go. What about Rostropovic?'

'*Keep him there for now and await further instructions.*'

Cunningham killed the call and bent over. With one hand on the back of Poliakov's shirt and the other on his bound wrists, he hauled the Russian to his feet. Poliakov's hair was dishevelled. The mole on his left cheek was bleeding slightly. He staggered, then started hissing away in Russian again. Cunningham drew his handgun, put it to Poliakov's head and put one forefinger to his lips to make a shush gesture. Poliakov's fell silent. 'Better,' Cunningham told him. 'You're coming with me.'

'You are not from Moscow?'

'Don't insult me, I'm from fucking Glasgow, you cunt.'

He guided Poliakov to the exit. The Russian's eyes bulged when he saw the wound in Rostropovic's shoulder, but he kept quiet as Cunningham manoeuvred him down the corridor. The door where the woman and kids were being held was half open.

One of the police officers was standing there, blocking the view in and out. The woman shouted something in Russian – she sounded distraught – and Poliakov shouted back. 'I said shut the fuck up,' Cunningham told him, and he pressed his weapon into the flesh of his neck.

Hunter and Parsons were in the lobby area. Hunter had the manager on his back, two fingers pressed to his neck. The two guards were still on the floor. 'Medics are on their way,' Hunter replied to Cunningham's unasked question. Hunter stood up. The guard with brown hair and the burn mark was face down a couple of metres away. Hunter bent over him, grabbed the hair at the back of his head and smashed his face hard into the floor. 'Never fucking try it on with me again,' he said. As he spoke, three more guys entered the room from the direction of the service lift: Cracknell, Finch and Knowles, the remaining men on Hunter's team who'd being keeping eyes on the building all day. Cracknell glanced at the bullet holes in the wall, the damaged painting and the smears of blood. 'Been busy?' he said.

'Clean up here,' Cunningham said. 'Deal with the medics, stick close to Rostropovic while we wait for the head shed to tell us what to do with him, and make sure the family's okay. Hunter, come with me. We're taking this fucker in.'

One of the guys must have reset the service lift while Cunningham had been dealing with Poliakov in the dining room. It was in its proper position and the doors were waiting open for them. Cunningham hustled Poliakov into the lift and he and Hunter escorted him back down to the basement. As soon as the lift doors opened, they were flooded with the flashing blue lights of an ambulance screeching down into the basement. More were coming – they could hear the sirens outside. The SAS men didn't get involved with the medics. They kept their heads averted from the lights that flooded the whole underground car park as they hurried their prisoner to the Amazon van. The engine was already turning over. Hunter opened up the back doors and Cunningham unceremoniously chucked Poliakov into the back. He lost his footing and fell heavily, unable to stop himself because his wrists were still bound. Cunningham and Hunter jumped in after him and slammed the doors shut. Total darkness. As the van pulled away, Cunningham took his Maglite from his pocket and pointed it at the Russian sprawled uncomfortably on the floor of the van. He looked back into the light. To Cunningham's surprise, he was smiling.

19.30 hrs, Amman.

Bethany and the General were on their third drink. Danny had no way of knowing if her apparent tipsiness was an act, but he knew for damn sure that it was having an effect on the General. O'Brien was becoming a good deal more touchy-feely. His flirtation was becoming more meaningful. He was leading up to something. Danny stood up and walked to the bar where he ordered another glass of water within earshot of Bethany and the General. 'You know,' he heard the General say, 'this is a pretty swell hotel. You seen the rooms?'

'No,' Bethany replied. She hesitated. 'But I'd like to. Do you have a minibar?'

'Do I have a minibar!' The General grinned.

Danny took his water back to his seat and carried on watching them. The stroke of Bethany's arm. The touch of her leg. Each time the General made physical contact with her, she seemed to lean in closer to him. She reciprocated. She gazed outrageously at him over the brim of her champagne glass. And when he leaned in and whispered something in her ear, she did something Danny had never seen her do before: she giggled. It was a masterclass.

The General stood up from his stool. He looked around the bar, absentmindedly correcting the stiff collar of his pink shirt, and caught Danny's eye. Danny cursed inwardly, but he didn't make the mistake of looking away. That would be suspicious. He held the General's gaze – there was absolutely no indication of drunkenness in his demeanour now – and made a cheers gesture with his glass of water. But by then the General had moved on. Danny restarted his pretence with his phone, while keeping an eye on the General. He was obviously looking for somebody. He found them at a table by the main entrance to the bar: it was one of the three army guys he'd walked in with. No words were spoken, but some kind of understanding passed between them. A pre-arranged signal. Danny recalled what Attwood had said about the General. *O'Brien will be well guarded in the hotel, but he has a weak spot. It's about six inches long and hangs between his legs.* The soldier at the entrance knew exactly what was going on and what his boss was silently telling him. *Let her come. We don't need any close protection for an hour or two.* The soldier inclined his head in acknowledgement. The General turned to Bethany. Said something. She smiled. The General, perhaps unconsciously, rubbed his right brogue against the back of his left leg, keeping it shiny, obviously concerned that he should look as good as possible. Bethany was quite a catch. He turned, walked back along the bar and exited the way he'd entered.

Bethany gave it five minutes. Danny noticed that she didn't touch the remainder of her drink. She examined herself in the mirror behind the bar and rearranged her hair. If she saw the smirk the soldier by the door gave her, she didn't show it. Nor did she acknowledge or make any eye contact with Danny. She just sat there, cross legged, straight backed, beautiful but unapproachable.

And then, when the five minutes were up, she stood and followed the General's path out of the bar.

There are some conversations between the authorities and a suspect that can safely take place in public. The 'do you know what speed you were doing, sir?' kind of conversation. Other conversations need the security and focus of a police station. The 'can you account for your movements on the night of the fifteenth?' kind of conversation. Sometimes the security arrangements require more heft: the basement cells of a secure central London location, perhaps, for the 'trust me, pal, right now we're your best chance of avoiding a rap for terrorism charges' conversations.

And then there was the kind of conversation that Alice Goodenough and Maxwell Stark needed to have with Dmitri Poliakov. The off-the-record, deniable kind of conversation. The kind of conversation that involved bruises. Split lips. A broken bone or two, if the suspect was being particularly uncooperative. Or worse.

Conversations like that take place in unofficial locations. An anonymous safe house, perhaps. Or, in this case, a prefab warehouse in an industrial park in west London. A bleak, grey, single-storey structure, surrounded by a high, sturdy wire fence, the entrance ordinarily padlocked and an old metal plaque with the words 'Park Royal Logistics' hanging off it at an angle.

It always amused Alice, on the rare occasions she had time to watch TV, to see spooks arriving in black cars with tinted windows. In real life they used cars like the one she and Stark had taken from the car pool in the basement of the MI6 building: a five-year-old Skoda Octavia, never-look-at-it-twice unremarkable. Stark was driving. The car suited him: they were equally shabby. He looked even tubbier behind the wheel, but Alice couldn't help noticing that he drove with a deft skill that she wouldn't have expected of him. As they approached the entrance to the warehouse, Alice saw a transit van with the Amazon logo printed on the side parked out front. The chain and padlock on the entrance gate were hanging loose. She got out of the car, opened it up and returned to her place in the passenger seat. Stark drove into the warehouse, parked up by the Amazon van and killed the engine. But he didn't get out. He seemed to be thinking. Alice gave him the space to do that. He took off his glasses and looked at her. It was the first time she'd seen him without those thick-rimmed frames, and she was surprised at how much younger he looked. Sharper, too. It occurred to her that his avuncular persona and all that business with the extra strong mints was an act. It was designed to put people at their ease and maybe to make them underestimate him.

But all of a sudden Maxwell Stark did not look like a man to be underestimated.

'You're going places, Alice,' he said finally. 'You're a bright girl. Bright enough to know that, I'm sure?'

Alice nodded.

'The trouble is, you're not the first to be in this situation. I've seen it happen before. A promising prospect, exactly the kind of person we need, but they never make it because there are certain parts of the job they can't stomach. Do you follow me?'

'I think so, sir,' said Alice.

'Sometimes the ends justify the means, Alice. The SAS have delivered Poliakov to us and he is now in the gentle care of two

MI6 operators in this building. It may be that he sings like a canary the moment we walk in. But in my experience, that rarely happens. It can take weeks, months even, to break these people down. We don't have that kind of leisure. We have active military operations all over the world. If General O'Brien has leaked intelligence on any more of them to Poliakov, it means we have men and women in danger of their lives right now.' He held up one finger. 'You're thinking that confessions extorted through torture are seldom reliable and you're right. Up to a point. But the men who are looking after Poliakov in this facility cut their teeth performing rendition during the Iraq War. They are skilled at enhanced interrogation techniques. They know what they're doing. If you have a problem with it, now would be the time to speak up.'

Alice glanced at the grey prefab. 'No problem, sir,' she said.

'Excellent. Peppermint?'

'I think you can stop offering me peppermints now, sir.'

Stark inclined his head. 'Shall we go?'

It was a warm night, but the temperature dropped a few degrees as they entered the building through a dented, green metal side door. They were in a large open space. The floor was a concrete slab, the walls concrete panels sapping any residual warmth. The strip lights hanging from the ceiling buzzed and flickered, but only over the far side of the warehouse. Alice and Stark were in shadow.

Two men stood under the flickering lights. They both wore black balaclavas. A third guy was tied to a high-backed chair, rope coiled around his body and arms, his ankles tightly bound to the chair legs. He was naked. He was trying to shout out, but his voice was muffled because he was gagged with something. The chair shook as he struggled against the ropes, and that was the only other sound in the room: the knock and scrape of the chair legs against the concrete floor.

'Shall we?' Stark said. He made an 'after you' gesture. Alice thought it was oddly gentlemanly, given the circumstances.

As she drew closer, Alice recognised Poliakov's face from his picture. Of course, he looked different. The rag in his mouth gave him the slight appearance of a goldfish. His eyes were bloodshot, his face pale. She couldn't help looking at the rest of his body. The pallid white skin, losing its definition with age. The triangle of dark chest hair. His penis, unusually fat. As she grew closer, she could smell something. Urine. There was a puddle under the chair and liquid dripped from the wood. The two balaclavad men stood silently behind him, hands behind their backs. Alice and Stark came to a halt a couple of metres from Poliakov, just shy of where a rivulet of urine was flowing from the puddle. Poliakov fell silent and stopped struggling. He looked at the two newcomers with wide eyes and started to shake his head.

'*Zdravstvuyte*,' said Stark in impeccable Russian. *Hello.* He nudged his spectacles further up the bridge of his nose. 'We happen to know you speak English, Mr Poliakov, so I suggest we conduct our conversation in that language.' He smiled. 'I say conversation. What I really mean is, we're going to ask you questions and you're going to tell us the answers. If we suspect that you're not telling the truth, we'll ask our friends here –' he gestured towards the two men in balaclavas – 'to persuade you to do so. In my experience, that usually involves fingers. Is that right, gentlemen?'

The taller of the two balaclavad man walked round to the front of the chair. His boots splashed in the puddle of urine, but it didn't seem to bother him. He held something up: a pair of garden secateurs with green rubber handles. He gave them a couple of test squeezes, then returned to his position behind the chair. Poliakov's eyes were bulging and he was shaking his head more frantically than ever; the chair scraped and banged and scraped and banged and Alice thought he might topple.

Stark raised a calming hand. 'Mr Poliakov, please, such a display helps neither of us. The calmer we can all remain, the more productive this conversation will be.' To Alice's surprise, his words had the required effect. Poliakov fell silent again, though he couldn't entirely suppress his trembling. 'That's much better,' said Stark. He removed a packet of extra strong mints from his pocket, popped one in his mouth and sucked noisily for a few seconds. 'Now then, we're going to talk about our friend, General Frank O'Brien. We're very well aware that he gave you intelligence about a British military operation in Syria.

For your information, that resulted in the death of thirteen British soldiers, and I have to tell you, the consensus is you should be thrown to the wolves for that. If you'd rather not spend the next thirty years in our frankly appalling prison system, I suggest you tell us right now what other operations, British or otherwise, are currently compromised.' He looked at the man with the secateurs. 'Would you mind?' he said, wagging a finger at the rag in Poliakov's mouth. The man walked to the front again and removed the gag.

Poliakov was talking almost before it was out of his mouth. 'You've got it wrong, you've got it wrong!' he said in Russian.

Stark sighed regretfully. 'Put it back, if you'd be so kind,' he said, and the man stuffed the rag back into Poliakov's mouth amid much muffled dissent. Stark took a step back and Alice emulated him. Stark bowed his head miserably. 'Go ahead,' he said.

The masked man didn't hesitate, other than to give the secateurs another couple of test squeezes. They didn't make a sound as the curved blades closed in on each other. Poliakov started to squeal, each squeal accompanied by another scraping of the chair. The man leaned over and moved the secateurs into position over Poliakov's right hand. Alice was relieved that she couldn't see it happen. Her view of Poliakov's hand was blocked by the masked man's back. She heard it, though. The same slice and crunch that she remembered from watching her mother cut up chicken in their tiny kitchen at home. And she heard the flat splash as the finger landed in the puddle on the concrete floor. Poliakov's squealing went up an octave. As the masked man stood aside, Alice couldn't help her eye being drawn to the detached digit. It looked much smaller now that it was no longer connected to the hand. Blood dripped on to it from the wound. Alice felt nauseous, but manage to remain impassive.

'We'll try again,' said Stark, his usual polite tone now had an edge. 'Which other military operations are currently compromised?'

He nodded at the masked man, who stepped round again and pulled the rag from Poliakov's mouth. Poliakov inhaled noisily and started to pant. Alice was reminded of a thirsty dog. But Poliakov wasn't thirsty, he was desperately trying to control the pain, or so it seemed to Alice. His eyes were clenched shut, his face screwed up. After thirty seconds or so, the panting stopped and his eyes opened. 'You've got it all wrong,' he said, and he was speaking English now, albeit with a thick Russian accent. 'Why do you think I am hiding in London? Why do you think the oligarch Rostropovic is giving me sanctuary?'

Stark and Alice exchanged a look then Stark's eyes flickered towards the finger on the floor. 'I suggest you tell us,' he said.

'I was not *receiving* intelligence from O'Brien. I was *supplying* it.' He grimaced horribly. 'My *hand* . . .'

'What do you mean?' Stark said. There was a catch in his voice.

'You don't understand what's *happening*. You don't know your friends from your enemies.'

'What the . . .'

Alice put a gentle hand on Stark's arm to silence him. Stark flicked her away, clearly irritated by her intervention. But she persisted. 'Sir, think about it. Number 10 were hesitant about us raiding Rostropovic's apartment. Surely that means he's more aligned to us than to the Russian administration.'

'Rostropovic *hates* the Russian administration!' Poliakov almost shouted. 'He was the only person I could trust to hide my family while O'Brien does his work!'

'Poliakov is a whistle-blower, sir,' Alice said.

Stark shook his head testily. 'We heard the tape of Poliakov and O'Brien talking,' he said. 'We heard O'Brien give him details of the Zero 22 operation.'

'We heard *fragments* of a conversation, sir,' Alice said quietly.

'I demand to see the British foreign secretary!' Poliakov shouted. 'This is no way to treat your allies! Untie me! Give me my clothes! Give me medical assistance!'

'We heard your conversation with O'Brien, Poliakov. Chapter and verse. He was giving you sensitive military intelligence so the Russians could ambush a British unit.'

Poliakov's wild eyes narrowed. 'Give me my phone,' he said.

'No phone calls,' Stark said.

'I don't want to make a phone call! Give it to me!'

Stark nodded at the masked man. He produced a phone and handed it over.

'I have only met O'Brien once,' Poliakov said. 'In Crete. I

recorded our conversation. You can listen to it. It will tell you what you need to know.'

It was a messy business, tapping the fingerprint sensor on the phone with Poliakov's bleeding hand. Stark did it with obvious distaste, holding the phone by the edge gingerly in an attempt not to become bloodied. Poliakov directed him to a recording app. 'June the twentieth,' Poliakov said. 'Play the recording.'

Alice was aware of a strange shift in power as Stark followed Poliakov's instruction. He put the phone on speaker. Two voices filled the room: Alice recognised General O'Brien and Poliakov himself. They were muffled. It sounded to Alice as though Poliakov's phone had been in a pocket as he was recording. But they were audible.

— *I don't feel good about this. I'm supposed to be on vacation. We shouldn't be seen together. Your people or my people work out we've been talking, it could blow everything apart.*

— *You think I would take this kind of risk without looking you in the eye? I need to know you mean what you say.*

— *You don't need to worry about that. I got the security of the whole damn United States in my hands. That son of a bitch in the Oval Office is unhinged and I gotta deal with him. And I can't do it without you, right?*

— *Right.*

A pause. The clinking of glasses. A low hubbub of voices in the background. Poliakov cleared his throat in the recording.

— *I have something for you.*

— *I'm all ears.*

— *The Americans have passed us information about a British military operation in Syria. I have details. Fourteen men. A night-time raid on a prison facility to collect some Kurdish militants. Operation call sign, Zero 22. My people have passed it to the Wagner Group. There will be an ambush. A massacre.*

Another pause.

— *Jesus. Fourteen men. Zero 22, you say?*

— *Zero 22.*

— *I can't do anything about it.*

— *You must tell the British.*

— Not possible. If my people have given your people hard intel, and the Brits suddenly change their plans, we got a whole world of problems. Both sides are going to know there's a leak, and our job becomes twice as hard.

— Maybe you're right. This is the biggest operation we've worked on. We need to be careful we don't make a mistake.

— I need to be careful nobody points a finger at me.

Pause.

— Damn, it bites. Fourteen men. SF, by the sound of the op. Fourteen good men. But what we're doing is more important, grand scheme of things. We got to accept there's going to be collateral. Casualties of war. Every soldier knows the risk.

Pause.

— Damn, it bites. You'd better get out of here. Anyone sees us . . .

The conversation was suddenly drowned out by the blare of loud dance music. But they'd heard enough. Stark killed the recording. Silence fell on them like a heavy weight.

'Untie me,' Poliakov said.

'Do it,' Stark said. He sounded slightly sick.

Poliakov's release was an unseemly business. Once the ropes were loosened, he slipped in his own urine, seemingly dizzy from the loss of blood from his wound. He refused any help to put his clothes back on, but it took an age as he awkwardly wormed his damaged hand into his shirt, smearing blood all over the material as he did so. Scruffily dressed, he turned back to Stark and Alice. 'Where are my family?'

'Safe,' said Stark.

'I don't *trust* you. I demand to see the foreign secretary and I demand to see my family. I don't say another word until I *see* them.'

'Forget it,' Stark snapped. 'You see nobody until I have more information. And if you don't give me that information, you know what will happen. You said Rostropovic was the only person you trusted to hide your family while "O'Brien does his work". What did you mean by that?'

Poliakov spat on the ground. Stark turned to the balaclavad man with the secateurs and nodded. He strode towards Poliakov, who shrank back into his chair. 'Get this animal away from me!'

Another nod from Stark called the masked man off. Poliakov clutched his bleeding hand. His eyes rolled, and for a moment Alice thought he might faint. Then he seemed to compose himself. He closed his eyes. Opened them again. 'My government is working with the American president.' The sneer on his lips made it quite clear what he thought about that arrangement.

'Collusion,' Stark said.

'*Collusion?*' Poliakov said it like it was an absurd word. 'You cannot even imagine the extent of it.'

'Enlighten me.'

Poliakov's eyes were rolling again.

'He needs to sit down, sir,' Alice said, earning herself an irritated look from her boss.

'Talk,' Stark said.

'My people . . .'

'When you say "your people", you mean the Kremlin? The FSB?'

'Elements within both. Close to the Russian president. They have been supplying—' He frowned for a moment and closed his eyes. Alice thought he was going to pass out and stepped forwards to help him. But then he opened his eyes again and she realised he had been searching for an English word. 'Deepfake,' he said.

'What do you mean?' Stark turned to Alice. 'What does he mean?'

'Deepfake video, sir. It's mostly a pornography thing. The faces of celebrities mapped on to porn actors. The technology is very advanced . . .'

'Pornography,' Poliakov spat. 'This is nothing to do with pornography. This is deepfake video footage of the American president's political adversaries meeting with known terror suspects.'

'I don't understand,' said Stark. 'Which terror suspects?'

'There *are* no terror suspects, sir,' Alice said. 'They're fake. Their faces are mapped on to the faces of ordinary people the President's political rivals might have met quite innocently.' Her mind was rushing. Dots were joining up. She realised she was several steps ahead of her boss, and an icy sensation hit her in the gut. 'Sir . . .' she said.

But Stark brushed her away. 'Do you have evidence of this?' he demanded of Poliakov.

'I gave it to O'Brien,' Poliakov said. 'The original footage and the deepfake footage. Separate files. Anyone looking at them side by side will understand what is going on.'

'You have copies?'

Poliakov looked at him like he was stupid. 'You think I would risk that?'

'*Sir* . . .' Alice said.

'You didn't upload it somewhere?'

Poliakov didn't even bother replying to what he clearly thought was a preposterous suggestion. 'I gave it to O'Brien,' he repeated. 'He knows what to do with it. But he must be fast. The American president is planning something. An attack. On his own soil.'

'When? Where?'

'I don't know where.'

'When, then?'

Poliakov swayed. He said something, but it was indistinct. Stark nodded at the masked man, who strode up to Poliakov, held him by both shoulders and shook him. 'When,' he repeated.

Poliakov's reply was hoarse. 'The fourth . . .' he said. 'Of July.'

'*Sir* . . .' Alice repeated, her voice urgent. The masked man was helping Poliakov to the ground. Stark was staring at him, apparently frozen by this new intelligence.

'Sir, if O'Brien is innocent, we need to move fast. Hereford have sent someone. To deal with him. It's happening, sir. Now. He might already be dead.'

Poliakov looked aghast at her, his face wracked with pain. Then, quite unexpectedly, he started to laugh. 'They've conned you into doing that?' He shook his head, as though he couldn't quite believe their stupidity. 'They've persuaded you to kill O'Brien? Then it's over. All the risks I took have been for nothing.' His eyes rolled.

'We need to stop it happening, sir,' Alice said.

Poliakov laughed again. 'You will *never* stop it happening,' he said. 'Don't you see?'

'We need to speak to Hereford, sir. Tell them to pull the op.'

'They don't make mistakes, these people,' Poliakov said. 'There is always a backup plan. *Always*.' His voice was fading. 'Where is

O'Brien now? Jordan? You're taking out a hit in Jordan? Trust me, if the American president has decided to eliminate him, it is with the knowledge of the Russians. They are the same, don't you see? And we will have someone else there ... the Wagner Group ... ready to finish the job if you call it off ...'

His eyes rolled again and he slumped heavily on to the balaclavad man, finally unconscious.

Stark stared at Alice. She could see a pulse in his jaw. He suddenly looked ten years older. He pulled out his own mobile phone, dialled a number and practically screamed into it.

'Get me Hereford on the line. *Just do it! Now!*'

FIFTEEN

The General might have instructed his guys not to follow her, but Bethany couldn't assume they'd obeyed.

It was seven forty-five. An hour and fifteen minutes since she had made contact with the General. His suite was on the third floor. He'd given Bethany – or Sophia, as she'd introduced herself – the room number, 318. Bethany took the plushly carpeted stairs but walked a circuit of the second floor to check she wasn't being tailed. Her destination was hardly a secret, of course, but if she *was* being followed she would have to tell the General – or Frank, as he'd introduced himself – so that he could dismiss the overenthusiastic guard from outside his door. She hoped the procedure she had in mind would be silent, but she had to plan for the unexpected.

No tail. Back in the stairwell she could hear two men speaking in Russian on the floor below. Should that concern her? Chances were she could find guests from twenty different nations staying here if she cared to look. She moved to the third floor, found the General's room and knocked.

She couldn't help but be inwardly revolted when he opened the door in his hotel robe. It was a patterned Japanese kimono, knee-length, flimsy satin material. The General was a big guy and the kimono was almost comically inadequate. His greying chest hair was visible where the lapels crossed and his military ID tags, which he wore around his neck, nestled half-hidden in the hair. The sleeves stopped a good couple of inches above his wrist. His shins were much paler than his face and hands, and, although he was well built, his legs had lost all their hair like some older men's do. But he seemed pleased with himself. Bethany forced herself to be outwardly appreciative, even though she found the pungent smell of aftershave and martinis unpleasant. 'I see you've slipped into something more comfortable,' she said.

'When you spend as much time as I do in uniform . . .'

'It must be stifling. Are you going to invite me in?'

The General raised an eyebrow, stepped to one side and gestured for Bethany to come in. The door clicked shut.

'Nice,' she said, looking around the well-appointed room. The blackout curtains were closed, blocking what Bethany's sense of direction told her would be a view of the square at the front of the hotel. There was a comfortable sofa and a dining table. A large TV and even a small cocktail bar. Two doors on opposite walls. 'I thought soldiers had to make do with grubby little barrack rooms.'

'Oh sure, I've seen my share of those.' He winked at her like a kindly uncle. Bethany had to stop herself cringing. 'But there have to be a few privileges of rank, don't you think?'

'Were you going to offer me a drink?' she said.

'Name it. Uncle Sam's paying.'

'He sounds like a very generous uncle.'

'Well, like lots of uncles, he has his good traits and his bad.'

There were tumblers, highball glasses and champagne flutes behind the bar. The tumblers looked sturdiest. 'I'll have a Scotch,' she said.

'A girl after my own heart,' said the General. He poured two whiskies and handed one to Bethany. She was right. The tumbler felt solid in her hand. If she smashed it against the counter, it would provide a sharp, heavy duty shard. Clumsy, but useable in the absence of any other weapon.

She took a sip of her whisky. Take it slowly, she told herself. Let him make the first move. The more he thinks he's in control, the less he is. 'You've a busy few days coming up,' she said.

'The peace talks? Lots of the heavy lifting has already been done, truth to tell. That's what all these meetings have been over the last couple of days. Hopefully we'll get some ink on paper at the main conference tomorrow. If I manage to stop the Turks and the Kurds shooting each other across the conference table, it'll be a goddamn result. Those are some crazy sons of bitches.' He gave a rueful smile. 'But they seem to listen to me, so I do what I can. And then back to DC. You ever been?'

'A couple of times.'

'It's a bear pit, Sophia. And it's about to get a helluva sight uglier, mark my words.'

'Oh yeah?'

'Oh yeah. With yours truly in the middle of it.'

'Sounds to me like you could do with relaxing before it all kicks off.'

He held up his whisky glass, winked at her again and took a sip. 'Hey, I don't normally do this kind of thing, you know.'

'Liar,' Bethany said archly. 'Mind if I freshen up?'

'Knock yourself out.'

She pointed enquiringly to one of the doors.

'That's the bedroom,' the General said.

'Well we don't want to jump the gun,' Bethany said, and she headed through the other door. She locked herself in the bathroom. A marble surround to the bath. Bright downlighters. The smell of aftershave. She stood for a moment with her back to the door, eyes closed, breathing deeply, calming herself, trying to keep her focus. She thought of her little boy and wondered what he was doing now. That thought got her focused again. The sooner she left this place, the sooner she could see him again. She made a quick audit of the General's toiletries. Hotel shampoo and shower gel. A tube of shaving cream. A bottle of Aramis. A packet of Viagra hidden behind a box of paracetamol. She had been prepared to crack open the plastic housing of a safety razor, but it seemed like the General favoured the old-fashioned way. There was a traditional razor on the glass shelf in front of the mirror, and a small white plastic box of spare blades. She slid one of the blades out and took off her shoe. She lifted the inner sole, hid the blade underneath it, then she put the shoe back on. She flushed the toilet and ran the tap for thirty seconds. Then she fixed herself in the mirror and returned to the main room.

The General had finished his whisky and was leaning against the bar. His kimono had slipped a little, revealing more of his chest hair. He appreciatively eyed Bethany up and down and there was an expectant silence. Bethany walked up to him, taking her time, her lips slightly parted, fixing him with the kind of stare that she knew made men helpless. There was something quietly pathetic about his puppy-dog eyes and the way his breath trembled as he exhaled. She approached him, and as she walked her mind was making tiny calculations. The General was at least half a head height taller than her. And though he had thirty years on her, he still had a powerful frame. There was simply no way she could overpower him physically. Even if she managed to attack him with the razor blade, he would likely still have the opportunity to call for help. It was essential, therefore, that he was entirely disabled before she made her move.

She stood just inches away from him. She could smell the booze on his breath, a mixture of the martinis and the whisky, neither of them masked by his aftershave. He started to say something, but she put one finger to his lips. With her other hand, she pulled the cord of his kimono. It fell open. He was completely naked underneath. Naked and grotesquely ready for action. His body was fit, but ageing. She slid her forefinger from his lips, down along his chin to his neck, along the centre of his chest, stopping just where his stomach protruded tightly. 'Which door was the bedroom again?' she said.

The hotel bar continued to fill up. It was busy now, but Danny had chosen his position wisely and could still see both exits: the one to his left by which he'd entered, and the one at the far end of the bar. He ordered another drink and waited. The General's guy was still sitting at the main table by the bar. Like Danny, he was sipping from a glass of mineral water, but now lacked the military stiffness that had been evident when the General was present.

He picked up his phone from the table. He pretended to scroll through it again while surveying the room and trying to work out how long he would need to sit there. Bethany had left ten minutes ago. How long would she need? Half an hour? Longer? He found himself thinking of the photographs he'd examined back in Hereford of her previous handiwork. He wished he'd told her not to get creative. The General just needed to be dead. There was nothing to be gained from putting on a show.

His phone buzzed silently in his hand. Number withheld. He frowned. Who the hell would be calling him? Only Hereford had this number, which answered the question. He took the call. 'Yeah?'

'*Black?*' He recognised the CO's voice and knew it was important for Williamson to be making the call himself.

'Go ahead.'

'*Abort. Immediately.*'

A beat.

'What do you mean?'

'*What the hell do you think I mean? Six have got it wrong. They're being manipulated. You need to get the General safely out of there. Whatever it takes.*'

'It might be too late.'

'*Make sure it isn't. Tell him that we know about Poliakov and the deepfakes. And Black, you can expect interference. Most likely Russian, possibly Wagner Group. They might be on site to finish the General off in the event that you're unsuccessful.*'

At the mention of the Wagner Group, Danny clenched his jaw. He glanced over at the two Russian men at the nearby table, and he flashbacked to the final moments of the Zero 22 op. 'Roger that,' he said.

The line went dead.

The alarm clock by the General's bed read eight o'clock.

There were two kimonos in the bedroom. There was the one that had slid from the General's shoulders to the floor as Bethany had undressed him. And there was the one hanging on the back of the door. Bethany had identified it the moment they had entered the bedroom, and her strategy for the next few minutes had formed itself.

The bedroom was large and comfortable. There was a dressing table and a writing desk and two deep armchairs. The curtains were closed. There was dusky pink mood lighting. His clothes were folded with military neatness on a high-backed chair. The shiny brown brogues were next to them on the floor, precisely square to the chair. The bed dominated the room. Emperor size, a modern four-poster frame without drapes. Plump pillows and embroidered cushions. Complementary chocolates on the pillows. The General was naked, apart from the military ID tags around his neck. He stood between Bethany and the bed, a schoolboy grin on his old face.

'Lie down,' she told him.

He did as she said, propping himself up on the pillows.

'I'm going to give you a little show,' she said.

'Sounds swell,' said the General. 'I like to take in a show.'

'You'll love this one,' she said, and she started to remove her clothes. Her jacket first, which she dropped on to the floor next to the General's kimono. Then her blouse, which she removed to reveal her black bra. She slipped off her shoes. One of them she kicked across the floor. The other, the shoe with the razor blade, she kept upright and accessible. She wormed her way out of her skirt so that now she was standing there in her underwear. The General's appreciation was evident on his face and elsewhere. Bethany gave him a girlish twirl, mussing her hair as she did so, and he said: 'Bravo! Hottest ticket in town!'

'I thought you'd enjoy it,' she said. She touched the tip of her tongue to her front teeth and made a coquettish look skywards as though a naughty idea had just come to her. 'Let's play a game,' she said.

Danny felt his blood burning. He had no way of contacting Bethany and he didn't know the General's room number. He was momentarily frozen, paralysed by his lack of options. What the hell was happening? How could he stop Bethany in time?

He looked across the room. The General's guy was still slouched in his chair, glass of mineral water in hand. He would know where the General was. Suddenly Danny had options. Could he be persuaded to give up the General's room number? No chance. Just asking the question would surround Danny with a cadre of suspicious American soldiers. Could he be coerced, physically? Perhaps. But that would mean getting him on his own and, if he was well trained, the process could take some time. Danny didn't have time. So he needed another idea.

He stood up and hurried towards the far exit and out of the bar.

★　　★　　★

The belts from the two kimonos were soft and satiny to the touch. But they were strong, too. Bethany could tell as she pulled one of them taut before wrapping it along one arm. She draped the other over her left shoulder so that it covered her bra strap. Then she walked towards the bed, where the General was breathing heavily. He reminded Bethany of a hungry dog waiting for his dinner. And just as a hungry dog will perform any trick for food, she knew that the General was now lost to the moment. The job was as good as done.

'Give me your hand, baby,' she said.

The General did as he was told. His palm was warm and a little sweaty. He was entirely compliant as she tied one end of the loose kimono cord to his wrist and the other to the corresponding bedpost. She put her face close to his, as if to kiss him, but drew away at the last moment, teasing him. She sashayed round to the other side of the bed, slowly unwrapping the other kimono cord from around her arm. She didn't even have to ask him for his other hand. He offered it to her and was silent and meek as she tied it to the opposite bedpost. She stepped back to look at him. His Viagra had done its work and it occurred to her that under other circumstances her best option would be to present this as a sex game gone wrong. But she didn't have the time for anything sophisticated. She wanted the job done, and to be out of here. So the razor was her friend.

The General's legs were still free, but without the use of his arms he was effectively out of action. She couldn't drop her pretence just yet; she didn't want his suspicions to be raised and for him to start struggling and making noise. So she continued to sashay as she turned her back on him and walked over to where his clothes were neatly folded, and picked up his pair of pale blue briefs. She turned and held them up, winking at him suggestively. His brow wrinkled, half confused, half amused, as if to say, 'what are you going to do with those?'

She walked back towards him.

Danny found the fire alarm call point in an instant. It was situated at the bottom of the stairwell, just to the right of the elevator. A glass panel framed in red, the instruction to break the glass in case of emergency written in both English and Arabic. He checked his surroundings. Nobody was watching, so he smashed his elbow into the panel.

The response was immediate: a deafeningly loud alarm, high pitched and quickly alternating between two notes. Danny hurriedly climbed the stairs to the first floor. A military man would know never to use the lift if there was a fire, and so he figured that the General's guy would be there any minute, either to head straight to a room on the first floor or to continue up the stairs.

It took about twenty seconds. Guests were already hurrying from their bedrooms, pushing past Danny as he loitered on the half-landing, trying to zone out the ringing sound of the fire alarm. The General's guy pushed against the tide, taking two steps at a time. He paid no attention to Danny as he passed. He was looking up, not back, so he didn't see Danny follow him.

Bethany stood by the side of the bed and leaned over. She squeezed the General's nose between her thumb and forefinger, and she knew that, at last, he was beginning to realise that something was not right. His body tensed up and, looking down, she could see that his excitement was waning. She held his underwear close to his mouth. He would open it eventually, either to breathe or to shout out. When he did that, she would stuff the briefs inside and silence him.

But the General was a smart guy. He knew what would happen when he opened his mouth. So for now, he kept it clenched. He started to kick violently and to strain against the kimono cords, but Bethany had tied perfect double constrictor knots. She noticed how his hands reddened as the blood supply to them became restricted. A minute passed. His face was becoming red too. His eyes bulged. She kept the pressure on his nose, keeping the nostrils shut. And then it happened. He needed to breathe. He parted his lips but kept his teeth clenched as he tried to inhale. That was all she needed. She stuffed the underpants hard inside his mouth, crumpling them into a ball, forcing them between his teeth and pushing them to the back of the throat. He tried to bite her fingers, but the pressure of the material against the back of his mouth made him gag and open his mouth even wider, so she was able to force all the material inside before withdrawing her hand.

He was kicking in a frenzy now, arching his body up as he writhed and struggled against the cords. The mattress shifted underneath him, but Bethany wasn't worried. He wasn't going anywhere. She hurried back round to where her clothes were piled on the floor. It would be better to put them on before she did it. Then she could get out of there the moment his throat was cut and she had confirmed that he was dead. She felt awkward as she dressed, and she realised she was nervous. She breathed deeply and slowed herself down. Buttoned up her blouse and smoothed her skirt. Then she bent over, folded back the inner sole of her shoe and withdrew the razor blade. She realised that the General had been making a regular, metronomic squeal which she had barely noticed as she prepared herself. It grew more frenzied as she held the razor up to the light, establishing that both sides were sharp. A numbness came over her. It was a familiar sensation. Her body and mind protecting itself from what was to come. She'd been holding up the razor for longer than she intended. She lowered it, focused on the squealing man on the bed, and approached him.

The blare of the fire alarm made her whole body jolt. The numbness instantly dissolved. She spun round, half expecting somebody to burst into the room. But there was nobody. Just her and the General. He had stopped squealing and writhing. He was staring round the room, as if the fire alarm was a physical presence he was trying to catch sight of, as if it was somebody arriving to rescue him from the horror. But then he seemed to realise that the opposite might be true. That the alarm might speed things up. His writhing became more extreme. His squeals more desperate.

Bethany reached the edge of the bed. With the heel of her left hand she pushed against the side of the General's head to expose his neck fully. The tendons were tense and strained, and she could just make out the high-pressure pulse of the carotid artery. One cut was all it would need. One deft slice. She raised a corner of the duvet with the free fingers of her razor hand, ready to protect herself from the initial spurt of blood.

'Good night, General O'Brien,' she said.

★   ★   ★

The General's guy left the stairwell at the third floor. The fire alarm was loudest in the corridors. Tiny red warning lights flashed in the ceiling panels. There were four other guests in the corridor, hurrying from their rooms towards the stairs. It was enough movement for Danny's presence to be unremarkable to the guy if he even noticed him. Danny followed him to the end of the corridor where he took a left and disappeared from Danny's field of view. When Danny saw him again, he was holding a key card to a panel three doors down on the left. The door clicked open and he entered.

Danny ran. He caught the door a fraction of a second before it clicked shut, and burst into the room. It was a suite. With a single glance he took in the furniture, the whisky glasses at the bar, the two doors leading off. Only one was open, and the General's guy was standing in the door frame. Danny could tell from his posture – shoulders hunched, legs slightly apart – that he was aiming a weapon. He hurled himself across the room towards the door frame and launched his whole body at the guy, slamming into him with a crashing momentum. The guy fell forwards to the ground, but not before releasing a round. It was a handgun round, unsuppressed, and its retort, merged with the fire alarm, was disorientating. Danny let the full weight of his body crash down on to the soldier to stop him getting to his feet again and taking another shot. As he fell, he took in the room. He saw the General, naked and tied to the bed. He saw Bethany, one hand on his head, something in her other hand, looking back over her shoulder. He saw where the bullet from the guy's handgun had slammed into the wall just behind her, throwing out a shower of plaster. And he saw Bethany turn to the General again and raise her right arm. He realised she was moving in to cut his throat.

'*NO!*' he shouted. '*LEAVE HIM!*'

The General's guy was strong. Despite Danny's weight on his back, he was pushing himself up with his free hand and he still had a good grip of his weapon. He was aiming at Bethany again, his finger on the trigger. Danny slammed a heavy clenched fist on to his elbow joint. The joint clicked as it broke, and the guy yelled in pain and the gun fired. But Danny had compromised his aim and the bullet flew harmlessly under the bed and splintered into the skirting board on the far side.

'What the hell?' Bethany shouted, her voice tense.

'Instructions from London,' Danny shouted back. 'He's not what they thought he was.'

The General's guy started shouting for help from underneath Danny, each word followed by a noisy inhalation of breath, shaky on account of his broken elbow.

Danny didn't have time to explain. He bore this guy no malice. He was Yank soldier, doing his job, and he didn't deserve to lose his life because of it. But Danny needed him out of the way. He raised his own elbow and crashed it down on the back of the guy's skull. His head jarred hard against the floor and his body went limp. He'd be out for a good few minutes. Danny loosened the weapon from his hand – it was a Sig Sauer M17, nine millimetre, sand coloured. He stood up and strode over to where Bethany was still perched on the edge of the bed. The General was still wearing his military ID tags, and his eyes were bulging. Something was stuffed in his mouth and his arms were straining against two dressing-gown cords tied to the timber uprights of his four-poster. Danny didn't need to know how Bethany had got him into this position. He just needed to get him out of it. 'Give me that,' he said, indicating the razor blade.

'What's happening?' Bethany demanded.

'No time,' Danny said. He grabbed the razor and quickly cut through the two cords. The General rolled away from them, almost falling off the bed. He regained his footing and removed the object obstructing his throat. He gagged as he pulled out a fistful of material and Danny realised it was his own underpants. He raised the Sig and aimed it at the naked man. 'Get your clothes on,' he said.

'What in the—'

'*Get them on!* I haven't got time to explain. I think there are Wagner Group operatives in the hotel, and I think they've been ordered to kill you if we fail.'

'Who the *hell* are you?'

'British SAS,' Danny said, figuring that it would hold some weight with a man like this. 'We know about Poliakov and the deepfakes.' He said it with bullish confidence, hoping to hide that the CO's instructions made no sense to him.

Whatever they meant, Danny's words hit their mark. The General nodded, but then he pointed at Bethany. 'What about her? Who the hell—'

'Long story, no time. Get dressed if you want to live. Do it. Now.'

He nodded and hurried over to where his clothes were neatly piled. He was plainly traumatised as he tried to get dressed. He was having trouble coordinating his limbs. When Bethany moved towards Danny, the General visibly shrank away even though they were separated by the width of the room.

'We need to get back to the vehicle,' Danny said. 'As long as the fire alarm is ringing, we should be able to leave by any exit. There's a fire exit at the bottom of the stairwell. That'll be better than the main entrance. Less people to see us go. But we might encounter hostiles on the way down, so I need you and the General to stay behind me.'

'Why?' Bethany said. Her voice had an edge. She was wired. Hardly surprising. 'Because I can't take care of myself?'

'No,' Danny said, and he held up the Sig. 'Because I'm the one with the firearm and I think we're going to need it.' He bent over the unconscious soldier and felt around his abdomen. He located two spare clips for the Sig. He could tell by the weight that they were standard seventeen-round magazines. That gave him thirty-four shots, plus whatever was already in the handgun. He stole the clips and put them into his pocket. The General was worming his feet into his shiny brown brogues. 'Ready?' Danny said.

'Ready,' they said in unison.

And as soon as they'd said it, the fire alarm stopped. There was a heavy silence. Danny swore. Getting out of here was suddenly ten times more difficult. He considered the possible routes. They were on the third floor. They needed to get to the ground floor. The lift was out of the question. Too confined. He knew from the hotel plan on the exhibition board that there was only one staircase. They would have to use it to get back down to the ground floor. Once there, it would be better to avoid the main entrance, but he didn't think they could avoid going through the bar. And that made him remember something. 'There were two Russian guys in the bar,' he said. 'One with sandy hair, polo neck, leather jacket. One with black hair and a black moustache. Anyone starts firing, get out of the way and let me deal with it. Understood?'

'I can handle myself in a combat situation,' said the General.

Danny looked meaningfully at the remnants of dressing-gown cord that were still hanging from his wrists. 'Let me deal with it,' he repeated.

The General's pale face reddened but he puffed out his chest anyway. 'I have guys in the hotel,' he said. 'American guys. Good guys. Any more of them get hurt, you're in the glasshouse for the rest of your goddamn days.'

'Mate,' said Danny, 'you've got a fifty-fifty chance of getting out of here alive. My advice is to do what I fucking say.' He gave his weapon the once over, checking that the safety lever was disengaged, and headed out of the room. 'Let's go,' he said.

SIXTEEN

Danny held the Sig with two hands. His left supported its weight. His right kept it in position. As his body moved, the firearm moved with it. It was part of him.

At the entrance to the General's suite, he stood with his back to the wall by the door frame. He listened. There was a residual ringing in his ears from the fire alarm. It got in the way of his thoughts and he had to concentrate hard to drown it out. Were there footsteps outside? Voices? He didn't think so. Silently, swiftly, he stepped out into the corridor. Looked both ways, the Sig leading. There was nobody in sight. He checked back over his shoulder at Bethany and the General. For a man who minutes previously had been naked and humiliated on a bed, seconds away from having his throat slit, he looked alert. There was no hint of the relaxed womaniser from the bar. He was a little dishevelled, but sharp around the eyes. You didn't get to his position in the military without a high level of operational awareness. Danny made a minute adjustment in his mind: he was not protecting an incompetent, but someone who could be relied on to manage a hostile situation. And as for Bethany? She had a steely aura. Danny knew what she was capable of. 'Follow,' he told them.

They moved at a jog, heading down the corridor back towards the stairwell. Where the corridor turned a corner, he stopped again and listened. The ringing in his ears had subsided and he could discern no other sound. He turned. The way ahead was deserted. Two bedroom doors were ajar, one on either side. At the end of the corridor, twenty-five metres distant, was the door leading to the stairwell. The trio advanced again, still jogging, Danny's weapon still raised. He stopped before they reached the first open bedroom door.

Checked for threats.

Clear.

They advanced to the second open door.

Checked for threats.

The sandy-haired Russian man with the polo neck and leather jacket never stood a chance. Danny recognised him immediately as the Russian stood there in the bedroom doorway, his weapon ready. He held it like a pro: like Danny, two handed. A Russian PL-15 pistol, suppressed. But unlike Danny, this guy, whoever he was, hadn't spent untold hours in the Killing House at Hereford, testing his reflexes against targets that appeared suddenly and from nowhere, until it became second nature to drill bullets into them with perfect accuracy. Danny didn't hesitate. It only took one round and it slammed straight into the man's forehead before he could discharge a bullet of his own. He fell heavily to the ground, his forehead a mess of entry wound. Danny maintained his firing position, hyper aware of the possibility of another threat from inside the room. But there was silence. 'Take his weapon,' Danny said.

There was jostling in his peripheral vision. Bethany got there first. The sandy-haired guy was slumped over his gun. She rolled him on to his back with her right foot, bent over and unwound his dead fingers from the pistol. Danny maintained the firing position while she did this. 'I'm a goddamn five-star general,' O'Brien said, his voice testy. 'What are you doing giving her a weapon ahead of me?'

Danny didn't bother to answer. He turned back towards the door at the end of the corridor and continued to advance. The General was right behind him. Bethany was behind the General, regularly looking back to check for threats from behind.

They reached the door. Opened it to access the stairwell. Danny could hear people now on the lower floors. They moved down the stairs, Danny covering the space in front of and below them, Bethany above and behind. The sound of voices grew louder as they descended. Danny knew that as soon as any hotel guests saw him, they'd be thrown into panic, but he wasn't about to lower his weapon. Not with the possibility of Wagner Group operatives round every corner.

They descended from the third floor to the ground floor before they saw anyone. A group of hotel guests in traditional Arabic dress were congregating around the elevator doors at the bottom of the stairs. Five men, three women. It was one of the women who noticed them first, she screamed and grabbed one of the men and suddenly there was a panicked hubbub and Bethany was shouting at them to get on the ground. Danny blocked that activity from his senses. He knew the people at the lift were not an immediate, active threat.

The immediate, active threat was straight ahead of him.

The Russian guy with the Tom Selleck moustache was approaching from the entrance to the bar. Distance: ten metres. Unlike the sandy-haired guy, he had no visible weapon, though he may have had a concealed carry. Danny had a decision and not much time to make it. Should he fire? The retort of the weapon would be audible across the ground floor of the hotel. It would potentially alert any further Wagner Group operatives to a fire-fight, not to mention the American soldiers in the building. Quieter to put him down manually. But slower.

Decision made. He upped his pace and bore down on the target. Within two paces he could see that his guy was reaching for a weapon. His right hand plunged beneath his jacket, feeling for whatever was concealed there. But Danny knew it would take him a minimum of two seconds to aim and fire. By that time, it would be too late. He braced himself as he ran towards the target and made contact just as the body of his firearm peeped out from under his jacket. There was a brutal thump as he collided with the Russian. As their bodies impacted, Danny wrapped his left arm around the man's neck. He squeezed hard and jerked his forearm upwards and back. There was a stressed clicking sound as his neck broke. His body went limp and Danny eased him to the ground. The woman by the lift screamed again. Like the others she was now face down on the ground, but the noise she was making was a problem. Bethany was standing over her, weapon engaged. She gave Danny a 'shall I?' look and for a moment Danny considered it. Her weapon was suppressed, and the woman could be silenced without immediate consequences. But he shook his head. The Wagner Group was one thing. Innocent hotel guests? That was another. Not to mention that the more bodies they left behind them, the tougher it would be for them to get the hell out of Amman. '*Move!*' he barked at Bethany and the General. '*Now!*'

They didn't have time to take even a single step. Three figures emerged from the bar area. Camouflage gear. Weapons. American soldiers. They took one look at Danny, Bethany, their firearms and the prone Russian, and they reached for their guns.

Two things happened. Danny and Bethany got there first, raising their weapons before the soldiers were able to engage, and held them at gunpoint. And the General roared a command: 'Hold your fire! That's an order!'

The soldiers hesitated, giving each other sidelong glances. They clearly weren't sure if the order was intended for them or for Danny and Bethany. One guy in particular, with a pockmarked face and a monobrow, looked especially twitchy. Danny kept his focus on him as the General strode up to the men. 'They're with me,' the General said. 'You need to get us out of the hotel immediately. You have my authorisation to engage anybody you see with a weapon. Go.'

Fair play to the soldiers: they didn't fuck around. They immediately surrounded the General and started hustling him into the bar area. Danny and Bethany were not their concern and they paid them no attention. They followed behind. Danny kept his weapon engaged, scanning the bar as they moved swiftly through it. Guests were returning now that the fire alarm was silenced. Mostly they were talking animatedly to each other. When they saw the armed soldiers hurrying the General across the room, and Danny and Bethany following with their weapons in plain view, they tugged at each other's arms and pointed. Awareness quickly spread. A path cleared as other guests hurried away from the armed personnel. Danny distantly heard the woman by the lift screaming again, but he zoned it out and concentrated on the people around him. He was searching for threats, suspicious activity, sudden movements, anything that triggered his finely tuned sense of hostile action.

So far, nothing. Maybe sandy-hair and Tom Selleck were the only Wagner Group operatives on site.

They burst into the main foyer where the exhibition boards were still erected. It was much busier than before. Guests were pouring in from the outside. American soldiers, the guys tasked to guard the entrance, were freaking out, shouting orders and trying to herd people into groups so they could be searched. Hotel staff were patiently trying to encourage people back to their rooms now the fire alarm had stopped. Incongruously, the cocktail piano music had started up again. The General's guys yelled at everyone in their path to make way. The piano player stopped playing. Receptionists retreated from their desks. Somewhere there was the sound of a baby wailing. The other soldiers, when they saw the General surrounded by three of his guys being manoeuvred towards the exit, started shouting at the other guests to get out of their way. Danny moved and scanned, moved and scanned. He had noticed something. An anomaly. His instinct was telling him something wasn't right, but his brain hadn't caught up yet.

Then he saw it. Twenty metres away, at his eleven o'clock, standing by a marble statuette on a burnished wooden plinth, was a man. White skin, deep-set features, greasy slicked-back dark hair, stubble. Russian? Possibly. Ordinarily Danny wouldn't have looked twice at him. But now he did, because unlike almost everybody else in this large, chaotic reception area, he looked entirely calm. And that made him stand out. He wasn't looking at the General, or his guys, or at Danny and Bethany with their handguns. He was looking across at the main entrance, where another man – blonde hair in a severe parting, shirt and tie but no jacket – was standing equally calmly.

Danny knew a set-up when he saw one. They were waiting for the General to get close to them so they could make a hit. He sprinted and put himself in front of the General's guys. One of them shouted at him to move, but he stood firm and pointed over to his three o'clock where, at the far side of the reception, there was a green emergency exit sign. 'That way,' he said.

The General's guys looked like they were going to argue, but O'Brien cut them short. 'Do what he says,' he instructed.

The soldiers probably didn't like the order, but they carried it out. They immediately altered their trajectory and headed towards the second exit. Danny watched the reaction of the two guys he'd clocked. They didn't look so relaxed all of a sudden. The blonde guy with the tie caught Danny's gaze. Something passed between them. The dead-eyed look of two pros acknowledging each other, respecting each other and warning each other. Danny knew he'd just looked at the face of his enemy. He lost sight of him as a crowd of hotel guests obscured his line of sight. He cut his gaze away and, still scanning the room for anomalies and threats, followed the General and his guys to the side exit. Here there were members of the hotel staff: a bell boy, two waiters, a female member of housekeeping. They receded as the General's guys kept yelling at them to move. Two American soldiers in camo were guarding the exit. One look at the situation and they opened the doors, letting in the night air. The General, his three guys, Danny and Bethany burst out of the hotel and into the street. The hot, humid night air hit Danny, a furnace wave after the air-conditioned atmosphere of the hotel. He quickly took in his surroundings. A busy urban street. Solid traffic. Fumes. A blur of light from cafes on the opposite side. People passing along the pavement, unaware of what was going on in the hotel. As soon as they saw the American soldiers, however, they kept their distance or crossed the road.

Danny turned to the General. 'You need to come with us. We'll extract you. Leave your men here.'

'They're good guys,' the General said.

'That's why we need them here.' He turned to the soldiers. 'Twenty seconds time, two men are going to walk through that door. Blonde guy with a tie, dark-haired guy with stubble. They'll probably be Russian and they want to nail the General. They most likely have accomplices. Don't let them get anywhere near us.'

The soldiers looked uncertain. 'Do as he says,' the General told them again. He nodded at Danny.

Danny, Bethany and the General moved away from the hotel's side entrance and crossed the road. Night had fallen. Car head-lamps glowed in the dark. Cars honked angrily when the trio cut in front of them. Danny knew that the sound of the car horns would highlight their position, but it couldn't be helped. If anybody were to fire on them from the hotel exit, the vehicles would act to some extent as a ballistic shield. Plus, they would slow the shooters down.

They reached the opposite side of the road. There were cafes here spilling out on to the pavement. Late-night fruit stalls. A guy selling dates. A few shops boarded up with metal grates. Two Jordanian men, seeing the handguns in Danny and Bethany's fists, shouted out in alarm and fled. Their reaction caused a stir among the other pedestrians, then a panic. Danny blocked it out. He needed to focus on getting the General to their vehicle. The crossroads was a hundred metres up ahead. When they reached it, they needed to turn left to get on to the road where their vehicle was parked. Total distance to the car: about eight hundred metres. He directed Bethany towards the crossroads. As they moved, he looked back across the road at the hotel.

So he saw it all happen.

The two men Danny had clocked in the reception area had emerged from the hotel exit on to the street. The General's three guys had surrounded them, displaying the body language of a hard arrest: weapons raised, standing round the targets in a close semicircle. There was no sign of the other two soldiers inside the hotel who had opened the door for them. The targets had their hands up. They showed no sign of alarm. Their body language was relaxed. The blonde-haired guy was almost smiling as he looked beyond his closest soldier. Danny followed his line of sight and saw two Western men weaving their way across the road towards the hotel, casually dressed in jeans and T-shirts. One of them was much taller and broader than the other. He had a black, buzz-cut mohawk – it looked particularly odd against the civvies – and pronounced scarring on his scalp. His nose looked like it had been recently broken. Pedestrians moved out of his way as he walked.

SAS scum. I killed two of your comrades with my hands. You will be an easy third.

'Turgenev,' Danny whispered. He felt a twinge in his shoulder.

He stopped. Calculated the distances. He was forty metres from the hotel exit. Much too far for an accurate handgun shot. Turgenev and his mate were fifteen metres from the soldiers. Too close for Danny to get to them before it happened. The street was noisy with traffic sounds. The soldiers wouldn't hear him if he shouted.

177

There was nothing he could do. He found himself momentarily frozen as he watched.

The three American soldiers had their backs to Turgenev and his accomplice. It meant that two of them never knew what happened. Turgenev and his companion only revealed their handguns when they were a metre away from the Americans. They raised them so each was pointing at the back of a soldier's head. They fired in unison.

Danny didn't hear the sound of the suppressed weapons above the noise of the street, but he saw the guys go down. They slumped mundanely to the pavement. The remaining soldier started to turn. Did he know what had happened? It hardly mattered. Turgenev nailed him in less than a second.

'Mother*fuckers!*' the General shouted. Danny saw that he and Bethany had stopped and seen the shooting too. He sensed that the General wanted to join the fray. That made two of them. The urge to sprint back across the road to the hotel and deal with the man responsible for so many Regiment deaths was almost overpowering. But he mastered it. He grabbed the General's arm and held him back. The shooting had taken place in full view of pedestrians. They scattered, creating several metres of open ground in the vicinity of the gunmen. The two Russian guys from the hotel pointed across the road directly at Danny and the others. Turgenev turned. He saw Danny immediately and he grinned. Again, Danny fought the urge to return. He saw Turgenev's mate put one sleeve to his mouth. He was obviously speaking on a covert radio. And that meant only one thing: he was communicating with other hostiles.

'There's more of them,' Danny said. 'We need to get to the car now.' Eight hundred metres. They should be able to get there within five minutes.

They ran in the direction of the crossroads, past open-fronted restaurants and a couple of souvenir shops. Danny was fit and fast. Bethany too. The General was older and slower, so they had to move at his pace. Mostly, pedestrians moved out of their way. Some didn't. There were collisions and angry shouts. Danny ignored them all. He blocked out the shock of seeing Turgenev too. He was scanning left and right. Up ahead. His tactical mind making a hundred tiny decisions every second. Of the people around them, who was harmless, who was hostile? These were Wagner Group guys, so he was looking for white skin. Only male? Not necessarily . . .

They reached the crossroads and sprinted left into the street where they'd parked. Distance to the vehicle: six hundred metres. The street was much busier than before. Arabic pop music rang out of cafes. Crowds of young people were congregating on the pavements in the warm night air. There was a smell of grilled lamb and a party atmosphere. It was harder to get through them all. Slower. Tougher to identify threats among all these people. The younger crowd were reluctant to get out of their way. Twenty-something men trying to impress their women were bolshy and shoulder-bargey. Danny moved through them like a bullet through steel, gripping the General, aware of Bethany at his shoulder.

He saw the car up ahead. Distance: thirty-five metres. He upped his pace, his focus now all on the vehicle.

And that was why he missed him.

The shooter was standing in the doorway of an electrical equipment shop on the other side of the road. White skin, brown beard, backwards baseball cap. He had obviously been waiting for them, and Danny only noticed him in his peripheral vision a fraction of a second before he took his shot. He threw himself and the General to the ground at the exact moment that the retort echoed across the street. The bullet missed Danny. It missed the General. But it didn't miss the old Jordanian guy they were passing at the moment. The victim was comfortably in his seventies and wore a cream dishdash. The bullet slammed into his stomach, and a red patch spread instantly across his clothes as he clutched the wound and staggered back. Danny was on the ground. He raised his Sig and aimed. He discharged three shots in quick succession. Each of them found their target and the gunman collapsed in the doorway.

Now there was real panic. Screams. Pedestrians jumping up from cafes and running from the scene. There were fifty or sixty people in their immediate vicinity. Danny hauled the General to his feet. Bethany was already halfway to the car and they sprinted after her. Danny made his gun very visible. It ensured any loitering pedestrians quickly moved out of the way. He half expected more shots, but they reached the vehicle unharmed after a few seconds. It had been boxed in by two other cars. Bethany was standing on the pavement, protected by the body of the car, her arms and weapon stretched out over the roof as she scanned left and right, searching for threats in the direction of Danny and the General. Danny found the car keys and quickly opened up. 'Get in!' he shouted. He pushed the General towards the rear passenger side, then opened the driver's door and threw himself behind the wheel. He stowed his Sig in the door, well out of the General's reach. Bethany took the seat behind him and the three doors slammed shut at the same time. He turned the engine over, revved it hard and knocked it into gear. He sharply nudged the car in front, then reversed into the car behind. Repeated the process twice to shift the vehicles boxing him in. Then, when it was possible to exit the parking space, there was a screech of wheel spin and the vehicle catapulted down the road.

Ordinarily, Danny's strategy would be to manoeuvre a vehicle as safely and calmly as possible. All that Lewis Hamilton shit was for wankers. But right now, he needed speed. There could still be more shooters in the vicinity. A single bullet in a tyre and they'd be in even more trouble than they were now. They were still in the centre of the city and they needed to get out as quickly as possible. One hand on the wheel, he slammed his free fist on the horn to clear the way of the few stray pedestrians ahead of him, then accelerated up through the gears. Average speed down a narrow street like this? Maybe twenty miles per hour. Danny hit fifty and continued to accelerate. In his rear-view mirror he could see the General looking behind them.

'Get down!' Danny shouted. 'Get out of sight!'

The General did as he was told, crouching down in the back seat. Just in time. A bullet hit the rear window. The glass splintered but remained whole. Bethany lowered her sitting position to protect herself. 'Stay down!' Danny shouted, and he kept his foot on the accelerator.

The road bent round to the right. Danny followed it with just the faintest whisper on the brake pedal. Blue emergency lights came into view. A police vehicle, blocking the road at right angles.

Distance: forty metres. He slammed the brakes and pulled a hard left into a side street. The rear tyres lost traction, but he went with it and was back in control in a moment. He heard sirens and knew that the police vehicle was making chase.

'You just killed two men,' the General shouted from the back. 'The police get us, we ain't getting out of Amman this side of Christmas.'

Danny didn't reply. The General was stating the obvious, and anyway, he needed to focus on the road. The side street continued for fifty metres before emerging on to another busy thoroughfare where the traffic, mercifully, was moving. Danny slammed the brakes, then merged more sedately on to the thoroughfare. He was sweating profusely and he could hear Bethany breathing hard. The General sat up. He looked back at the cracked window rather gingerly, then faced forwards again. 'I think you owe me a goddamn explanation,' he said.

'Quiet,' Danny said. With one hand on the wheel he located his phone and dialled in to Hereford.

'*Go ahead.*'

'We have him. We're still in central Amman but we're heading out.' He didn't mention Turgenev.

'*Make for your original drop zone. We're sending in a stealth chopper to pick you up at 04.00 hours. Does that give you enough time?*'

Time check: 20.37 hrs. He estimated they had forty miles to travel, and some of that was off road.

'Roger that.'

He killed the line and dropped the phone into his lap.

'I said,' the General repeated, 'you owe me a goddamn explanation. That crazy bitch was one cut away from killing me.'

'Call me that again, lover boy, and I'll finish the job.'

'Cut it out,' Danny said. He realised he had to choose his next words carefully. The message from Hereford had been cryptic. *Tell him that we know about Poliakov and the deepfakes.* When he'd said it, O'Brien had become immediately compliant. But what the hell did it mean? 'I'm getting you out of Jordan,' he said. 'Right now. But you have to tell me everything about Poliakov.'

'Tough shit, soldier,' the General said. 'That's need to know, and you don't need to know.'

Danny glanced in the rear-view mirror. The General looked like he meant what he said. Through the cracked rear window, he saw the distant glare of flashing blue neon. 'The Amman police are on high alert,' he said. 'Easiest thing in the world for me to pull over right here, wait for them to catch us up.'

'What are you, stupid?'

'I just saved your life, pal, a couple of times over. Don't make the mistake of thinking that means I give a shit about you. We pull over now, I like my chances of getting away better than I like yours.'

'Don't be an idiot.'

'For a guy who had his dick hanging out half an hour ago,' Bethany said, 'he's got a gob on him.'

'Just tell me about Poliakov,' Danny said, changing lanes to get ahead more quickly. 'I can't guarantee your safety, so if you have intel that needs sharing, now's the time to share it.'

A moment of silence. O'Brien frowned. Taciturn. Unsure of himself. He looked back at the neon light. 'Fine,' he said, with great reluctance. 'I'll tell you about Poliakov.'

SEVENTEEN

'Poliakov's an FSB agent, but I guess you know that, right?' The General didn't wait for Danny to confirm or deny. 'He came to me with certain information.'

'Wait,' Danny said. 'He came to you?'

'That's what I said, Einstein. He was blowing the whistle on the Russians. Hard intel about the Kremlin's collusion with the Oval Office. It's hardly a secret that I'm no fan of the President, so he figured I was the guy to approach. He figured right.'

'No,' Danny said. The General was obviously lying. 'I read a transcript of your conversation with Poliakov in Crete. You gave him intel on the movements of the Zero 22 unit in Syria. I read it with my own eyes.'

'You read it wrong. Or you read what somebody *wanted* you to read. Zero 22 was the SAS operation, right? Poliakov told me the Russians were going to ambush it and that they'd had the intel from the White House. I couldn't act on that information. If I had, if I'd warned the British, the Kremlin and the White House would have known there was a leak. Couldn't do it. Poliakov's intel was too big. Had to accept that there'd be some collateral damage.'

'That collateral was my unit mates,' Danny said. It was a task to keep his voice level.

Silence.

'You were on the op that was compromised in Syria?' the General said.

Danny nodded.

'I'm sorry for your loss,' the General said. He spoke the platitude with a bland expression.

'That all you can say?'

'What's your name?' the General asked.

Danny didn't reply.

'I'm a goddamn five-star general in the United States Army. You think I can't find out your name?'

'Danny Black.'

'Okay, Danny Black. In case you didn't notice, I just lost three good men to a couple of Russian hoods. They've got wives and families, too. Not to mention that this psychopathic bitch was a split second away from killing me. So spare me the victim act, huh? Truth is, Poliakov's intel is bigger than all of us. If I had to compromise Zero 22 again, or put my men in the line of fire, I'd do it.'

Danny breathed deeply. Felt the air travel into his lungs and back out again. Forced himself to stay calm because he knew anger was no use to him. 'So what was it?' he said.

'Poliakov's intel?'

'Right.'

'The deepfakes,' the General said, as if that explained everything. Danny glanced at him in the rear-view mirror and saw that he was smiling. 'You don't know about the deepfakes, right? You were just passing on a message from London.'

The bustle of Amman was all around them, but they were on a fast-moving northbound flyover. There was no sign of police and no indication that they were being followed yet Danny couldn't relax. 'The Regiment is picking us up in the desert,' he said. 'Close to the Israeli border. We're going to have half the Jordanian police force looking for us, not to mention the Wagner Group. I'm going to do my best to get you out of here alive, but there's no guarantees. If this intel is so important, you should tell me what it is now, in case you don't make it out.'

'You're a smart guy, Danny Black. I've met a few of you boys from Hereford and I can't say the same for all of them.' He leaned back in his seat, and all of a sudden he was no longer a scared target fleeing from danger. He was the alpha male who had wasted no time hitting on Bethany in the hotel bar. It occurred to Danny that it took a special kind of self-confidence to go from being naked, tied up and humiliated to this. O'Brien was not a guy to let stuff get in his way. He cleared his throat. 'Collusion between the Oval Office and the Kremlin, that's no big story, right? The Russians helped the President get elected in the first place, they encouraged him to withdraw support from NATO and Europe. Sure, we haven't seen a smoking gun, but we all know it's been happening.'

Danny said nothing. He was a soldier, not a politician.

'What we didn't know, what *nobody* knows, at least not publicly, is the extent of it. Our president has developed a taste for power. I guess that when you have more money than you can spend in several lifetimes, your appetites become more rarefied. Fortunately for the United States, the founding fathers predicted just such an eventuality. They wove certain checks and balances into the US constitution. No president of the United States is permitted to serve more than two four-year terms.'

The General obviously liked the sound of his own voice. But he was talking, that was the main thing. Danny kept quiet and let him continue.

'Of course, you tell an autocrat that he's not allowed to do something, you can be pretty certain he'll start trying to find a way to do it, right? Look at that ex-KGB jackal in the Kremlin. The moment his tenure as president comes to an end, he fixes his sights on the post of prime minister and starts increasing the scope of prime ministerial authority. He frames it as the will of the people. It's how tyrants work. Bit by bit, they chip away at the structures intended to prevent the abuse of executive power. Bit by bit, they whip the people up into a frenzy of paranoia. They tell them that their livelihoods and their safety are under threat by external forces. Think Hitler and the Jews. They persuade them that the only solution is more authoritarianism. It's a seductive message. It works. History tells us that the result is never happy.'

'Poliakov,' Danny reminded him.

The General nodded. 'Poliakov's your regular FSB careerist. But when he found out what the Kremlin and the Oval Office were plotting, it was too rich even for his Russian blood. He came to me because he knew I was a vocal critic of the President, and because I might be in a position to do something about it.'

'About what?'

The General pointed at Bethany. 'Can she be trusted?' he said.

Bethany was staring straight ahead. She showed no sign that she was even listening to the General, nor did she react to his question in any way. 'Yeah,' Danny said. A short answer, because the long one was complicated and couldn't be spoken out loud.

'Okay then. This is what I believe to be happening. The Oval Office is planning what I can best describe as a right-wing coup. To do that, the President needs a scapegoat, and the Kremlin is helping him make one. There will be a terror attack. My understanding is that it will take place on the fourth of July. That's an important day for us Americans. Independence Day, right? A terror attack on the fourth of July is like, I don't know, bombing Buckingham Palace on the Queen's birthday. It's an affront to all patriots. And patriots, or at least those who make a song and dance about how damn patriotic they are, they're the President's base. They're the ones who will be most outraged, and most susceptible to what comes next.'

'I don't get it,' Danny said. 'If the Americans know there's going to be an attack, what are they doing to stop it?'

'You're not listening, soldier. They don't want to stop it. They're making it happen. They're actively manipulating known jihadists. Funding them. Planning the whole damn thing. And then, when the outrage is at its highest, and the President has addressed his rallies, and the crowd are baying for Muslim blood, that's when they release the deepfakes.'

'What are the deepfakes?'

'Video footage of the President's political rivals meeting with known terror suspects. He has form, right? Smearing his rivals, any means necessary. But this takes it to the next level. The meetings are fakes. They take totally innocent footage of totally innocent meetings between the President's rivals and ordinary folk, and they map the faces of terror suspects on to the images. It's completely convincing. You wouldn't know the difference. Even the top tech guys analysing the footage wouldn't be able to tell it's a deepfake. So, the Oval Office makes this footage public and the narrative writes itself. The liberals and left-wingers are hopelessly compromised, they'll say. There's an existential threat to the United States, they'll say. It requires a change in the constitution to give the President a firm hand, they'll say. You ever seen one of those goddamn rallies of his? Well I have, and trust me, he whips those people up. They get this idea in their head, they'll never let it go. It'll happen.'

'I don't get where the Russians come in,' Danny said.

'They made the deepfakes.' It was Bethany who spoke, not the General. She was still looking straight ahead and her voice was emotionless. 'When I was working at MI6, we knew about it. They've been on to the potential of deepfake technology for a long time now. It's a natural extension of the way the Kremlin thinks. Fake news, electoral interference, social-media manipulation. We thought they were developing the technology for black-mail purposes. We were wrong.'

'But why the Russians? Why would they be doing this?'

'Isn't it obvious? The President is their puppet. They can't believe their luck. They're pulling the strings of the man in the Oval Office. They want him in there as long as possible.'

'Right,' said the General. 'And if I know the President – which I do, unfortunately – he'll be quite certain this is all his great idea, and completely oblivious to the fact that he's been totally played. And I guess I don't need to tell you what a threat it is to global security to have a Russian stooge in the White House?'

'No,' Danny said. He was thinking of poisonings on the streets of the UK. He was thinking of the horrors he'd seen in Syria. He was thinking of the Wagner Group, and Turgenev. 'You don't have to tell me that.'

They were doing a steady thirty miles per hour along a north-bound dual carriageway. The lights of Amman glowed all around them. The traffic was fluid and the dual carriageway well lit. He checked his mirrors, making a mental note of the cars surround-ing them. Then he said, 'The fragment of conversation between you and Poliakov that ended up with MI6 ...'

'Doctored to fit their narrative,' the General said. 'Look, I don't know what MI6 and Hereford have been told, but the fact they sent you two to assassinate me means they're playing you Brits as if they were the goddamn New York Philharmonic.'

'It means they know you're on to them.'

'Not necessarily. He's got other reasons to want me out of the way.'

'What reasons?'

'You think a coup like this happens by itself? Who does every tinpot dictator in every banana republic need on side before they make a power grab?'

And immediately it became clear. 'The army,' Danny said.

'Right. And you know what? In the US military, the President is pretty popular. Talks the talk, finds the funding, and he's developing a taste for battle. But he's got one big pain in the ass.'

'You?'

'Me. Without my support, it's hard for him to keep the military on side. He'd like to get rid of me, but I'm a tough guy to fire, even for him. He'd face a revolt from the joint chiefs for a start. I've been expecting some dirty tricks to oust me so he can install one of his own in my place. I was on the lookout for it. I didn't expect this.'

'And by making the British complicit in your assassination, it keeps us quiet if we ever find out what's really going on.'

'Like I said, New York Philharmonic. And if you fail to finish the job, the Wagner Group are on site to finish it for you, as you say. Thanks for dealing with those guys, by the way.'

I haven't finished dealing with them, Danny wanted to say, but didn't. Instead, he responded to the General's acknowledgement with a curt 'You're welcome.' He slowed down as they approached a large roundabout. Danny circled it three times, maintaining his vigilance of the vehicles around him, checking for trails. He saw none. He left the roundabout and accelerated back up to thirty. 'So the fourth of July attacks happen and you go on CNN to say the President was behind them,' he said. 'You'll get laughed out of town.'

'Sure. Unless I have evidence.'

'Do you?'

'I have the footage. Before and after. The raw material and the deepfake. Look at it side by side, nobody's going to be in any doubt about what's going on.'

'So you do what? Let the attacks happen? Let the President release the deepfakes and then out him?' He couldn't hide the distaste in his voice. 'More collateral?'

'No,' the General said. 'Military targets are one thing. Civilian targets, that's a whole other can of worms.'

'So what's your tactic?'

'A pre-emptive strike. I release the footage in advance. Use whatever weight my name and authority carry to accuse the President of planning a coup.'

'But nobody's going to believe you,' Danny said. 'The President will deny it. Straight out. It'll give him an excuse to remove you from office. You'll be totally discredited.'

'Discredited? I'll be more than discredited. I'll be a laughing stock. Paranoid. A fantasist. It'll be the end of my career. But it'll stop him doing it, right? Guy can hardly deny the whole thing and then go through with it. And deep down, the man's a coward. Trust me. I've sat in a room with him. Looked him in the eye. He's a draft dodger. Spends his life blaming other people for his own mistakes. If he knows someone's on to him, perhaps he'll think twice before trying something like this again.'

They drove in silence for a minute.

'I don't believe you,' Bethany said.

'Well, sweetheart, I guess I'll have to learn to live with it. I believe your guy here has his orders to extract me from Amman, so I suggest we—'

'Why wait?' Bethany interrupted him. 'If you know the President's been trying to oust you, why haven't you released the footage already, while you're still in office?'

'Isn't that obvious?'

'Not to me.'

'The peace conference,' Danny said.

'It's a big deal,' the General said. 'The Turks and the Kurds keep knocking chunks out of each other, it destabilises the whole region.'

'It's destabilised anyway,' Danny said.

'Right. So any chance we have of calming tensions goes to the dogs if these peace talks fail. Like it or not, I can bring the warring factions to the table. I know the decision makers. I can appeal to their better natures. End of the day, peace doesn't happen through military action. It happens round the table. It happens with hand-shakes, not mortars. You just need to get the right guys in the room. Better or worse, I'm one of those guys.' The General looked out of the side window. 'Well,' he said, 'I *was* one of those guys. I guess they're on their own now.'

There was silence as they drove on.

'It's what the Russians want,' Danny said.

'Huh?' the General replied. His thoughts had obviously been elsewhere.

'The Russians have been supporting the Syrian regime. The Syrians want the Kurds out of the way. So destabilising the peace process by taking you out – it's what the Russians want.'

'Oh sure,' the General said. 'Two birds, one stone. The President gets to put in a puppet to control the army, the Russians get to control the conflict in the Middle East. Lot of good reasons for sending a hot chick with a razor blade into my hotel room. Doesn't mean they know I'm on to them about the deepfakes.'

'Where's the footage?' Danny said. 'Have you uploaded it somewhere?'

'I guess there's a reason you're a soldier and not a software engineer,' the General said.

'What are you talking about?'

'He can't store it on the cloud,' Bethany said. 'Not something like this. The FSB, the NSA, they'd be all over it.'

'Your little lady's right,' said the General. 'Only time to put that material on the internet is when I want to make it public. And that has to be at a time of my own choosing. Poliakov gave me the footage on a memory stick, and that's where it stays. I don't transfer it to any computer or any device connected to the internet.'

'So where's the memory stick?' Danny asked.

The General didn't reply.

'You're going to have to tell us sometime,' Danny said. 'Sooner or later. You know we'll get it out of you if you don't.'

'You threatening me, soldier?'

Danny didn't reply. Another silence filled the car.

'It's back in DC,' the General said finally. 'Safe.'

'Where in DC?'

'You're persistent, Black,' the General said. 'I like that in a soldier. But you might as well stop asking me that question. It's somewhere safe is all I'm saying. And before you make any more veiled threats of enhanced interrogation, remember that as soon as you deliver me up to your superiors, this ceases to be your problem. I'm still a five-star American general, and right now your bosses are working out how to stab each other in the back and shift the blame for ordering an assassination attempt on me. They're not going to make a bad situation worse.'

Danny thought of Sturrock and he knew the General was right.

An overhead road sign directed them towards various suburbs of Amman, including As-Salt, which told him that they were heading in the right direction: north-west. Time check: 20.58 hrs. Seven hours till they needed to be at the pick-up point, which Danny estimated was still thirty miles away. There were tenement blocks on either side of them, but the road ahead was clear, and he had just increased his speed from thirty to forty when it happened.

The vehicle was a BMW X5. It had been on Danny's shoulder in the other lane of the dual carriageway for no longer than thirty seconds. But in that moment, every instinct he possessed shrieked at him. Everything was wrong. The X5 was accelerating up the inside. Its windows were tinted and, as it sped up, the rear passenger window was sliding down. '*Duck!*' Danny shouted. '*Now!*'

Both Bethany and the General reacted quickly. Bethany slumped in her seat. The General crouched. Danny had only a fraction of a second to strategise. He could accelerate further, but the X5 was the faster vehicle and would surely catch them up. Better to slam the brakes. Force the X5 to overtake at the moment of Danny's choosing. It would put them momentarily and unexpectedly in the line of fire as the two cars came alongside each other again, but the shooter would be disorientated and the shot would be almost impossible. Danny checked his rear-view mirror. The car behind – a white hatchback, no indication that it was hostile – was twenty-five metres away. He allowed the X5 to creep closer in the adjacent lane. Its nose was in line with the back of his vehicle. In his wing mirror, he could just see the muzzle of firearm protruding half an inch from the open window, preparing to take the shot when they came alongside.

He hit the brakes hard. The tyres screeched on the road and the handling became loose. The X5 whizzed past. Danny caught sight of the shooter: shaved head, leathery skin. Not Arab. More than likely a Wagner Group Russian. He had a long-barrelled pistol, suppressed. Then he was out of sight ahead of them and all Danny could see was the firearm protruding from the rear passenger window. A muzzle flash as it fired, too late, across the road.

There was the sudden, urgent sound of a horn increasing in volume from behind. The white hatchback was closing in fast. He yanked the steering wheel to position the vehicle into the other lane, behind the X5. The white hatchback shot past, its horn still blaring. The X5's brake lights lit up. The distance between the two vehicles quickly closed from fifteen metres to five. The shooter was leaning out of his window, now aiming backwards towards Danny's vehicle, weapon raised, ready to take a shot directly at the windscreen.

There was an exit up ahead. Thirty metres. Danny yanked the steering wheel again, manoeuvring his vehicle to the exit. He saw another muzzle flash in his peripheral vision and this time the pistol's bullet was not harmless. It slammed into the windscreen of another small car that had innocently found itself behind the X5. As Danny accelerated towards the exit, he saw the windscreen shatter. The small car veered sideways and collided with another vehicle. A third car smashed into the back. A pile-up was happening on the dual carriageway behind them, but Danny couldn't focus on that. The driver of the X5 had realised that Danny was making for the exit. He was swerving too, heading for the same exit. But he was too far ahead. He couldn't cross the traffic to make the exit in time. Danny could. As he left the dual carriageway, he half-watched the X5 speed out of sight, away from the pile-up. Then the exit road twisted round to the left and Danny had to brake heavily to avoid a collision of his own with another vehicle in front.

'What the hell?' the General shouted. 'Won't you keep a handle on this goddamn vehicle?'

Danny didn't answer immediately. His ears were filled with more horns sounding at him as he brought the vehicle back down to a safe speed while checking ahead, back, behind for any more threats. They were on a much narrower road now, which was winding uphill into one of the busy districts on the outskirts of Amman. They were heading south-west, which took them in the opposite direction to their route out of the city centre towards the RV point. Sweat was collecting in the nape of Danny's neck. His mouth was dry. He inhaled deeply to bring down his pulse, forced himself to think rationally. Only then did he speak.

'They know which vehicle we're in,' he said. 'They're tracking us somehow.'

'A tracking device on the car,' said Bethany. She sounded a damn sight calmer than the General.

'It's possible. Even if there isn't, they know our registration number. We can't guarantee they don't have contacts in the Amman police.'

'What do we do?' Bethany said.

'We need a different car,' Danny said. 'And we need it now.'

EIGHTEEN

Cincinnati, Ohio. 13.30 hrs, Eastern Standard Time

Hamoud and his family were not used to airports.

They stood close to each other as if for protection. Almost touching, but not quite. Even Melissa was quiet. They had a single shabby suitcase between them, the only one they owned. Rabia had carefully packed it with the family's clothes, old but clean and neatly pressed. They each wore more layers of clothing than they really needed, to save space. Hamoud himself had eschewed the robe he normally wore to prevent his scars hurting, in favour of three tops and a jacket. They were all too large for his bony frame, as were his jeans. He would be much too hot when they arrived in Orlando, but the concourse here at Cincinnati Airport was air-conditioned and he was so thin that he sometimes found it difficult to keep warm. For now, he was glad of the extra layers.

He carried the suitcase in one hand and the FedEx package in the other, gripping both of them tightly as if somebody might rip them from him. Crowds bustled past the family, swerving round them and making no attempt to avoid staring at Hamoud's gruesome facial scar, as they stood gazing up at the departure screens. The 15.25 flight to Orlando was there, sandwiched between flights to Los Angeles LAX and New York JFK. 'We need to go to the check-in area,' said Rabia. 'Come on, children. Stay close.'

There was a line to check in. Maybe twenty or thirty people. It took half an hour to reach the desk, but it felt longer than that. Anxiety burned in Hamoud's chest. Surely they would be turned away. Or worse. The lady at the check-in desk looked kind, but would she call for security when she realised Hamoud and his family were trying to board a flight under false pretences?

Hamoud was understandably nervous of men in uniform. Each time he saw one of the airport security guys, with their peaked caps and their weapons on display, he suppressed a shiver. He had to stop his mind flashing back to the prison camp. He had to look at his wife and children, to remind himself that everything was much better now.

There was a tremor in his hand as he gave the lady the documents. She didn't seem to notice. 'Where are we travelling to today, sir?' she asked.

'Orlando,' Hamoud said. He had to repeat himself because the word stuck in his throat first time round. '*Orlando.*'

She was silent as she checked the documentation. Hamoud scratched his palms hard. His children were either side of him, looking up at the desk, wide-eyed. He realised they were nervous too. Nervous that this was all a mistake, and their trip wasn't really going to happen. The woman kept looking up from the documents to glance at Hamoud, and he knew she was looking at the scar on his face. Then she smiled at the children, and it was as if the whole family exhaled at the same time. Hamoud lifted the suitcase on to the conveyor belt to be weighed. Rabia took the boarding passes and gave the children a grin and a thumbs up, and they were clearly so excited Hamoud thought they might hyperventilate. And as they walked away from the desk, asking their mum a thousand questions about where the airplane was and how long it would take to get there and if they would be allowed on all the rides or just some of them, Hamoud felt a little lighter. As they walked towards security, he listened to the children's chatter and Rabia's patient responses, and it all felt real.

Then something made him stop. The security area was very busy. There were more lines at the luggage and body scanners. Airport staff were shouting instructions over the crowd. Belts and shoes off. Tablets and laptops out. A man in a suit stood at the far end of the scanners. He appeared official, but he wasn't shouting like the other members of staff. He was looking across the security area directly – or so it seemed – at Hamoud and his family. Hamoud caught his eye and inclined his head. Then a large African woman in a colourful headdress stepped in the way and Hamoud couldn't see him any more. When the woman moved on, the man in the suit had gone. Hamoud searched for him, but there was no sign.

Rabia touched his arm tenderly. She gave him that enquiring expression that he knew meant 'are you okay?' He smiled and nodded. He was okay. Everything was fine. He took his son's little hand and together they walked to the body scanner.

Finding a car would be easy. Finding the *right* car? That was a different matter altogether.

Danny ditched the Passat in a dark, quiet alley. On either side were the back entrances to restaurants, cafes and shops. Bins overflowing with rubbish. 'What about our suitcases?' Bethany said.

It was true. Danny was still in his suit, Bethany in her jacket and skirt. But this wasn't the time or place to change, and they could hardly move quickly and carry their cases at the same time. 'We'll leave them,' he said, even though leaving such evidence of their presence breached just about every standard operating procedure Danny could think of for a covert op like this. Question of priorities. If they were being tracked, they had to move fast.

'What do we do?' the General said. 'Rent something?'

Danny gave him an incredulous look. 'You've been a General too long,' he said.

'Then—'

'We steal something. But not just anything. The driver needs to be in it so that we can get the keys. And it needs to be something run down.'

'Crap,' the General said. 'If we're going to take a vehicle, we'll take something modern and reliable that we can count on to get us the extraction point.'

Danny shook his head. 'The better the car, the richer the owner. The richer the owner, the more likely the police are to take him seriously.' He opened up the boot of the Passat and located his night sight, which he stowed in his shoulder bag along with the Sig. He turned to Bethany and the General.

'Hold hands,' he said. 'Look like a couple. It'll stop people interfering with you. Follow me at a distance of about twenty metres. I need to be able to see you every time I look back. Stop if I stop.' He pointed at some litter in the gutter and some Arabic graffiti scrawled on a nearby wall. 'Looks like we're entering a rough area. Keep your heads down, don't make eye contact with anybody, don't get into any arguments. We don't want anyone to remember us.'

If Bethany and the General felt patronised by his comments, they didn't show it. But the General did look uncomfortable, and Danny guessed he wasn't relishing the idea of holding hands with the woman who'd been seconds away from slaughtering him like a pig earlier that evening. It was Bethany who made the first move, grabbing his hand in hers. It occurred to Danny that as foreigners they would attract attention despite presenting as a couple, and that maybe he should leave them here, in this deserted street, while he found them a new vehicle. Not an option. The operation had been turned on its head. The General's safety was his responsibility now. And he wanted to keep Bethany White close at hand. He cleared his mind and focused on his strategy for the next couple of hours. They had to get out of this Amman suburb and return to the drop zone in the desert – the sooner they got out of country, the better.

'Let's move,' he said.

They walked to the end of the side street and took a left into a much busier road. It was narrow and cobbled and on a steep hill. Danny was right about this being a rough area. There was nothing overt, but the signs were all there. Groups of young Jordanian men in Western clothes, congregating outside grotty bars. Music seeping from third-floor windows, flung wide open against the heat of the night. Shops closed up with sturdy metal grates. The stench of drains.

There was traffic, too. A constant line of cars crawling up the hill in the darkness. Danny's sense of direction told him that this route was still heading south-west–north-east. He suppressed a moment of anxiety at the need to get back on to the main north-westerly route out of town. It was important that they lost the Wagner Group trail, otherwise they'd be leading them directly to the RV point.

Exhaust fumes were thick in the air. Appropriating one of these vehicles on the main road through this suburb was out of the question. There were too many people around to see it happen.

He considered looking for a taxi and getting the driver to take them to a deserted area before overcoming him and stealing his car. Bad move. Vehicles for hire could routinely have tracking devices fitted. They wouldn't know until they saw the Jordanian authorities bearing down on them. No, he needed a private car, nothing fancy, just like he'd told the General.

He checked behind him. Bethany and O'Brien were following. Danny himself was drawing attention from passers-by. In this district his suit marked him out. He took care not to catch anybody's eye. A misinterpreted glance could easily lead to trouble. He couldn't quite be the grey man, dressed like this. But he could at least be monochrome.

Danny had been walking for a couple of minutes when he spotted an opportunity. Up ahead, a young man was leaving a bar. There were two things that made Danny notice him. The first was the set of car keys in his hands. The second thing was his gait. He was having a little difficulty walking in a straight line. He'd been drinking. Danny felt a moment of gratitude that alcohol was not frowned upon in Jordan to the same extent as in some other Muslim countries. He locked on to him like a guided missile. He was the perfect target: a driver, easy to overcome and unlikely to go to the police, at least until he'd sobered up. By which time Danny and the others would be in a stealth chopper out of here.

He had to slow his pace to keep an unremarkable distance from his target, who was still weaving erratically as he walked. When the guy turned into a side street, Danny loitered for a few seconds at the corner. He watched his target stop to take a piss against a closed-up shop before continuing along the street and stopping by a parked vehicle. Danny couldn't see what type of car it was at first, because his view was blocked by another vehicle parked in front of it. He upped his pace, striding over the stream of urine that trickled down into the gutter. He checked once to see that Bethany and the General had appeared at the street corner and were waiting there for a moment, just as he had. The guy was fumbling with his keys and seemed completely unaware of Danny as he approached. Danny could smell the booze on him from a good three metres away. He instinctively sized the guy up. He was five inches shorter than Danny, for a start. He was wearing Western clothes. The loose material of his badly fitting leather jacket told Danny that he had a light frame, was unlikely to be strong. Danny bore the guy no ill will. He just happened to be in the wrong place at the wrong time. He didn't want to hurt him, but he did need to put him out of action for a while.

He checked his surroundings. Other than Bethany and the General, Danny and his target were the only people in the street. He approached him from behind and, before the target even knew what was happening, wrapped his right arm around his neck and covered his mouth with his left.

The secret was to asphyxiate him sufficiently that he passed out, but not so much that he would suffer any long-term consequences. It meant waiting for the precise moment that his body went limp, then releasing. He struggled, of course. A flailing of the arms. A writhing of the body. But he was entirely helpless against Danny's strength and skill and he soon passed out and dropped the car keys on to the ground. Danny allowed the body to relax into his grip. He held the guy under both arms and dragged him away from the car to a nearby doorway. Danny sat the guy down so that he slumped into it. Just a drunk, sleeping it off. At least, that's what any passer-by would see.

He picked up the car keys and turned to signal to Bethany and the General that they should approach, but they were already halfway up the street. They'd dropped the pretence of being a couple and were no longer holding hands, but striding purposefully in Danny's direction. Danny opened up the vehicle – it was a yellow Nissan, maybe ten years old – and took the wheel. The interior stank of stale tobacco. The windscreen was grimy with dust. That suited them well. He turned the engine over and checked the fuel gauge. It was three quarters full. Enough, he hoped, if they had a straight run.

Bethany took the passenger seat. The General sat in the back. It was a smaller car than the Passat and the General looked correspondingly larger in the rear-view mirror. Danny retrieved the GPS unit from his shoulder bag, switched it on and set it to direct them to the drop zone. He handed it to Bethany behind him. 'Guide me,' he said. He placed his Sig in the door and then pulled out into the road. He glanced at the drunk guy still out in the doorway but put him from his mind. It would be a while before he raised the alarm, and longer before anybody acted on it.

'Left at the end of the road,' Bethany said. He accelerated. It felt good to be in an anonymous car. Untracked. Unmarked. He knew not to let his guard down, but the worst of the job was probably behind him.

They drove in silence, punctuated only by Bethany's directions as she read them off the GPS. It took them through back streets of Amman that Danny would never have navigated without help. He was glad of Bethany's calm co-piloting. It meant he could concentrate on his driving and his situational awareness. Not that it proved necessary. There were no trails. No SUV with hidden gunmen pulling up alongside and taking shots. It was an ordinary, uneventful journey up and down the hilly urban terrain of Amman. And so Danny allowed a corner of his mind to wander, to consider everything the General had said. If he was right, and was telling the truth, it meant Danny now found himself at the centre of a global conspiracy that led all the way to the Oval Office and the Kremlin. A foolish American president plotting an atrocity on his own people in order to justify a power grab, and all this orchestrated and masterminded by the Russians. Danny was no politician. He was just a soldier who did as he was ordered, most of the time. But this sickened him. It also made him wary. Knowledge like this was dangerous. Powerful men would kill to keep it secret. He glanced at the General, who was looking thoughtfully out of the window at the passing street scenes. The conspirators wanted him dead because of who he was and not because of what he knew. Just imagine the energy they would put into assassinating him if they realised he was on to them.

The same went for Danny, of course. To the Oval Office and the Kremlin, an SAS grunt was a thousand times more expendable than a five-star general. They'd kill him without thinking. And as for Bethany. He glanced at her beautiful face as he drove. She was incredibly calm, given everything that had happened. But for her to have this knowledge would make MI6 even more determined that she should be silenced permanently, for fear that she would use it as leverage. Had Bethany worked that out? She knew how the security services thought and operated. If she shared any of Danny's intuition, however, she was hiding it well. Not for the first time, he felt a certain grudging respect for her. He would still do what he was told, when the time was right. But his enthusiasm for that particular part of the job was waning fast.

It took an hour for the urban sprawl of the city to subside. They found themselves on a straight motorway, clusters of buildings here and there on either side, moderately busy traffic in either direction. Danny settled into the slow lane: sedate, unremarkable driving. 'We follow this for about forty miles,' Bethany said. 'Then we have to go off-road. You think the car's up to it?'

'It's going to have to be,' Danny said. 'We'll make it.'

As he spoke, he was checking the vehicle behind him in the rear-view mirror. He couldn't discern its make or colour because its headlamps were bright, but he could see that it was starting to overtake.

Rapidly.

It drew up alongside the Nissan. Its passenger window was open. The man in the passenger seat looked too big for the car. He had a buzz-cut mohawk. Turgenev. His scarred scalp was sweating and he was looking directly at Danny with that gloating grin.

And then, quite suddenly, Turgenev's vehicle veered into Danny's.

It was just a nudge, but the other vehicle was larger and the momentum was such that Danny momentarily lost control. The Nissan screeched to the side of the road, the steering wheel spinning through his hands. 'What the *fuck* . . .' he hissed, as he gripped the wheel again and drove into the skid just in time to regain control of the vehicle and bring it back into the lane. 'Did you see him?' the General shouted. 'It was the asshole who wasted my guys!'

'He's done a lot more than that,' Danny growled. Turgenev's vehicle was twenty metres in front, but its brake lights were on and the gap was closing. Danny couldn't work it out. They'd switched cars. How could anybody still be on to them?

And then, just as Turgenev was alongside them again, he realised what was happening, and he cursed his own stupidity. 'They're going to hit us again!' Bethany shouted. All her calmness had deserted her and there was real panic in her voice. Danny maintained his speed, staying level with the other car, holding his nerve. If he was going to avoid a collision, he had to time it just right.

Just right.

He accelerated. Turgenev's car did the same in order to keep level. He accelerated some more. Same deal. The cars behind them were hanging back, clearly aware that something dangerous was going on. That suited Danny just fine. He needed the space. He accelerated a third time. Waited for Turgenev's driver to catch up. And then he waited for it to swerve. He could see that Bethany's knuckles were white as she gripped the GPS unit.

Hold it.

Hold it.

The vehicle closed in. Danny waited until the two cars were separated by barely a metre. Then he hit the brakes. The Nissan slowed. Turgenev's vehicle shot ahead and swerved into Danny's lane. But the resistance it was expecting from the Nissan wasn't there. It overshot the lane and careered into the hard-baked terrain at the side of the road. Danny knew the driver had lost control when he saw the wheels on one side of the vehicle rise from the ground as the Nissan sped past them. In his rear-view, he saw the car roll. It landed on its roof and slid ten metres across the ground away from the road. Then it spun and its momentum righted it again, but pointing in the wrong direction. Smoke was belching from its engine. Danny reckoned the vehicle was out of action.

'How did they know where we were?' Bethany demanded. 'What the hell's happening?'

Danny didn't answer. He was looking for a place to stop by the side of the road where there would be some cover. There was something he had to do, and he only had a few minutes to do it before his pursuers caught up with him again. He saw a suitable location soon enough: an abandoned petrol station, run down and boarded up, no sign of any pumps. He manoeuvred off the road and brought the vehicle to a halt behind the main building, where weeds and debris littered the ground, the kind of place most sensible people would avoid. He killed the engine. Killed the lights. Grabbed his Sig and jumped out of the car. Opened the rear passenger door and pointed the Sig at the General. 'Get out,' he said.

'What the hell—'

'*Get out, now!*'

The General hesitated for a second then did as he was told. 'I don't know what you think you're—'

'Take your clothes off.'

'You're insane.'

'Do it now.' Bethany had also exited the Nissan and was staring at Danny, a questioning look in her eyes.

Danny ignored her. '*Now!*' he repeated.

The General started with his sports jacket. As he wormed his body out of it, Danny took the jacket and felt inside the pockets. There was an asthma inhaler and a wallet. He removed the canister from the inhaler and checked the plastic casing. Nothing. He looked through the wallet. Several credit cards, some American dollars. Nothing else. He dropped the jacket on to the ground and indicated with a wave of his Sig that the General should remove his pink shirt. He scowled at Danny as he unfastened the buttons and handed it over. The shirt was crumpled and sweaty. It smelled bad. It was not the crisp, clean article of clothing he had been wearing when he entered the hotel bar six hours earlier. Danny checked the breast pocket and the hem. Nothing. He dumped the shirt with the sports jacket. 'Trousers,' he said.

Wordlessly, the General kicked off his brown brogues. They were still shiny. He removed his trousers and handed them over. Danny checked them: pockets, lining, hem, belt buckle. Nothing. The trousers joined the rest of the General's clothes pile. O'Brien was standing in his socks and underpants – the same ones that Bethany had stuffed in his mouth – and his humiliation was plain to see in his face. Danny was about to tell him to strip completely when he remembered the brown brogues. He pocketed the Sig then bent down to pick them up. They smelled of boot polish and foot odour and were warm and moist inside. Danny removed the inner sole from the right shoe. Nothing. The inner sole from the left.

There it was.

The tracking device was no bigger than a mobile phone sim card, but thicker. It was stuck into a recess in the sole of the shoe.

Danny picked it off with his nail and held it up. 'It wasn't the car they were tracking,' he said. 'It was you.'

'How the hell did they plant that thing on me?' the General said.

'I don't know. Doesn't matter now. Get dressed.'

Bethany walked towards Danny. The General was scrambling to get his clothes back on, seemingly embarrassed to be seen by her. But she showed no sign of interest in the older man. She was interested in the tracking device. 'Destroy it,' she said. 'Or just leave it here on the ground. They won't be able to track us then.'

'Yeah,' Danny said. She was right. No tracking device, no trails. He dropped it on the ground and prepared to grind it with his heel.

But then he stopped.

He looked back along the road. He could just see the head-lamps of Turgenev's car blazing into the darkness a couple of hundred metres away. He squinted. There was no doubt about it. A figure was standing in front of the burning car. Even at this distance, Danny could tell that he was taller and broader than the average man. 'Turgenev,' he muttered.

'The guy with the mohawk?' the General said.

'Yeah,' Danny replied. 'The guy with the mohawk.'

He thought of the Zero 22 operation. Of Bullethead and Chinese Mike. Of Dougie and his daughter. He remembered the ambush and the air strike and the burned and butchered bodies littering the blast site. The carnage that Turgenev had orches-trated. He thought of their fight, and of Turgenev's promise to kill Danny with his bare hands. He thought of the two SAS patches he had on his jacket, and of Turgenev holding the heads of decap-itated SAS men.

Danny Black was a Regiment man. It was in his blood. And from his very first day in Hereford, one rule had been instilled in him: there are consequences to killing SAS men.

Two hundred metres, he thought. I could deal with him now.

It wasn't an option. Turgenev was likely to be armed and would see him coming. Not to mention that the police would likely be on the scene at any moment, as well as any Wagner Group backup.

If Danny wanted to deal with that mohawk-headed fucker, he'd have to think a bit smarter.

He checked his watch. 22.59 hrs. The stealth chopper would be at the pick-up point at 04.00. That gave him five hours. He consulted the geography of the area in his head. Their current location. The drop zone forty miles to the north-west of Amman. The location of the ruins where they'd hidden the smuggler's lorry. If he was to go back there, it would involve a ten-mile detour to the south. He had enough time, just.

He bent down again and picked up the tracking device.

'Get dressed,' he told the General. 'And get back into the car.'

NINETEEN

It was a short hop from Cincinnati to Orlando. The children had squealed at take-off and landing, and had been almost unreasonably excited when the kind air stewardess had handed them a complimentary Coke from the drinks trolley. Rabia did not ordinarily allow them to drink soda, but today she did so with an indulgent smile. It was almost enough to make Hamoud forget about the unpleasant stares he and his family had received from some of the passengers on this Delta flight. There was something about airplanes in America that made those stares more aggressive. It was probably a 9/11 thing, Hamoud supposed. At least, and as far as he was aware, none of the other passengers had demanded that his family leave the plane before take-off. He had heard of that happening.

When they arrived in Orlando, the children's excitement was irrepressible. Even Malick, who was normally so quiet. Almost every poster at the airport showed an image of the Cinderella Castle, or thrill-seeking kids on a rollercoaster, or Mickey Mouse. Malick and Melissa pointed at every single one. Hamoud and Rabia gently ushered them along the corridors of the airport towards the exit, through the crowds and out into the departure area.

A man was waiting for them here. He wore smart clothes – a blazer and dark trousers – and he held up a blackboard with the name 'Hamoud Al Asmar' clearly written in white chalk.

Hamoud stopped. The man's face was familiar. He tried to place it, but it eluded him.

'Hamoud, are you alright?' His wife and children had gone on ahead for several metres before realising that Hamoud was not with them. They had turned back and rejoined him. 'Hamoud, what is the matter?'

Hamoud smiled. 'Nothing, my love,' he said, and he tousled his son's hair as the little boy stared up at him. 'Look, there's our transfer.'

Rabia preened herself. They would never take a car service in the ordinary course of events. 'It's like being the President of the United States,' she told her children rather grandly. 'Come along!'

They made themselves known to the driver, who was very polite. He offered to take their bag for them but Hamoud declined. He wasn't used to such service and it made him uncomfortable. The driver led them out into the hammer-blow heat of a Florida summer. Hamoud felt a bead of sweat dripping precisely along the vertical scar on his face. They headed into the parking lot where the driver's minivan was parked. 'Make yourself comfortable folks,' he said as he slid the door open for them. There were two rows of seats in the back of the minivan. The children took the back row to themselves – another thrill for them – while Hamoud and his wife took the front row. It was pleasantly cool in the air-conditioned van, and a country music station played softly as they exited the parking lot and headed away from the airport.

But Hamoud couldn't relax. He could see the driver's face in the rear-view mirror and was even more certain now that he recognised him. He thought hard. The harder he thought, the more the man's identity slipped from him. Relax, he told himself. Try to forget about it. If you're not thinking so hard, maybe it will come.

'We're nearly there, children,' he said. The kids squealed with joy and Rabia laughed fondly to hear it.

And it was as she laughed that it came to him. He hadn't been able to place the face because he'd only seen it for a split second earlier that day, watching Hamoud from a distance as he and his family passed through security at Cincinnati. He felt a twist of anxiety in his gut. What could this mean? Were they being followed? Did this man mean them harm? He didn't *seem* harmful. He was driving calmly at fifty miles per hour, eyes forward, paying no interest to Hamoud and his family.

It was paranoia, he told himself. Nothing more. It couldn't be the same person. Why would an Orlando transfer driver be loitering in the security area of Cincinnati airport? He wouldn't. Hamoud was mistaken. It was as simple as that. He was being foolish. He wasn't well in his mind. He had to remember that, for his own good and for the good of his family.

He held his wife's hand and tenderly squeezed it. They were going to enjoy their holiday, and his confused thoughts were not going to get in the way.

'This is fucking insane,' the General growled. 'You were one of my guys, I'd have you court-martialled.'

Danny said nothing.

'You should throw that goddamn tracker out of the window,' the General said. 'Any one of these vehicles.' He pointed vaguely out of the Nissan's windows to indicate the other cars on the motorway. 'Any of them could be one of these Wagner Group nut jobs. You want them to try to take us off the goddamn road again?'

'They can try,' Danny said.

Bethany kept quiet. Danny guessed she was conflicted. Like the General, she no doubt wanted to get to the pick-up point as quickly and as safely as possible. She was surely thinking about her kid, and getting home to him as quickly as she could. But at the same time, if anybody understood the desire for revenge, it was her. She had killed for it in the past. Risked everything for it. Bethany White most certainly understood how Danny was feeling.

The traffic was thinning out. They were heading west, back towards the Israeli border. Desert terrain faded into the night on either side of them. Danny had reset the GPS unit to guide them back to the Roman ruins where they'd met their fixer and left the smuggler's lorry. It would mean, any minute now, going off road and heading across the desert. The Nissan was hardly the ideal vehicle for such a journey. Danny didn't care. It would do. He would make it work.

'It's insane!' the General said again.

'You want me to leave you by the side of the road, say the word.'

Silence. Danny could tell the General was considering a different line of argument. 'You any idea how important it is I get out of here in one piece? You think your goddamn side show is more important than the security of the United States of America?'

'You'll get out of here in one piece.'

'It's a war crime, you know that? It's a bona fide, black and white, cut and dried war crime. Jesus, I'm trying to expose a conspiracy at the highest level, and you're off on some personal vendetta?'

'It's not a personal vendetta,' Danny said.

'I'll tell you what it is – it's a disaster in the making. You got any idea what will happen to me if it's discovered that I've been involved in this madness.'

'Nobody's going to discover anything.'

'How do you know that? How can you possible say that?'

'Because the Russians won't want anybody asking questions about why they were trying to assassinate a five-star general, an SAS man and a former MI6 officer. In any case, we don't have a choice. We *have* to deal with these Wagner Group guys. It's an operational necessity.'

'The hell it is,' the General said.

'We're heading to a covert RV with a British chopper in the Jordanian desert close to the Israeli border. If we don't deal with these guys, we'll lead them straight to it. They're serious players. I've seen them in action. I'm not going to compromise the guys coming in to pick us up. I'm not going to risk another massacre.'

'You're finding excuses,' the General said.

'The guy with the mohawk is called Alexander Turgenev,' Danny said. 'He's smart enough to orchestrate an ambush on an SAS unit. He's smart enough to track us this far. You really think we should underestimate him? Not to mention that you just watched him shoot two of your men in the back of the head. Are you seriously telling me you don't want to see him dead?'

'Of *course* I want to see him dead,' the General said. 'But there are more important things at stake.'

'They're not more important to me,' Danny said. 'And anyway, we'll make the RV. Trust me.'

The General fell silent.

'The ruins are ten miles due south,' Bethany said quietly. She was holding the GPS unit and reading the screen. Danny nodded.

Despite everything, he appreciated her implied approval. He slowed gradually and pulled up on the side of the road. Cars were passing now at a rate of about one every thirty seconds. He couldn't risk anyone seeing them take the Nissan off-road. He waited a full two minutes before there was a suitable gap in the traffic. Then he killed the headlamps and eased the vehicle off into the darkness.

Luckily the moon was bright enough for him to see his way. The lights of the motorway receded behind him. The desert stretched out in front. He drove at a steady speed. Not so fast that the weak chassis of the Nissan would be damaged by the pitted terrain. Not so slow that the Wagner Group would catch them up before he had a chance to welcome them. The hard-baked earth crunched monotonously beneath the tyres. Sure, the quad bike they dropped in with had been by far the better vehicle for terrain like this, but Danny had been trained to adapt to circumstances.

He had been trained, too, to maintain his observational skills at all time, and he did that now. He was being tracked. He knew that, beyond question. But there were unknowns. How many guys were tracking him? What vehicles were they using? How were they armed? Would they realise that Danny was leading them into a trap? What kind of countermeasures would they deploy? As Danny drove, he maintained an acute awareness of his surroundings. At the same time, he put himself into the heads of his enemies. They would know that he was off road now. They'd be following him, but they'd also be wary of a guy who'd already dealt with two carloads of their men. They would be persistent and uncompromising, but they would plan their approach and their attack a little more carefully. That would give Danny the time he needed. He hoped.

They cruised across the desert, the silence only broken by Bethany's occasional suggestion that Danny alter his trajectory to keep on track. It took the best part of an hour for their destination to come into view: the stone remnants of the Roman ruins protruding from the ground, the copse that hid the smugglers' lorry, the rough road leading away from the ruins back towards Amman. Danny stopped the car fifty metres from the edge of the ruins, took his night sight from his shoulder bag and exited the vehicle. The ancient stones glowed a pale grey in the moonlight, which was bright enough now to cast stubby shadows on to the ground. It was absolutely silent. There was no breeze. No sound of desert animals. The whole area was as still as a photograph. He scanned a full 360, searching minutely for movement, threats, anything that indicated the Wagner Group was close. Nothing. He got back in the car and drove further into the ruins.

He needed to choose his position carefully. Somewhere in the centre of the ruins, because he wanted the low stone walls and protruding columns to act as a kind of camouflage. The busier and more broken up the area looked from a distance, the easier it would be to hide the objects Danny had in mind. He also wanted to be close enough to the stone walls that he could make tactical advantage of them. So he parked up in a circular open area with a diameter of about fifteen metres, a section of wall forming the perimeter, but broken up here and there to allow access. He parked the car to one side of the circle, blocking a gap in the perimeter. Then he turned to the others. 'This is going to take me half an hour to set up,' he said. 'Maybe forty-five minutes. You need to position yourself at the edge of the copse and keep stag. I need to know the moment you see anybody approaching. You can do that?'

The silent stares he received from Bethany and the General told him exactly what they thought of the suggestion that this task might be beyond their abilities. 'If we're going to do this,' the General said, 'let's get it done.'

Danny left the tracking device in his footwell. Then they left the car and ran towards the copse. Bethany took up a position behind the treeline facing the road, the exact position from which they'd watched the fixers approaching the previous night. The General moved across the copse, checking the view from various positions. Danny noted that his footfall was soundless. He might be top brass, but he still had a soldier's stealth when he needed it. Danny himself headed to the smugglers' lorry. It was exactly where they'd left it, on the far side of the copse from the road. He recovered the keys from where he'd buried them beneath the tree with the distinctive knot and shook them clean. He opened up the back, climbed up into the lorry and allowed his eyes to adjust to the darkness inside. He saw a long-handled torch and closed the door of the lorry before switching it on. The light was filtered red and it gave the interior of the truck a fiery glow. Danny took stock.

His memory of the contents of the lorry hadn't failed him. There were Claymore mines and huge spools of wire and heavy-duty sets of wire cutters. There were blocks of C-4 plastic explosive. There were detonators. There were two Dragunov sniper rifles. There were Kalashnikovs with underslung grenade launchers. There were pistols. There were wooden crates filled with RPG warheads. With a grim smile, he saw that the crates were wrapped in old woollen blankets to protect them. There were boxes and boxes of ammunition. It was a heavy-duty arsenal. Enough gear to cause death and destruction on a massive scale. Danny wondered about its original destination. Had he stumbled across hardware intended for some gruesome, sickening act of terror? Was it intended for the people of the West Bank to be able to defend themselves? It was impossible to know for sure. But one thing was certain. This gear was about to be repurposed. It belonged to Danny Black now.

Before he made use of it, however, he needed a fire.

It was the work of a couple of minutes to gather an armful of deadfall from the floor of the copse, and a pocketful of dried leaves that crumbled almost to dust at his touch. He carried it to the centre of the circular clearing and made a wigwam of smaller twigs. He stuffed the dried leaves at the bottom of the wigwam. He patted down his pockets and found the wallet of hotel-branded matches he'd taken from the bar. He struck one, lit his tinder and gently blew on it until the wigwam caught.

During jungle training, it had been instilled in him that the most important ingredient for a good fire, after fuel, oxygen and heat, was patience. Look after a fire when it's young, it'll look after you when it's old. It wasn't always easy to be patient. As the twigs smouldered, he looked out across the desert, checking for a sign of anybody approaching. Nothing yet. He knew it was a matter of time. He added larger bits of firewood perhaps a little earlier than he should, but he got away with it. The wood was desert-dry and burned readily. In four or five minutes it was burning well enough to leave.

He hurried back to the lorry, climbed inside and turned on the torch. He took the longest, heaviest spool of wire. There was several hundred metres of it, at a guess. Certainly sufficient for his purposes. He hauled it over his shoulder, grabbed a set of wire cutters and killed the torch. Then he exited the vehicle, locking it behind him to make sure nobody else got a chance to raid the sweet shop. He ran with it to the part of the treeline that was closest to the Nissan and the circular clearing. Distance: about thirty metres. He started rolling out the wire towards the clearing. The wire was very fine and, once it was on the ground, almost invisible if you didn't know it was there. When he reached the clearing, he looped the wire around the low stone perimeter wall. Where it crossed the gaps in the wall, he camouflaged it further by covering it with loose grit. Once he'd made a full circle, he rolled the wire back towards the copse, laid the spool next to the beginning of the wire and made a cut. He stripped the ends. Now he had two terminals, ready to deliver an electric charge to his hastily constructed ring main.

Danny ran through the copse to check with Bethany and the General that they hadn't spotted anybody approaching. Negative from them both. He returned to the lorry and opened it up again. Switched on the torch. Red glow. He helped himself to an armful of detonators and plastic explosives. Closed up the lorry. Sprinted back to where he'd left the spool of wire. Slung it over his shoulder, pocketed the wire cutters and took his armful of gear to the circular clearing.

Danny's hands were large, his fingers thick. But he worked with the deft skill of a seamstress. He moved round the loop of wire and made a cut every couple of metres. At each break in the wire, he spliced in two more lengths of several metres. Some of these he laid outside the perimeter of the circle, some inside, so now there were ten branches of wire leading in and out of the circle, each ending in a double terminal. One of the interior branches snaked to the underside of the Nissan. He connected a detonator to each of these terminals, then sunk the blasting fuse of each detonator deep into a block of C-4 plastic explosive.

He was sweating heavily now and breathing deeply. A good fifteen minutes had passed since he had started laying his trap. The fire was burning well. He laid some more fuel on the flames, then took another moment to check his surroundings through his night sight. Nothing. Just the still, silent, wide expanse of the desert. He turned his attention back to the primed explosives. He needed to hide them better. He quickly moved the C-4 nearest the Nissan to underneath the vehicle's fuel tank. The remainder he either dug into the ground, or positioned close to the stone perimeter wall, on the inside of the circle. The wall would force the blast to focus in one direction, doubling its efficacy.

But that wasn't enough for Danny. He was a Regiment man, and he had the Regiment's approach. When he attacked, he wanted that attack to be sudden, brutal and instantly deadly. He didn't want a fair fight. He wanted to dominate the field of conflict utterly. So he ran back to the lorry, opened up, shone the torch and went to work on the wooden crates containing the RPG warheads.

He loosened the blankets wrapped round the crates – he'd need those in a bit – then turned his attention to the boxes themselves. Normally they would require a tool to jemmy them open. Danny didn't bother with that. The wooden cases were dry and brittle. Their lids came off with a vigorous tug, splintering as they came away from their bases. He carefully lifted out the warheads. They were solid and heavy, their metal casings strangely cool in the warm night. Danny carried them two at a time back to the ring main. The air smelled of smoke and the fire was burning brightly. He placed a warhead next to each block of plastic explosive. When the C-4 exploded, the warheads would detonate. Anybody in the vicinity would know about it. For a few seconds, at least.

'We've got company.'

Danny looked up from where he was placing the last warhead. He hadn't heard Bethany approach and he didn't like that she'd managed to creep up on him like that. She pointed across the desert and Danny followed her hand. He immediately saw the lights.

They were distant, probably a couple of miles off, and they disappeared as soon as Danny saw them. He knew what they were, though. Headlamps. A single set. One vehicle, which had driven into a dip so that the headlamps were no longer visible from Danny's position.

'Get back in position,' Danny said. 'Keep watching.'

'If I didn't know better, I'd think you wanted me out of the way. You don't need me keeping stag. You know they're coming.'

'Fine,' Danny said. 'You still have your pistol?'

'Of course.'

'Few minutes' time, we're going to have a lot of dead Russians on our hands. Your job is to make sure they really *are* dead, when the time comes. You can do that?'

'Of course.'

'Then get back behind the treeline.' He pointed towards the copse, to a position about twenty metres from where he was setting himself up. 'Make sure you're out of sight. There might be shooting and I want you out of the line of fire.'

'How chivalrous.'

'That's got nothing to do with it. You're no use to us with a bullet in the head. Go.'

Bethany headed back into the copse. Danny checked the time: 00.29 hrs. Three and a half hours till they needed to be at the pick-up point. Danny still had items to set up. He ran to the Nissan and found the lever by the driver's seat to open up the bonnet. The battery was at the right-hand side of the engine block. He carefully removed both terminals, then lifted the battery out of the engine and closed it up again. He ran with this back into the copse and left it by the two loose ends of the ring main. Back to the lorry. He gathered up the blankets that had been cushioning the RPG crates. There were ten in all. He only needed nine.

He carried the blankets back to the clearing and arranged them carefully around the fire. The flames had subsided now. The embers glowed and crackled. He kept a distance of a couple of metres between the fire and the material. He made three piles of three blankets. One blanket rolled lengthwise to mimic a body. One blanket bundled to mimic a head. The third blanket draped over the two to make the whole ensemble look like a sleeping person. It was a crude pretence, but Danny knew that people would tend to see what they expected to see. A campfire in a deserted location would likely be surrounded by sleeping people. Nobody would think it remotely unusual.

Yeah. Any luck, they'd see what they wanted to see.

He returned through the copse to the lorry. He took a Kalashnikov, grenade launcher, ammo and box of tubular grenades, then delivered them back to the car battery and the ring main terminals. He loaded the Kalashnikov with a full magazine of 7.62s and a grenade. Back to the lorry, where he grabbed the Dragunov sniper rifle and a box of rounds. Back at the car battery and in the shelter of the trees he took another look through the night sight. And he allowed himself another grim smile as he saw what was happening.

Now there was more than a single vehicle approaching. He counted four. No, five – one more had appeared. They had turned off their headlamps and were advancing on the Roman ruins from Danny's ten, eleven, twelve, one and two o'clock. A formation advance, centred on the tracking device that was currently broadcasting its position from the driver's footwell of the Nissan. Danny looked around. No sign of Bethany. She was well hidden. He ran through the copse and found the General, who was keeping stag in the opposite direction. 'Any vehicles from your direction?' he asked.

'Zip,' the General said. Danny could tell he was still pissed off, but he was taking his lookout duties seriously.

'You know your way around a sniper rifle?'

'You kidding? I was US Army champion three years running.'

Danny checked the terrain from this direction through his night sight. He had a good view and there was no sign of any approaching vehicle. 'This way,' he said.

He led the General back to where the battery, the ring main terminals and the weaponry were stashed. He pointed to the Dragunov. The General eyed it hesitantly. Danny crouched down by the battery and gripped the two terminals of the ring main. He looked out from the treeline. Even without the benefit of the night sight he could see figures approaching. Ten guys, silhouetted in the moonlight. He could see the outlines of their bodies, and of the weapons that were slung across their chests. He tried to pick out Turgenev's distinctive height and physique. He couldn't, and he felt a dig of disappointment. He told himself to focus on what was ahead of them. The men were advancing carefully on the clearing. Current distance from the kill zone: sixty metres.

'In case you're coming down with a bad case of ethics,' Danny said quietly, 'might be worth remembering that those ten guys think they're about to kill you. We don't put them down – all of them – that's what they'll do.'

The General still didn't pick up the Dragunov. Danny felt a grudging respect for him. The guy obviously wanted to do the right thing. He clearly took the view that they should have escaped these Wagner Group operatives, rather than massacre them. But he hadn't been on the ground when Zero 22 walked into the Russian ambush. He hadn't seen his mates butchered and mangled. He hadn't fought Turgenev. Danny glanced sidelong at the General. In that moment, he didn't see a powerful man who had a seat at the table with the most influential people in the world. He saw a soldier, in the dark, on ops, and he knew what he had to say. 'You saw them kill your men outside the hotel, right? You watched them do it? And you don't want them to answer for that?'

Danny didn't need to watch for the General's response. He knew what it would be. As he remained crouched down by the battery, looking out across the Roman ruins, he heard the General load and prime the sniper rifle before putting himself down in the firing position.

There was total silence. The fire glowed a burnt orange, occasionally spitting sparks into the air like fireflies. The figures approached slowly. Moving with stealth. Distance: fifty-five metres. Danny could see now that they had their weapons raised, the butts pressed into their shoulders. They looked like pros: a good amount of space between each man so that they didn't present a bunched-up target, approaching on foot from a distance to avoid disturbing their own targets with the sound of their vehicles. But Danny could tell were making a big mistake. Their weapons were all pointing in the direction of the clearing, at the fire and the dummy bodies. They had fallen for his staging. They *were* seeing what they wanted to see, without expecting the unexpected.

'Who actually is the broad, anyway?' the General said very quietly. 'Not one of yours, that's for certain, knowing how you SF guys are about chicks in your ranks.'

Danny didn't answer. He kept his focus on the approaching men. Distance from the kill zone: fifty metres.

'Where is she?' the General asked.

Danny tensed up. 'Close.'

'I'm going to level with you,' the General said. 'If she didn't make it through this ambush, I wouldn't be weeping at her graveside.'

'Keep your mind on the fucking job,' Danny said. The truth was, it had occurred to him that now was a good time to take Bethany out. She wouldn't be expecting an attack, not when they were working together like this. And one more body in the massacre that he was planning would cause fewer questions to be asked. Like hiding a branch on a log pile.

Why, then, was he resisting the idea? Why was he persuading himself that, in the light of the mission change, he needed direct confirmation from Hereford before taking Bethany out of the picture? He couldn't answer that question and now he put it from his mind.

'Your silence speaks volumes,' the General said. 'I gotta tell you, I don't like her being in possession of that pistol she took in the hotel. You should have seen the look in her eyes when she was in my hotel room . . .'

'Just shut the fuck up and don't move,' Danny said. 'They see movement behind the treeline, they'll know it's a trap.'

The targets were still approaching very steadily. There was a sudden breath of wind. The fire embers flared. A cloud of sparks drifted towards the copse, and with them a warm smell of wood smoke. Danny held the ring main wires close to the battery terminals, ready to make the connection when the moment was right. His hands were completely steady. Unlike the General, he had no compunction about what he was about to do.

Distance from the kill zone: thirty metres.

Twenty.

They were among the Roman ruins now. The moon cast their shadows over the standing stones and dilapidated walls and columns. As a unit, they were breaking up a little. Five guys were moving ahead to the clearing. The remainder lagged behind, covering their mates, but still advancing once there was a gap of about seven metres between them. They continued their advance in two lines. Danny was pleased he'd placed his explosives both inside the ring main and outside it.

The first two guys were inside the clearing now. Their weapons were pointing down at the dummy blankets and they glowed slightly in the light of the embers. Danny touched one end of the ring main to the negative battery terminal. Three more guys entered the clearing. The remaining five were just outside it, almost in a semicircle, covering their unit mates.

A shout. Russian. It rang out across the desert. One of the guys in the semicircle had lowered his weapon. He was pointing at something on the ground. It was clear he knew something was wrong. He'd seen Danny's trap.

It was too late.

Danny touched the loose wire to the positive terminal.

The explosion was instantaneous and immense. The detonation of ten blocks of C-4 was enough to send a shock wave through the air and emitted a crack so thunderous that it momentarily numbed Danny's ears. It was nothing, however, to the harsh, brutal clatter of the RPGs. They detonated in such quick succession that the individual explosions almost became one. Danny's view of the clearing became completely obscured by the vast geyser of dry earth and shrapnel that spat violently up from the ground, scorching and impenetrable. The sound of raining shrapnel followed the noise of the detonations, like nuts and bolts hammering on a steel roof. But this too was quickly drowned out by a third explosion. Danny had laid one RPG under the fuel tank of the Nissan. It did its work. A black and orange flash flowered deep in the cloud of dust and shrapnel. There was a deafening crack of combusting fuel, a thick plume of black smoke and a crunch as the Nissan itself shifted position and its chassis crumpled.

Then the screaming started.

Danny couldn't see the men. The cloud of smoke and grit was still impenetrable. He had to rely on his ears to tell him how many were dead and how many – unfortunately for them – were still alive. He could make out four individual screams. They were the mindless, desperate screams of men in such agony that it blocked out all other thought. They were shrill. They were hoarse. They oozed panic and pain. When, after twenty seconds, the cloud started to dissipate, Danny saw why.

One guy was on his knees. The skin on his face was shredded and burned. He no longer had features. Just a red mask of blood and bone. As he screamed, he brought his fingertips up to his face, but he plainly couldn't bear to touch the wounded flesh.

A second guy was staggering by a low wall. He had a jagged piece of shrapnel embedded in his chest. The shrapnel was too large to have come from the RPGs. It must have flown off the Nissan, which Danny could now see lying on its side, shrouded in hot flames and burning smoke.

A third guy was on fire. He must have been close to the Nissan when the fuel tank exploded. His hair was ablaze. His clothes too. He was running around in a circle like a demented dog. His screams were the most hoarse, but no quieter for it.

A fourth guy had lost his arm just above the elbow. His screams were more of a whimper, breathless and staccato like the individual rounds of a semi-automatic. He was holding the stump with his good arm, staring at it with a burned, blistered face. There was no blood. Danny assumed that the heat of the blast had instantly cauterised the wound.

The dead were the lucky ones. Killed instantly, they didn't have to endure these agonising final moments before the inevitable came. Their bodies were strewn around the ruins, some of them partially dismembered. One guy was half covered by the dummy blankets. Another was slumped against the burning Nissan, his body smouldering as the flames began to eat it. Danny watched, listening to the agonised shouts and the crackle of the flames and he remembered the bomb site in Syria and the state of his dead mates and he couldn't help feel a surge of satisfaction.

The General was shifting position. Danny could tell he was about to take a shot, most likely to put one of the screaming men out of his misery. '*Hold your fire!*' he hissed.

'These guys need finishing off. It's inhumane.'

'Not yet,' Danny said. '*I mean it. Not yet!*' He was looking past the kill zone now, at the line of vehicles in which the Wagner Group had arrived. These guys might be mercenaries, but they were also soldiers, and among soldiers there was a code. You help your mates when they're in trouble. If there were any further targets still in the vehicles, these screams would most likely bring them running. But if they thought there were shooters behind the treeline, they would have no choice but to retreat. Danny's job would only be half done.

It happened after a minute. A long minute, filled with the diminishing screams of the men and the greasy stench of burning fuel. Three car doors opened. Five more guys appeared. Danny felt his stomach lurch. One of them was substantially taller than the others. Danny could just discern the outline of his buzz-cut mohawk.

Turgenev was here.

Like the others, he was armed with a rifle. Danny guessed they'd been waiting to check if any enemy personnel showed themselves. But they didn't have Danny's patience, and the sound of their companions screaming was too much for them. Turgenev's four mates sprinted towards the kill zone, but Turgenev was smarter and held back a little. As they ran, Danny picked up his Kalashnikov. He aimed so that the dull grey tubular underslung launcher would fire a grenade between the two left-most guys. When they were ten metres from the clearing, he fired. The launcher made a hollow, echoing pop as it spat its contents, and the stubby grenade flew visibly through the air. When it exploded, its effects were as devastating as Danny intended. Shrapnel peppered the two guys in a sudden, shocking burst. They went down, their screams adding to the bitter yells of their mates. They writhed on the ground, entirely out of action, minutes or even seconds from death.

Now, however, the remaining three Wagner Group guys knew they were going to come under fire. They hit the ground, Turgenev about ten metres behind the other two, and crawled to cover behind bits of protruding ruins: Turgenev behind a column, the other two behind a low wall about twenty metres away. They were out of sight, but Danny knew their counterattack would come at any moment. He threw himself to the ground, Kalashnikov by his side, and pressed himself into the earth alongside the prostrate general. They were hidden in the darkness behind the treeline. Danny also knew that the gunfire, when it came, would be the random spray of shooters hoping for the best ...

The wounded men stopped screaming almost at the same time. A dense silence settled. Then the gunfire came. It was the harsh cough of two automatic weapons releasing short bursts towards the copse. Danny was aware of bullets slamming into the trees above him, of bark splintering and falling to the ground. He saw two muzzle flashes from the shooters' firing points behind the low wall to his one o'clock, about metre from each other. A bullet ricocheted from a nearby tree. He felt a vibrating thud pass through his arms and for a moment he thought he'd been hit.

But he hadn't. The gunfire stopped. Silence returned. The muzzle flashes had given Danny their precise location. Bad mistake. They were close enough for Danny to take them out with a single burst once they showed themselves again.

He moved, very slowly and quietly, up into the firing position. Aimed his Kalashnikov, set to automatic, and rested his finger lightly on the trigger. Kept his breathing shallow. Waited.

Thirty seconds passed.

Forty-five.

The shooters popped up like jack-in-the-boxes. Danny fired.

There was nothing. Just an impotent click. His rifle had a stoppage. He swore silently, and went through the motions of clearing the stoppage, a process so familiar he could do it in seconds. He tried to fire again. Nothing. He realised that the vibrating thud must have been a stray round hitting the weapon. It was fucked. The targets started firing again. Danny slammed himself back down to the ground. The incoming was more on point this time. Was it luck? Had they seen him? Danny didn't know, but now Turgenev's two mates had emerged from their hiding position. They were firing in turn, short bursts towards the copse as they approached. Danny was pinned down. Unable to move. Unable to defend himself.

Distance: twenty metres. They closer they came, the more danger he was in because they would spot him if he moved. His rifle was out of action, but the grenade launcher could still be okay. The grenades were stashed several metres to his left. Could he risk rolling to them, reloading and firing? How long would that take? Several seconds, by which time the advancing guys would only be ten metres away and they would see him for certain.

Rounds landed left and right of him. Too close. *Much* too close . . .

'Put them down!' he hissed to the General.

From somewhere to his right a shot rang out. The single dead thump of a sniper rifle. He saw one of the guys fall, and even before he hit the ground, there was a second shot. A bullet hit the head of the second guy, causing a grotesque fountain of blood and brain matter to spurt from the shattered skull as the man slumped heavily to the ground.

Which left Turgenev himself.

He appeared from behind thirty column thirty metres distant, his weapon engaged. He had clearly made an accurate judgement of the General's position and he fired a burst. For a sickening moment, Danny thought the bullets had hit their mark, but then he heard a third shot from the sniper rifle. The General wasn't hit, but his third round went awry, and Turgenev was still standing, huge and hulking, and about to fire again.

What he didn't know was that his hesitation had given Danny the time he needed.

He rolled over towards the stash of grenades. Grabbed one and loaded it quickly into the underslung launcher on his Kalashnikov. In a single deft movement, he pushed himself upright and aimed at Turgenev. There was another almost silent click as he launched the grenade. It fizzed towards the target and hit him directly in the upper leg before he was able to fire on the General. The grenade exploded, knocking him on to his back. Danny couldn't see the extent of the wounds, but he didn't need to. He could hear the screams, worse than any of the others. Even Turgenev was in no position to fight back with an injury like that.

Neither Danny nor the General moved. Together they'd put down fifteen men. There was no guarantee, however, that there were no more enemy personnel waiting in the vehicles. The Nissan was still burning, still pumping out black smoke. There was a second, smaller explosion. The burning corpse that was slumped against the side of the car fell forwards. Danny waited a minute, ignoring Turgenev's screams, then lowered his Kalashnikov and grabbed his night sight. He focused in on the cars. The glow of the burning Nissan compromised the NV capability a little, but he was able to check each vehicle for the sign of occupants. There was none.

'We're good,' he said.

Both men stood up. Danny saw something in the General's face that he recognised. The wired, bright-eyed excitement, tinged with relief, that routinely followed a successful firefight. 'Nice shooting,' Danny said.

'You looked like you could use a hand,' the General replied. He grinned. 'Been a while since an old timer like me was allowed on the front line.' He nodded towards the clearing. 'That was quite a trap you laid.'

'If a job's worth doing . . .' Danny started to say. He peered at the screaming Turgenev. 'We should talk to him,' he said. 'See if he has any intel we can use.'

The General nodded. Danny lowered his Kalashnikov – it was useless now – and drew his Sig. He kept it raised, two handed, as he approached the screaming man, then stowed it as he stood above him. The burning Nissan was just five metres away. It radiated immense heat. Enough heat for it to scorch Danny's skin. Turgenev was lying between him and the fire. The network of scars on his scalp almost glowed red in the night and the mohawk was crisping up in the heat and giving off the acrid stench of burning hair. It didn't seem to bother Turgenev. What bothered Turgenev was his leg. The grenade had exploded against his quad. His trouser leg had burned away and the leg had split open. The meat of the muscle was fully on display and Danny could see a narrow shard of bone extending from thigh to knee. There was not much blood. The skin, and what remained of the trouser leg, was smouldering. Danny reckoned he had a bit of life in him yet. He knelt down by his side, aware of the General looking over them. He put one hand over the man's mouth to muffle his screams. 'Hello, Turgenev.'

Turgenev's pained eyes widened. Perhaps he was surprised that Danny knew his name.

'I've got medical supplies,' Danny continued, 'and a way out of here. You do what I say, you'll live. You don't, I'll throw you on that fire while you're still alive. Up to you. You understand what I'm saying?'

Danny removed his hand from Turgenev's mouth. Turgenev took a large intake of breath. Danny thought he was about to spit at him, but he didn't.

'Name your target,' Danny said.

Turgenev panted some fast, shallow breaths. An attempt to start speaking. 'O'Brien,' he whispered finally.

'Who gave the order?'

'You think they tell us that?' He closed his eyes and shuddered.

'What do you know about a fourth of July terror hit?'

Turgenev opened his eyes again. 'America,' he whispered. And he managed a grin. The same grin he'd given Danny in the Syrian desert. The same grin he'd worn in the picture they'd shown Danny of him holding the decapitated heads of two SAS men. Danny wished he could waste him right then, but he held back.

'I'm going to give you some pain relief real soon,' he said. 'But you've got to tell me everything you know first. What's happening on the fourth of July?'

Turgenev's grin became even broader.

'The fourth of July,' Danny pressed. 'What's happening on the fourth of July?'

'Not the fourth of July,' Turgenev rasped.

'What do you mean, not the fourth of July?'

'They changed it.'

Danny looked up at the General. O'Brien had a sick expression on his face. 'When?' he said

'Today,' Turgenev said, and his grin became a sneer of complete contempt.

'Where?' Danny said. 'Where's it happening, Turgenev?'

Turgenev looked from Danny, to the General, back to Danny. 'Fuck you,' he said. 'Just shoot me now.'

Danny nodded slowly. He stood up. 'We've got everything we're going to get out of him,' he said, but the General didn't even seem to be listening any more. He looked stricken. Panicked. Danny stared down at Turgenev who was still grinning madly at him. Then he bent down again and mustered all his strength. He needed it to roll Turgenev towards the burning Nissan. He had to grip the huge man's clothes and use his feet as well as his hands to move him. Two rolls would do it, he reckoned. He grunted and Turgenev struggled, but the grenade wound had sapped his strength and he was now no match for Danny, who grimaced against the heat of the flaming car as he manoeuvred Turgenev closer to it. When Turgenev was just a metre from the car, Danny had to jump back because the heat was too intense.

Turgenev started screaming again, in Russian this time, so Danny had no idea what he was saying. He didn't care. He watched with grim satisfaction as Turgenev's clothes caught alight, followed by what remained of the hair on his head. Turgenev writhed and shouted. He tried to wriggle from the flames, but now he *was* the flames. His whole body was burning. The scarred skin on scalp shrivelled and smouldered. His face seemed to melt. The open wound on his leg, wet and fresh, was the last to burn. His screams faded and though there was still some movement in his body, he was as good as dead. Danny didn't need to see any more.

He turned to the General, who was watching Turgenev in horror. He seemed to shake himself out of it. 'I thought I had plenty of time before the hit,' he said. 'We need to get the deep-fakes out there.'

'You have to tell me where the footage is.'

'I already did. Washington DC.'

'That's not enough. Not now. *Exactly* where is it?'

'I'm not going to tell you.'

'Why the hell not? You heard what he said.'

'I have my reasons.'

'They'd better be damn good, because people are going to die.' And before the General could point out that they were standing in the middle of a bloodbath, he added: '*Civilians* are going to die.'

'I can still get there in time. They're seven hours back.'

'Tell me where it is, we can get someone there right now.'

'Not going to happen, soldier.' The General's face glowed in the light of the flaming vehicle. 'I tell you, you tell your superiors, this goes all the way up to the highest level of government, and you'll forgive me for being suspicious about the motivation of governments, right? Your prime minister is in no position to stand up to my president. This thing will get swept under the carpet. I'm not going to let that happen.'

Danny knew determination when he heard it. It crossed his mind that the General might need a taste of the medicine he'd just given the Wagner Group, but he instantly dismissed that thought. What he needed was the General's trust. He wasn't going to buy that with violence. 'Get your clothes off,' he said.

The General raised an eyebrow.

'We need to put your clothes on one of these bodies,' he said. 'Your ID tags too. It won't fool anybody for long, but if the Russians think they've nailed you, it might make them look in the wrong direction.' He turned his back on the General and looked at the bodies strewn around the clearing. The guy with the butchered face was closest in build to the General. He was wearing khaki trousers and a black T-shirt, both torn and blood-spattered. There was a bad smell about the body where it had started to leak fluid from its various orifices. Danny removed the garments. The corpse was heavy, the process fiddly. When he turned, he saw that the General was down to his underwear again. They swapped clothes and Danny went about the even more cumbersome business of re-dressing the corpse. It took a couple of minutes, by which time the General had put on the dead man's clothes. They were a tight fit, and a mess, but they would do. 'Give me your tags,' Danny said. The General unclipped the necklace with his military ID and handed it over. Danny put it round the corpse's neck. Then he grabbed it under its arms, hauled it to its feet and manoeuvred it on to his shoulder in a fireman's lift. He and the General turned to face the copse.

'*Jesus!*' the General whispered.

Danny froze.

Bethany was standing at the treeline, facing them. Her right arm was extended, pistol in hand. She was pointing the gun in their direction. The two men stood side by side, Danny with the corpse still over his shoulder, as she strode towards them.

'What the—' Danny started to say.

Bethany was ten metres from them when she started to fire. Five shots in quick succession. Danny was aware of the General looking down at his chest, as if expecting to see bullet wounds.

But there were none. Danny realised a moment later that she was not shooting at them. She was shooting beyond them, and he quickly turned in time to see one of the Wagner Group guys who had been put down in the original blast. He was a mess. His face was burned and blistered and one arm was hanging off. But the other was raised and he had a handgun aimed at Danny.

Not for long. Bethany released another round and it slammed straight into the hostile's chest. He slumped heavily to the ground and there was an immediate, heavy silence.

The General was breathing heavily. Danny too. 'Thank you,' he muttered.

Bethany glanced calmly around the Roman ruins. The burning Nissan. The butchered bodies. The corpse on Danny's shoulder. 'And they say I'm sick,' she said. 'If you boys have quite finished playing, do you think we should get out of here?'

Danny ignored the sarcasm and surveyed the scene. He had the strange sensation of seeing it for the first time, as though a mist of rage and determination had fallen over him prior and was only now clearing. The Roman ruins were a death site. The state of the corpses was shocking. Turgenev was a smouldering husk. Bethany was right that they needed to move quickly. If the sounds of gunshots and grenade explosions didn't attract people, the plume of black smoke snaking up from the Nissan certainly would. 'You want to finish your job?' he said.

Bethany displayed no qualms about delivering precautionary headshots to each of the remaining dead men. She made an uncompromising sight, silhouetted by the moonlight, arm straight, head slightly inclined. The retort of each gunshot clapped across the terrain. Each corpse juddered slightly. The stench of Turgenev's burning body filled the air as she quickly went about her work. 'Maybe it's not such a bad thing she's still with us,' the General said.

'Maybe,' Danny said. He turned his back on the ruins. The Wagner Group were no longer his concern. He knew that word would get back to their paymasters of what had happened here.

Maybe they would think twice before putting the Regiment in their sights again. He thought of the Zero 22 crew and felt a moment of grim satisfaction that he'd done right by them.

Bethany and the General followed him back to the copse. Back behind the treeline, where the Dragunov was lying on the ground, he dumped the body. It fell on to its back and stared at the tree-tops, mouth grotesquely open. Danny examined the face. The hair was burned away and the skin scorched down to tissue. Yet it somehow still retained a whisper of its previous features, and those features were not the General's. He drew his Sig and aimed at the face. Fired two rounds directly into it. The retort of the shots clattered loudly around the copse and across the desert. The bullets did their work well. Even Danny, no stranger to such sights, was repelled by the sight of the gouged flesh, exposed skull and bleeding eyeballs. He didn't linger on it.

The General was standing behind Bethany, grimy, sweating and blooded in the corpse's original clothes. He looked at her, then at Danny, a questioning look on his face. Danny made no response. 'Pick up all the gear,' he said, indicating the sniper rifle and the ammo. 'Get it back in the truck. We'll take that to the pick-up point.'

Without waiting for a reply, he grabbed a couple of ammo crates and turned his back on the ruins. The glow of the burning Nissan cast his shadow long into the trees, which faded as he walked back to the lorry.

TWENTY

The children had never stayed in a hotel. Every aspect of it delighted them. The ice machines in the corridors. The foil-wrapped cookies on the coffee tray in their twin room. The bouncy single beds and en-suite shower room. The interconnecting door that led to their parents' double, and which Rabia insisted must be propped open at all times. Hamoud didn't mind. They hadn't been intimate since his return from Guantanamo. It was impossible for him, and she was very patient.

The hotel was vast. A triangular mirrored building with calming lakes in the grounds. Hamoud knew it was not the most expensive hotel in the resort. It was separate from the parks themselves. They would need to catch the free shuttle bus each day. But that was alright. The truth was that he shared his children's excitement. He smiled as he watched Rabia examine the miniature bottles of shampoo and body lotion in their own en suite. She wasn't accustomed to luxury.

There was no hope of staying in the rooms for long. The children were desperate to head straight to the parks, even though it was gone six in the evening. Hamoud found their passes in the FedEx package and, before Rabia could even unpack their suitcase, they walked to the bus stop outside the hotel that would shuttle them to the Magic Kingdom. 'I'd like to go on Space Mountain,' Malick said quietly as they walked. He tugged gently on his sleeve.

'Me too!' Melissa agreed, more buoyant than her brother as usual. 'Me too!' Hamoud and Rabia smiled at each other and held hands as Melissa chattered happily. She fell silent once they reached the bus stop, however. There were three other families waiting. White, American families. They sat in the early evening sun, all baseball caps and Mickey Mouse T-shirts, all chewing gum and sun-kissed skin, and they stared at Hamoud and his wife and children as they approached, and shuffled further up the bench to avoid having to sit too close to them. No words were spoken. They weren't necessary. The difference in skin colour between Hamoud's family and the others said it all. That and the overt expressions of distaste on the faces of the American holiday-makers. Hamoud's children sat silently between their mum and dad. They understood, perhaps without even knowing why, that it would be unseemly of them to make an exhibition of themselves. Hamoud wished he could persuade them otherwise. But that would be hypocritical, because he and Rabia shared their discomfort and their reticence. How could they not, when they received this treatment wherever they went? Hamoud felt self-conscious about his beard. The scar on his face, which made him look so suspicious and unsavoury, throbbed in the heat. They all sat in silence, Hamoud scratching his palms, as they waited for the bus.

The back seats were free. The family settled into them and soon the children became animated again. They could see crowds congregating around the entrance to the Magic Kingdom and the turrets of the Cinderella Castle peeping into the sky. They held the children's hands firmly as they stepped off the bus. There were hundreds of people here, all bustling to pass through the entrance turnstiles. It would be very easy to get lost.

There was music playing. A brass band. Hamoud couldn't see it but the jaunty, happy music made him smile again. The family stuck close to each other as the momentum of the crowd swept them towards the turnstiles. Hamoud fumbled one-handed for their passes. He experienced a moment of anxiety. What if they didn't work? What if it was all a con? But the turnstiles allowed them through and suddenly there they were, inside the park, the crowds dispersing around them, his children trembling with anticipation. They could see the castle directly up Main Street. The brass band was louder and, up ahead, there were people in character costumes waving and greeting all the new arrivals. Donald Duck put his arms around a delighted toddler. Mary Poppins, complete with umbrella, was surrounded by young girls. Captain Jack Sparrow held aloft a wooden cutlass.

Hamoud turned to his children. Their cherubic faces stared up at him. 'Where first?' he asked.

'Space Mountain!' they squealed. 'Please, Daddy!'

'Let's go then!' Hamoud laughed. 'I bet you'll scream more than I do.'

Malick cocked his head and gave him a queer look. 'Dad,' he said, 'you're *never* like this.'

Hamoud understood what his boy meant. That he was never *happy* like this. His innocent observation made Hamoud catch his breath. He crouched down so that he was at his son's level and put one hand on his cheek. He said nothing, but realised he was experiencing a moment of clarity, of lightness, that had eluded him for years. For the first time almost since he could remember, there was no feeling of anxiety, or dread, or paranoia in his chest. There was just gladness and optimism, and he made a pact with himself to try to keep hold of those feelings.

But they didn't last long.

As he stood up, he saw another character standing by a kiosk that sold Coke and corn dogs. Hamoud only knew that the character was called Goofy because the kids had watched him on TV. Goofy was alone. None of the other punters had approached. There was something about this character that kept people away. Hamoud could feel it. He had comedic, oversized white gloves. He had removed one of them and was clutching it under his other arm. With his free hand he held up a cell phone. Hamoud had the unnerving feeling that this man was taking his photograph.

If that was true, it was done in a second. Goofy dropped his phone into the front pocket of the waistcoat he wore. Then he slipped the glove back on to his hand. He made no obvious attempt to get away immediately. Instead, he did the opposite: he stood his ground and waved enthusiastically at Hamoud and his family. The children waved back. Goofy threw back his head in a gesture of hysterical laughter. He rubbed his ribs as though deeply tickled. Then, with another wave, he skipped off, and disappeared into the crowds.

'Did you *see* that?' Hamoud asked Rabia.

'See what?'

Rabia's expression stopped him. *Please don't do this*, it seemed to say. *For the children's sake.*

He looked back after Goofy, but the character was nowhere to be seen. His son was pulling him by the arm, desperate to get started. 'Nothing,' Hamoud said. 'It was nothing. Space Mountain!'

The family made its way further into the park.

The smugglers' lorry handled the desert terrain far better than the Nissan had. They sat in a line at the front, Danny at the wheel, the General next to him, Bethany by the passenger window. The atmosphere had changed. Bethany, who up until now had been engaged and proactive, was distracted. She once again held the GPS unit, and occasionally gave Danny an instruction to alter his direction of travel. Other than that, she gazed out of the window and said nothing. Danny guessed she was thinking about her boy, and when she might next see him. Until this evening she'd had a road map: kill the General, escape Amman, get home, see the kid. That plan had been blown apart. No wonder she was pensive. She would be wondering what was going to happen next. If she would be allowed home. Danny had quickly briefed her about the intel they'd extracted from Turgenev. She had listened intently, but he suspected she was merely calculating how it affected her. She couldn't know that the change in circumstances had led to a change in her own fortunes. Danny wasn't going to waste her now that the nature of the mission had changed. He would wait until his orders were updated.

The vibe between Danny and the General had changed too. There's a closeness you only get from fighting alongside someone. It wouldn't make them friends for life. Nothing like. Danny was a Regiment grunt, O'Brien was top brass. Different people, different worlds. But there was a bond of sorts. A wary camaraderie. They had respect for each other, even though it was not articulated. Danny didn't agree with the General's refusal to reveal the location of the deepfake footage. But he knew he wasn't going to change the old guy's mind and, deep down, he couldn't deny the General had a point. Leaving a job like that to the politicians was not a way of making it happen. Some jobs you just had to do yourself.

The glow of the burning Nissan soon receded from the rear-view mirror. Danny once more negotiated the desert terrain by moonlight. He estimated that it was forty-five klicks to the drop zone where they could expect their pick-up. Two hours drive, off road. It was 01.30 hrs. It would get them on target with thirty minutes to spare.

'Why would they move the date of the attack?' the General said after they'd been driving in silence for half an hour.

Danny had no answer. Who could guess why people who would dream up a plan like that did anything?

'It's a common strategy,' Bethany said. 'If you bring forward the date of an attack at the last minute, it mitigates the risk of an information leak.'

'Either that,' the General said, 'or they knew I was on to them.'

'Maybe,' Bethany said.

'We still don't know where, who or how,' Danny said.

'That's why it's so important I get to DC. If I expose the deepfakes before they happen, there's no way they can go through with it.'

Danny put his head down and continued to drive.

He would never have recognised the drop zone at first. It was just a featureless patch of flat desert terrain. Hard-packed earth with a few scraggly weeds struggling their way through the cracks. Once they'd disembarked from the smuggler's lorry, however, he noted the wadi where they'd dug in the chutes and he knew for certain they were in the right place. He scanned the surrounding area with his night sight, checking for threats. But there was nothing. The drop zone had been chosen for its isolated location, and it had been chosen well.

'When they get here,' Danny said, 'they're not going to want to stick around. They're sending in a stealth chopper, so my guess is they'll have breached Israeli and Jordanian airspace without permission. They won't want anybody to get a whiff of what's going on. Be ready to board as soon as the skids are on the ground.'

The General leaned against the front of the lorry. He stared at his shoes, his eyes narrowed, his face calculating.

Bethany said, 'Where will they take us?'

'My guess would be Cyprus,' Danny told her.

'They'll put me on a flight home from there?'

'That's up to them. Not my call.'

'You'll tell them that I was going to do what they wanted?' For a killer, she sounded weirdly vulnerable. 'You'll make sure I see my son again?'

'I'll tell them what happened,' Danny said. They fell into silence.

Danny didn't expect to hear the chopper until it was almost upon them. The stealth capability of a Black Hawk kept the noise of the rotors to an absolute minimum. He saw it, though, a black ink spot against millions of stars, flying low towards their position. And gradually, the sound became audible. The flight crew selected an LZ approximately thirty metres from their position. As the chopper touched down, Danny could discern the pointed, angular shape that allowed it to cause minimum radar splash. The side door was closed, of course. That was necessary for the stealth capability. It opened the instant the chopper was on the ground, by which time Danny, Bethany and the General were jogging towards it. Two members of the flight crew in camo gear ushered them urgently into the aircraft. If they were surprised by the sight of this mismatched trio – Danny still in his battered, dirty business suit, Bethany dishevelled in her once glamorous two-piece, the General in the bloodied gear they'd stolen from the dead Wagner Group guy – they didn't show it. They simply secured the chopper again. By the time Danny and the others were seated in the dark interior of the Black Hawk, they were already airborne and speeding west out of Jordan.

If Alice Goodenough had been allowed to talk about her job to her friends in the pub – which she wasn't – she would have to admit that it was not nearly as intriguing as it sounded. Most of her time was spent in her tiny office at her computer or on the phone. Sure, she dealt in secrets, but those secrets had to be typed up and analysed and shared with the appropriate personnel. Intelligence work was ninety-five per cent admin.

At least, that was what she'd have said before now.

Everything had happened so quickly. Stark had arranged it all with a few phone calls from the echoing Park Royal warehouse. The paramedics who had arrived in an unmarked ambulance within ten minutes to take away the unconscious Poliakov, guarded by the two MI6 operatives who specialised in that type of work. The car that had taken both her and Stark to Heathrow, their nearest airport, and directly on to the tarmac without the need for passports or security checks. The Learjet that had been waiting for them. What would her friends have thought if they'd seen her travelling like a pop star? What would her mum say? Not that they were on board to enjoy the facilities of the private jet. It was simply, Stark explained, the quickest way of getting from A to B. A being London, B being the British military base in Cyprus. 'We have an operative extracting O'Brien from Jordan as we speak,' Stark told her. 'We need to be the first to debrief him.'

It was Alice's first time on an army base. As they stepped off the Learjet into the warm Mediterranean air at four in the morning, local time, she was surprised at how busy it was. A military vehicle was waiting for them as they disembarked, one of many that were driving across the tarmac, their headlamps glowing yellow in the darkness. There was the thunder of a jet taking off, and Alice saw the lights of two helicopters circling overhead. The soldier driving the truck looked to Alice barely old enough to shave. He, for his part, couldn't hide his surprise at the arrival of young black woman with colourfully braided hair, painted nails and a nose stud, accompanied by a stout, dapper, balding older man. He drove them to a secure area cordoned off by armed soldiers. There was a single-storey building here, constructed from sectional concrete panels. Another armed guy at the entrance. Alice could tell from Stark's confident stride that he'd been here plenty of times before. He led her into the building, and she found herself in a busy military ops room. Maps on the walls. Soldiers in camo gear with headphones and boom mikes at laptops. All male. Unlike the driver, these men barely seemed to notice Alice's arrival. They were too focused on their work. Stark walked up to an older guy on the far side of the room and had a brief conversation with him. The older guy looked over at Alice, who stood by the entrance feeling awkward but trying not to show it. He nodded and pointed to a door leading to another room.

It was a sparse waiting room. A couple of uncomfortable sofas. A broken coffee machine. Alice and Stark sat down. Stark put a peppermint in his mouth and hummed a tune.

'What now?' Alice said.

'Now?' Stark sounded surprised at the question. 'Now we wait. And we hope our chap in Amman is up to the job. There was an RV scheduled in the Jordanian desert at 04.00 hours. We should expect them back here at about five thirty.'

They sat and waited. Exhaustion overcame Alice's adrenaline and she found her chin dropping often to her chest, her eyes closing. Each time she jerked herself awake again, she saw that Stark was sitting calmly opposite her, his hands on his stomach, eyes open. She wished she could match his alertness, but she simply couldn't. When six thirty came, he had to shake her awake. 'They've arrived,' he said. 'I've asked for them to be brought directly to us.'

Alice roused herself. She was angry that she'd fallen asleep, but Stark didn't seem to care. He was pacing the room now, hands behind his back, throbbing with anxious energy.

'Is the General alive?' she asked.

The question was answered for her as the door opened. Three people entered. They brought with them a stench of sweat and fuel.

If Alice thought *she* was an incongruous sight, she was nothing compared to this mismatched trio. She could tell which one was General O'Brien. Well built, well tanned. A thick head of silver hair. Handsome, no doubt about it, but he had a slightly wild look in his eyes you might not have expected. He wore an ill-fitting pair of khaki trousers and a black T-shirt. Both were torn and the trousers spattered with something dark. Alice had a nasty suspicion it was blood. His skin and hair were dirty and there were bags around his eyes.

There was a woman. She was blonde and very beautiful, in her early to mid-thirties. She was as dishevelled as the General. She was wearing what had once been an elegant shirt and jacket. Alice couldn't imagine what she had been through to make her outfit look as it did now. As beautiful as she was, there was something about her that Alice didn't like. Could she detect a coldness? Alice prided herself on being a good judge of people. She decided that this was a woman to be avoided if possible, and respected if not.

The third person intrigued Alice the most. He was tall and broad shouldered. Scruffy black hair and a day's stubble. He wore a suit that was a little tight. It was torn in places and the shirt was spattered with blood and dirt. He had a steely frown. Dark eyes. A square jaw. She couldn't stop looking at him.

'Welcome to Cyprus, General O'Brien,' Stark said. 'Would you like a peppermint?'

'No, I don't want a damn peppermint. Who the hell are you?'

'I'm a representative of Her Majesty's Government,' Stark said, smoothly avoiding having to say his name. 'I hope you haven't been overly inconvenienced?'

'Overly inconvenienced?' O'Brien laughed harshly. He pointed to the dark-haired man. 'This guy hadn't been so quick off the mark, Her Majesty's Government would have assassinated me a few hours ago.'

Stark smiled blandly, admitting nor denying anything.

The dark-haired man stepped forward. 'I'm Black and you know the rest,' he said. 'We need to talk. That is, I'm going to talk, you're going to listen. Sit down.'

Alice could tell Stark didn't like being spoken to like that. His cheek twitched but he said nothing. Just sat back on the sofa. Alice did the same. The other three remained standing.

Black spoke. Alice listened, first in astonishment at the extreme nature of their insertion into Amman, in alarm when she understood the role the blonde woman – it transpired that her name was Bethany – had to play in all this, in horror at the gravity of the conspiracy the General had revealed to them, and finally with a sense of growing panic when she learned that a major terrorist atrocity was going to take place today. She wasn't stupid, of course. She could tell he was glossing over parts of his account. Why, for example, did he lead the Wagner Group into an ambush when he could have simply discarded their tracking device? She realised that she might have to accept that the reality of operations on the ground did not always align with the MI6 playbook. And anyway, if he hadn't done that, they wouldn't have learned that the attack had been brought forward.

Stark didn't seem to share her concerns. He had his fingers pressed together and his eyes closed. She knew he was listening intently. When Black finished, Stark remained like that for a full thirty seconds, silently processing. Then he opened his eyes.

'I take it, General O'Brien, that you are unwilling to share the location of the deepfake footage with me?'

The General pointed at Stark with a 'this guy knows what he's talking about' gesture. 'Damn right,' he said. 'Can you blame me?'

'Not in the least,' said Stark. 'It seems to me that you have precious little reason to trust politicians. But you can perhaps trust me?'

'Don't blame you for trying, buddy, but that's not going to happen. How quickly can you get me to DC? No Homeland Security, obviously.'

'In time for you to stop a terror attack that's going to happen today? That's going to be a challenge, even for us, but I'll make some enquiries.'

'Make them fast. With the time difference, today hasn't started yet in the US. But if these guys can change their plans once, they can change them again. If we don't publicise these deepfakes, the attack could happen any minute. We might even be too late as it is.'

Stark inclined his head and left the room. Nobody spoke. Alice sat silently, trying not to stare at any of this strange trio, without success. She was shocked by what she'd heard. Astonished by the dangers they had encountered in and around Amman. Faintly sickened by the idea that, but for her investigations into Poliakov, the General might now be dead. The silence in the room thickened. She found it almost unbearable. She jumped, but was relieved, when Stark entered again.

'It's in hand,' he announced. 'We'll get you into DC at the earliest opportunity. But I have one or two conditions. The first is that we keep all knowledge of this operation from Number 10. They're simply too compromised, too reliant on the approval of the American administration. I can't guarantee that they wouldn't put the brakes on the operation the moment they hear of it.'

'Suits me,' said the General. 'What else?'

'Danny Black and Bethany White will accompany you.'

As he said it, Alice happened to be looking at Bethany. She was standing behind Danny and the General, and Alice was certain she was the only person in the room to notice Bethany's reaction to this news. It was quite brief. Barely a flicker before she regained her composure. But like all MI6 officers, Alice had been trained to observe, to read and interpret people's responses. There was no doubt about Bethany's response: shock, suspicion, the dawning realisation of something sinister that she forced herself to suppress. Then it was gone. She was expressionless again.

'I see no reason for that,' the General objected. 'Once I'm in DC, I know what to do. This is my play, not yours.'

'Forgive me, General,' said Stark. 'I don't blame you not trusting us. But right now, we have only your word, and a forced confession from Mr Poliakov, about the matter in hand. You'll allow me a little mistrust too, I hope. It seems to me that you work well with your new friends, and I'd feel much more comfortable if they were with you, just to make sure you do what you say you're going to do.'

'This is an American matter.'

'No, General. You claim your president is planning a right-wing coup. You claim he is prepared to sacrifice innocent civilians in the process. You claim two of the world's superpowers are intimately entwined in a conspiracy to subvert democracy and the rule of law. This is a matter for us all.' He smiled. 'You should be thanking us. I'm assigning one of our top SAS operatives for your protection, not to mention an extremely experienced MI6 officer should you need any intelligence expertise on the ground.'

'Ex-MI6 officer,' Bethany White said.

A beat.

'My understanding,' Stark said, 'is that you have very good reasons for remaining on-message.'

The look of poison that Bethany White gave Stark was chilling. But there was no evidence of that poison in her voice when she said: 'I suppose I do.'

'And I might remind you, General O'Brien, that there is absolutely no possibility of you re-entering the United States without our help. Your face is well known after all. And if the Homeland Security officials fail to recognise you, their facial recognition systems most certainly will.'

The General didn't immediately reply. Alice watched him intently as he stared into the middle distance. He was clearly thinking deeply. Eventually he nodded his agreement. 'How do we do it?' he said. 'How do we get into the States without anybody knowing.'

'May I say,' Stark said, 'that I admire what you're doing. When you release the deepfake footage and expose the conspiracy, you will of course be—'

'Laughed out of DC. Spare me the Oscar speech, will you?'

'No Oscar speech, General O'Brien. Far from it. If you fail to locate the footage in time, questions will be asked as to whether you refused to tell us its location because you were too concerned about your own position.'

'You saying I'm risking civilian lives?'

'I'm saying questions will be asked. It won't be a good look.'

'I don't care what it looks like. I'm just a soldier, end of the day. We do what needs to be done.'

'How do we get into the US?' Danny Black asked.

'I'm a humble intelligence officer,' Stark said. 'Such matters are not my area of expertise. The military personnel in the next room will brief you.' He raised one hand to indicate that they should go through to that room. 'Good luck, gentlemen. And lady, of course.'

Danny Black, Bethany White and the General exited wordlessly. Stark watched them go, his eyes half closed, his face unreadable. Alice waited until the door was closed. Then she waited a moment longer. Then she asked a question that was perplexing her. 'I understand why Danny Black needs to accompany the General,' she said. 'They need to make a covert border crossing, and the SAS are trained to do that. But why does Bethany White need to go? Surely her role in all this is over.'

At first she thought Stark hadn't heard her. He was still staring after the others, as though he could see through the wall. Then he seemed to shake himself out of a reverie. 'You're a smart young lady, Alice,' he said. 'If they manage to stop this conspiracy, it will be in large part down to your efforts. But I'd advise you not to ask too many questions from here on in. There are some things you're better off not knowing.'

He stared through the wall again. Alice remembered the fleeting expression on Bethany White's face when she learned she was to be part of the insertion into DC, and a suspicion formed in her mind.

TWENTY-ONE

The briefing occurred on the move.

Danny, Bethany and the General strode across the tarmac to a waiting Land Rover, accompanied by a thin man with a thin moustache, whose camo gear seemed too big for him, but who was clearly in charge of the ops centre in the adjoining room where they'd met with the spooks. He'd introduced himself by his surname, Forshaw, and he spoke as they walked. 'We're in direct contact with Hereford. They're fully aware of your projected movements.'

'Great,' Danny said. 'Be good if we were too.'

Forshaw let the sarcasm pass. 'We have a Royal Navy frigate currently heading into NS Norfolk.'

'What's that?' Bethany asked.

'Naval Station Norfolk,' the General said. 'Biggest naval station in the world. Three and a half thousand acres of Norfolk Virginia, home to a hundred and fifty thousand military personnel and their families. Hell of a place. Home for the US Atlantic Fleet.'

'The frigate is scheduled to dock at Norfolk in about two hours. We've sent word to the captain to delay that for several hours. We have a C-17 incoming from Brize Norton as we speak. We'll give her the chance to refuel and then we'll get wheels up. She should be able to get you across the Atlantic in about eleven hours. You'll board the frigate and then it'll dock.'

'This gives us hardly any time,' Danny said. 'What if the hit's already happened by the time we get on to US soil.'

'We have to take that chance,' the General said. 'I'm not revealing the location of the memory stick. I don't trust anyone but me with it.' He frowned. 'If the hit's on the west coast, that buys us a bit more time.' He didn't sound optimistic.

'Hang on,' said Bethany. 'How do we get from the plane to the boat?'

'We freefall in,' Danny said.

'Onto the boat?'

'No. Into the water.'

She gave him a slightly sick look.

'Don't worry about it. You did fine last time.'

'It's only the last inch that kills you,' the General said with a grim smile. The old joke was received about as well as it had been when Danny had told it before they dropped into Jordan. 'A long time since I did a freefall into the ocean,' the General added.

'We have a four-man Special Boat Service team on standby to freefall in with you,' Forshaw said. 'SBS headquarters in Poole are making a request to the Americans to allow a training drop in the vicinity of the frigate. Story is that it's an anti-terrorist training exercise to recreate a similar scenario to the QE2 incident back in the seventies, when the Regiment dropped some guys in to the Atlantic to deal with a bomb scare on the ship. The aircraft has permission to land in the USA, refuel and take the four SBS guys back home. You'll actually be seven, of course, but with three sets of tandem jumpers, it'll look like four guys on the radar splash. If the Yanks want to make any enquiries, the four SBS guys will be on-site to answer their questions. They'll tell them they dropped in solo. The frigate will have a RIB in the water to load you up. That's a rigid inflatable boat,' he added, for Bethany's benefit. 'Once you've docked, you can pose as Royal Navy, and you'll be able to get off the naval station quickly.'

'I thought you said it was home to the US Atlantic Fleet,' Bethany said.

'Right,' said the General.

'So won't security be off the scale?'

'Sure, if you want to get on to the base. Getting off's much more straightforward.'

'There's going to be hundreds of crew members on that frigate that want to get straight off the base and into the nearest town to start drinking,' Danny said. 'Men and women. They'll be bussing coachloads of them off site. We'll be able to lose ourselves in among them.'

'But there'll be cameras, right?'

'I'll deal with that.'

'Once you're away from the naval station,' Forshaw said, 'you'll have a vehicle waiting for you. Then it's over to you.'

'What's the journey time from Norfolk to DC?' Danny asked. He was working out timings in his head.

'Three to four hours,' the General said. They had reached the Land Rover. The driver had opened all the doors and was waiting behind the wheel to drive them off.

'How long till the C-17 gets here?'

Forshaw didn't immediately answer. He looked at the sky for a few seconds, then pointed to the west. Danny saw the lights of an aircraft in the distance. 'That's your ride,' said Forshaw. 'Let's get going.'

They climbed into the Land Rover and drove across the tarmac.

It was midnight in Florida and Hamoud's family were asleep. If he lay very still, he could hear his children breathing in the next room. Hamoud and Rabia had carried them, half asleep, back to the hotel from the nightly firework display at Magic Kingdom. They'd seemed to grow heavier the sleepier they became. Hamoud felt ashamed that he'd appeared to find it more difficult to carry Malick than Rabia did Melissa. He reminded himself that he was not, even now, back to his full strength, but it didn't really help.

To cheer himself up, he thought back over their evening as he lay next to his sleeping wife. The wonder on the children's faces as they walked through the park, absorbing the sights and the sounds. Their sweet patience as they stood in line for the rides, and their screams of excitement for the few minutes that each ride lasted. The way they craned their necks and widened their eyes during the firework display. The way they begged to be allowed to come back and see it again the following night.

The fireworks! Hamoud had never seen anything like it. It was astonishing to him that such an extravagant display could take place every night. He remembered reading somewhere that gun crime always increased in the vicinity of Walt Disney World during the firework display, because the sound of the fireworks masked the gunfire. He didn't know if that was true or not, but he did know that somebody could have exploded a small bomb this evening and the sound would have been quite well camouflaged. The thought unnerved him. He pictured his family standing in that enormous, cooing crowd, eyes aloft, unable to defend themselves against an explosive device ...

He shook his head against his pillow. He was not in control of his thoughts. Sometimes it was as if a person with a remote control was switching the channel in his head. Why would he want to imagine such catastrophes when they were almost certain not to happen? He was torturing himself, and he'd had quite enough of that from other people.

Hamoud was naked, but still very hot. He climbed out of bed – quietly, so that he didn't wake Rabia – and put on the Mickey Mouse robe that he had found hanging in the wardrobe. He crept into the adjoining room and looked at his children. Moonlight was shining on them through the window and they looked very peaceful. He took his key card and tiptoed out into the corridor.

The lights were dim, but still brighter than the dark room, so he couldn't see very well as he made his way to the ice machine. It buzzed noisily ten metres along the corridor. There was a tube that dispensed plastic cups. Hamoud took one and half filled it with ice. He was about to take it back to the room, where he would fill it with water from the bathroom tap, when he stopped. His eyes had grown used to the dim light now, and he saw a man standing at one end of the corridor. Was he of Middle Eastern ethnicity? He didn't seem to be looking at Hamoud, or even to have noticed him. But it was strange. Even stranger when he turned and saw another brown-skinned man at the other end of the corridor. Why would they be standing there, as though guarding the place?

Hamoud felt an urge to be back under the covers next to his wife. He shuffled hurriedly back to his room, head down, clutching the plastic cup, avoiding eye contact with the man he was facing. He reached the door to his room and tapped the key card to the sensor. A red light turned green and he was about to open up when he glanced both ways along the corridor. The men were still there, still ignoring him, but he noticed something else. The room opposite, number 297, had a strip of light leaking out where the door met the floor. Two dark shadows interrupted it, the width of feet. Hamoud imagined somebody standing on the other side, listening. His spine froze, as cold as the ice in his cup. He hurried back into his room. He could sense Rabia sitting up in bed. 'Are you okay?' she asked. 'Where have you been?'

'Ice,' he said. 'I was hot.'

He didn't fill the cup with water. He climbed straight back into bed, still wearing the dressing gown.

They lay there, each of them aware that the other was wide awake, but neither of them wanting to break the silence.

Inside Room 297, a man stood listening.

He had brown skin. He wore a grey T-shirt and jeans. He heard the door of the room opposite open and close. Then a voice in his earpiece said: 'Clear.'

He turned and walked back into the room and nodded at the other man sitting cross-legged on the floor.

He was a weird-looking guy. It wasn't something you could easily put your finger on, but the man in the grey T-shirt had spent a long time with him, encouraging his crazy jihadist tendencies, and so he'd had plenty of time to work out that it was something to do with the shape of his face. It was unusually long and thin. When he'd had a beard, the face had seemed even longer and thinner. Like a cartoon character. It had worried the man in the grey T-shirt because the face was so distinctive. It was hard to go unnoticed in a crowd when you looked like that. Now, though, he had a smart new haircut and was clean shaven. He still looked a bit odd, but not *totally* peculiar. Without the face fungus, he at least wouldn't turn heads. The only problem was the way he kept touching his chin, clearly not used to the unfamiliar absence of a beard. Read any of the counter-terrorism manuals and you'd learn that was a classic indicator. Tonight, however, nobody in the crowds would be observing the tics of the people around them. They'd be too busy looking at the sky.

The guy had apparatus spread out on the thin hotel carpet in front of him. Orange blocks of plastic explosive. A detonator. A coil of thin cable. A small battery pack. A knife. Several transparent bags of nails. A needle and thread. And a baseball jacket, a few sizes too big for him. It had white arms and a black body and, on the back, a cheerful picture of Donald Duck and his cheeky nephews. As the man in the grey T-shirt watched, he turned the baseball jacket over and started to cut neatly into the lining.

'You know what you're doing, brother?' the man in the grey T-shirt said. He took pains to disguise his American accent.

The man on the floor didn't look up. But he nodded as he reached for one of the packets of plastic explosive. 'I have done it many times before,' he said, before adding, more quietly: 'But never for myself.'

'You'll be a martyr,' said the man in the grey T-shirt. 'Inshallah, people will say your name for a hundred years.'

'My rewards will not be in this world,' said the man on the floor. 'They will be in the next.'

'Your place in paradise is assured,' said the man in the grey T-shirt. He watched him for a moment, then quietly left the room. He walked along the corridor towards one of the men standing watch.

'Is he doing it?' said the man quietly.

'You bet,' said the man in the grey T-shirt. No need to drop his American accent now.

'You think he suspects?'

'He thinks we're his best buddies. It's like he's blind to everything except . . . you know, the *thing*.'

'The *thing*?' His companion was clearly amused by the euphemism. 'He shaved his body yet?'

'Just his face.'

'He'll shave his body. Tonight probably. Ritual thing, you know? Chest, arms, legs.' His companion pointed to his groin to indicate another area that would be shaved. 'So you're in for a treat, watching him do all that.'

'We could always swap.'

'Not a chance, my friend.'

They stood in silence for a moment.

'This is a crummy hotel.'

'I've seen worse.'

'Oh yeah?'

'Sure. But it doesn't matter. We'll be out of here tonight. Nine fifteen tonight, we'll have earned ourselves enough dough to get the presidential suite in the Grand Hyatt.'

'I guess. Going to be quite the firework display, huh?'

'Couple of extra bangs. That's what the tourists come for, right? Bangs.'

'Right.' A beat. 'I'd better get back to him.'

'Sure. Bit of luck he'll be getting lathered up already. Allahu Akbar, huh?'

'Yeah. Allahu frickin' Akbar.'

The man left his companion and walked back down the corridor towards Room 297. He stopped just outside it and drew a deep breath. Put himself back into character. The white jihadist. Sympathetic to the bomber's cause. His friend. His brother.

He touched his key card to the sensor and re-entered the room. His 'brother' was packing plastic explosives into the baseball jacket. He stood and watched.

07.00 hrs. It was a bright, sunny morning but Danny felt anything but. His body ached with tiredness. He realised he was losing track of the days, as well as running out of time. The hit could happen in a matter of hours, and they were still on the wrong side of the Atlantic.

The C-17 was on the ground. Surrounded by vehicles. Engineers called to each other across the tarmac, checking the landing gear, moving up and down the open tailgate. Nobody paid Danny, Bethany or the General much attention as they made their way up into the dimly lit aircraft. 'Home from home,' Bethany said, looking around at the interior which was just as stark and utilitarian as the Hercules they'd used for their insertion into Jordan. There was a triple line of uncomfortable-looking seating up front, and a number of hammocks fixed to the sides. A few wooden storage crates. Danny didn't know what they contained. Otherwise, this personnel carrier was close to empty.

'Don't get too comfortable,' Danny said. 'An insertion into water is a little different.'

'How so?'

Danny was about to explain when he saw four figures in Crye Precision camo gear walking up the tailgate, slightly silhouetted by the morning light outside. Their clothes, and the huge waterproof bags they were lugging, told Danny that these were the SBS guys who'd be accompanying them. He left Bethany and the General and strode forwards to meet them. As he drew closer, he recognised one of the guys: Damien Parker had been on a few training exercises with Danny in the past. He had a ruddy face and looked a hell of a sight younger than he was, but he was a good man. Danny held out his hand. 'How you doing, mate?'

'Fucking busy times, Danny,' Parker said. He introduced the rest of his team: Alex Lewis, Rob Emerson, Dave Gordon. Danny shook hands with each of them in turn. 'Did you come straight from the office?' Emerson asked, indicating Danny's suit.

'Something like that,' Danny said.

Parker peered into the aircraft. 'I don't want to know what you're up to,' he said, 'but do you mind if I do the briefing once we're up and running?'

'We're in your hands getting into the water and on to the ship,' Danny said. 'However you want to play it.'

'Let's get up in the air first,' Parker said.

Danny led them back up into the body of the C-17. Once they were inside, he could tell that the SBS guys recognised the General's face, even if they couldn't quite identify him. But they said nothing about it. Their gazes lingered on Bethany. It wasn't often that someone as beautiful as her found their way on to a mission like this. Their appreciation went unremarked upon, however. They were too professional for that.

A loadie approached them. 'We'll be refuelling twice in mid-air,' he told them. 'Once over UK airspace, once mid-Atlantic. Wheels up when you're ready.'

'Have you jumped before?' Parker asked Bethany and the General. They nodded

'So here's what you need to know about landing in water.' Parker pointed at Lewis, Emerson and Gordon. 'These three guys are going to jump first, Lewis and Emerson in tandem, Gordon solo. I'll be in tandem with you.' He indicated the General. 'We'll follow Lewis and Emerson. Danny and the lady will follow Gordon. We get into any kind of trouble, they'll be waiting for us in the water to help out. We'll be jumping from about fourteen thousand feet, and we'll cut away our chutes when our feet hit the water. You need to expect to go straight under the water. We're expecting the sea state to be calm, but don't let that fool you. The water will be cold and your natural instinct will be to breathe in. Unless you want a lungful of salt water, and you don't, you need to clamp your mouth shut and concentrate hard on not inhaling. You'll be wearing a life vest. As soon as you're submerged, you need to inflate it. It should bring you to the surface in a few seconds. Once we're above the water, Lewis and Emerson will help us unclip our tandem harnesses. We'll then wait in the water until a RIB from the frigate picks us up. Bit of luck, it'll only be a couple of minutes, but it might be longer. The most important thing is that you keep away from the cut-away chutes and avoid getting tangled in the lines. Is that all clear?'

Bethany and the General nodded again.

Parker pointed at one of the waterproof bags they'd brought aboard. 'We have the dry suits and rigs here. We'll get changed when we're about an hour out. Questions?'

There were none. They all strapped themselves in for take-off. As the C-17 accelerated along the runway, Danny realised that for the first time in days he felt a sense of calm. There was something reassuring about being in transit. Here, in the belly of an RAF flight, surrounded by military personnel, he could be sure of one thing: for a few hours at least, nobody would be trying to kill him. That thought made him glance at Bethany. They were separated by a couple of empty seats. She was sitting upright, staring straight ahead. She displayed no emotion. Danny couldn't read her. He wondered if she seemed even more brittle than usual. He felt a moment of respect for her. She'd pushed on through this mission and kept her head. Very few people could manage that. He felt a pang of guilt for what was to come.

They gained altitude. Danny unclipped himself from his seat and made his way to one of the hammocks. He lay on it and succumbed to the weariness that had been pressing in on him. He was asleep in seconds.

Parker woke him. It felt like only minutes had passed, but Danny could tell from the SBS man's demeanour that they were closing in on the drop zone. 'We're an hour out,' he said over the noise of the jets. 'Time to brief and prep.' He checked his watch. It read 16.46 hrs. He put it back the requisite seven hours. 09.46 hrs, local time.

Parker handed round dry suits. There was nowhere for Bethany to have any privacy as she changed. She took herself up to the front of the aircraft where there was an area less illuminated by the dim interior lighting. It didn't stop the men all glancing over as she undressed in the shadow and awkwardly pulled on the tight dry suit. Even the General watched, which surprised Danny. He'd have thought the old boy would have wanted to forget about the sight of Bethany semi-naked. Danny kept her in his peripheral vision. She still had the pistol she'd taken from the Wagner Group guy back at the hotel in Amman. He saw her stow it in a waterproof pouch in the dry suit. He did the same with his Sig as he changed. His phone was dead. He found an external power pack in Parker's rucksack and plugged it in to recharge.

The SBS team were already rigged up: life vests, fins hooked to the front of their dry suits, freefall rigs for Parker, Emerson and Gordon, tandem harnesses for Parker and Emerson, helmets. Parker was talking intently to the General, clearly repeating the details of the jump. Gordon handed Danny a tandem harness, a helmet and a freefall rig. 'It's been checked,' he shouted.

Danny didn't care who had checked. There was no way he'd use a chute without giving it the once-over himself. He checked the packing and the strapping and, once he was completely satisfied all was as it should be, he put the rig on his back. He unplugged his recharged phone and put it in the waterproof pouch with his Sig.

They had forty-five minutes to kill before the jump. Danny and the others took seats along the sides of the aircraft. The time passed quickly. A loadie gave them the signal and he walked over to Bethany. 'You ready?' he shouted over the engine noise.

She smiled at him. The brittleness had suddenly gone. She seemed softer. It made him wary. 'This is getting to be a habit,' she said.

'Different to last time,' Danny said. 'A lower jump. No oxygen. But we still have to fall stable. You remember what to do?'

'I'm a fast learner.' They moved further to the back of the aircraft before clipping themselves together. Parker and the

252

General were waiting for them by the tailgate. The remaining three SBS guys were packing up gear at the front of the plane, but they soon joined them. Lewis and Emerson clipped themselves together, while Gordon remained solo. Seven people. Four radar splashes. The Yanks would have no idea that this seemingly routine training jump was actually a covert op.

The tailgate opened. They had flown west with the sun, so it was a morning light that entered the C-17. There was a brisk, biting chill as the cold air entered the plane, and the external noise of the jets doubled in volume, making it impossible to speak. The Atlantic stretched out to a hazy horizon. There was no sign of any ships below and that figured: the guys planning the drop would have made sure the DZ was out of view of shipping, in case anybody noticed that three of the chutes were carrying personnel in tandem. The loadie by the red jump light held up five fingers and then, two minutes later, three. The parachutists positioned themselves according to Parker's previous instructions. The tandem team of Lewis and Emerson to the left of the tailgate, with Danny and Bethany close behind them. Gordon to the right, with Parker and the General behind him.

The jump light turned green. Lewis, Emerson and Gordon fell from the C-17 out into the clear air. Danny, Bethany, Parker and the General followed close behind. The sound of the aircraft instantly disappeared, replaced by the rush of wind as they accelerated through the air towards the Atlantic, which sped up to meet them. Danny saw, in the distance, the dot of a ship and he knew that must be the frigate. But he kept his main focus on Lewis and Emerson and, when they deployed their chute, he deployed his just seconds later. The rush of air dissipated. The chute flapped open above them and then they were drifting. Danny used the steering toggles to follow Lewis and Emerson's path. He could feel a wind blowing from the south. Lewis and Emerson turned into it. Danny did the same.

He had performed freefall jumps into water not nearly so often as onto land. Maybe six or seven times in his whole career, and never operationally. He knew, however, that one of the greatest dangers was cutting away too early. In the past, the SOP had been to cut the chute away when the parachutist was a couple of feet above sea level, but distances over water could be deceptive and Danny had heard of guys cutting away a hundred feet too soon. Not a good idea, especially in a tandem rig. Nowadays, the trick was to cut away as soon as your feet hit the water. So, as well as concentrating on Lewis and Emerson's position, he focused on the ocean. The glint of morning sunlight on the surface. The curling flash of an occasional white horse. He estimated that he and Bethany were separated from the SBS guys by a hundred feet of altitude. He saw them cut away as they hit the water. 'Get ready,' he told Bethany. 'Remember what they said about not inhaling.'

Bethany didn't reply, but he could feel her chest expand as she drew a breath and held it.

Thirty feet.

Ten.

Five.

Water.

Danny yanked the cutaway handle at his shoulder. He felt the chute separate from his body.

The cold was no less shocking for being expected. The silence no less sinister. Even though he was prepared for the darkness and the sense of disorientation that naturally accompanied a sudden submerging, he had to work hard to prevent the instinctive panic. He was good at it. Bethany, still attached to him, wasn't. As they plunged deeper, he felt her flailing with panic. She wasn't dealing with the sensory overload. He could tell that she was trying to find the inflating cord on her life vest but she couldn't work out where it was, and was desperately grabbing different bits of her apparatus. Danny was experiencing the overload of his senses too, but his muscle memory kicked in and he yanked the inflating cord on his own life vest. He felt the pressure of the vest against his abdomen, but it wasn't immediately sufficient to stop their downward momentum. He opened his eyes. Bethany was little more than a shadow in the underwater gloom. She was fumbling for her own inflating cord, unable to find it. He stretched out one arm, located it immediately, and tugged.

The second life vest made the difference. They rose towards the surface. The gloom dissipated. Seconds later, they broke through the water into the open air. They both inhaled deeply, and it felt as though Danny's ears were inhaling the sound of the ocean too. The SBS guys had predicted a calm sea state, but there was a noticeable swell that blocked his view not only of the horizon but also of his immediate surroundings. He couldn't see the frigate. He couldn't see the SBS guys. He couldn't even see the cutaway chute.

'You're okay!' he shouted. 'We're safe.' She replied with a nod. Danny noticed that she was shivering as she gasped for air and he felt protective. 'I've got you,' he told her. 'Move your limbs. Arms and legs. Do it.'

She started treading water and Danny copied her movements so they were bobbing in sync. The current turned them and the swell raised them, and Danny saw their chute and its lines just a couple of metres away from them. They kicked away from it.

And then Lewis and Emerson were there, appearing as if from nowhere. They had unclipped themselves from their tandem harness and had obviously donned their fins because they were cutting speedily through a mound of swell. Emerson reached them first and helped them unclip from each other. Lewis moved close to Bethany, ready to help her if she got into trouble. Danny caught sight of her face for the first time since the jump. Her skin was very pale, her blonde hair plastered to her cheek. She looked vulnerable, bobbing in the vastness of the Atlantic. And although Lewis stuck close, it was Danny she looked to.

He could feel his own body temperature dropping and was relieved to hear the approaching buzz of an engine. It grew louder very quickly and, as the swell raised him again, he saw a large black RIB approaching. Beyond it he caught a glimpse of the frigate, grey and immobile in the distance. Then the RIB was alongside them. A coxswain leaned over the side, shouting at them to board. Danny kicked his way to the RIB and remained in the water as the other guys helped Bethany. He clambered over the side. The RIB only had one other crew member at the wheel. He followed the coxswain's instruction to sit behind him next to Bethany. He could almost sense the relief coming off her.

It only took a couple more minutes to collect the others. The General looked in pretty good shape for an older guy. He swam powerfully towards the RIB and barely needed any help boarding. Then they were speeding back towards the frigate, bouncing on the waves, spray everywhere, the air a mixture of salt and fuel fumes. Apart from the Royal Navy vessel, the ocean was deserted in all directions. Their insertion into American waters might have registered as a radar splash, but he was confident that no American eyes had witnessed it. He couldn't help noticing, though, how the General scanned the horizon constantly, as though searching for some unseen watcher.

They were travelling against the current, so it took longer than Danny expected to reach the frigate. Maybe fifteen minutes later its vast hull loomed above them, and the ocean itself seemed to shake with the rumble of its idling engines. Overhead, a crane jutted out over the deck railings. It supported a heavy winch, which lowered a set of ropes and carabiners down to the bobbing RIB. The SBS guys fastened the ropes to anchoring points on the RIB, and in seconds they were hauled aloft. Danny saw Bethany gripping her seat so hard that her knuckles turned white. The SBS guys almost looked bored, this manoeuvre was so routine for them.

The crane lowered them on to the deck. A man stood there to greet them. He was dressed in blue naval uniform, and wore a full black beard, flecked with grey. His eyes were sharp and blue, and he spoke cheerfully with the remnants of a Liverpudlian accent that sounded out of place here in the middle of the ocean. 'I'm Captain Mitchell,' he announced, 'and you're very welcome aboard.'

Danny stood and shook hands with him. 'How long till we dock.'

'Four hours?' He seemed to notice Danny's frustration. 'Sooner if possible. I've a got a boat full of men and women who've been at sea for several weeks and we've just delayed their arrival into Norfolk by eight hours. I'll be honest with you. They're getting thirsty.'

With a twinkling smile, the captain turned and led them along the deck.

TWENTY-TWO

The chef at the breakfast bar made the children pancakes shaped like Mickey Mouse's head and flecked with chocolate drops. They stared at their breakfast in awe, as if unable to process that something so extravagant and delicious could be theirs to eat. Rabia nursed a bowl of fruit and a glass of orange juice and fondly watched the kids take their first bites and close their eyes in ecstasy as they chewed.

Hamoud had nothing but a small cup of strong coffee. He wasn't hungry but he was tired. He hadn't slept.

The dining room was very large but only half full. Perhaps a hundred people, half of them children, none of them sitting anywhere near Hamoud and his family. A young child had pointed at his scar and started crying. His parents had hurried him along to another table much further away.

Disney characters, in their huge, colourful costumes, were moving from table to table. There was Baloo, the bear, pretending to steal a young boy's chocolate milk. There was Cinderella, white gloves up to her elbows, gracefully curtseying at a table of wide-eyed girls. Chip 'n' Dale were messing around at the far end of the restaurant. They had frightened a baby in a high chair and were putting their hands to their mouths in false alarm.

Hamoud was sweating. He was scratching his palms under the table. He was looking from character to character and he realised he was searching for Goofy. For the Goofy who had taken his picture yesterday.

Or had he?

'Is everything alright, my love?'

His wife put one hand on his and he smiled in return and took a sip of coffee. There was no Goofy. None of the characters were paying him or his family the least attention. He was about to point at Chip 'n' Dale because he knew their antics would make her laugh, when something caught his eye. It was a security camera, positioned over the entrance to the restaurant and angled so that it was pointing directly at Hamoud's family.

A surge of panic rose in his chest and he fought to control it. He shut his eyes. In an instant he was elsewhere. He was sitting alone in a foul cell, cross-legged on the floor, a tray of food that only a starving person would countenance eating. A camera above the door, pointing at him. The flashback was sharp. Vivid. He could see every streak on the concrete walls and every tiny dot of rodent droppings on the floor. He could smell the toilet in the corner and taste his thirst. He could hear the footsteps of the guard outside.

And then he opened his eyes and was back in the restaurant, his family staring at him as he continued to scratch his palms under the table.

'My love?'

'I'm sorry,' he said. 'I think I have an upset stomach. I'm going to the washroom. Shall I see you up in the room?'

The children were munching again. Rabia squeezed his hand. 'See you up there,' she said.

Hamoud left the restaurant. The elevator that would take him back up to his room was straight ahead. The reception desk was to his right. He stood for a moment, contemplating the two. He looked over his shoulder to check that his wife couldn't see him. She was out of view. He walked up to the reception desk. There was a small line and he had to wait a couple of minutes to be seen. Long, sweaty minutes. His mouth was dry and his palms itched. He forced himself not to scratch them because that would make him look even more nervous than he already did. He had never tried anything like this before.

'May I help you, sir?'

The woman behind the desk was plump, with bleached hair scraped tightly back. She smiled, of course, but it was the fixed, forced smile that Hamoud recognised so well. The smile of a prejudiced American attempting to hide their true feelings. Her eyes kept flickering to his scar, and Hamoud could tell that she was making unfavourable judgements without even talking to him.

'I'm very sorry,' Hamoud said, keeping his voice low so that the person behind him in the line would not overhear, 'but I've lost my key card. May I have another?'

'What room number would that be, sir?'

He hesitated before delivering his lie, then cursed himself for hesitating, and so he stuttered and had to repeat himself. 'Room 297,' he said.

He knew he'd blown it the moment the words were out of his mouth. The receptionist couldn't hide her suspicion. She typed at the terminal in front of her and said, 'I'm sorry, sir. The guest in Room 297 checked out this morning.'

'Room 298' Hamoud said, a bit too quickly. 'Mr Al Asmar.' He patted down his pockets. 'I'm sorry,' he said. 'I've found it.' He pulled out his key card and showed it to her. 'I'm very sorry.' He could feel the heat of embarrassment on his cheeks. He bowed slightly and shuffled away from the reception desk, hurrying towards the elevator. What had he been thinking? Even if he had somehow managed to persuade the receptionist to give him a key card to the room opposite, what then? Would he really have entered? What was he hoping to find?

He stopped. He had seen something out of the corner of his eye. He turned to get a better view.

It was one of the men he had seen in the corridor last night. He was striding towards the exit. Another man was following him. He looked Middle Eastern. He was wearing a baseball jacket with Donald Duck on the back that looked rather too big for him. But it wasn't the colour of his skin that made Hamoud stop, or the clothes he was wearing. Hamoud *recognised* him. He knew that face. He had seen it before. He tried to think when and where, but the memory was slippery and he couldn't grab it.

The guy in the baseball jacket exited the hotel. Hamoud stood where he was, his face screwed up as he tried to remember. Then he noticed people watching him and he felt self-conscious. He hurried over to the elevator and called it. On the second floor, he forced himself not to look at the door to room 297. He was embarrassed by his clumsy attempt to get the key card. Inside his own room, he sat on the edge of the unmade bed, scratched his palms and waited for his family to return.

Captain Mitchell had assigned them a dedicated ops room: a sparse, windowless area below decks that vibrated with the frigate's engines. The SBS guys didn't join them. They hadn't asked why Danny, Bethany and the General needed a covert insertion into the US, and Danny had the impression that they were determined not to find out. A wise call, in the circumstances.

There was a trunk of mismatched clothes waiting for them in the room. Danny and the General stood outside to give Bethany the privacy to strip out of her dry suit and change. When they re-entered, she was dressed in nondescript jeans and a loose-fitting T-shirt. Her hair was matted from the salt water and she still looked cold. Danny found an oversized jumper among the clothes and gave it to her. 'Keep warm,' he told her, and she didn't argue. She turned her back as Danny and the General changed. At first, the General put on chinos and an open-necked shirt, but that didn't work for Danny. 'You look too much like yourself,' he said. 'We don't know if or how the media are going to present your disappearance from the hotel, but we've got to assume you're going to be on most TV sets in the States. You have to disguise yourself better.' He found a black hoodie emblazoned with a New York Yankees logo. The General put it on and raised the hood. He had a day's stubble and dark rings under his eyes. The effect of the hood was to make him look like the kind of guy most people would want to avoid. He certainly didn't look like top brass.

Danny found a hoodie for himself. This one had a Harvard logo. Pretty much the closest he'd ever get to a university. It wasn't very clean. It reeked of another man's sweat. That didn't matter. In fact, it was an advantage. It meant people would avoid him, too. He put an old denim jacket on over it. He took his Sig and phone from the waterproof pouch in his dry suit. He checked the pistol over. All good. The General pointed at Bethany. 'I want her weapon,' he said.

Danny stowed his Sig in the inside pocket of his jacket, and his phone in his jeans. He took a moment to consider the General's request. It made sense. As soon as they stepped foot on American soil, O'Brien was in danger. He might need to defend himself. And maybe Danny had been too trusting, allowing Bethany to be armed in the first place. She wasn't reliable. And the time was surely approaching that he needed her to be unarmed in any case.

'Hand it over,' he said.

He expected an argument, but it didn't come. Bethany handed the pistol to the General.

They waited. Time crept slowly. An hour. Two. Three. The General paced the room small room anxiously. Eventually, there was a knock. Danny opened the door. A naval rating stood there, red-faced and pimply. He looked barely young enough to be out of school and his acne spread all the way down his neck. 'Secure comms from Hereford,' he said. 'I'm to take you to the bridge.'

'Wait here,' Danny told Bethany and the General. 'Try not to kill each other while I'm gone.'

The bridge was busy but quiet. The captain sat at his control post watching his men as they went about their business of preparing the frigate for docking. Danny could see the eastern seaboard of the United States up ahead through the windows. There were three other naval ships in his field of view. A vast mackerel sky suggested that the weather was about to change. The rating led him to a comms post where Danny put on a headset with a built-in boom mike. 'Go ahead,' he said.

He recognised the CO's voice, every word crisp and clear despite the distance of several thousand miles. '*I've been briefed,*' said Williamson. '*Sounds like you've had a busy night.*'

'Roger that, sir.'

'*Some time, you and me are going to have a little chat about your detour.*'

'Yes, sir.' A pause. 'It was the Wagner Group, boss. The same people who targeted the Zero 22 convoy.'

'*Understood,*' said Williamson. A beat. '*You have Bethany White with you?*'

'Yes, sir.'

'*You understand why?*'

'Not entirely.'

'*Because now that the op has evolved, US soil is the best place for her to end up dead. The Yanks are going to sweep this whole thing under the carpet. If they can do some of our tidying up for us, so much the better.*'

'Understood, sir.'

'*Prioritise the General. The frigate should get your feet on solid ground at about 15.00 hours local. It's crucial that he broadcasts those deepfakes, even if it happens after the terror attack. We have no lead on when or where the attack is going to take place. This is the only way to put the skids on the President's conspiracy. But when it's done, finish your mission.*'

Danny stared through the window of the bridge. Naval Station Norfolk was fast approaching.

'*Do you copy?*' the CO asked.

'Yes, sir,' said Danny. 'I copy.'

The line went dead. Danny removed the headset. The rating was standing nearby. Danny could tell he was trying to glean something from his end of the conversation, but was disappointed. He was just a kid, and Danny had learned that kids were often a little starstruck in the presence of an SF guy. He gave him a friendly smile. 'What's your name?' he said.

'Jack,' the kid said.

'Do me a favour, Jack? Find me a pair of binoculars. Meet me on deck?'

Jack reddened at the neck. Not from embarrassment, Danny perceived, but from pride at being included. He scurried away. Danny left the bridge and went to fetch the others.

There was not a cloud in the sky. It was the perfect weather for a day in the parks. They were busier than yesterday. The crowds made Hamoud more nervous than usual. They seemed to have the same effect on his children. They stayed closer and were less exuberant. Perhaps they were just tired.

Hamoud made a special effort. He shouted with mock glee as they sped round the Big Thunder Mountain Railroad. He cooed and pointed as their sedate boat bobbed its way around It's a Small World. He had his picture taken with a pirate, whose ar-harghs became less enthusiastic when he saw the real scar down Hamoud's right eye. But whenever he knew his family was not looking, he was like a lighthouse, the beam of his gaze rotating in circles around him. What was he looking for? Another cartoon character taking his photograph? Familiar faces out of place? A brown-skinned man in an oversized baseball jacket whom he still simply could not place, no matter how hard he urged his brain?

He saw none of them. As they sat at a refreshment stall and guzzled Coke from enormous cups – a rare treat for them, of course – he maintained his surveillance under the guise of taking in the view. He saw children, some dragging their parents by the hand, others wilting in the heat. He saw adults, some of them so enormous that they required the use of mobility vehicles. He saw Walt Disney World staff, all tans and smiles. He saw characters clowning around with the visitors, animated despite the heat.

But he saw nothing suspicious.

Why, then, was the urge to scratch his sweaty palms so overpowering that he felt the need to cool them down on his Coke cup?

It was the face. The long, curious face that he recognised but could not identify. He was so close. But each time he thought he had it, it slipped away again. He felt like a drowning man grabbing at a life raft, only to find that the touch of his fingertips perpetually nudged it out of reach.

They finished their Cokes and the children, revived now, grabbed their parents' hands and dragged them off to the next amusement, whatever that might be.

Danny, Bethany and the General stood on deck as the frigate docked. There were very few other crew members outside. Those that were, walked with purpose. They clearly had jobs to do and they paid the trio scant attention.

The docking was an impressive manoeuvre. The ocean churned all around them. There was spray and the vast grind of engines. But for all its bulk, the vessel moved with an almost delicate precision as it drew up to its berth alongside one of a long line of concrete piers. There was an aircraft carrier at the next berth. Beyond that, huge grey destroyers and a variety of supply vessels. As they docked, Danny watched the conning tower of a sleek, black diesel-electric sub break the water to the north-east. The activity wasn't limited to the water. An aircraft of some description was circling in the distance. Closer by, three Seahawks were coming in to land. Beyond the pier was a huge area where at least 200 military vehicles were parked up. There were more vehicles moving along the pier itself: supply lorries mostly, but also armoured trucks and three buses. It was these that drew Danny's attention as the frigate came to a halt by the pier and vast ship-to-shore mooring lines were thrown from the vessel. The buses were parked in a line. It was hard from a distance to judge accurately the space between them, but Danny estimated about twenty metres. In front of the leftmost bus was a tall post and it had something mounted on it. Danny could quite make it out, but he thought he knew what it was. Right then Jack appeared with the binoculars Danny had asked for. 'Good man,' Danny said. He took the binoculars. Jack stood a respectful distance of a few metres while Danny put the binoculars to his eyes.

NS Norfolk appeared through the lenses in greater detail. It was huge. A vast, flat area, dotted with hangers and runways and roads and accommodation blocks and all the infrastructure of a busy military base. Danny couldn't see its boundaries. He adjusted the binoculars and focused in on the buses and the post in front of them.

The object mounted on the post was a camera, as Danny expected. Security would be high on a naval base like this. He doubted there would be airport-style facial recognition, but there would be some level of CCTV surveillance and he was seeing evidence of it now. He had no means of knowing whether his attempt to stage the General's death back in the Roman ruins outside Amman had worked. He needed to plan for the worst-case scenario, and that meant avoiding all video surveillance if at all possible. He scrutinised the position and angle of the camera. It was pointing downwards and just to the right of the leftmost bus. The middle bus was likely in its field of view. Not the bus on the right.

Danny lowered the binoculars and turned to Jack. Gave the spotty rating his friendliest smile. 'Do me a favour, bud,' he said. He pointed in the direction of the buses. 'You see those three buses?'

Jack nodded.

'I'm guessing they're to take crew members off site.'

Jack grinned. 'Party time,' he said. 'We've been a long time at sea. They'll be hitting the bars the moment they open. You joining them?'

'Bit early for me,' Danny said. 'But you see the bus on the right? I need you to get a message to whoever's in charge that we need to be on that bus, and once we're off site the driver's going to have to stop for us when I tell him to. Can you do that for me?'

It was almost comical, the way Jack nodded casually, as if this was something he did every day, then turned and almost sprinted back along the deck. Danny raised his binoculars again and monitored the activity on the pier. There was much to-ing and fro-ing. Military vehicles approached, and service lorries. Already there were people disembarking from the frigate. Danny focused in on them and saw a couple of official-looking US Navy men leading the four SBS guys to a vehicle. Just a quick word, no doubt, to confirm that their training exercise was just that. Danny knew he could rely on them to keep quiet about their extra tandem loads.

Jack was slightly out of breath when he returned. 'This way, guys,' he said, before remembering that Bethany was one of their group, and flushing a little. He led them below decks. There was much activity now. Sailors hurriedly squeezed their way through the narrow corridors, plainly eager to get off the frigate and paying Danny and the others almost no attention. Jack led them down into the noisy, dirty hull of the ship, where the grinding sound of the engines vibrated through their bodies. Here there was an exit, where a metal platform had been laid between ship and pier. A group of crew members had congregated here. They were full of boisterous good humour and although Danny and the others drew a few glances from them, they were clearly more concerned with their trip on to land than with this mismatched trio who had joined them. One guy stood slightly apart from the others. Jack went to talk to him, pointing out Danny, Bethany and the General. He nodded, made a quick head count and then divided the sailors into three groups, before indicating which bus each group should board. Danny, Bethany and the General were in the right one. Danny winked his thanks to Jack, who ballooned with pride, and then they walked down the platform and along the concrete pier towards the buses. The trio walked in the middle of their group, heads down. The bus's engine was already turning over when they reached it, an impatient and rather sweaty driver sitting at the wheel flicking through his phone. Danny took a seat next to Bethany. The General sat in the seat in front, next to a sailor who obviously had no idea who he was and was more interested in talking excitedly to the guy across the aisle from him. The bus filled up quickly. The doors hissed shut. There was room enough on the enormous pier for the bus's wide turning circle. It trundled away from the frigate and made its way towards the exit of Naval Station Norfolk.

It was a fifteen-minute drive around a perimeter road that passed inlets on the left and the outskirts of the huge naval station infrastructure on the right. This was just a blur in Danny's peripheral vision. He kept his eyes forward, head slightly down, avoiding any interaction with the other passengers.

They reached an exit – a lowered barrier manned by several US Navy personnel. The bus came to a halt. The doors hissed open again and Danny felt a lurch of anxiety. 'What's happening?' Bethany whispered.

Danny stopped himself from peering down the aisle to check. His mind turned over. Had the SBS guys messed up? Did the Yanks have some way of knowing that the four-man drop wasn't what it seemed? Getting out of this naval station ought to be straightforward. Had they hit an obstacle? Danny felt hemmed in. The bus offered only a single exit. Even if they managed to get off, leaving the naval base when it was on a security lockdown was a whole other proposition . . .

A man walked along the aisle. He had a square face and a humourless expression, as though this busload of boisterous Brits was somehow beneath him. He was doing nothing, however, but counting heads. Danny tensed up as he approached the General. Would a member of the US military recognise O'Brien at a glance, despite his hoodie.

He didn't. Nor did he look twice at Danny and Bethany. A minute later he had alighted, and the bus was driving through an open security cordon and out of the base.

Danny stood up. There was a lull in the buzz of conversation on the bus as he moved up the aisle and towards the driver. It was a wide road, but mostly deserted. Any vehicles Danny saw were military not civilian. The sky was changing. The mackerel clouds had become stormier. Bad weather was on its way. 'You've been told to stop for us?' he asked the driver.

Just a surly nod by way of response.

Danny stayed standing at the top of the aisle. He didn't have to wait long. After a couple of minutes he saw a black SUV parked up on the side of the road. It was an anomaly: a civilian vehicle abandoned here in the middle of nowhere. 'This is it,' Danny told the driver.

At first he thought the driver wasn't going to stop. Then he understood his passive-aggressiveness for what it was. The driver only hit the brakes once they'd passed the SUV. The bus came to a halt fifty metres beyond the vehicle. The driver opened the doors without taking his eyes from the road. Bethany and the General joined Danny up front. They alighted together and the doors hissed shut almost before they were out of the bus, which immediately eased back out into the road.

The General sniffed the air. 'A storm's coming,' he said.

Danny nodded. 'You need to tell me where the memory stick is,' he said.

'I already did. DC.'

'Where in DC?'

'I'll show you when we get there.' A couple of heavy raindrops hit the tarmac, leaving wet splodges the size of military medals. 'We going to stand here and get wet, or we going to drive?'

Danny looked at the sky again. Dark clouds were rolling in from the south. 'We're going to drive,' he said.

Danny found the keyless entry fob hidden behind the nearside front wheel. He took the driver's seat. The General sat next to him. Bethany in the back. The car was new, modern and comfortable. There was a full tank of gas. As Danny turned on the ignition, the General made to key directions into the built-in navigation system. Danny stayed his hand. 'We put our destination into that, anybody can read it if they get hold of the car.'

'Nobody knows we're here,' the General said.

'Plenty of people know we're here. Hereford. MI6. You think none of these people have contacts with Washington? We'll find our own way.'

The General considered that for a moment, then nodded. 'Route 64,' he said. 'We'll take the bridge-tunnel up into the Hamptons. North from there. I'll direct you.'

That was all Danny needed to know. He turned on the wipers, pulled out into the road and drove.

The weather deteriorated. The spots of rain became more frequent and fell so heavily that they started an irregular drumming on the roof of the SUV. Their route took them over a long bridge spanning the waterway between Norfolk and the Hamptons. By the time they crossed, visibility was barely a few metres on either side. Thunder rolled overhead. Lightning cracked. The sky became twilight dark. Danny kept his foot on the gas.

The storm followed. It was as if the elements were tracking them. They sat in silence, not only because they were tense in each other's company, but because the hammering of the rain and the crashing of the thunder made conversation impossible. It slowed them down, too. Whenever Danny saw the speedometer dip below forty miles per hour, he felt a twist of anxiety in his gut. The day was passing. It was already 16.00 hrs. That made it 13.00 on the west coast. The terror attack might happen there, which gave them a few extra hours. He turned on the radio and found a news station. A news anchor spoke in a brash, booming voice of a power struggle between the President and congress, as if he was discussing the latest celebrity tittle-tattle. But there was no talk of a hit.

Not yet.

Time crept by. They turned north on to Interstate 95. The storm turned north with them. That was how it felt, at least. The General had said three hours to Washington. Danny estimated that they needed to add another hour to that. Maybe more.

The afternoon waned. The weather deteriorated further. The closer they grew to the capital, the heavier the rain became. The wipers were on high, necessary but barely effective. A grey mist of road spray surrounded every vehicle on the highway. Evening came. The overhead signs for Washington DC became more frequent: 150 miles, 100 miles, 75 miles. The traffic became heavier. Danny kept his speed at a safe level. It was a challenge. His urge to reach DC was strong, but they'd get nowhere if they came off the road: a distinct possibility for anyone travelling at speed in these conditions.

By 19.00 hrs they were twenty miles out of DC and the neon of emergency lights glowed through the downpour up ahead. The traffic slowed to a halt. They crawled past a four-vehicle RTA. Danny knew at a glance that there were fatalities, but his attention was not on the crash or the ambulances. It was on the six police vehicles parked up around the crash sight, and the police officers in foul-weather gear, some of them dealing with the crash, others waving the traffic jam on. Rain pelted heavily against the windscreen and the side windows. It would be difficult to see into the SUV from outside. It didn't stop Danny's skin from tingling as they drove past the police lights. Next to him, the General pulled up his hood and stared straight ahead. Nobody spoke until they were well past the accident and the traffic moved a little faster. Even then, tension bit at the air. 'We'll head for the centre of the city,' the General said. 'Then I'll tell you where we're going.' He looked at his watch. 'Couple of hours and we'll get this done.'

Danny drove.

TWENTY-THREE

The children were grouchy. Staying up late the previous night watching the fireworks was all catching up with them. They had begged their mum and dad to be allowed to watch the fireworks again this evening, but Rabia had only agreed on the condition that they went back to the hotel for a late afternoon rest. Her decision was unpopular, but as soon as the children had lain on their beds, they had fallen asleep.

Now it was half past seven. The fireworks wouldn't start until a quarter past nine. Hamoud lay on the bed, watching television to ease his racing thoughts. Fox News played quietly. It was broadcasting footage of a presidential rally somewhere in the south. Hamoud watched, half transfixed, half appalled. The President had a kind of rictus grin and was rambling so incoherently that Hamoud simply could not follow his line of thought, if indeed he had one. The audience didn't appear to share Hamoud's lack of comprehension. They cheered. They waved American flags. They held banners aloft with the President's name and his jingoistic slogans. They punched clenched fists in the air. The audience, more than the President, interested Hamoud. There were only white faces. The camera didn't settle on a single person with brown skin. Each time the crowd roared its approval, he felt unnerved. He imagined himself among those people. Would he feel safe? He would not.

Rabia came out of the bathroom wearing a robe, her hair wrapped in a towel. She checked on the children through the interconnecting door, then sat on the edge of the bed next to Hamoud and stroked his hair. 'I don't know why you watch that man on television,' she said.

'Look how popular he is,' Hamoud said. 'Look how they cheer for him. Maybe, if that's what it is to be an American, we should listen to what he says.'

'No,' said Rabia. 'He won't be president for ever, even if he would like to be. When he's gone, things will change.'

'It doesn't feel like things will change,' Hamoud said. 'You've seen how people look at us. They don't trust us. They think our children will grow up into terrorists.'

'Then we will show them that we are good people,' said Rabia. 'That our children are good people.'

She was right, as always, and he smiled at her. 'I think,' he said, 'when we get back home, I would like to find some work. I think I'm ready.'

Now it was her turn to smile. One of those smiles that was almost a cry. She squeezed his hand and then went to look out of the window. On the television, he saw two adoring members of the crowd hold up a banner which said 'POTUS 4 EVA'. The President smirked and nodded. Hamoud switched the television off.

19.45 hrs.

Lightning flashed over the skyline of Washington DC. Thunder cracked and the rain lashed down. Lines of headlamps and brake lights glowed hazily through the elements. There were no pedestrians on the sidewalks. It was the kind of rain that made it difficult to breathe.

Danny followed the General's directions, which took them to the heart of the capital. They queued over the Potomac River, where the water seethed and shone with each fork of lightning. 'Jefferson Memorial,' the General said, pointing out an illuminated domed building with classical columns.

'We don't need the full sightseeing tour,' Danny said. 'Just get us to the thing.'

Danny's curt response didn't stop the General pointing to the right a few minutes later. 'United States Capitol,' he said. Danny looked at the huge, impressive building, lit up in the darkness, the illuminations burning through the thick curtain of rain. A couple of minutes later, the General pointed ahead and to the left. 'You know what that is,' he said.

It was the first time Danny had ever been to Washington DC, and so it was the first time he had seen the White House in person. The atmosphere seemed to boil around and above it. A double fork of lightning streaked the sky, framing the White House on either side, and Danny couldn't help a hot sensation of bile rising in his throat. He wondered how many operations he'd been involved with had been discussed in that building. How many men had been sent into action, and to their deaths? He thought of the Zero 22 team, and the taste of bile grew more bitter. He could just make out the American flag perched atop the White House, and the muscles in his face pinched. He suppressed a fantasy of breaking into the place, finding his way to the Oval Office and letting the President have it. That would be an impossibility, even for him. His only option was to help the General release the deepfakes. And quickly.

'Where's the memory stick?' he said. And before the General had time to refuse to tell him again, he added: 'We're here now. We've got you into the country. We've got you in to DC. We can't fuck around any more.'

The General was also staring at the White House. He didn't take his eyes away from it as he spoke. 'I have a lady friend,' he said. 'I keep an apartment for her downtown. On the QT, you understand? It wouldn't be seemly for a man in my position to be involved in any kind of indiscretion.' If he was aware of the ridiculousness of his comment, given what had happened with Bethany in Amman, he didn't show it. 'I hid the memory stick at her apartment.'

Danny felt himself deflating. How stupid was this guy? 'You asked some random bit on the side to look after the most important intelligence object in the world right now?' he demanded, incredulous. 'How the hell do you know you can trust her?'

'She doesn't know I hid it there,' the General said. 'I didn't tell her anything about it.'

'What if she finds it?'

'She won't. She won't even be there tonight. She works in New York during the week, flies back weekends. The apartment will be empty.'

'You hope.'

'I know.'

Danny gave that a moment's consideration. 'Tell me about the apartment,' he said.

'What you want to know?'

'What kind of building?'

'Terraced townhouses. Four storeys. The apartment's on the second floor.'

'Entrances? Exits?'

'One entrance. There's a fire window at the back with an external staircase. Don't think it's ever been used, at least not since I bought the place.'

'Is there a concierge?'

'No.'

'Do you have a key?'

'Don't need one. Smart entry system. There are access keypads at the entrances to the building and the apartment.'

'Are you known there? Will people recognise you?'

'They'd recognise me if they saw me, I guess. I go in and out late nights and early mornings. I don't think anybody knows I'm a regular.'

'Where can we leave the car?'

'Out front, if there's space. Otherwise, a parking lot a couple of blocks away.'

Danny thought his way through this information. He didn't like it much. A second-floor domestic apartment with only one entrance and one exit. If anybody was expecting them, it would be simple to surround the place. A couple of guys on the floor above, a couple on the floor below. Mark the entrance and the exit. Eyes on the street to see them approaching. If Danny had a team of his own, he could establish some countermeasures. But he didn't. It was just the three of them. And it didn't matter that the General thought his liaisons with his mistress were discreet. If Danny knew the intelligence community – and he did – they would be fully aware of O'Brien's supposedly secret trysts. They would know about his apartment, what time he tended to arrive and leave. They might even have surveillance equipment installed in the walls and other hidden places. If they had even the slightest suspicion that the General was still alive, the vaguest notion that he had re-entered the country, the three of them could be heading straight into a death-trap.

'Stop.' It was Bethany. Her voice was a shocked whisper. They were driving along a street lined with shops. 'Pull in,' she said. 'Back up.'

'What the . . .'

'Do it, Danny. I think I just saw something. You need to see it too.'

The road was busy. Danny earned himself some angry beeps as he put two wheels up on to the sidewalk and reversed several metres, past a drug store and a McDonald's. He came to a halt in front of a TV shop. There were several large screens in the window. Had they been any smaller, the rain lashing against the glass would have completely obscured them. But they were huge, and they all displayed the same image: Danny and Bethany, in the clothes they were wearing in Amman. Their faces looked grim and purposeful. It would not be obvious to anybody looking at the image for the first time, but Danny could immediately see that this was footage that had been taken as they strode along the corridor of the General's hotel.

'How the hell—' the General started to say.

'The hotel's CCTV,' Danny said. 'Your people have hacked it. Or they've leant on the Jordanians. One or the other.'

The picture disappeared. The news reel moved on. Danny silently pulled out into the traffic again. He felt sick. He tried to work out what it meant. Were they reporting that the Brits had launched an op to assassinate the General? The President's Wagner Group contacts would have seen Danny and Bethany leave with him. They would be wondering who they were and what they were doing.

'My bet is the President's people want to know why we didn't go through with our op to take you out,' Danny said. 'They want to know what you said to us to make us change our mind.'

'I didn't say anything.'

'They don't know that.' He frowned. 'The question is, do they think you're dead? If they do, why are they looking for me and Bethany? And if they don't, will they have someone waiting for us at your apartment?'

'Nobody knows about that apartment,' the General said, his voice testy.

Danny gave him a sidelong 'don't be so naive' look. The General fell silent. A muscle twitched in his jaw as he clenched his teeth.

'If the media controlled by the President is circulating that footage on the news networks, it means they're very nervous,' Danny said. 'They're going to make sure their hit happens quickly.' He inhaled. 'I don't like this,' he said. 'Every military instinct tells me we should hold off. Put in some surveillance on your apartment. But I don't think we have time. I think we have to deal with whatever comes. And Bethany and I need to make sure nobody sees our faces.'

They drove in silence for a moment. Then the General said: 'We're about forty-five minutes away.'

The television was on mute. Rabia was in the children's room, getting them ready. Hamoud could hear her kind cajoling and it made him smile. He crossed the room to join them, but the picture on the television screen made him stop. An eight o'clock news bulletin showed a slightly blurred CCTV image of a man and a woman. The man had dark hair and dark features. He wore a suit that looked a little small for him across the shoulders. The woman had blonde hair and a dark jacket. There was something about them that made Hamoud stare. A sharpness in the eyes. A ruthlessness. A caption across the bottom of the screen read: 'American troops killed in Amman, Jordan. Footage of suspects released.' Hamoud felt a chill as he looked at them. He didn't really know what a killer was supposed to look like, even though the American authorities had accused him of being one. But if he had to guess, he imagined they might look like these two.

He caught himself. What a terrible assumption he had just made, judging somebody on their appearance. Others did that to him all the time. Perhaps these two people were completely innocent, like Hamoud had been completely innocent, like so many others at Guantanamo had been completely innocent. He thought of his box of newspaper clippings back home, with pictures of other inmates he had never met. How many of them had been falsely accused? But, he told himself, the news networks must have a reason for broadcasting such an accusation against this man and this woman. Perhaps Hamoud was being too sensitive. Perhaps they really were bad guys.

The news reel moved on. Hamoud switched off the television and put the image from his mind. He was determined to have a pleasant evening with his family.

It was a warm, clear Florida night. The buses that took people from the resort hotels to the park were packed full. Hamoud's children gripped his hands tightly. He could tell that they felt claustrophobic, pressed in on all sides by the other passengers. There was not so little room, however, that those around Hamoud couldn't manage to put a little space between them and him, especially when they caught sight of his beard and vivid scar. Hamoud gave both his children a little reassuring squeeze. He hoped they would not realise that he felt the same as they did. Sweat dripped down his back. His mouth was dry. He held his breath.

Then the bus spat them all out at the turnstiles and he could breathe easily. The children were more relaxed too. Hamoud and Rabia ushered them into the park and towards the now familiar sight of Main Street. It glowed with activity. There was a juggler who twirled luminous batons high into the air. Mickey, Donald and Goofy were enthusiastically greeting children as they passed. The Cinderella Castle dominated everything, its spires glowing. Rabia stopped him for a moment and pointed at it. 'This,' she said. '*This* is America. Not that awful man and his awful rallies.'

She was right, of course. She always was.

They walked through the castle and onto the main drag. Here it was even busier. An enormous carnival float made its way slowly towards them. The characters – more than Hamoud could even recognise – stood on the float, waving and dancing. There was a full brass band with trumpets and trombones and an enormous bass drum with a picture of Mickey Mouse on the skin. Young women with twirling batons and epaulettes marched glamorously in front of the float, and everyone cheered and waved as it passed. Rabia and the children waved too, and he felt a sudden and indescribable surge of happiness. It took him by surprise. He looked around and realised that, for the first time in ages, he felt like he was living in the moment, like he was part of something. He started to wave at the float. He grinned. He even shuffled from one foot to the other, in time with the music. His children laughed delightedly to see it, though he couldn't hear them because the music was so loud. They danced with him and waved at the float with two hands and Hamoud didn't even stop dancing when he saw a woman dressed as Snow White taking photographs of people in the crowd. She was taking photographs of *everyone*, so what did it matter that, as the float had almost passed, she stood at the edge, looked back and scanned the crowd as though searching for someone in particular? What did it matter that as her gaze fell directly on Hamoud, there seemed to be a flicker of recognition? That a look of intense concentration replaced that of vacuous jollity as she raised her camera and took his picture, lowered it again and waved at him with a big cheesy grin, and then was gone?

Hamoud was breathless. He was excited. He felt like a new person. 'What shall we go on first?' he said, speaking loudly because the noise of the brass band hadn't faded away yet. The children shouted a barrage of incomprehensible suggestions and Hamoud laughed again and took them by the hands and led them up Main Street with Rabia also laughing by his side.

And then he saw him, and he stopped.

The man with the strange, long face was standing on the opposite side of the road outside a souvenir shop. Three young girls with blonde ringlets were standing to one side of him clutching cuddly Minnie Mouse toys. He was wearing the same baseball jacket that looked just a little too big for him, and he was distractedly touching his cheeks. Was he nervous? He certainly appeared to be. One of the Minnie Mouse girls bumped into him and giggled. He gave her a look of such fury that Hamoud was shocked. Frowning, the man turned and stormed away, disappearing into the crowd.

All Hamoud's joy drained out of him. He felt a crushing sense of impending doom. Who *was* that man? How did he know him? Because he *did* know him. He was certain of it.

The children had noticed his sudden change of demeanour. They looked up at him, wide-eyed. Rabia gently touched his arm.

'This way,' he said. He pushed through the crowd, his family close behind, heading in the direction he had seen the man storm away. He caught a glimpse of Donald Duck on the back of the man's baseball jacket. Then he lost sight of it again. He picked up his pace and continued to follow.

20.30 hrs.

The SUV was stationary. At the General's instruction, Danny had parked it on a quiet street. It was lined with yellow street lamps. They beamed geometrical shapes of light into the heavy rain that hammered on to the roof of the vehicle and sluiced over the windscreen. They sat in the darkness, barely able to see out. Shadows flitted past on the sidewalk, hunched under umbrellas or wrapped in heavy raincoats. Across the street a line of four-storey terraced townhouses loomed above them. Danny couldn't make out the roofline or the doorway through the rain. Just the window-glow of the rooms that had lights on inside.

The car windows were misting up. The General cleared his with one hand. His skin squeaked across the wet glass. He pointed at the house directly adjacent to them. 'That's it,' he said. 'The one with the black door.'

Danny couldn't make out the colour of the door, nor any other feature of the house. It was in complete darkness. There was no lamp post in front of it, no lights on in the windows. He strategised. If he were putting in surveillance on this place, where would he do it from? Easy. He would set up an OP on the roof of the townhouse opposite. In weather like this, nobody would look up, nor expect anybody to be out in the elements. But he knew how the average surveillance guy thought. They were not Regiment trained, willing to endure any amount of physical discomfort in order to get the job done. They would take the easier option, which would be to set up behind one of the windows of the building opposite. Danny wiped away the condensation on his side of the car and examined that building. He observed that each floor had a light on. But if there was surveillance on any of those floors, they would keep all the lights off in case they unexpectedly had to move into another room.

'Wait here,' he told the others. He stowed his Sig, raised his hood and exited the vehicle. The rain soaked him to the skin in seconds. He strode twenty metres along the sidewalk, head down, checking out the other vehicles parked on either side of the road. He was looking for something that stood out as a surveillance vehicle. A van, marked or unmarked. Even a larger car with blacked-out windows. He saw nothing suspicious, so he turned 180 and walked back past the SUV and twenty metres in the other direction. Still nothing. He returned to the others and sat behind the wheel again. His clothes were cold and clammy. Rainwater dripped from them on to the seat and floor. There was another fork of lightning. As it flashed, Danny saw Bethany's face reflected in the rear-view mirror. It was pale. Almost gaunt. She looked more tense than he'd ever seen her.

'I'm going in by myself,' Danny said. 'I can move quicker and more quietly alone, and if something goes wrong it means you have another chance to retrieve the memory stick. Once I get into your apartment, I'll check it's empty. I'll turn on a light overlooking the road for five seconds if everything's clear. If you haven't heard from me in ten minutes, you need to get the hell out of here. I'll leave the fob with you. Any questions?'

'I guess I should tell you where the memory stick is,' the General said.

'Damn right,' Danny said.

'It's taped to the underside of a unit in the kitchen.'

'You'll find it quicker than me,' Danny said. 'Get up as quickly as you can when I give you the all-clear sign. What are the access codes for the flat?'

The General told Danny the codes. 'Apartment three,' he said.

Danny nodded. 'Ten minutes,' he reminded them. 'No longer.'

He stepped out into the rain again. Looked left and right. There were no pedestrians. Still no sign of surveillance. He crossed the road quickly and approached the front door of the General's house. He was weirdly reminded, by the black paint, the brass fittings and the ornate detailing above the frame, of the door of Number 10 Downing Street, which he'd only ever seen on television. To the right there was a keypad. He entered the numeric code the General had given him. The door clicked. He gently opened it, just an inch, drawing his Sig at the same time.

He waited. Listened through the torrential rain. Tried to discern any other sound behind the door. There was nothing. He kicked the door open, gripping his weapon two-handed. Entered.

He was in a tiny hallway. To his left, four locked cubby holes for mail. Straight ahead, a door with a brass '1' plaque. Ahead and to the right, a carpeted staircase winding steeply into gloom.

He closed the door. Allowed himself a few seconds for his eyes to grow accustomed to the dark. Water dripped from his clothes on to the stone floor. Not ideal. It meant his presence could be detected. But as long as he was aware of that, he could take steps to mitigate the risk.

He moved across the hallway to the staircase. Aimed the Sig up and at an angle. Searched the gloom for shadows and movement. Nothing. He advanced.

The stairs were steep, the treads shallow. He trod lightly but couldn't help them creaking as he walked. His hyper-acute senses amplified each creak. He stopped at the first landing. Breathed. Scanned. Tried to listen beyond the thumping of his heart. Kept his weapon raised, his finger on the trigger. Noted the door on his right with a brass number 2. Advanced again.

The next set of stairs creaked louder than the first. Every sound seemed exaggerated in the silence of the stairwell. He paused after each step, checking ahead of him and behind him. There was no sign of anything, or anyone.

The second landing was almost identical to the first. The only noticeable difference was the number on the door of the apartment.

3.

He approached the door. Listened hard. Heard nothing. He removed his shoes to keep his footfall silent. Felt for the keypad with his left hand, gripping the Sig with his right. Keyed in the code. Opened the door just a couple of inches. Listened. Stepped inside. He closed the door behind him and stood for a moment in the darkness. He was in a square entrance hall. Three doors leading left, right and straight ahead. All shut. A posh, high-backed armchair in one corner. An occasional table with an internet router, two green lights glowing, and a vase of tall flowers that emitted a pungent, floral odour. He couldn't make out the flower heads in the darkness, but the smell suggested they were past their best. Evidence that nobody had been here for a couple of days. There was something else on the table, but he couldn't quite make it out.

No sign of any break-in. Absolute stillness.

Danny raised his Sig. Breathed slowly and deeply to control his pulse. Somewhere at the edge of his senses he could hear distant traffic. But nothing else.

He stepped towards the table, his feet making no sound. The other object on the table was an antique mahogany letter-writing set. Next to it was a silver letter-opening knife, blunt but pointed.

And there was something else.

On the edge of the table was a circular mark where somebody had placed a glass – or more likely a bottle – of water. Danny touched it. The ring was wet. Fresh.

Someone was in here. He was certain of it.

And he would be waiting for Danny behind one of three doors. Question was: which one?

Thunder cracked outside, so loud that the house seemed to shake with it. Danny analysed the layout. The window looking out on to the street where Bethany and the General were waiting would be through the door to his left. That meant the room with the rear fire exit would be to his right. Perhaps the door opposite the main entrance led do a bedroom or bathroom. If Danny was lying in wait for someone, he would definitely choose the room with an extra exit. Basic tradecraft. But would his guy think the same way?

The sound of a toilet flushing answered that question for him. It came from the room Danny had identified as the bedroom and he knew the door would open any moment. He didn't want to fire his weapon. Not if he could help it. It was not suppressed, and the sound could bring people running. He grabbed the silver paper knife in his right hand and moved over to the door. He stood to the right of the door frame, back to the wall, Sig now in his pocket.

There was another crack of thunder.

He waited.

Five seconds passed. The door opened. A figure appeared. He was taller and broader than Danny, which was unusual. He had a handgun in his belt, but was still doing up his fly. He didn't see Danny until it was too late. Danny's strategy was to hit him hard and fast. Not too much of a swing, because that would waste precious seconds and he knew he could achieve the power and momentum he wanted without it. He grabbed the man's neck with his left hand and drove the tip of the paper knife into the bottom of his skull. The knife sank halfway up to the hilt before the tip hit something hard and gristly. He gave it a good wriggle and felt the man's legs collapse beneath him. Danny eased him down on to the ground, one hand still on the hilt of the knife. There wasn't much blood. Each time the knife moved position, the guy's legs flickered uncontrollably. Once he was on the ground, Danny kept wriggling the knife until the nerve movement stopped and the dead man was completely still.

Silence.

Danny straightened up and drew his Sig. He checked the flat. The bedroom had a lingering smell of perfume and a neatly made double bed with lots of cushions. An en-suite bathroom was filled with cosmetics, but nobody was hiding there. The door to the right of the main entrance was a sitting room. Sofa and more armchairs. A TV. Various cabinets. A wide window with a sturdy locking mechanism. No people. The third room off the hallway, overlooking the road, was a large eat-in kitchen. And empty. He switched on the lights for five seconds, then returned to the hallway. He retrieved his shoes, put them on and waited by the slumped corpse of the man he'd killed, weapon raised.

Thunder cracked. The lights flickered off and back on again. Danny shivered. His wet clothes were bringing down his body temperature. He ignored it.

It took them two minutes to arrive. The General's face went pale when he saw the dead man on the floor. Bethany barely seemed to notice him. She calmly closed the door behind them as the General led them into the kitchen. There were no curtains and Danny didn't like being illuminated. He took up position to the side of the window and half watched the road, half watched the General as he removed the kick board below a line of kitchen units and felt underneath. A moment later, he heard the rip of tape. 'Let's get out of here,' Danny said.

'You kidding me? We've got to broadcast this stuff now.'

'This place is under surveillance.'

'It'll only take a minute,' the General said. 'I keep a Chromebook in the other room. Come on, let's get this done.'

Danny hesitated. He felt uneasy. But maybe the General was right. The sooner he could broadcast the deepfakes, the better their chance of stopping the hit. He nodded.

'I need to use the bathroom while you gentlemen save the world,' Bethany said. Danny understood that she was seeking his permission, and he nodded. She left the room, then Danny and the General crossed the hallway, past the dead body with the knife still protruding from the back of its neck, and into the room opposite. The General switched on the light and moved over to a desk against the far wall. There was a mirror over the desk. As the General located a laptop in one of the drawers, Danny looked at his own reflection. Several days' stubble. Black bags under his eyes. He looked like he needed to sleep for a week. The General opened up his computer and sat in front of it at the desk. Switched it on. Inserted the memory stick. 'You got to see this,' he said.

There were two video files on the memory stick. The General clicked on the first. Footage ran. Danny crouched down to watch it.

The footage was completely unremarkable. It appeared to have been taken by a surveillance camera in a busy street. Danny could tell from the US registration plates on the passing cars that it was an American street, but Danny didn't know the registrations well enough to identify which state it was in. The surveillance camera pointed across the road to a stretch of sidewalk where there was a fast-food joint, a thrift store and a massage parlour. Clearly not the best part of town. A man stood outside the massage parlour: a white guy, perhaps in his mid-thirties. He stood there for twenty seconds or so as other pedestrians passed by without looking at him. Then somebody approached. A woman. Also white. Dark shoulder-length hair. They spoke for perhaps thirty seconds, then shook hands. The woman walked away. The man remained outside the massage parlour for a few more seconds then walked off in the opposite direction.

The footage stopped. The General clicked on the second file. The same piece of footage ran. The same street. The same cars. The same angle onto the same shops. But the man was different. At least, his face was. Brown skin. An Arab-style beard. And a peculiar, distinctive feature: a scar that started above his right eye and extended vertically, over the eyelid and down on to his cheek. Danny knew that he was watching a deepfake. He knew to expect authenticity. But he was astonished at how lifelike it was. If he hadn't seen the original footage, there was simply no way he would have guessed that this had been doctored. It was completely convincing.

The woman approached. The same woman, only not. This face was also different. Older, with highlighted hair. Danny thought he perhaps recognised her. From TV maybe? Then he had to remind himself that he was not watching a real person. He was watching a lie. Whoever it was that he was supposed to recognise, she had not walked up to this man with the strange scar on his eye. She had not spoken to him. She had not shaken his hand before walking away. The event unfolding on the screen simply had not happened.

But nobody watching it would believe that, if they hadn't seen the original first.

The footage stopped running. There was silence.

'The woman on the deepfake is Madeline Doherty, or at least that's what we're supposed to believe,' the General said. 'Democratic congresswoman, chair of various select committees, frontrunner for the Democratic nomination. She has a strong following among the Black and Hispanic communities. Makes her the President's biggest threat, come election time.'

'What about the bloke with the huge scar on his eye?' Danny said.

'I haven't been able to find out. But whoever he is, he's being set up. By the CIA, probably. Or at least a faction within it. They have a unit, you know? Its sole purpose is to target jihadist sympathisers who wouldn't ordinarily be a credible threat and encourage them to cross the line and plot actual terror attacks. They let them get ninety per cent of the way, then they pass the intel on to the Feds to make the arrest and everybody's happy.'

'You think that's what's happening to him? You think he's been encouraged to carry out an attack?'

'Maybe. There's another possibility though. The attacker could be somebody else. They might be making sure this guy is on the scene when it happens. They'll want a scapegoat, and a living whipping boy's better than a dead one, right? This guy sure looks the part, with the beard and the eye and all. The President's base? They'll be a pack of wolves over a hunk of raw steak if they think a guy like that is involved in a terror attack. And if they think the liberals have been fraternising with him? He'll be able to spin whatever the hell he wants. We'll never be rid of the guy.'

'So let's stop him,' Danny said. He felt faintly sick.

'I've already set up a YouTube account,' the General said. 'And a mailing list with the news chiefs of all the major networks. I'll distribute the footage, then make some calls. There should be time to get me on to the late bulletins. The White House machine will get straight into motion. The story will lead the news cycle in the morning, I'll be discredited by lunchtime. But by then, the Oval Office and the Kremlin will be sufficiently spooked not to try this line of attack again.'

His fingers hesitated over the keyboard. Danny felt a moment of profound respect for him. For all his faults and foolishness, he was a good man doing the right thing, despite the personal consequences.

Thunder rolled overhead. The lights in the apartment flickered off then on. There was a flash of lightning.

'Let's do it now,' the General muttered, and he opened up a web browser.

It was the last thing he ever did.

TWENTY-FOUR

If he hadn't crouched down to watch the footage on the General's laptop, perhaps Danny would have seen Bethany earlier. As it was, he stood up just in time to see her reflection in the mirror. She was standing just a couple of metres behind them. Both her arms were extended. She held a pistol – a Glock 17 – two-handed, right forefinger on the trigger. She must have taken it from the belt of the dead man in the hallway. It was aimed directly at the back of the General's head and she was close enough for an accurate pistol shot.

Everything happened in an instant. Bethany released a single round. It slammed into the General's skull. The General slumped heavily on to his laptop as a spatter of blood and scorched hair spat from the entry wound. Danny reached for his own weapon, but he saw in the mirror that Bethany had immediately turned her Glock on him, and he half expected to hear the shot that would kill him.

Instead he heard her voice. 'Hands up, Danny. Let's not make a mistake.'

He raised his hands.

The General's laptop was quietly beeping due to his face pressing down on the keys. Blood seeped from the wound. It dripped down the side of his head and on to the desk. Danny watched Bethany in the mirror. She was completely in control. Her arm didn't shake. Her expression didn't change. She spoke calmly. 'Here's what's going to happen,' she said. 'You're going to very slowly take your firearm and place it on the table. Then you're going to put your hands on the back of your head, and you're going to walk over to the window. You do anything else, any sudden movements, you get what the General got. Understood?'

'Bethany—'

'*Understood?*'

Danny didn't reply. He considered his options. Could he draw his weapon, turn and fire on Bethany before she had a chance to shoot? No way. Could he dive out of the way and hope to get the better of her in the confusion? Perhaps, but he wouldn't bet his life on it. And that was exactly what he'd have to do. Bet his life. He had no option but to do as he was told.

Very slowly he lowered his hands, removed his weapon and placed it on the table. The computer stopped beeping. Maybe the General's blood had seeped into the mechanism. He walked over to the window. Bethany kept the Glock trained directly at him. 'You think I'm stupid?' she said as he moved.

'You know I don't think that,' Danny said.

'Then why do you behave like it?'

'I don't know what you mean?' He glanced over at the General's body. 'Why did you do that?'

'That's my job, isn't it? That's why I'm here. Oh no, plans have changed, haven't they? You don't need the crazy psycho-bitch to do your dirty work for you any more. So why *am* I here, Danny? What possible reason could your people have for sending me into the US with you and –' she inclined her head distastefully in the direction of the dead general – '*him*?'

Danny said nothing. He could feel his heart beating. He cursed himself silently. For leaving the dead man's Glock in his belt where Bethany could swipe it. For taking his eye off her at the critical moment. And for underestimating her. For failing to real-ise that she would work out the real reason she had been told to accompany him on this part of the mission.

'When were you going to do it, Danny?' she whispered. 'When you'd finished saving the world? Put a bullet in the head of the stupid woman, then have a good laugh about it with your new friend the General?'

'You've got it wrong,' Danny said. 'Put the pistol down. We need to get out of here. Someone will have heard the gunshot. They'll have called the police.'

'Shut up,' she hissed. 'Don't patronise me.' She edged towards the laptop. She released one of her hands and pulled the memory stick from the side of the computer. Put it in her pocket.

'What are you doing?' Danny said.

'What does it look like?'

'It looks like you're taking the evidence. Bethany, there's going to be a hit. You know that. We can stop it ...'

'I'm not taking evidence,' Bethany said. 'I'm ensuring my son continues to have a mother. Your people want this footage, they'll need to deliver my son and guarantee our safety.'

'Bethany—'

'Don't insult me!' she snapped. 'Don't tell me you had no plans to kill me when this was over. Don't tell me that's not what they told you to do. I know how they work. I know how *you* work.'

She moved her free hand back up to the weapon. Danny judged the distance between them. Five metres. An unskilled shooter could easily miss at that range, but he knew she'd had weapons training. She was likely to hit him.

'You're wrong. We can sort this ...'

'You think I'm mad?' she said.

Danny shook his head.

'I'll *tell* you what madness is,' she continued. 'Madness is performing the same action and expecting a different result. I let you go once before, and you turned up again like a bad penny. I'm not crazy, so I won't be doing *that* again.'

'Put the gun down, Bethany ...' Danny started to say, but he knew there was no point. He could tell when somebody had made the decision to kill. There was a unique flatness in the eyes. She was going to do it. '*Bethany, I can sort things for you ...*'

'*Don't lie to me!*'

'If you shoot me now,' Danny said, 'you make it *harder* to see your son again, not easier. I can make it happen, Bethany. You *know* I can.'

There was, for the briefest instant, a flicker of doubt. She glanced at the General, then bit her lower lip, as though pondering whether she'd made a mistake. But she didn't lower the weapon. Her hands didn't tremble. And when she looked back at Danny, he sensed that her determination had doubled.

He felt a sickening ball of heat in his stomach. She looked like she was going to do it.

Somewhere outside the building there was the sound of a police siren.

Bethany's lip curled contemptuously, but she glanced sidelong, clearly registering the siren.

'Sounds like someone's already phoned in the sound of gunshot, Bethany,' Danny said carefully. 'The police are on their way and chances are they'll be putting in a cordon on the roads round the apartment. Our faces are all over the news networks. We don't know what instructions they've been given if they see us. If you want to see your son again, you need to stick with me. I'm your best way out of this.'

'You make me sick,' Bethany spat. 'I don't need your help.'

There was another roll of thunder that caused the lights in the apartment to flicker momentarily.

Danny grabbed his chance. He dived to the ground in the half second of darkness. He heard the retort of the Glock, and the familiar splintering sound of bullet against glass. He rolled behind the cover of a sofa as the lights returned. He heard Bethany hiss with frustration and prepared himself for her to appear and take a second shot.

But she didn't.

He heard her footsteps as she sprinted out of the apartment. Had the siren spooked her? He didn't know and didn't have time to think about it. He pushed himself to his feet. Ran to the table to grab his Sig. He was no stranger to death, but the sight of the General slumped and bleeding over his laptop angered him. A good man trying to do the right thing. And Danny had let him down.

He sprinted from the apartment. On the landing, he took a second to consider whether Bethany would have gone upstairs. He decided not. In two minutes, this place would be full of police. She knew that. She wouldn't risk it. He hurtled down the stairs, his feet thumping heavily on the treads as he took them four at a time. The front door to the house was open. The rain was still falling heavily. It stung his face. He looked left and right. No sign of her. But to the left, neon lights. Sirens. Would Bethany have run that way to double-bluff him? No. She was too careful. The risk was too high, especially when she was holding the gun that had just committed a murder, and her face had been on national TV. She had turned right. He was certain of it. He sprinted after her. He tried to calculate how far ahead of him she would be. He estimated he had left the apartment twenty seconds after her. He was fitter and probably faster. A hundred metres? He peered ahead through the rain as he ran. Visibility was poor. He couldn't see her.

He upped his pace, half closing his eyes to stop the rainwater blinding him. The sirens were screaming behind him. His feet slapped against the wet path. He kept looking straight ahead. He could see a street crossing, one at right angles. Distance, seventy-five metres. And in the yellow light of a street lamp, which illuminated the rain pelting at an oblique angle, he saw a figure turning the corner to the right. A small frame. A glimpse of blonde hair. It was her.

Rain everywhere. In his mouth. Down his neck. It saturated every thread of his clothes. It seeped in between his palm and the handle of his Sig. He wiped it from his eyes with a soaking sleeve as he reached the corner and turned right. It was another residential street, almost indistinguishable from the last. Townhouses loomed on either side. Parked cars lined the road. And there was the flashing neon of police lights, too. Danny had been right about the cordon. They blocked the road, 150 metres distant. Danny scanned through the rain and the glare, searching for Bethany. There was no sign of her, but she couldn't have simply disappeared. She would be avoiding the police lights. She would be hiding somewhere between his position and theirs.

He slowed to a jog. Advanced along the street, scanning left and right. He didn't really think she would be hiding between parked cars or in the porch of a townhouse. Too easy to see, but he checked those locations anyway. No sign of her.

The flashing lights didn't move. The police vehicles were stationary at the end of the road. Twenty metres ahead, Danny saw a side street leading off to the right. More of an alleyway, really. Narrow: no more than six metres wide. He put himself into Bethany's head. Police in front of her. Danny behind. No other place to hide. She wouldn't know if the alleyway had an exit, but it looked like her only option. He stopped at the corner by the black railings in front of the end of terrace. Listened through the pounding rain. Raised his weapon two-handed.

Turned.

She was there. Fifty metres away.

She wasn't running. Perhaps she had realised that he would catch up with her eventually. But Danny didn't understand what she was doing. There was a high brick wall on either side of the narrow alleyway. There seemed to be an exit route at the far end, but the rain was too heavy for him to see it clearly. Bethany herself was crouching on the ground to the left-hand side of the alleyway. The slope of the road was such that a rush of rainwater was streaming towards her. She seemed to have one hand in the stream. She held her gun in the other and was pointing back down the alleyway towards Danny.

There was no way she could fire reliably from that distance. Danny advanced, his own weapon raised. There was a clap of thunder, then another flash of lightning. It illuminated the wet hair plastered to her pale face. Even from a distance, she looked desperate. Crazed.

Distance to Bethany: twenty metres.

Fifteen.

What was she doing? Why was she crouching there?

Ten metres, and Danny understood. The stream of rainwater was gushing into a drainage grate. He could now see that Bethany was holding the memory stick over it. Ready to drop it. And if Danny took her out, her grip would immediately loosen and it would be lost.

Stalemate.

Rainwater streamed down Bethany's face. Danny couldn't be certain that there weren't also tears. They stood in silence, weapons pointed at each other, for a full thirty seconds. Danny knew he had to choose his words with great care. He had to talk her round. He had to be persuasive. He took a single step towards her.

'Don't move!' she screamed.

He froze. Kept his weapon raised. Evaluated his position. He knew she was right-handed. She was holding her weapon in her left hand. She was in a heightened state of emotion. Her chances of an accurate shot at this distance were low. His chances were pretty high. How far would the sound of gunshot travel? With the cacophony of the rain pelting the ground and the rooftops, not far.

'We can sort this out,' he shouted over the hammering of the rain. 'Put the weapon down. Give me the memory stick.'

She shook her head. He saw that she was shivering.

'If you don't put the weapon down, this only ends one way,' he shouted. 'Work with me, I can get you out of here.'

Another shake of the head.

'We can deal with the General,' he shouted. 'We can say he was killed by the guy waiting for us in the apartment. They'll believe me even if they don't believe you. We can fix it.'

He risked another step.

'*I said, don't move!*' Bethany screamed. She waved the weapon threateningly and put her fingers into the gaps in the grate, so the memory stick was out of sight. 'I want to speak to my son!' she shouted. 'I want to see him. Get him on the phone. Otherwise this footage is gone.'

Danny didn't move.

'Don't you understand me?' Bethany shouted. 'I don't care about anything else. I don't care about this footage. I don't care about the terror attack. I don't care about you. I just care about my son and I want to speak to him right now.'

Danny heard sirens. A glimpse of blue neon as a police car passed the opening to the alleyway forty metres behind him. *What are my options?* He could continue trying to talk her round. But she wasn't in the mood to be persuaded. Or he could do what she asked. Get the kid on the phone. It would give him the opportunity to approach her. Get close. And when he was close, he had a much better chance of overpowering her.

Decision made.

He released his left hand, while keeping the Sig raised in his right. Felt inside his jacket for his phone. It told him that the time was 21.00 hrs. Beads of rain collected on the screen, making it unresponsive as he swiped. He had to try a few times. But he accessed his encrypted calling app and dialled the access number into Hereford before putting the phone to his ear.

It rang. Bethany stared. He was sure that it wasn't just rainwater welling in her eyes.

'*Go ahead.*'

'Get me the CO.'

'*Say again. The line is bad.*'

'Get me the damn CO!'

'*Wait out.*'

The line went silent. Danny's focus moved to other sounds. The distant sirens. The boom of thunder. The rain fizzing all around him.

'*Black?*' The CO's voice sounded curt. '*What's happening? You're all over the fucking news networks ...*'

'I need Bethany's kid,' Danny said. 'On the line. Right now. Video call.' He judged the level of his voice carefully. Clear enough to be heard over the line. Not so loud that Bethany could hear him.

Silence.

'Boss? Did you hear me?'

'*I heard you,*' the CO said. '*Black, I don't know why you're asking this, but it's not going to happen.*'

'It has to. Bethany has the memory stick with the footage. She's going to destroy it if she doesn't see her kid.'

More silence.

'*You have to find another way,*' the CO said.

A crack of thunder. A flash of lightning. It lit Bethany's face up again. There was a kind of hunger in her expression. She looked wild. Desperate.

'There's no other way,' Danny said, and he meant it.

'*There has to be. Don't you get what I'm saying? The kid can't get on a call. It's impossible. His getting-on-a-call days are done. He's dead.*'

Danny could almost taste his revulsion. It was bitter and acrid. It made him sneer. 'How?' he said.

'*The team that picked him up got heavy handed. We couldn't tell you. Not when he was all the leverage we had with her. You get that, right?*'

Yeah. Danny got it. He got that he was on the side who would think nothing of using a dead kid to their advantage. He killed the call and lowered the phone.

'Well?' Bethany demanded. 'Are they going to do it?' Her voice was shaky. It had turned hoarse. '*Are they?*'

Danny didn't know what it was that communicated the truth to her. The crease of his frown, perhaps. The self-loathing down-turn of his mouth and eyes. Maybe it was the way he distractedly failed to raise his left hand up to his weapon again, as he should have done. Or maybe it was simply his silence. His inability to say anything, for fear of revealing the one fact he knew he had to conceal.

All he knew was that she understood.

She shook her head. The faintest shake. More of a twitch, as though she couldn't quite believe the truth that had just struck her. Her lips moved. Danny could tell what she was whispering to herself. Her child's name, perhaps. She closed her eyes briefly. Danny experienced a curious sense of time slowing down. He saw raindrops splash in slow motion from her eyelashes. Then she opened her eyes again and it was as if she was a different person. Everything about her had changed. She was not the Bethany White who had been on ops with him over the past days: ruthless, certainly, but calm and in absolute control. It was the Bethany White he had seen back at Brize Norton, caged in the guarded Portakabin, raw aggression and fire.

She screamed. It was pure emotion and it cut through everything: the sirens, the rain. He could tell that instinct and fury had taken over her. He knew she was going to fire.

He hit the ground just as she released her round. And as he dived and rolled on the wet pavement, he fired his Sig. The two retorts followed each other in quick succession. It was only after Danny released his round that he felt a sting in his right arm and realised Bethany had clipped him. The impact had compromised his own ability to shoot straight. His round had hit her in her right forearm. She screamed again and pulled her arm up. The memory stick fell from her grasp, into the grate, washed away with the torrential flow of rainwater. Danny clasped one hand to the wound. It wasn't bad, but it wasn't good. It felt like there was some blood loss and the arm was shaky. Bethany was on her feet. Her own arm hung loosely by her side and rainwater washed off the blood that dripped on to her hand. She staggered back and fired again, but the bullet went loose, Danny didn't know where. She turned to run towards the far end of the alleyway. The exit was about thirty metres away and, so far, there was no indication of a police presence there.

Danny took another shot. But she was a moving target and the graze on his arm affected his aim. He cursed as his own bullet missed his target. He steadied his hand. Fired again. But Bethany was running fast, at an angle from his line of fire, and she was beyond his effective range.

He pushed himself to his feet, ready to chase her. But then he heard voices and he looked back. Blue lights flashed at the entrance to the alleyway behind him, no doubt drawn to the sound of gunfire. Silhouetted figures moved in front of them. Four, maybe five. Armed? This was America, so yeah, armed. He couldn't tell what they were shouting through the noise of the rain, but he could guess.

Decision time. The footage was lost. Bethany was gone. Those American police officers would be trigger happy, especially if they recognised his face.

He had to get out of there.

He ran in the same direction as Bethany, towards the far end of the alleyway. Fast.

TWENTY-FIVE

Five past nine and the park was so busy. Much busier than during the day. Everyone was here for the fireworks at nine fifteen and the streets were packed. It was difficult to move through the crowds. But Hamoud did it. Rabia and the children struggled to keep up.

Every now and then, he caught a glimpse of the man with the long face. Or at least of his back, and the Donald Duck baseball jacket. The sighting never lasted more than a few seconds before the crowds closed around him. Hamoud was aware of Rabia calling at him to slow down. He couldn't. He was drawn to this man, desperate to see his face again, desperate to identify it. Maybe it was someone from his past. He had to know.

He stopped.

He had reached the edge of a large circular fountain that blasted water twenty metres into the air, lit up by lights of all colours. On the far side was a set of steps leading up to a cafe. A crowd several people deep enclosed the fountain. Hamoud's children cupped the water in their hands and naughtily splashed each other. Rabia was giving him her concerned look. Hamoud was staring over at the steps. The man with the long face was there. He was almost at the top, so he was visible above the crowd. He was scanning it, as though looking for someone. The baseball jacket really did look too big for him, and he was muttering to himself and absentmindedly touching his face, as though he was somehow unfamiliar with it.

Hamoud blinked and realised what he was seeing.

He was seeing a man unaccustomed to being clean shaven. A man used to wearing a beard. That thought made Hamoud touch his own beard, and it made him envision what the man with the long face would look like if he had one.

And then, instantly, he knew.

Hamoud closed his eyes. He pictured himself back at home, sitting at the table, opening up the box of newspaper clippings that he kept on the top shelf of the bookcase, and which Rabia wanted him to throw away. The clippings about former Guantanamo Bay prisoners Hamoud had never met or even seen, but with whom he felt a connection. One of them was a man with a long face and a long beard. In his picture, he had looked friendly and appealing. Hamoud had found himself wondering if in another life they might have been friends.

He opened his eyes. Superimposed a beard on the man's face. It was him. There was no question. Only he didn't look friendly and appealing now. He looked nervous and dangerous. Nausea flooded through Hamoud's gut. He thought of the man and the woman who he'd seen on TV. How he'd told himself not to be too quick to judge. And he realised he had been misjudging the man in the clipping. Perhaps he was not innocent, like Hamoud. Perhaps his case was *not* a miscarriage of justice.

And it was suddenly, strikingly, horribly clear to Hamoud why the man's jacket was oversized, and why he had shaved his beard. He was absolutely certain that if he looked under the man's clothes, he would discover that he'd shaved his body hair too. He remembered the urban myth that had come to him the previous night, that the fireworks coincided with a spike in gun crime nearby. Was that true? Perhaps, perhaps not. But there was no doubt that the best time to set off an explosion was when everybody's attention was on the sky, not on those around them.

The man walked down one step towards the fountain. He was still muttering to himself, as if praying. Why could nobody see what Hamoud could see?

Dizziness almost overpowered Hamoud. He had to grip the edge of the fountain to stay upright. He couldn't hear anything. The people in the crowd were a blur, with the occasional face suddenly crystallising into absolute clarity. A young woman with a shaved head. A black man with his son on his shoulders. A couple of teenagers kissing. All of them unknowingly seconds from horror.

'Hamoud! *Hamoud!*'

His hearing returned. The excited buzz of the crowd, and Rabia urgently saying his name and pulling at his sleeve.

'What's the matter? What's going on? You look ... you look *terrible*.'

He stared at her. She had tears in her eyes. He looked down at his children. They had stopped playing with the water. They were watching him, their adorable eyes so wide.

And all of a sudden everything made sense. The free holiday. The people watching him, taking his photograph. He hadn't been imagining it. He wasn't paranoid. He was seeing things as they were. Hamoud had been manipulated into being in this very place at this very time. His presence was being documented. Because then, when the horror happened, he would be the scapegoat. A former Guantanamo inmate, a man looking like him, at the site of a horrific terror attack. An accomplice to the crime. He thought of the presidential rally he had watched on TV: those white faces with their American flags and their fists punched in the air. Who among them would believe Hamoud was not involved? Not a single one. He was the perfect suspect, oven ready. And would they believe him when he declared that he had been set up? Of course they wouldn't. A dead suicide bomber would soon be forgotten. But a live accomplice, dragged through a sensational trial and awarded a lifelong prison term or even a death sentence? Hamoud would become a symbol, a focus for their bile. Living, breathing proof that their hatred of outsiders was justified.

Hamoud looked at his watch. Ten past nine. The fireworks would start in five minutes.

He took Rabia's hand. Held it between his. 'You have to go,' he said.

She frowned. 'Hamoud ...'

'No,' Hamoud said. 'Do not talk. I beg you not to argue with me. Take the children and go. Now. Get out of the park. Get as far away from here as you can. Do not look back. Run if you can. Don't stop running, even to look at the fireworks. *Especially* to look at the fireworks.' He bent down to Malick and Melissa and embraced each of them with a fierce hug. 'Look after your mother,' he said. 'And remember that I love you.' He stood again. 'Now go!'

Rabia obviously understood his urgency. He was grateful that she didn't try to talk him round, or tell him he was paranoid or unwell. He could see his own panic in her face. She took the children, one in each hand, and squeezed back through the crowd, earning some shouts and unkind comments from those whose good humour did not extend to letting through this brown woman and her children. For once, the comments didn't anger Hamoud. For once he was pleased that people didn't want to be too close to his family. It meant they passed through the crowd more quickly. They were out of his sight within seconds.

Hamoud moved just as quickly. He half considered jumping into the fountain and splashing across its diameter, which was only about fifteen metres wide and so was the most direct route to the steps. It was not a possibility, of course. To do that would draw attention to himself, and that was the worst thing he could do. So he squeezed his way around the perimeter, ignoring the same comments and complaints that his family had received. He kept the man on the steps in his peripheral vision. Hamoud didn't want him to see that he was under observation, nor did he want to lose sight of him. He saw the man take another step down towards the fountain.

Classical music filled the air, a tune that Hamoud recognised but couldn't identify. He knew what it meant, though: the firework display was about to start.

He was sweating heavily. His palms were more irritated than they had ever been. He scratched them with his fingernails whenever he was not using his hands to clear a path around the fountain. The scratching brought no relief. It increased the irritation. By the time he had made a semicircle and was standing in front of the steps, his palms were burning. The sweat felt like blood.

There was a heart-thumping series of bangs. Hamoud felt them at his very core. He thought, for a sickening moment, that it had happened. Then the crowd oohed and aahed, and the sky lit up a multitude of different colours, and the fireworks continued with their squeals and cracks and techicolour explosions. Hamoud zoned it all out. He heard nothing but his heartbeat and the rise and fall of his lungs. And he focused in on the only other person in the vicinity whose eyes were not raised to heaven.

The man with the long face was still scanning the crowd. He had reached the fountain and was looking across it. He was only four metres from where Hamoud was standing, and as a red firework burst overhead, Hamoud saw beads of sweat on his forehead, reflecting the glow. Thanks to the curve of the circular fountain wall, Hamoud saw that he was muttering to himself. Although no lipreader, he could make out what the man was saying.

Allahu Akbar.

Allahu Akbar.

Allahu Akbar.

Hamoud hesitated for a moment, but only for a moment.

A moment in which he thought about his family. His children. How he knew that they would always bear the stigma of their father's imprisonment. How they would always be under suspicion. The children of a man everybody thought was a terrorist, even though he was not.

But what if he could alter the story for them? What if, instead of being the children of a pariah, they grew up as the children of a hero. What if he gave them the one thing Hamoud had looked for but never found: a new life.

He raised his eyes. The fireworks bloomed above him and he felt, for the first time since the camp, serene. His palms had stopped itching. His breathing was steady. His heart beat at its usual rate. He kept gazing up, but edged around the perimeter of the fountain, keeping the man in view. His awareness had never felt so heightened. He saw and heard everyone and everything with complete clarity. An elderly couple, hand in hand. A baby cooing in a stroller. Twin girls, no more than ten years old, in identical outfits. All these people unaware of the threat in their midst.

He was only two metres away now. The music swelled. The man with the long face turned so that his back was facing the fountain. Hamoud realised what that meant. The blast would come from his front and he didn't want the deserted area over the fountain to take the brunt of it.

There was no point being a suicide bomber if you didn't take as many people with you as possible.

Hamoud could see his right hand. It was clenched, as though he was grasping something. The pad of his thumb was circling. It looked like he was preparing to press a button.

Hamoud took another step towards him.

They were just a metre apart.

The man with the long face closed his eyes. Hamoud hesitated. He saw the crowd, a blanket of raised heads spread out around the fountain and far beyond it. He saw the sky, a riot of light and colour and smoke. He saw, from the corner of his eye, the glowing fairy-tale castle, and he made a wish: that what he was about to do would make his children's dreams come true.

And then he did it.

Hamoud stepped in front of the bomber, facing him. He wrapped his arms around the bomber's abdomen, as tightly as if he was holding on to his own children. He was aware of rapid sequence of firework explosions overhead, and of someone shouting nearby, and of the bomber roaring in frustration as Hamoud forced them both over the edge of the fountain. He was aware of a splash as they hit the water and a muffled cry of anger as he twisted hard, so that the bomber was lying face down in the water, and Hamoud was beneath him, face up, submerged.

And then he was never aware of anything, ever again.

The fireworks were loud, but the explosion of the suicide bomber's homemade device was louder. The kind of deep boom that vibrates the core and deadens the hearing. The kind of shock that paralyses the muscles and the senses, for a few seconds, until the panic starts.

The panic started.

There were screams, of course. They mingled with the fireworks and the classical music, and were a catalyst for more screaming, which radiated through the crowd from the epicentre of the suicide bomber. Within seconds people were screaming and running without knowing what they were screaming about or running from.

Even the people in the vicinity of the steps could not know it all.

Some of them, distracted from the firework display by the sudden movement, had seen Hamoud grapple the bomber into the fountain. They had seen, as well as heard, the explosion. It was a sight that would remain with them as long as they lived. Hamoud's body had taken the force of the blast. He could not absorb it all, of course. The force of the explosion had thrown the bomber himself up into the air in a shower of blood, water and shrapnel. Those closest to the blast were thrown outwards from it, their skin burned, their hair scorched. A nail flew into the shoulder of the black man with the kid on his shoulders. Another pierced the leg of a young woman. Yet another blinded an old man in his left eye.

But they could not know, amid the panic and the chaos and the injury and the blood, that the bulk of the shrapnel in the bomber's jacket had torn into the flesh of Hamoud's thorax and abdomen.

They saw dismembered body parts, flying through the air and lying on the ground, mangled, wet, cauterised and smoking, and the sight revolted them. It revolted them not only because the limbs were gruesome to behold, but because they were the limbs of an extremist. A fanatic. A killer who wished harm on them and their families.

But they could not know, as they gathered their weeping children into their arms to protect them from the vision of these body parts, that the body parts floating in the fountain belonged to a man who had sacrificed himself to save them.

They could smell the rank, acrid stench of burning flesh and it made some of them sick.

But they could not know, as the fireworks continued to flower in the sky, and the music continued its inappropriate counterpoint to the screams, that a woman holding hands with her two children had suddenly stopped hurrying to the exit, and the sickness in her stomach was more profound than any of theirs. The screams had reached her ears. She closed her eyes. When she opened them again, there were tears, and her children were looking up at her. She bent down to hug them each in turn, and drew some comfort from the warmth of their bodies and the way they wrapped their little arms around her and held tight.

Then she said: 'We must do what your father asked.' She took them by the hand again and led them to the exit.

TWENTY-SIX

For the first time that night, Danny was thankful for the rain. It offered cover from the police officers behind him. And he had to outrun them.

The alleyway extended for another thirty metres. Danny sprinted along it, ignoring the pain in his right arm where Bethany's bullet had grazed him, his feet splashing heavily in the flood of water on the ground. The cops would be following, forty metres distant, perhaps less. He didn't need to check behind him to be certain of that. If they got close enough, there was every chance that they would take a shot. Distance was essential.

At the end of the alleyway he could turn left or right. Both led to busy streets, with the hazy glare of car headlamps moving through the rain. There was nothing to choose between his two options. Bethany could have gone in either direction, but she was not his primary concern now. She no longer had the memory stick. The footage was lost. His attempt to stop the President's conspiracy had failed. He turned left at random and emerged, soaked and panting, on to the busy road.

A police car screamed past. Danny pulled his wet hood further over his face and hurried in the opposite direction. There were still no pedestrians out in the rain. He was a lone figure as he pounded the path, and although his head was down and his weapon concealed, he knew he had to hide. The police were everywhere, and there were no crowds in which to lose himself. It was impossible to be the grey man when you were sprinting alone along deserted pathways.

He soon came across a right-hand turn which led down a side street filled with large commercial rubbish bins. It was dark, dingy, unwelcoming and stank of debris. The places nobody wanted to go were the perfect places to hide. He ducked down the lane and secreted himself behind one of the huge plastic bins. There was rotting litter on the ground and rain streaked down the wall behind him. He crouched in shadow, his wet clothing clinging to him, and removed his weapon, ready should he need to use it. He listened hard through the rain. The distant sound of sirens came and went. He thought perhaps he heard the sound of voices shouting. But the rain washed away these fragments of sound, and Danny remained undisturbed and undiscovered.

Defeat did not sit well with Danny Black. He had the mindset of a Regiment man. A mindset that valued operational success at all costs. Bethany White had denied him that success. Thwarted his operation. There was a part of him that wanted to hunt her down and finish the job the head shed had given him. Another part of him, however, felt as much anger with the head shed as with Bethany. They'd killed her boy. He hadn't deserved that, whatever his mother might have done. Danny didn't know what made him feel more bitter: that he was in some way complicit in the death of a child, or that they'd kept him in the dark about it while he carried out their instructions. Either way, they'd been playing Danny as well as Bethany. He knew he shouldn't be surprised after all these years. He was just a soldier, after all, there to do a job and not ask too many questions. But the head shed's deception had an unintended consequence. Despite everything, Danny felt a strange complicity with Bethany. He was not going to go looking for her. She could be anywhere in Washington DC already, in any case. She was somebody else's problem now.

The rain continued to fall. Danny stayed where he was. His body temperature was dropping. His arm was in pain. He was cramped and wet and uncomfortable. But he could wait here, hidden in the darkness, for as long as he needed while the police moved on and he worked out his next move.

Bethany White did not know where she was. She had run, and run, and run. Everything was a blur. She was clutching her right forearm with her left hand. There was blood and it hurt, but she didn't care about that. Rain streamed into her face, but she didn't care about that either. There had been tears for a while, washed away by the downpour, but now there was just a hot, burning mass of pain in her chest. A desperation and an anger like she had never known. They had intended to take her life. She could cope with that. She could even understand it. But to take the one thing that meant more to her than that? She could never forgive them for it.

She stopped running. She was breathing heavily. Her surroundings came into focus. She was outside a liquor store in a small street with barely any traffic. She had no phone and no money, but these things were not so hard to come by, especially if you had a Glock 17 in your fist. She looked through the window of the store. There was just one customer: a lanky young guy with a ponytail and a thin raincoat, wet from the weather and slightly unsteady on his feet, buying beer. The cashier was putting the beers into a brown paper bag while the young guy placed some bills on the counter. Moments later, he was heading to the exit. Bethany could tell he was drunk. She gripped her handgun behind her back, checked to see that the street was empty, then stood to one side of the store and waited for him to step outside.

The young man paused for a moment in the doorway, looking out at the rain with a bleary expression of distaste. Then he shrugged, stepped out into it and walked in Bethany's direction. He didn't even appear to notice her until she was standing right in front of him, her weapon raised and inches from his chest.

He stopped. His jaw dropped.

'Give me your cell phone,' Bethany said.

He stared at the gun. Then at Bethany. He shook his head, emboldened perhaps by the booze in his system, which she could smell.

She didn't have time for this. She pulled the trigger. There was a sharp recoil as she discharged a round, but the bullet drilled directly into the young man's chest and he crashed heavily to the ground. Bethany felt nothing. No compassion for the victim, no fear that the gunshot would attract attention. She found his phone in ten seconds and took his wallet while she was at it. The phone required facial recognition to unlock it. She held the screen over the young man's dead face then swiped it up and she was in. She disabled the locking function, then heard sirens in the distance.

She pocketed the phone and the wallet, and then she started running again.

Danny had made a plan. He would head to the British Embassy. It was the only place he would be safe. There he'd demand to see the defence attaché and the suits could do the rest of the work. He checked the location of the embassy on his phone. Memorised the route. Then he stood up. His joints were tight, his limbs numb. Pain radiated from the bullet graze. He hadn't heard a siren or a voice for twenty minutes, however, so he was ready to risk moving.

He slowly emerged from behind the bin and wiped rain from his eyes. There was nobody about, so he moved to the end of the side street where it met the busier road. The traffic had died down a little but there were still no other pedestrians in this torrential rain. He had to force his aching legs into action. He had the uncomfortable sensation of his body letting him down.

His route took him north. He estimated that he'd need an hour, plus any time required to put in surveillance on the entrance to the embassy to check the US authorities weren't lying in wait for him. He'd only been moving for ten minutes, however, when two police cars appeared up ahead, screaming down in his direction, forcing him to change his strategy. He was just passing a sports bar: green neon signage and a cartoonish decal of an American football player on the window. He quickly entered.

It was a relief to be out of the rain. It was warm inside. It made his soaked clothes feel even more clammy. There was a staircase leading down into the basement where the bar was. He could hear the regular thrum of music from below. Here on the ground floor were toilets. He entered the gents. Two of the cubicles were occupied, but he was able to check himself in the mirror without anybody watching. He was a mess. His hair and clothes and stubble were soaked. There were dark bags under his eyes. His main concern, though, was his sleeve. There was a tear in his jacket where the bullet had grazed it, but any blood had been soaked up by his hoodie. He looked scruffy, but he didn't look as though he'd been shot. If the police cars had passed, he'd leave. If necessary, though, and in the dim light of a bar, he could pass as a loser who'd got caught in the rain. He put one hand through his hair, then exited the gents before the cubicle occupants emerged.

But the police cars had stopped outside the bar. Their lights were still flashing. Had he been seen? He didn't know. But his decision was made for him. He couldn't leave, at least not this way. His only option was to head down into the bar itself. Perhaps there would be another exit.

The volume of the music increased as he descended. Some heavy guitar band. He pushed his way through a set of double doors and entered the basement. There was a square bar with three bartenders serving in the middle. Dim lighting. Thirty or forty punters, all men, most of them at the bar, but a few standing at high tables. The walls were covered with framed pictures of sports stars, some of them signed. On one wall, there was a large, smirking picture of the President in front of the stars and stripes. There were numerous screens hanging from the ceiling. Some were showing the golf, others baseball. The music was not quite loud enough to drown out people's voices, but nobody seemed to be talking to each other. They were just staring up at the screens, or down at their beers. Nobody even noticed Danny as he entered. He looked for alternative exits. There was another set of double doors at the far side of the bar. They swung open and a fourth bartender entered. He caught a glimpse of a washing-up area, but couldn't be certain that it would lead to an exit.

He approached the bar and pointed at a Coors beer tap. An unsmiling bartender poured him a beer. Danny didn't want it. He wanted hot, sweet coffee to raise his body temperature, but it was more important to blend in. He took a sip and looked up at the golf. He only saw five seconds of it, because it suddenly changed. A news anchor appeared, and a banner across the bottom of the screen read: *Suicide bomber latest.*

Danny pushed his beer away and stared. The image changed. There was shaky camera-phone footage of terrified crowds jostling each other. There were fireworks overhead. The wording changed. *Walt Disney World terrorist attack. Two dead. Many injured.*

A guy sitting at a stool to Danny's right said: 'Fuckin' A-rabs.' His speech was slurred.

The image changed again. A face appeared. Danny recognised it. The beard. The vertical scar across the face. It was the man in the deepfake footage, and he braced himself for what might come next.

'Fuckin' *look* at him,' slurred the guy on the next bar stool. 'They got the chair in Florida and that's too good for him ...'

Danny zoned him out. He read the rolling news banner across the screen. *Former Guantanamo Bay suspect throws himself on suicide bomber. Foils terror plot in heroic act of self-sacrifice.*

Danny blinked. He didn't understand. He glanced across the room at the picture of the President smirking down on them. He pictured him sitting in the Oval Office, watching the same news flash, also wondering what the hell had happened. He imagined a room deep in the heart of the Kremlin, where men in suits would be having the same bewildered reaction. He looked to his right and saw the guy by his side properly for the first time. He was white, of course, and he wore a baseball cap with the words: *Make America Great Again!* He was frowning, as though what he was watching made no sense. Then he looked at his beer, downed it, left a twenty-dollar bill on the bar and walked out.

Danny pulled out his phone. The implications of what he was watching were not fully clear to him, but his duty was. Hereford needed to know that the guy with the scarred eye was the same guy in the General's deepfake footage. He was about to dial into base when the phone vibrated and the screen lit up with an unfamiliar number.

Danny hesitated. Should he answer? It was a US number and that made him edgy. The golf had returned to the screen. The punters were still staring at it like zombies. Danny accepted the call and put the phone to his ear but didn't speak.

He had to listen hard. The music in the bar was a distraction. He blocked his left ear with one finger and could make out the sound of traffic and rain on the other end of the phone. Whoever this was, they were outside. He still didn't speak. If this unknown caller wanted a conversation, they would have to identify themselves first.

'Hello, Danny,' said Bethany White.

Danny felt a chill, and it was nothing to do with his wet clothes. The hysterical distress in her voice had gone. Menace and ice had replaced anger and fire. She sounded cold and determined.

'I don't know where you are,' Bethany said, 'and right now I don't care. Don't bother trying to track me. I'll be miles away by the time your people find this phone. But I want you to know something.'

She paused, as if waiting for Danny to speak. He remained silent.

'You and your people have taken everything from me. First my husband, now my son. I have nothing left. If I died tomorrow, I wouldn't care. You need to understand that, Danny. *I wouldn't care.*'

Another pause.

'What do you want?' Danny said.

'I want you to suffer. Like I've suffered. And believe me, you will. You'll feel what I'm feeling now. I'll take your loved ones from you, one by one. And I'll let you live to mourn them because that's what I'll be doing, every day for the rest of my life.'

It occurred to Danny to argue with her. To tell her that what had happened to her son was nothing to do with him. That he'd been as much in the dark as she was. But he saved his breath. When Bethany White saw Danny Black, she saw all members of the Regiment and Security Services, and she blamed him for all their betrayals and shortcomings.

'She sounds like a gorgeous little girl, your daughter Rose,' said Bethany. 'It would be a shame if something terrible happened to her, wouldn't it?'

The line went dead.

Danny stared at the phone. A hot, tingling nausea spread to his stomach. He was aware of nothing else. Not the music, not the screens, not the other people in the bar. He was only aware of Bethany's words, which were ringing in his head like funeral bells.

He stood up. Pulled a damp banknote from his back pocket and placed it on the bar without even checking its denomination. As he walked to the exit, he could feel the weight of his Sig in the inside pocket of his jacket. He hoped, for their sake, that the police had moved on.

Danny Black needed to get back home. He had business there, and nobody was going to stop him.

★   ★   ★

Two miles to the west, Bethany White stood in the yellow light of a street lamp, rain lashing against her skin. She lowered her phone and stared into the middle distance for a moment. Police sirens had started up again, but she didn't care.

She saw her boy in her mind's eye. His gentle smile. His soft, innocent face. A sob escaped her throat and her hands shook and she felt herself bending over with the anguish of it. But she quickly straightened herself and took several deep breaths. She looked around. Rainwater was gushing into another nearby grate. She strode up to it and dropped the mobile phone into the drain, just as she'd done with the memory stick. She thought of the General and his crazy conspiracy. Was he right? Were the most powerful men in the world manipulating the gullible to tighten their grip on power?

She didn't care. She only cared about her son and righting the wrongs that been done to her.

She put her head down and disappeared through the rain and into the darkness.